PSI

Book One
Manifest

Ric Bruce

Talent Forge Publishing—Las Vegas, Nevada
ISBN: 979-8-9898203-0-6
Library of Congress Control Number: 2024900938
Title: *PSI: Book One: Manifest*
Author: Ric Bruce
Digital distribution | 2024
Paperback | 2024

Dedication

~ iii ~

To all my family and friends who encouraged me to create this world.
And for Omi, who taught me what it means to be an Empath.

Chapter One
Psychic 101

"Telepathy, telekinesis, pyrokinesis, and empathic projecting. Are these fiction or actual scientific fact?"

The lecture hall wasn't the biggest on campus, but it still held a considerable number of students, especially considering the subject matter. The man teaching the class captivated the students' attention with a lecture on the workings of the human mind and the possibilities of expanding its potential. He spoke of not only increasing short and long term memory, but also touched on the notion of psychic abilities. Even those students who may not have believed in such things, couldn't help but pay close attention to every word he said.

Dr. Ross Burton was a true scholar of his time. Having been voted the most respected educator by the graduating class of 1952, he was easily one of the most respected men at the prestigious Worthington University. It was obvious to his students and colleagues that he was a true man of science, just by his appearance alone. Although he was not the bumbling genius, as most movies portray such men, his appearance was that of a man who was more focused on his work than having a crisp crease in his pants. A true child prodigy, he excelled all through school and had always been fascinated with the human mind. He focused first on psychology, then neurology, and even into the lesser charted areas of psychic possibilities.

He began lecturing in 1949 at the age of 36. He had attended Worthington University in Connecticut for most of his academic career, traveling abroad between semesters and taking classes in universities around the globe. His appearance made him look wiser and slightly older than his age, mainly due to the premature gray peppered through his thick brunette hair, his round spectacles, and ever present cardigan sweater. For him, teaching was not only a way to earn a living, it was also a way to work out his thoughts and theories. Whether by writing them on the black board or by lecturing to his students, it allowed him to press even further into his studies. Periodically a student may present a fresh approach or idea for him to explore that he had previously passed over or had missed entirely. This was another benefit to his teaching.

"Throughout time, many great rulers, leaders, and conquerors of the world have based their decisions on the guidance of their advisors." Dr. Burton spoke loud and clear, his voice ringing through the lecture hall. "History, and legends, have described some of these advisors as having military positions or experience. While others had been characterized as oracles or mystics who read the stars and runes to base what their advice would be. An example of this would be the legend of Merlin to King Arthur. But consider if their ability to give guidance wasn't based in magic, but instead in science. What if these mystics were actually using an unknown force in their brain to advise their leader's on tactical strategies or basic decision making?" He paused to allow his students to absorb the question he just posed to them.

"Sound a bit too fantastic to be real?" He continued, adjusting his glasses to watch the reactions of the students as they listened intently. "History tells us that some of the world's greatest conquerors would consult with those who were not considered military advisors. Alexander the Great, Napoleon, even Genghis Khan… Would it surprise you to learn that Adolf Hitler was exploring the use of mental abilities to further his victories on the battlefield? He believed he could apply the use of psychic phenomenon to influence his strategies. Imagine the possibilities of soldiers who could…" he was interrupted by the sound of the bell signaling the end of class.

The students began to stir, gathering up notebooks and backpacks, to make their way to their next class. Dr. Burton shouted over the bustling noise to remind the departing students of what to review to be prepared for the next class.

He began to gather up his notes for the class, sliding them together into a stack so he could place them into his briefcase. A few of the notes detailing his findings on the Nazi soldier experiments slid off the desk onto the floor. He quickly gathered them up and replaced them in the stack along with his schedule for using one of the science labs after regular school hours.

Dr. Burton would occasionally hold study groups after hours for studies and experiments. He would include students who showed a great deal of interest in this field, or better yet, those with possible psychic potential. A small group of students, usually 4 or 5 of them, would meet him in the science lab that connected to his lecture hall.

One such meeting took place during the early evening hours in early October, 1952. They were granted the use of the lab used for Earth Science 101. Being that it was mainly used for first year students, there wasn't too much activity there for late night studies or experiments. It was set up as most basic college science lab classes would be. There were pictures on the walls of various species of animals and their skeletal structures. A large diagram of a microscope was on the chalk board, labeling all of its parts. Instead of desks there were larger tables, able to accommodate 2 to 4 students at a time, which stood taller for easier access if the experiments required the students to be standing. Although standing wouldn't be necessary because all of the tables were supplied with their own tall stools for students to sit on.

As the participants arrived, they positioned their stools next to one of the lab tables that had a deck of playing cards on it, and began to settle in. Dr. Burton turned off one of the two rows of overhead lights as he explained the instructions for how the exercises would be conducted.

"Now our first exercise will be for Jonathan to be in our 'sender' position." He gestured to the stool on one side of the table where Jonathan was to sit. "He will take one of the cards from that deck on the table, stare at it, and hopefully transmit it to our 'receiver.' Connie, will sit in the receiver spot." He pointed to the chair on the other side of the table, across from where Jonathan sat. "She will hopefully be able to know, and not just guess, what card it is."

Jonathan, a young man with short, sandy brown hair and horned rimmed glasses, moved to the chair as instructed. He was still 3 years from graduating and had initially joined this group hoping it would count as extracurricular credit. By the time he discovered that it did not count, he had developed a genuine interest in the subject and decided to stick with it. He sat on the stool and removed his glasses, placing them gently on the table, picked up the deck and shuffled through it. With all the cards face down, he carefully slipped one card out and set the rest of the deck down. He held up the single card so only he and the students seated near him could see it. He took a deep breath, slowly exhaled, and stared intently at the card in his hand. It was the five of hearts.

Across the table from Jonathan sat Connie. She was slowly twisting her blonde hair around her right index finger. That was the only movement in the dimly lit and silent lab. Dr. Burton kept it dim and free from distracting noise to keep everyone in a calm state so their minds would be more open and receptive to the "thought waves." At least, this was his theory. But even with the calming environment, Connie was feeling a little anxious and wanted so badly to succeed in this experiment.

"Concentrate on the card Jonathan," Dr. Burton said in a low even tone. "Really concentrate on the card. Picture it in your mind."

Jonathan did as Dr. Burton instructed. He held the card in front of his face, closed his eyes and attempted to picture it in his mind.

Connie sat across from Jonathan, staring at his forehead. Could she see an image?

"Ummm," Connie said as her eyes started to squint, as if the answer was printed in tiny letters on Jonathan's forehead and she was trying to read it. "Is it ... uh, a nine ... no, a four of clubs?"

As everyone sighed, Jonathan held the card up for Connie to see. She felt the disappointment of having failed to help prove Dr. Burton's theories. She was hoping for his theories to be true and to be one of those chosen to help prove them. She wanted to be special.

"Ok then," Dr. Burton started, "this is only the first test tonight. Consider it a warm up of sorts. Let's try another. We're going to try something new tonight. We have a new person joining our group experiment. His name is Paul. We'll keep Jonathan in the sender position and have Paul move into the receiver spot."

Connie reluctantly got up from her seat and let Paul sit down. He looked a bit younger than the other students, a lanky boy, maybe 16 years old. The other students had noticed him when they first arrived and had talked amongst themselves as to why such a young kid had been invited into the group. No one recognized him as one of Dr. Burton's students and didn't know how he would have gotten involved.

Paul settled onto the stool. The few lights in the room cast a shadow across his smooth young face and blond hair. Connie stared at him as she took her new seat. Even though he had a seemingly innocent face, there was something odd in his eyes. She couldn't place it, but it made her slightly uncomfortable.

"Alright, let's begin," said Dr. Burton, again in a soft voice to keep the feel of the room relaxed. "Go ahead and pick another card Jonathan."

Just as before, Jonathan singled out a card in the middle of the deck and carefully pulled it out. Holding it up as he did before, he stared intently at it for a moment and closed his eyes.

"Are you concentrating on the card?" the doctor asked.

"Yes sir," replied Jonathan with his eyes shut tightly, as if trying to keep the image from escaping through his eyelids.

"I'm sorry," said Paul after a moment of staring at Jonathan. From the perspective of the other students, it appeared as if he were looking through Jonathan. "I can't see anything clearly."

One of the students moved from his chair and made his way to the side of the table. He moved silently, in his light blue button-down dress shirt, making sure his shoes didn't make any noise as he walked. He leaned across the table in between the two young men. His name was Martin Sellers. He was careful not to make any noise as his dark brown eyes looked back and forth between them a few times and then stood up straight.

"Jonathan, open your eyes." Martin spoke using the same soft tone as Dr. Burton had. "Now concentrate on the card with your eyes focused on it."

In less than 5 seconds Paul stated, "Jack of diamonds." Jonathan held the card out to Paul and turned it over to confirm that he had, indeed, named the correct card.

The students began to applaud. The results were the same each time a student sat in the sender position and Paul was kept in the receiver position. He was able to clearly identify what card they were holding. When they attempted to switch Paul into the sending position, the results were 50/50 with the person in receiving position getting a clear image of which card was being viewed or not being able to envision it at all. So, they tried putting him back into the receiver's spot. Ending with Connie concentrating on the two of hearts card and Paul responding with, "Who is Bobby Fremont? I am not a freak. And the two of hearts."

When the session ended the students put the stools back to their original spots at each lab table, making sure to reset the room as it was before they started. They discussed the night's events while restaging the room.

As the students left the building and headed off to their dorm rooms and homes for the night, Dr. Burton called out and stopped Martin from leaving.

"Mr. Sellers!" Dr. Burton called out. "Martin, hold a moment. I'd like to talk to you."

"Me? Sure, sir, whatever you need."

"I wanted to ask you something in private," he began walking with Martin as they exited the building onto a path that led away from the campus. "What prompted you to see if Jonathan's eyes were open, and why did you think that would make a difference?"

"I'm not exactly sure, sir. I first leaned in front of them to see if I could intercept something. A look or a signal… anything. Just to prove or, I'm sorry to say, disprove what we were trying to accomplish. I thought, maybe those two had some kind of secret code to signal what the card was."

Dr. Burton seemed puzzled by Martin's honesty at trying to prove this was some sort of hoax. "Why would you think that the experiment was not genuine?"

They continued to walk as Martin tried to explain. "Well, we hadn't seen that boy, Paul, before. Some of us thought he might be a fake brought in to try and fool us." Martin looked away from Dr. Burton's direction, feeling slightly embarrassed. He ran a hand through his short, curly dark hair and sighed lightly. He kept his eyes on his feet as they walked and Dr. Burton began speaking.

"Paul is a young man that I have been working with for some time," the doctor said with a little hesitation. "Based on my past experiences with him, I thought he would be a good candidate for our experiments. I'm afraid I can't go more into detail about Paul right now. But, please continue about your theory."

"Oh, well alright," Martin tried to continue his train of thought, "After I had looked at each of them a few times, I don't know, something just clicked in my head. I have a couple classes with Jonathan, and he's a bit of a scatter brain. Don't get me wrong, he's a nice guy, I just know he has a problem staying focused sometimes. It seemed to me if his eyes were closed, I just thought his mind might wander a bit. And…and, well, this sounds silly, but it almost seemed as if I could hear Paul saying that it was too dark and he couldn't see anything. So, I just said open your eyes."

"Extraordinary," Dr. Burton said this as if it confirmed something other than just the experiment they performed tonight. "Martin, I realize that there is no class tomorrow, but I would like to ask you to meet me at my office. I have some information I would like to share with you that I think you would find fascinating and that your input could prove very helpful on."

"Wow. Sure thing, sir. I didn't have any plans anyway."

"Excellent. Meet me at my office at 11 am."

They had reached the end of the path leaving the campus as they said good night. Martin stood for a moment and watched at Dr. Burton walk off towards his parked car. He felt a great sense of validation. Even though this course wasn't part of his major, it was one that he felt a passion for. It didn't seem likely to him that the medical world and psychic phenomena would ever cross paths. But it was a subject that continued to fascinate him.

Chapter Two
Starting on the Path

The alarm clock began ringing its alarm bells promptly at 9 am. It did its job, waking Martin out of his sound sleep. He reached over to his side table next to the bed to turn it off before rubbing his eyes and pulling himself out of his sleepy state.

Martin made sure he was awake on time that morning. Although this wasn't an official academic meeting, he wanted to make a good impression. Normally on weekends he would wear denim pants and one of his plaid, short sleeve, buttoned up shirts. But not today. He would be exchanging ideas with a man who was a respected doctor and educator. He pulled out his khaki pants. The type of pants usually worn for the formal dinners with his parents when they would come to visit him at the University. Luckily, he had hung them up carefully and they were still sharply pressed. He glanced at the clock and realized he would be late if he didn't hurry. He slipped on his shoes while pulling on an undershirt and then buttoning up his white dress shirt. He made sure not to have misaligned the buttons. He grabbed a large notepad, just in case he needed it, and headed out the door.

It was just a quick sprint across the campus from the dormitory housing to the science building, where the offices for that department were located. He reached Professor Burton's office right on time. Just as he raised his hand to knock, he realized he hadn't put on a tie.

"He'll think I'm a stupid kid," Martin thought to himself. "It's too late to run back and get one."

He knocked on the door and heard Dr. Burton on the other side beckon him to enter. He stepped through the doorway into the modest office. It was a simple square room with a desk, two chairs in front of it, and a couple filing cabinets behind it. As soon as he saw the doctor, he knew he didn't need to worry about not wearing a tie. Dr. Burton was hunched over his desk staring at the sheets of papers spread across the top of it. He was dressed in his usual attire, the cardigan and spectacles were the same.

"Ah, Mr. Sellers, thank you for coming," Dr. Burton said, peering over the top of his spectacles, barely raising his head from the direction of the papers. "I was just reviewing some of my data and trying to sort it out. Maybe it is something you will be able to assist me with."

Martin was feeling that sense of validation again. "Of course, I would. If I'm able, that is."

"Now then, Mr. Sellers," Dr. Burton started to speak but stopped when he saw Martin was slightly stunned by how he was being addressed. "Martin, I wanted to see you today to further discuss the events of last night. I have some data that may further my discoveries in the experiments we've been holding. I have been noticing your continuing interest in the course and some of the excellent observations you've been making. Observations, not only during our experiment last night, but some you've made in your essays and tests as well." He raised his head up to fully make eye contact with Martin. "Now, I would like to share some information with you, but it must be kept in the strictest confidence. Can I trust you, Martin?"

"Of course you can, Dr. Burton. I swear I won't tell a soul."

"The boy from last night, Paul, I have been working with him for a number of years. He is a most fascinating case. More than a few years back I was fortunate enough to be approached by his mother who had been told by many therapists that her child was going mad. You see, Paul had been hearing voices in his head and it was something that threatened to drive him insane. These voices were not present all the time, but when they were he found it impossible to shut them out. He said that at times he would hear so many at once that he could not clearly make out what any of them were saying. It seemed to be at its worse when his mind was not focused on a specific activity or if he was highly agitated."

"That's why you keep the lab so peaceful during the experiments," Martin interrupted. "Sorry sir, please continue."

"That's quite alright, Martin. I can appreciate your enthusiasm. Yes, that is the reason I keep our test environment in that serene state. It helps the mind be more attuned to the psychic waves being sent out from our minds. Paul's case was what led me to this conclusion. After an extensive series of questions throughout different times, I was able to conclude that Paul was indeed hearing the thoughts of people nearby.

"I continued studying Paul, during active times and times at rest. Comparing when the voices were quiet for him and when he was in a great deal of pain by the noise in his mind, I began to see certain patterns. Those patterns have allowed me to help him in controlling how and when he hears the thoughts of others."

"That is amazing sir. Will you be writing a paper chronicling his condition?"

"Unfortunately, I won't. Even though his mother is entirely grateful for my help, it has taken a great deal of persuasion for her to allow me to study Paul further and have him participate in my experiments. She does not want his condition to become public knowledge."

"What about Paul's mother?" Martin asked. "Can she hear voices like Paul can? Or does he have any brothers or sisters?"

"No. No to all your questions, I'm afraid. The research is leading me to believe we all have the ability to send out our thoughts. But only a special few, like Paul, are able to receive them. That was an interesting question about his family though. I also thought of the possibility that this may be a trait inherent in other family members."

Martin felt a small sense of pride hearing that his path of logic was on the same course as this brilliant scientist. "Have you come to any conclusions?" he asked.

"Nothing conclusive. Neither of his parents had ever shown any signs of having any abilities and he doesn't have any siblings. Although, during a meeting with his mother, she did say that his paternal grandmother was rumored to have been diagnosed as clinically insane, though never formally treated. And she is no longer alive, so we'll never know for sure if she heard the voices just as Paul does."

Martin had barely noticed that while Dr. Burton was speaking, he was also shuffling the papers on his desk. It wasn't apparent if he was trying to find something or hide something. Although, he did begin to produce pieces of paper that he presented to Martin for him to look over.

"This is another case I worked on briefly," he said as he handed the paper to Martin. "This is just a short account of a young girl I met with in Maine. After many talks with her I came to the conclusion that it was not a small coincidence that her family had a house at the beach."

Martin looked at Dr. Burton with a puzzled expression. "I don't understand."

"Look at my findings." He pointed to the paper in Martin's hands, "There. You see, she could start fires with her mind."

"Unbelievable," Martin could barely keep his jaw from hitting the table.

"Yes, I would think unbelievable as well if I had not seen her do it with my own eyes. Her family had this house on the beach in case she had an episode where she couldn't control her fire-starting ability. When this instance arose, they would rush her out onto the beach where she was surrounded by nonflammable sand, or even take her into the ocean."

"Why haven't you brought her into the lab? Or into the class? This would be amazing!"

"A couple of reasons. The first is that the act of starting these fires would cause her terrible headaches. I can't be sure, but I think each time she used her abilities she was causing some slight damage to her brain. I was not able to examine her thoroughly enough to determine if this was true. I never had the chance to do so. She, along with her family, moved. Well, they disappeared, actually. That is the second reason I never brought her in."

"They just left? No note? No, 'Thanks for the help, Doc'? Have you tried to find her?"

"Of course, I have. But, without any luck. And she isn't the first."

With that, Dr. Burton handed Martin a folder. It had the letters P - S - I on the front of it.

"PSI?" asked Martin. "What is this folder?"

"PSI is short for Psychic Studies Initiative. It encompasses all the various abilities I've discovered. Psychic, psychometry, telepathy, telekinesis, pyrokinesis, and others. This is one of the folders that contain some of the cases I've studied. Some have proven very enlightening. Some were hoaxes. While others were inconclusive due to the subjects disappearing."

"You're giving it to me to read over?"

"Indeed, I am Martin. Last night was a most simple, yet extremely important example of just how close I am to my work. Sometimes it is beneficial to get a fresh perspective. And, I think, you may provide that perspective. I think you might be able to find something I've missed or come to a conclusion that I did not. Or, who knows, you may reach the same destination I have."

"I'll read every one of them, sir," Martin said with great

enthusiasm. He was honored to be considered for such an important role in this man's research. "I'll get started right away and have them back before you know it."

Dr. Burton chuckled lightly, "I do not expect you to read them all tonight. As I said, this is just one folder of the cases I've studied. There are a few more as well, spanning the many years I've spent researching many different cases." He leaned in a bit closer to Martin as he continued to speak. "Even though I do not doubt that I can trust you with this information, I must ask you to only review my work here in my office. I cannot have these files leave the premises. There are people who, if they knew these files existed, would have no problem stealing them from me. And that would leave me with nothing to show for all my years of work."

This statement made Martin realize just how much the doctor trusted him. "Uh... may I ask why you are entrusting me with all this? I mean, I'm just a student."

"Martin Sellers, I have been watching you in my class for some time now. When I first realized you had the same passion for this subject that had started me on this path, I took a closer look at your academic career. Your file is very impressive. I saw how easily you have been able to process information and excel in your classes. Your academic transcripts practically mirror my own. I believe, that if you continue with your studies, I will be calling you Dr. Sellers in less than two years, and that you could become an invaluable asset to furthering research in this field. That is, if you have a continued interest in this field of research."

Martin stood speechless for a moment, holding the folder and reflecting on what this man just said. He smiled at Dr. Burton and nodded. After years of questioning if he had chosen the right path in college, in life for that matter, he felt as if he had finally gotten his answer.

"If it's ok with you Dr. Burton, I'd like to start reading these now."

"No time like the present to get started, hmm? Sounds like a good plan to me. Please place the file back in this filing cabinet when you are finished. You'll notice that there is a small number in the upper right corner to keep them in order." He gestured to the tall filing cabinet that was against the wall to the far side of his desk.

Martin took note of his instructions and began looking through the papers in the folder he was holding. As he was reading, out of the corner of his eye he noticed the doctor taking some of the papers from his desk. They were the ones he had placed on the bottom of the stack. He pulled them out and turned towards a separate filing cabinet, one behind his desk, in one smooth motion. Still pretending not to notice, Martin watched him place the papers in the filing cabinet, close it, and lock it.

Martin simply dismissed the action but made sure to make a mental note of it, and continued reading the case studies. Each was more fascinating than the last. One such case started in New York, involving a supposed spiritual medium who claimed she could communicate with the dead. When, in actuality, she appeared to be using telepathy to read the thoughts of her clients for information on the deceased. She didn't even realize that she was doing it. She believed she was getting the information relayed back to her from beyond the grave.

The case file on this woman said that when she had gone missing, Dr. Burton enlisted the aid of another woman who claimed to be medium as well. Her talent was getting "psychic vibrations" off personal possessions of missing persons in order to find them. Dr. Burton surmised that she was actually using a phenomenon called psychometry. She was tuning into the same psychic vibrations of the object's owner in order to track them. Much like a hunting dog uses scent trails to track its target. Apparently, when the trail led to an abrupt dead end, the 2nd medium abandoned the search. The doctor stated in his notes that she was visibly shaken and frightened by whatever the trail had led them. Something about additional, and aggressive, residual psychic vibrations that had been left behind. But she refused to elaborate as to what that might have meant.

Martin read the file on the girl who lived on the beach and could start fires. That story's ending was the same. There was no trace of her or her family. The house was bare, as if they had packed everything they owned and simply vanished.

Another case consisted of the talents of a 7-year-old boy. His parents claimed that upon his first time sitting at the piano he was able to play as if a master pianist. His parents, both expert pianists, one a piano teacher and one a concert pianist, figured he was just a natural child prodigy. Dr. Burton was not able to determine whether the boy was using telepathy to read the minds of his parents and apply the knowledge, or if he was using psychometry to pull the "psychic residue" off of the much-used piano and get the knowledge that way.

When Dr. Burton proposed further study based on these possibilities, the parents sternly refused to believe their child was anything but a prodigy and denied the doctor access to him.

Case after case read like this. Incomplete findings seemed to have the same ending in every file. Whether by mysterious disappearances, or families of individuals who refused to believe the scientific explanations of their situations. It seemed most people were more comfortable believing in magical explanations and religious divinity than scientific theories. Martin had been reading for hours when Dr. Burton interrupted him.

"I think the files can wait for a bit. We should get something to eat. It is well past our lunch time."

"Hmm... I think you're right. I am getting a little hungry."

As they left the office, Dr. Burton pulled the door closed behind them and locked it. But not before Martin turned around in time to steal a quick glance at the locked file cabinet behind the desk. And he feared that not knowing what was in it could make it his very own Pandora's box.

Chapter Three
Student

Almost two months had passed since Dr. Burton had asked Martin to meet him at his office and shared his information on the rare cases of psychic phenomena. Now Martin had started reading the cases in the fifth large folder. As he began reading these cases, he found himself wanting to make notations and create a more fluid timeline of the events in each case. He decided to go back to the first folder and reread it. This time he took careful notes on each case. With Dr. Burton's permission, he also began to rearrange the files and added these notes to each one. Although the original method of organizing all these cases did have a specific method, Martin's new plan would make finding and referencing any case at a later date much easier. Now and then he would have to backtrack into previous files, or cases, and reorganize them as new information presented itself.

The work was a bit time-consuming, but he enjoyed it. There were a few nights when he had to tear himself away from the files to go back to his dorm room and get some sleep. He still had his other classes and studies to keep focused on as well. Of course, when time allowed, he and Dr. Burton would still hold the after-hours study groups and experiments. With these cases to reference and use as inspiration, Martin was able to suggest new ideas for the groups to try.

The doctor was resistant to many of Martin's ideas. The suggestion to bring in some of the subjects from the files, for example, those who had not vanished, had been immediately dismissed by Dr. Burton. He did not want to risk the possibility of exposing those people to whatever had caused the disappearance of some of the others.

"But Dr. Burton," Martin argued, "you brought Paul in. He is a consistent success in every experiment testing telepathy, but not in any of the other areas."

"Indeed. We have established that Paul only possesses the telepathic ability. His involvement in the group is a special case. He needs these exercises to help aid him in the control of his telepathy."

Martin tried to keep his frustration hidden. "That's my point, sir. His participation has helped him immensely. He seems to be gaining more control and even getting stronger the more he learns how to use it. Imagine if we brought in someone else who needs that help. We could help them to control it. And further your studies at the same time."

"I do not doubt that you would wish to help someone, Martin. I feel that bringing someone in for the sole purpose of learning control could prove more harmful than helpful to them. Right now, the motivation for these experiments is more on understanding the nature of these gifts. Maybe as a way to neutralize them. Not the control of them or the people who have them."

"Sir, I can understand your view on this, but I..." Martin was interrupted before he could finish.

"Enough, Mr. Sellers! I must deny your request on the matter. It is not up for further discussion at this time."

Martin was suddenly aware of the teacher/student relationship. He was not on equal footing with this man. It was Dr. Burton's program, not his. So he would respect the man's wishes.

"Yes sir, Dr. Burton. I understand."

Martin continued his work just as he had been. But, it was at this point that he suddenly realized that he had not come across any file concerning Paul. He couldn't help but wonder why there was no documentation on this mysterious young boy when there had been whole files on people they could no longer track down.

Chapter Four
Discovery

Martin sat in the library alone. It was towards the end of Christmas break, and most students were still off campus enjoying time away with their families. Martin did not go home for the holidays this year. Even though his father had recently become ill, his parents had assured him that everything was alright. Money had become very tight for his family and traveling home for the Christmas break wouldn't be in the budget. Martin had thought of trying to raise enough money on his own, but couldn't find a way to afford a round-trip ticket to make it back to the college in time for when classes started again. It was something that was out of his control. So he decided to make the most of his time and keep his mind off of it by researching Dr. Burton's findings and refining the possible causes and effects of psychic phenomena. A task made easier since Dr. Burton had given him a key to his office. Unfortunately, it was not the key to the locked file cabinet.

He recalled what Dr. Burton had told him about his theories on witchcraft and magic. He believed that the myths about wizards and witches were misunderstandings about the use of psychic abilities. Of course, the cultures of those periods in history didn't have the science to explain such powers and simply explained them by means of magic. Some of the examples and stories Martin uncovered were easy enough to categorize. Making objects fly through the air would be telekinesis. Meaning, it was the use of one's mind to move objects without physically touching them.

The myth of throwing fireballs and causing objects to burst into flames would be an example of using pyrokinesis. Defining the use of telepathy was a tricky one. This was the talent of picking up the thoughts of others, and sometimes also the ability to send out thoughts to others as well. It even included the ability to have limited control over the actions of others.

Then there was an odd subset, which seemed to be able to detect or project emotions without a clear message transmitted. Martin had discovered that this gift belonged to those with empathic abilities.

These became the explanations that correlated with most of the myths and legends. Some of the stories were either so fantastic or unbelievable that he had to hope that they had just been exaggerated over time. Or, they were pure works of fiction.

With all this in mind, Martin began drafting out a chart. He was determined to find some kind of example of when these occurrences were the strongest in relation to a myriad of other events. There did seem to be times when the tales were more popular. Certain times in history were heavier with stories of wizards and witches. Was it just a coincidence of these gifted people being noticed? Or were these points in time an example of when a greater number of them had been born? Those were the questions he was searching for the answers to.

His searches led him to the tales of ancient Egypt. He spent hours hunched over historical reference books. As he read the historical recount of the pharaohs and their devotion to their gods and legends, he cross-referenced it with all of the myths and legends of the time as well. He followed that trail to the Greeks, Romans, Chinese dynasties, Native American tribes, and even the legends of the Norse gods and their stories. He was attempting to decipher what might be based on actual people and events but had been spun into fantastical tales because they lacked the scientific knowledge of what these people actually were.

Martin sifted through the fictional stories, trying to separate what might have been based on factual truth. It was no small task, and he welcomed it to consume his entire Christmas break. And it did just that. He had spent his vacation obsessed with this task. Focused on compiling and completing this area of research. The feeling of accomplishment came when he was able to return to Dr. Burton's office to properly file his findings and charts for review.

Dr. Ross Burton always enjoyed the crisp winter air. The cold never bothered him much. He felt a certain comfort of always being covered by his warm cardigan sweater. If he was just walking from the lecture hall to his office, as he was today, an overcoat wouldn't be necessary. It was just a short distance outside. There was a moderate covering of snow on the ground which made a pleasant crunch under his stride. He would exchange greetings with any of his colleagues or students he happened to pass along the way.

"Good afternoon, Dr. Burton," said a man wearing a knee-length wool trench coat.

"And a good afternoon to you, Dr. Clark," replied Dr. Burton. He noticed Dr. Clark's gloved hands. One hand was holding a steaming cup of coffee, and the other hand clutching the handle of his briefcase.

"I hope you had a restful Christmas vacation," said Dr. Clark.

"I did. Very quiet, as a matter of fact," said Dr. Burton. "I trust you did as well? Prepared to return to our task of educating these young minds?"

"I'm not sure that I'm ever fully prepared for some of these students. I must tell you, Ross," said Dr. Clark, "I am rather envious of that assistant of yours."

"My assistant? How so?"

"Well, I had returned to campus early from Christmas break and found him in the library practically every day. He is, clearly, a dedicated individual. I've had him in my class for the past year and he is a very brilliant young man."

"Yes, he is." Dr. Burton quickly began to think of a reason to explain why Martin was assisting him. "He has been a marvel at helping me to reorganize some of my files. You know course curriculum and exam papers."

"You may be a genius Ross, but I've seen your office. I'm sure he has his work cut out for him. As a matter of fact, I believe he is at your office now. Probably buried under an avalanche of papers."

The men both chuckled. Dr. Burton realized it was a slight attack on his organizational skills, but he took no real offense from it.

"Well, I suppose I should see just how efficient he has been in my absence. Have a good day Dr. Clark." Dr. Burton waved to the man as he renewed his journey onward.

Dr. Burton continued to his office thinking of how Martin had spent all of his time. He was both impressed and concerned that Martin had not left for Christmas break. He couldn't understand why he had been on campus the entire time. When he reached his office, he did find Martin there.

"Good afternoon, Martin."

"Good afternoon, sir. I'm glad you are here. I'm very eager to show you some of the discoveries I've made."

Martin shared his findings and how he believed the occurrence of psychic phenomena happens in cycles. He retrieved a graph he had drawn up from one of the files and handed it to Dr. Burton.

"Even though I believe people with these abilities are born all the time, it seems that greater numbers of them occur in cycles. And the number of occurrences seems to get greater with each cycle." Martin spoke with great enthusiasm.

"This is amazing, Martin! I cannot believe you were able to discern all of this on your own. Truly amazing!"

"Thank you, sir. It was simply a matter of lining up all the facts and times, counting them back, and charting it all out. I already filed the charts for you to look over when you are ready."

"Martin, this is some impressive research you have done here. I am a little saddened that you gave up your entire Christmas break to do all of this."

"No need to worry about it, sir. I didn't have plans for the break and I am grateful for having something to do while I was stuck on campus. My father has been sick and this has been a good distraction. I think it all leads to some very enlightening discoveries."

"My boy, you are truly a man of science," the doctor said with a smile on his face. He was astonished by the amount of work Martin had accomplished in such a short time. "I am sorry to hear that your father is not well. If there is anything I can do to help, please let me know." He could see the sadness and need for approval in the young man's eyes. "I am looking forward to reviewing all of your research. In the meantime, I believe you have a class to attend. You don't want to be late."

"No sir, you're right." Martin smiled at Dr. Burton and gathered up his books for his class. "I guess I'm a bit off schedule. Too used to being on break."

As he left the office and began to close the door, he saw the doctor go to the locked file cabinet, unlock it, and place some papers inside. Martin stopped for a moment and watched as he closed the drawer but did not relock the file cabinet. Martin silently closed the office door and headed off to his class.

There was a slight breeze that night. It was just enough to keep the snow from falling straight down. The moon was bright enough that Martin could see the entire courtyard from the window in his dorm room. He had been sitting and staring out the window for an hour now, hoping the serenity of the night scene would relax him enough to fall asleep. He hadn't been sleeping lately, the concern about his father's health was weighing heavily on his thoughts. Most students wouldn't be able to handle the difficult classes on such a short amount of sleep, but he had no problems keeping up with the classwork and assisting Dr. Burton. Occasionally, he squeezed in a little time for food and rest.

The moon was full and bright that night. Even with the lights off, it provided enough light for him to see the features of his dorm room. The bed his roommate slept in was empty, he hadn't returned to school from Christmas break. Martin wondered if he was going to. It was usually after these breaks that some students decided that college wasn't the route for them. Maybe his roommate discovered the same thing. It would be nice to not have the distraction of a roommate.

His mind wandered from his roommate to his work with Dr. Burton. He was wondering if the file cabinet was still unlocked and began contemplating going to the office to check.

"Curiosity killed the cat," he thought. It was locked for a reason. But if it had more data on Dr. Burton's research in it, it could help further their findings. What if he just went and looked? If the information was useful then he could figure a way to make it look like he had discovered it somewhere else. It was a terrible risk and he knew he shouldn't do it, but Martin was going to do it anyway.

He quickly put on some denim pants, a sweat shirt, and his winter jacket. Even as he was putting on his athletic shoes, he debated in his head if this was the right thing to be doing. He continued to get ready as he weighed the options in his head. It seemed the decision was made when he grabbed the key to the office and left his room.

The walk across campus didn't take him very long. The night air felt crisp and fresh against his face. The snowfall was very light now, just a smattering of snowflakes floating down in the gentle breeze. As Martin drew closer to the building that housed Dr. Burton's office, he noticed fairly fresh foot prints in the snow leading to the main door. Two separate sets of foot prints. It was late enough that there shouldn't be anyone in there, but not so late that it was an impossibility.

"What if Dr. Burton is in there?" Martin thought. "How will I explain my being here this late at night?" He no sooner thought this when he heard the doors begin to open.

Martin quickly ducked behind a snow-covered bush and watched two figures emerge from the doorway. One was visible in the moonlight. It was Dr. Burton. The other, a shorter figure, walking close to him in his shadow, was all covered up in a heavy coat, scarf, and hat. Martin couldn't recognize who it was. The two figures continued to walk, in silence, away from the building towards the parking lot. They were leaving the campus.

Martin watched as they got into Dr. Burton's car and pulled out of the campus parking lot. His mind began to race with questions. Why was Dr. Burton there so late? If he was doing research, why wasn't Martin included in it? Who was that person with him? He desperately wanted the answers to all of his questions, but knew he'd have to follow him immediately if he was going to get any answers tonight.

Just as Martin wondered how he was going to follow, he saw an abandoned bike sitting by itself on the bike rack. Some student must have decided it was too cold to ride their bike and either got a car ride with a classmate or took a bus home and left it there. This was a terrific break for Martin. It wasn't locked up, so he brushed the snow off of the seat and hopped on. It was a bit of an effort to get it going. Riding on snow was tricky enough, but the ice and snow on the chain and tires weren't helping matters.

Moments later, Martin was quickly trailing after Dr. Burton's car. Luckily, traffic lights and the snow had him driving a bit slower than normal. It seemed the destination wasn't going to be far from the college. There weren't many other cars on the road, so he was able to follow them fairly easily. He took shortcuts through parking lots and cut across the street corners where the car had turned. His breath fogged out of his mouth into the night air like exhaust from a steam engine. A testament to how hard he was straining to pedal fast enough to keep up with the car.

Martin continued to follow the car into an average-looking neighborhood. The street was lined with small, "cookie cutter" type, middle-class homes, one next to the other. Each house, like the one next to it, with its snow-blanketed shrubs in the front yard. These shrubs provided a perfect place to hide the bike and watch as the car parked in the driveway of one of the homes.

Both figures got out of the car and walked up to the front door of the house. Dr. Burton reached out and opened the door for the other person. They both wiped their feet and headed inside.

"So he didn't knock on the door," Martin thought to himself, "he just opened it. I thought the doctor's house was farther away than this.

So, the other person must live here."

He had one small piece of the puzzle. Although, he was now questioning his decision to follow Dr. Burton, as he was beginning to feel the cold night air work its way through his coat, and his pants were becoming damp from the snow. He would have picked a heavier jacket if he had known he was going to be outside longer than just the walk to the doctor's office.

Martin looked around to be sure no one had seen him and made a run for the house. The neighborhood was quiet, it seemed everyone was in for the night, so he wouldn't be spotted as he reached the house. He found a window on the side of the house, out of view of the main street, that was illuminated by the lights inside. He had an unobstructed view from the window, allowing him to look into a large room. He began rubbing his hands together for a little warmth as he tried to catch a peek at who was inside. A male figure turned on another lamp and walked right in front of the window. It was Dr. Burton. He was speaking loudly to someone in another room.

"His control is so much better. He is able to receive and send now. I could actually hear him clearly. That is, when he takes the time to concentrate properly. We barely spoke out loud the whole way here."

A woman came into the room and handed Dr. Burton a mug. Martin assumed, from the way he held it, it was coffee or hot cocoa.

"She must have been who he was talking to," Martin thought to himself. "But she couldn't have been the one in the car. The body isn't the same build." He tried to maneuver himself to get a better look. Yes, there was a third person just barely sitting out of his sight. It was Paul!

"I was concentrating just fine," Paul said. "Maybe *you* needed to concentrate harder," he said jokingly, but with a slight edge of sass to it.

"My concentration does not matter as much as yours. I am not the one with the ability here, you are," said Dr. Burton.

"I'm just glad he can control it and keep the voices quiet now," added the woman as she walked up to the doctor and put her arm around him. It was a very intimate and familiar move on her part. They seemed very familiar with each other.

"That was our goal," Dr. Burton stated, "but we have surpassed that and gone even further. It reacts like a muscle. The more he practices, exercises in using it, the stronger his ability and control become. I am very proud of you," he said to Paul.

"Thanks, Dad."

"Dad? Did Paul just call him Dad?" Martin's thoughts shouted in his head.

"Dad? Did Paul just call him Dad?" Paul said very loudly. He sounded almost in a panic.

"Paul? What did you just say?" asked Dr. Burton. He looked very stunned by Paul's sudden exclamation.

Martin panicked. He must have been so overwhelmed hearing Paul call Dr. Burton "Dad" that he shouted his thoughts out in his head. And Paul heard it!

Dr. Burton emerged from the front door with Paul right behind him. The lights from the inside of the house escaped from the open door and cast their shadows down the path to the front door. Paul turned on the porch light as Dr. Burton stepped further outside. Dr. Burton looked from side to side, standing on the front porch, trying to discover whose thoughts Paul had overheard.

"There!" Paul shouted. Pointing towards the side of the house where Martin had been hiding.

Paul narrowed his eyes and focused on the sounds in his brain. He reached out with his mind and touched into Martin's. Martin could feel a small tingling sensation in his skull, almost like his balance had been thrown off for a split second.

"It's your assistant, Martin," Paul announced, "and he's hoping you don't discover that it's him."

"Come out Martin," shouted Dr. Burton, "we know it's you."

Martin cursed in his thoughts, hoping Paul would hear it (and he did), and slowly walked around the corner to the front of the house to reveal himself to his mentor, who was still standing at the front door.

"Come inside, Mr. Sellers. I think we need to have a talk."

As he entered the house, the woman took Martin's coat and hung it up. Dr. Burton showed Martin into the living room and gestured for him to have a seat. The furniture wasn't overly elaborate. Two rose-pink-colored wing-backed chairs sat near each other. They were separated by a small table that supported a simple lamp. Both of the chairs sat across from an oval coffee table and past that was a couch that matched the chairs. Paul sat on the couch, keeping his eyes fixed on Martin the whole time. Martin sat in one of the chairs, and Dr. Burton sat in the other. He positioned himself in the chair, turning so he was facing Martin more than the chair would have originally intended. The woman entered the room, handed Martin a warm mug of hot chocolate, and took a seat on the couch next to Paul.

"Uh, thank you," Martin paused, not knowing what to call this woman.

"This is Carol," Dr. Burton said to Martin. "Carol is Paul's mother. And she is my ex-wife."

They all sat in uncomfortable silence for a moment. Though it felt like much longer. Martin's eyes shifted nervously between Carol, Dr. Burton, and the warm mug he was holding. He avoided eye contact with Paul.

"Well, I suspect your following me here has to do with your questions about Paul." Dr. Burton shifted in his chair to get more comfortable as he spoke. "I suppose it is time I told how this all started."

Dr. Burton began to relay the story to Martin of how he and Carol had married at a young age and had a child. Martin could see the emotion on Dr. Burton's face as he spoke.

"I had been more focused on my academic career than my home life with my new family. I wasn't giving my family the presence of a husband and father, like they deserved. So, Carol and I divorced. Not long after that, Carol remarried. Around the age of 6, Paul started suffering from terrible headaches. He would describe it as a noise similar to a large crowd of people all talking and shouting in his head. Carol's new husband was not very understanding of all of the doctors' appointments and trips to specialists who attempted to diagnose this mysterious ailment. They thought it could be anything from an inner ear problem to mental instability. They prescribed Meprobamate and Miltown, to help Paul with the pain and to keep him calm. Carol's second marriage ended when one of the voices in Paul's head whispered, through the effects of his medications, and alerted him of a time, place, and a woman's name. And since none of it made sense to him, he announced it and questioned this information… at the dinner table. Carol's husband had been cheating on her and was planning on leaving her and Paul. Paul had heard his thoughts of infidelity and plans to abandon them and exposed his plans."

Dr. Burton paused for a moment and took a sip of warm liquid from his mug. He glanced over at Carol. His eyes conveyed a silent apology to her, and she returned it with a small smile and a quiet acceptance.

They were still friends and still cared deeply for each other.

"Regardless of a new husband or not," Dr. Burton continued to speak, "Paul is my son, and I have always wanted to be there for him. But Carol did not tell me the severity of his situation until she found herself alone and in need of help."

"I didn't want Ross's help at first," Carol added to the conversation, "I had initially blamed him for Paul's condition and was afraid he would look at Paul as a subject to study. I knew of Ross's interests in psychic abilities and mental disorders. I had felt as if that was the reason why this was happening to my son. That Ross's obsession had magically caused it. I didn't want my son to be one of those examples in his files."

"You see, Martin," Dr. Burton began to explain, "My interests in this field did not start with my son. It was my grandmother who suffered from similar headaches for much of her life. She claimed to hear voices and attempted to drown them out with alcohol. The rest of my family thought she was insane and a drunk. I knew better. Deep in my heart, I knew there had to be another explanation."

"Sir, I have to apologize," Martin said. "I honestly did not have the intention of following you tonight. I was on my way to your office..." he paused suddenly remembering why he was going there. He couldn't possibly tell the truth about why he was out tonight.

"He was going to see if you left your file cabinet unlocked, Father." Paul snitched him out. All of their attention was so focused on Martin that they didn't see the smirk on Paul's face.

"My what? Martin, you were planning on breaking into that filing cabinet?"

"No, sir. Well, not technically breaking into it. I think you left it unlocked. I was just curious as to what you kept in there. I wanted to know if it was information that could prove useful to your research and cases. Well, that is, information that could help me find something useful to present to you. I'm sorry, sir. I am truly sorry."

"Well that much is true," said Paul, as he continued to glare at Martin.

"That is enough, Paul. I thought we agreed that reading someone's thoughts without their permission was something you were not going to do," Dr. Burton said with a stern tone. "Martin, if you will get your coat, I will drive you back to the campus. I need to think on tonight's events and decide where we stand as far as your continued involvement in my research."

Martin put on his coat, thanked Carol for the hot chocolate, and made his way outside. He ran over to the shrubs where he had stashed the bike. He took hold of the handlebars, all too aware of how icy cold they were, and walked it over to the car. He waited as Dr. Burton used his key to open the trunk, and Martin placed the bike inside. He sat in the cold car alone for a few moments while Dr. Burton went back to say his goodbyes to Carol and Paul.

The ride back to campus was quiet and felt like it took longer than it did. Neither of them spoke a word. They were both very deep in thought, and at this moment, Martin was very happy that Paul had not accompanied them on the ride back. Martin could see Dr. Burton's face, barely lit by the dim light coming from the car's dash gages. Dr. Burton kept his eyes focused on the road while contemplating how to handle Martin's actions. A great deal of trust had been placed in this young man, and now a good measure of it had been broken.

The car pulled up to the front of the dormitory. Martin waited a brief second to see if he was going to be spoken to. He just sat, facing the road.

"I suppose we should get that bike out of the trunk," Dr. Burton finally spoke.

They got out of the car, meeting again at the trunk. Once the bike was out, Martin held on to it, trying to think of something he should say.

"I will speak with you tomorrow, Mr. Sellers." Dr. Burton said.

"Ok, sir. Thank you for driving me back. Good night." Martin said quietly.

Martin stood with the bike and watched Dr. Burton get back into the driver's seat. He shut the door and drove off into the winter night.

Martin walked the bike back to the bike rack where he had originally found it. The cold air was more obvious now than when he had first taken the bike. He wrapped his arms around himself and headed to his dorm room. Knowing he would not sleep well with the huge amount of disappointment he felt for himself.

Dr. Burton spent the next morning sitting at his desk, keeping himself busy with paperwork. It was approaching 11 a.m. when there was a light knock on the door. He barely looked up from his work when he told the visitor to enter. He assumed it was Martin Sellers, and he was correct. He gestured his hand for Martin to sit in the chair opposite him on the other side of his desk. When Martin was seated, the doctor took in a deep breath, sighed slightly, then began to speak.

"Mr. Sellers…..eh, Martin, I believe we have some trust issues that need to be worked out here."

"Sir, please, let me just say," Martin tried to interject, but Dr. Burton cut him off.

"No, Martin. Let me finish," he kept an even, level tone of voice as he spoke. "I was saying we have some issues with trust that must be dealt with. Not only from your spying last night, or the possible desire to pry into areas of my office that you are not permitted," he paused for a moment and removed his round glasses. "There is the issue of why I did not trust you with those details as well. I have been so guarded about my reasons for this research, and my son's involvement, that I may have lost sight of the real goal. I do not find myself having to separate the roles of being a father and a doctor too often. But in this instance, I must look at the events as a man of science with logic, not emotion. You have contributed an unbelievable amount of time and knowledge to my work. I must realize the level of dedication and passion you have for this research. Your reasons may be more pure than my own for starting down this path. I must also acknowledge how much more efficient the filing system has become since you became involved. I can only imagine how much further along we might be if I had allowed you access to all of my files and all of the information.

"So, I think that all of the events of last night should be forgotten, and we should continue forward from this point. You now know the history and reason for Paul's involvement and my past with his mother. As long as I can trust you with that information, then you can trust me to make all current and future information available to you."

"You can definitely trust me, sir. Of course, you can. I'm so sorry about last night. I want so much to be a part of all of this. It won't happen again."

"It's agreed then. We shall continue forward from this point."

Dr. Burton reached out over the desk with his right hand. He had a small smile as he clasped hands with Martin. They shook hands, both confident that this new understanding of trust was a move in the right direction.

Chapter Five
Doctor Martin Sellers

It was unusual that Dr. Burton would be running late. Even though he was not speaking at this year's graduation ceremony, it was important that he attended. Today, graduating with the class of 1954, was the day Martin Sellers would become Dr. Sellers. It was a great accomplishment.

Dr. Burton arrived in time to find a seat and get situated before the ceremonies began. The graduating students made their way to their seats, with the audience cheering and applauding already. The events played out as they do every year. The dean of students gave a speech that no one would be able to recall in later years. The same would hold true for the guest keynote speaker. Then, Martin took the podium as valedictorian. His speech was inspiring. Of course, no one, except Dr. Burton, would understand his true meaning when he spoke of "a hidden potential in all of us," or "the unseen mysteries of the world that have yet to be discovered." But Dr. Burton knew.

After the ceremonies had concluded, the students found their families and began taking group photographs. The proud parents were standing next to their children, who were dressed in the customary caps and gowns. A sea of hopeful young people, standing proudly in the light of the summer sun, posing for pictures and receiving congratulatory hugs from their loved ones.

Dr. Burton found Martin standing with his mother. The day was bittersweet for Martin and his mother since his father had passed away a few months earlier.

"Congratulations Mr. Sellers," Dr. Burton stopped himself and smiled. "I mean Dr. Sellers." He reached out and shook his hand.

"Thank you, sir."

"Dr. Burton, would you mind taking a photograph of my son and me?" Mrs. Sellers asked.

"I would not mind at all, Mrs. Sellers." Dr. Burton took the camera from her and stepped back a few paces. He looked through the viewfinder on the camera and placed them squarely in the frame. With the push of a button, the moment would be saved forever.

"Mom, could you take a picture of me with Dr. Burton?"

He was both shocked and honored as the young man handed the camera to his mother and stood next to him. He put his arm around Dr. Burton's shoulder and smiled for the camera. It was a proud moment for them both.

What neither of the men saw was the figure in the distance, glaring at them both. Paul watched from the edge of the crowd. His eyes were narrowed and he felt jealous of the attention Martin received from his father. He was attending classes at Worthington University now. He had enrolled in the most advanced classes he could, and received the best grades possible, but he still did not get the praise from his father that he desired. Unknown to his father was the fact that he had accomplished almost all of it by using his telepathic abilities.

Over the years, with much practice, he was able to single out the thoughts of the smartest students in class, or even the teacher. Then he could pull the information he needed to write the perfect essay or ace the exam, directly from their minds. His father had been correct. His ability was like a muscle. The more he used it, the stronger he became. But it never seemed to be good enough to compete with Martin Sellers.

It was situations like this when Paul's temper would flare and he was not able to fully stop the thoughts of those around him from flooding into his mind. Even with his improved control, he could be weakened we his emotions would break his concentration. Being in such a large crowd, that much noise could prove very painful. Knowing the intense pain that would follow if he stayed, he left Martin to bask in his father's praise. He wouldn't challenge Martin. Not today. Not yet.

The night after graduation, after his mother had left to return home, Dr. Martin Sellers asked Dr. Burton if he would join him for dinner. To celebrate his graduation.

They sat across from each other in a local Italian restaurant. Martin wanted to thank Dr. Burton for all his encouragement and help, especially during the past year.

"You were really there for me after my father passed away. Well, really the whole time he was ill, these past couple of years. It meant a lot. Your being there made it a great deal easier for me to stay focused on my classes and our research projects."

"Think nothing of it, Martin." Dr. Burton responded. "I consider you a friend. And I suppose, from this point on, a colleague as well... Dr. Sellers. Your father would be very proud, indeed." He lifted his glass to toast the young man and the memory of his father.

They continued their dinner and talked about various subjects ranging from recent motion pictures to plans for the future.

"I know I have brought this up before, sir. But, I believe that if we are going to press further into your research and make more notable advancements, we need to bring in some more of the case subjects from your files. Paul is great, but he is distracted by his studies, and frankly sir, I don't think he cares for me much. I believe the research has gone as far as it can with Paul and the other few subjects you've brought in. I feel that we need to broaden the subject base."

"You know my feelings on this," Dr. Burton said but took a moment to reflect on what was just said to him. "I think at this point you may be right though. It seems our research will come to a standstill if we don't start to include some new possibilities. We will have to carefully select the subjects from the files who will not only give us good results, but will benefit the most, and will also be able to be tested in our facilities."

"Of course, sir. I ... uh... I already have a few in mind. I wanted to be prepared if you ever said you wanted to go ahead with the idea. I'll have the possible subjects' files on your desk for you to look at tomorrow. I've also been thinking of ways we might find others who aren't already in your files." Martin said quickly with excitement.

Dr. Burton stared at him for a moment with a smirk on his face. He was not surprised by this. If Martin Sellers had proven anything over the past two years it was that he always plans ahead. He smiled and shook his head, and raised his glass to toast him once again. "To the future," he said.

"To the future," Martin echoed.

Chapter Six
The Agents of '61

Martin ran as fast as he could down the campus hallway towards Dr. Burton's office. He cursed in his head that his leather dress shoes did not have the traction that his gym shoes did. A point made all too clear as he tried to dart around the students who blocked his path down the hallway. Normally he would not be dressed so formally, unless teaching a class or assisting Dr. Burton in his classes. But since the whole department had been under the watchful eye of the Board of Directors, because of their application for a grant and a spot in the new Medical Center, he had to keep up a more professional appearance.

The new Worthington University Medical Center was state-of-the-art. It had access to the best scientific equipment and medicine that 1961 America had to offer. Being given grant money and a prime spot in the Medical Center could mean great advancements in their research. It would also mean that they would be taken more seriously by the scientific community.

He had just received the message that Dr. Burton wanted to see him and that it was urgent. It could only mean they got their answer about the grant. Hopefully, this time, it was a positive one. They had already been turned down twice before. The first time was in 1959 when the Medical Center was in its planning stages. The second, was at the end of 1960, when the construction had been completed.

When Martin reached the office door, it was slightly open, so he burst into the office. To his surprise, Dr. Burton was not alone. Two men were standing just inside the office in front of Dr. Burton's desk. Luckily, Martin's quick reflexes stopped him from running right into them. Dr. Burton stood behind his desk across from two other men. Both of these men wore the same dark blue suits, and Martin didn't recognize either of them.

"Dr. Sellers, I see you received my message," Dr. Burton said. "This is Agent Brown and Agent Warner. Gentlemen, this is..."

"Dr. Martin Sellers." The man introduced as Agent Brown spoke. "Yes, Doctor, we are well aware of who he is. We know he has been assisting you for some years now. But your answer is the only thing we are interested in at the moment." He was a very tall man and his dark blue suit was tailored to accentuate his broad shoulders. He stood with one hand in his pants front pocket and the other at his side. He had a strong square jaw, which looked freshly shaved. His counterpart, who was a little shorter, but equally as intimidating looking, stood next to him. He stood perfectly still, with his hands hanging at his sides.

"Dr. Sellers is no longer my assistant, gentlemen. He is now my colleague," stated Dr. Burton. "My answer to you and your agency remains the same as it has always been. Good day to you, gentlemen."

"This isn't the first time you've been extended this opportunity," it was Agent Brown speaking again, "but it may be the last time. We could make it possible for you to work with other doctors and experts and equipment that you otherwise would never have access to. Think about it carefully. I doubt your school here can make you the same offer Uncle Sam has." The agent looked at his watch and then at the other agent. "If you'll excuse us, we have another appointment to keep." With that said, they both nodded, turned and left. Martin closed the door behind them.

"Sir, what was all that about? They're government agents?" Martin was still a bit stunned and not quite sure what he had just witnessed.

"Yes, yes. Their kind have been by before. They want my research... *our* research, with the promises of huge funding and support. I don't believe they have our best interests at heart. They want to set up science and medical labs that would, supposedly, be dedicated completely to our cause. Their agenda is to use our findings and turn them into tools for control, spying on foreign countries, or into weapons. Who knows! But they can try and succeed without us. We got our grant! We are moving to the Medical Center and setting up shop there! This is all due mainly to your research linking all our findings into medical and biological aspects."

"That is fantastic news, sir. But don't you think we should consider the offer from the government? That has to afford us more possibilities than what the University can offer us."

"No. They aren't men of science, Dr. Sellers. Their purpose is to twist our goals and what we have accomplished into something that isn't for the benefit of those with abilities. It is for their benefit that they try to lure us away from here. All the main reasons why I have kept so much of our research a secret. They are not truly aware of just how much we have discovered. We must stay the course."

"But how can you be sure? Ross, don't you think..." Martin stopped short of finishing his sentence. Both men silently realized he just called Dr. Burton by his first name.

"Yes, Martin, I do think," he said in a slightly cold tone of voice. "I think all of the time. I have thought long and hard on this subject many times. Do you remember my class lectures about how those in power sought to use these phenomena to control the masses and shift the tides of war? Even as recently as Hitler trying to incorporate it into his strategies. Have you ever stopped to consider what may have happened to those files of missing people? Do you not think that those men, and the organization they work for, might be involved in that? I realize you have had some very brilliant suggestions that have led us in amazing directions with the experiments. I was wrong in fighting you on bringing in new subjects. All of the data we have obtained because of it and the number of subjects… people helped because of it is quite an accomplishment. In that instance, you were correct," he then leaned in closer to Martin to emphasize his point, "But make no mistake on this particular subject. I do not wish to *ever* hand my work over to those men or the people they work for. Am I understood?"

"Completely, sir."

Despite being verbally confirmed as a "colleague," it had just been made apparent that they were not equals.

"Excellent. Let's not let that unpleasant business spoil our good news. I'd say we have more important things to worry about, Dr. Sellers. Now, let's figure out how we are going to put this grant money and new space to good use."

The two government agents left the building that housed Dr. Burton's office and headed to the parking lot. They put on their dark sunglasses as they approached a new Ford Galaxie. It was the same dark blue as their suits. Agent Warner got into the driver's seat and started the car. As they drove away Agent Brown pulled a file from the glove compartment.

"We've got a bit of information on this one," Agent Brown said to Agent Warner. "He's not too old and seems to excel at every type of intellectual endeavor. But, not at all in the area of sports. So, I'd say it is safe to assume he's using some serious brain power to accomplish this. He's the one we'll be meeting at the café today. Supposedly, he might be able to help us finally snag Dr. Burton."

It was a sunny day out. Not too hot, but not breezy either. They only had to drive a few miles from the university to a small café. Agent Warner pulled the car into the small parking lot. They both kept their sunglasses on, to shield their eyes from the bright afternoon sun, and walked to a small cluster of tables located outside of the café.

"There he is," said Agent Brown, pointing at the only young man sitting at one of the café tables. "Stay alert. We're not sure what kind of tricks he may try to pull."

They both walked up to the table, Agent Brown was a few steps ahead. The young man sitting at the table slowly looked up from his cup of coffee as they approached.

"Paul Burton, I am Agent Brown and this is Agent Warner. We're with the United States Government, Science Division of the FBI. Do you mind if we take a seat?"

"Not at all," Paul said with a smirk on his lips, lightly dabbing the coffee off of them with a small napkin. "It's not that bright out, why don't you take off your sunglasses."

Both men sat and slowly removed their dark sunglasses. Moving slowly, as if in a slight trance.

"That's better," Paul said. "I find it much easier to talk freely when I can look someone in their eyes."

Chapter Seven
PSI Department

The labs, medical rooms, and offices, of which Dr. Martin Sellers now had an office of his own, in the new Worthington Medical Center were amazing. In no time at all they had everything moved in and set up. There was no longer a need to hold meetings and experiments after school hours. They had students signing up and were testing for new subjects every week. Being housed in an actual medical facility, they had new cases coming in from across the country. Families who had children who were suffering, as Paul once had, were coming to them for help. Even adults with abilities were seeking them out. The cases were arranged by order of importance. Those who needed the help, those who could provide crucial data, and then those who showed signs of having any abilities at all.

The first year was filled with trial and error. In order to handle the larger case and research loads, a full medical staff was implemented. Consisting of resident doctors, interns, and even visiting experts in every considerable medical field. Dr. Burton resisted the addition of all the new people since he had become accustomed to keeping a low profile when conducting his personal research. But he soon realized that in order for this to grow, they would need additional help. He stayed completely involved in every decision-making process concerning any test subject or case. Over time, though, he found it easier to share and exchange information and ideas, especially with the esteemed visiting professionals. He soon recognized the new respect he was given from the scientific community during all this growth and expansion. The years of having his research thought of as superstition, hoax, or ridiculous were ending.

The most valuable asset gained from all of this was the expansion into drug testing. This was Martin's area of expertise. His fascination in this area had him searching across the globe to find doctors who might shed more light on the subject of what medication would mean to those with psychic abilities.

When he contacted some of these experts, Martin realized that their department did not have a formal name. They were glad to be part of the Worthington University Medical Center, but they wanted to stay a separate entity as well. It had gone back and forth from "Psychic Research" and "Research of Psychic Phenomena," to "Department of Parapsychology." Those were just a few of the names they were trying to decide on. They wanted to pick a name that would be respected by their peers. Trying to encompass all the various abilities was not an easy task either. Finally, almost a year and a half after establishing their department in the medical center, he discovered one of the original files from Dr. Burton's old office. On the front, in bold print letters, it read "PSI." It was the inspiration he had been looking for. Psychic Studies Initiative. Their department would now be known as the "PSI Department at Worthington Medical Center."

Martin was finishing up his notes on the effects of mild tranquilizers on dampening the abilities of a PSI subject when there was a knock on his office door. It was Dr. Burton.

"I am leaving for the night." He walked into Martin's office carrying a folder. "I just wanted to drop off this data to you before I left."

"Thank you. You have plans tonight?"

Martin took notice that Dr. Burton was wearing a nice overcoat and hat. It wasn't his typical attire when he left work.

"As a matter of fact, I do. My son, the stock market wizard, is in town and taking me out to dinner."

"That sounds very nice." Martin couldn't care less that Paul was in town. He was well aware of Paul's hatred towards him. And with Paul's telepathic abilities, he preferred to stay clear of him. "Have a good time, sir. Tell Paul I send my best."

"I will. Good night, doctor." With a tip of his hat Dr. Burton pulled the door closed behind him as he left. Whether he was aware of the rivalry between Martin and Paul, or if he just chose to ignore it, was not apparent. Both rivals believed he just preferred to fake ignorance in order to stay neutral.

Martin also believed the same blind eye was turned regarding Paul's amazing career pertaining to the stock market. It had to be obvious he was using his talents to gain knowledge on how to excel in his job. Martin figured it must have been some guilty feeling on Dr. Burton's part, that he owed this leniency to Paul for cursing him with this gift.

Martin could clearly remember when he threatened to expose Paul's technique for cheating on exams to Dr. Burton. He had figured out that Paul was reading minds to gain the information he needed to pass classes and didn't think it was fair when compared to all the hard work he had to do. The argument didn't last long. As soon as Paul realized he had been discovered, he countered with a threat of his own. He unleashed a telepathic scream inside of Martin's head that was so loud it left him with an hour-long headache.

"IF YOU TELL MY FATHER," Paul's inner voice boomed at the base of Marin's skull, "I WILL SCREAM IN YOUR MIND UNTIL I KILL YOU." The whole time, Paul never let an expression of what he was doing show on his face. Just a slight flare of his nostrils.

Martin sat for a moment clutching his head. The words echoed in his skull even after Paul had left. He was angry, furious even. He would have stormed out and told Dr. Burton what had happened, and of his son's deceptions, but he stopped and thought it through. What would he truly gain from this? The wrath of an immature telepath and the possible alienation of a trusted friend. He couldn't be sure Dr. Burton would side with him over his son. And even if he did, he didn't have the means to stop Paul from continuing to cheat or acting on his threat. The best plan was to wait.

It wouldn't matter anyhow. Paul soon decided he didn't need to continue wasting his time, and talents, in college. He had somehow been hired at a prestigious firm on Wall Street and announced to his father that he would be applying his energies to his career instead of school. Dr. Burton was powerless to change his mind and had to accept his decision.

Martin shook the memory from his head and continued with his work. He hoped with Paul traveling so much he would be "out of sight, out of mind." Quite literally.

Dr. Burton handed his coat and hat to the attendant inside the restaurant. He was informed that his son was not there yet and was shown to their table. He sat in the restaurant quietly, waiting for his son to arrive. He had been seated at a table near the back of the restaurant. It was a bit fancier than the places he was used to dining in. Truth be told, he spent most of his meals at the university's cafeteria. He wasn't used to the pressed tablecloths and dimly lit chandeliers. There was even a man softly playing a piano on the other side of the restaurant.

He did not mention to Martin that this wasn't just a family dinner with his son. When Paul called to invite him to dinner, he said he wanted to discuss a business proposition. Surely, he wanted his father to invest some money in stocks. A venture that always seemed a bit shaky to the doctor. The idea of it appeared more of a gamble than scientific. It was something he couldn't wrap his head around. Still, any excuse to spend some time with his son was a good one. Dr. Burton pushed the thought from his mind as his son approached the table.

"Hello, Father. Sorry that I'm late." Paul said as he put his tan overcoat on the back of the chair and sat down across from his father. His clothes were new, stylish, and expensive. Paul was the picture of a successful man.

His boy was a young man now. What was once bright blond hair was now maturing into a sandy tone. His face was filling out and even if he had shaved that morning, there was a small shadow of stubble on his jaw. His body, though still lean, had a more mature build to it as well. It was obvious, he paid as close attention to his body as he did to the detail and fashion of clothes he dressed in. He sat with poise and authority. Chin in the air, shoulders back, as if he were interviewing an employee instead of dining with his father.

"No need to apologize. I've only been sitting for a few minutes. I had the waiter bring two menus."

"We'll order first. That will give us some time to talk before the food arrives." Paul seemed a little too comfortable giving orders and had forgotten to whom he was speaking.

"I am quite hungry. Very well." Dr. Burton uncomfortably agreed. He

They looked over the menus, and ordered when the waiter came to their table. Dr. Burton also ordered a glass of wine before the meal. Paul declined, preferring to keep a clear head.

The silence at the table was awkward, so Paul spoke first, and got right to the point.

"Look Dad, I've done some digging on one of the scientists that recently paid a visit to your facility. He works with a chemical development company that has some great investment possibilities. They have been getting ready to release a new medication to the market, and it is going to cause their stock prices to soar."

"Paul, I don't think it would be appropriate for me to invest in a company that is so closely connected to the university. At some point, it may appear that our department had shown some sort of favoritism to their product because of my personal investments in their company."

"That's nonsense, Dad. Besides, all the paperwork and legal matters can be done through my firm. You wouldn't be directly connected at all. As one of the investors in their company, it may allow you to make sure your facility is the first to run their tests or even become their main source of research and development. You could be the first to run their clinical trials and get the patents on new drugs. Maybe even secure government contracts."

Dr. Burton sat back in his chair. He removed his glasses and gently rubbed his eyes. Even though he loved Paul dearly, the boy never really understood the workings of science and how human nature can corrupt its progress. His son did not understand that his passions did not lie in the pursuit of money, but the discovery of knowledge.

"I appreciate your generous offer," Dr. Burton began, "and for thinking of me for this opportunity. But I'm sure Dr. Sellers would agree with me that, at this point, the PSI Department, and its personnel, cannot use its connections or influence for personal gains. Even if he and I were to discuss this, as we do all things concerning the department, I'm sure he would think the same as I do. And I don't think that using my personal funds to profit from this information would reflect very well on the university itself."

"Frankly, Dad, I don't give a damn what Martin Sellers thinks! He may have the title of Doctor now, but you are still the one who runs this show. You are the one who makes the decisions. You don't need his approval or permission to do any of this. Do you honestly believe that he is as focused and dedicated to all of this as you are? Here you sit, telling me about integrity and ethics in the lab, when your star doctor has been dating one of your subjects for the past 5 months. Hmm… how do you think that would reflect on the university?"

Dr. Burton was silenced by this information. It has always been an unspoken rule that all relationships involving anyone being studied were to be kept strictly professional. The same rule applies to teachers and students. Emotional bonds cannot be made with the subjects. It can affect the way the data is perceived or the way the tests themselves are administered. Or, in some cases, it can lead to great emotional turmoil.

As he silently sat across from his son, spectacles still in his hand, he asked himself who this test subject could be.

"Janet Talbot," was gently whispered into Dr. Burton's mind. Paul's Cheshire grin spread across his face as he confirmed what Dr. Burton thought he heard in his head.

"Her name," Paul now said aloud, "is Janet Talbot."

Paul flagged down the waiter. He sat back in his chair and crossed one leg over the other. He had a slight smirk on his lips.

"I think I will have that glass of wine, after all."

Janet sat at the vanity in her bedroom, slowly brushing her hair. She was savoring each moment of each brush stroke through her long brunette hair. It would be her last night at home. Tomorrow she would be moving to the women's dormitories at Worthington University.

She was both excited and scared about the move. She had never lived away from home before. She had always been with her father. Even sleepovers at a girlfriend's house had been extremely rare, and visits to relatives always involved her father going along with her.

Her father had fought her on this decision to move to the university. But, she argued her point that she couldn't live with him forever and would eventually have to learn to live outside of his home. He couldn't refuse her. He never could.

He knew her decision wasn't solely based on the fact she was dating Dr. Martin Sellers. Though he didn't completely agree with someone employed by the school dating his daughter, a student, he had met Martin and thought him to be a very upstanding young man. He liked him, and how well he treated his daughter.

Martin made her feel secure. He had given her the knowledge and tools to feel safe with herself. A lifetime of fear, of standing on the edge of a cliff, all seemed like a bad dream since she had met him.

She remembered a time, not so long ago, during her senior year of high school, when she wasn't secure in herself. She was beautiful but withdrawn. Her large brown doe eyes, high cheekbones, and full lips stood out, even when she tried to hide her beauty. It made her a target for the girls who were jealous of her good looks, and the boys who didn't get their attention towards her returned.

One of those times, in the cafeteria, was especially traumatic. A small group of the popular girls began to taunt her. First teasing her on her style of clothes. Accusing her of being mentally retarded because of how secluded and anti-social she was. Then accusations that she probably didn't date because she was romantic with her father, and that was why her mother left them. The girls laughed at her.

That last remark triggered the hurt feelings she had toward her mother. It triggered her anger. It triggered her pyrokinetic ability.

As one of the girls began to flick at Janet's hair, there was a noticeable rise in the temperature in the cafeteria. Some of the students became uncomfortable and attempted to take their lunch trays and leave. Only to discover some of the trays were stuck to the tables. They were melted to the tables. Random plastic trays were starting to bubble as the heat increased. The students, seeing they couldn't grab the trays for fear of burning their hands, abandoned their unfinished lunches and began to exit the cafeteria. The formica on a nearby tabletop began to warp and made a loud "POP" as it dislodged from the top of the table. More tables began popping as the heat rose. The students began to panic, jumping up away from the tables and running to the exit of the cafeteria. In their haste to run out, one of the girls who had been teasing Janet was pushed down onto the bench next to Janet. She screamed in pain as she fell on top of her hands and forearms. All of her lower arms were burned and blistered by the heat of the bench.

Janet sprang to her feet and ran out with all of the other students. She ran from the school towards her home. She ran until she was exhausted. Only when she slowed to a walk did she turn around and see what effect she was having on the world around her. The weeds growing through the sidewalk browned, shriveled, and slumped over. The sidewalk itself had scorch marks and yellowing spots trailing back to the school. In the distance, she could spy smoke bellowing up from the school.

"What have I done?" Janet thought to herself. Her hand clasped over her mouth, muffling a scream.

A fire truck, with its siren blaring, roared past her, startling her out of her daze. She turned towards home and began running again.

When she finally reached home, she was lucky to find her father was there. She ran inside and collapsed in his arms, sobbing. Trying to tell him what had happened.

He held her tight, even though he was afraid of what her state of distress might do to him. But she was simply too physically spent to exert any heat at this point. He held her, and gently rocked her as if she were still a little girl. He looked at the scars their home bore as a testament to her turmoil over the years. There were burns on the dark green shag carpet and the old furniture. Spots on the walls where wallpaper had been replaced or taken down completely and painted over. He didn't know how to help her.

A glimmer of hope came a couple of years later. She was between classes at Worthington University when she heard some fellow students talking about studies being done at the medical center.

"Sounds like they're looking for people with crazy superpowers or something." She heard one student say to the other.

"Well, I heard you can get credit for it, or they're paying, or at least a free lunch. It can't hurt to sign up, right?" said the other student.

Janet had nothing to lose. Maybe they could cure her. Maybe they could take out whatever this was inside of her and she could be normal. She skipped her next class and headed right over to the medical center. That's where she met Dr. Martin Sellers.

He had gentle eyes, soft curly brown hair, and a soothing tone to his voice when he spoke to her. He gave her the paperwork to fill out and explained how the testing process would go. She was almost too mesmerized from staring at him to hear what he had to say.

She wanted to tell him about what she could do, but feared it would scare him away. She decided to let them proceed with their normal testing and let it come out on its own.

First, they would see if she had any telepathic abilities. They did the card test and the "think of a number test." When she wasn't able to send or receive any mental messages, they marked it as a "no."

Next, they tested for telekinetic abilities. Objects of various weights and sizes were laid out in front of her. She was then asked to concentrate on each object separately in an attempt to make it move. Again, she was not able to make any objects move with her thoughts. Another "no." She didn't mind all the testing, and the "no" responses. If the actual test wasn't conducted by Dr. Sellers, he was at least there to observe her progress, and his presence put her at ease. Not to mention, she was very taken by the way he looked.

They were going to test her for empathic abilities next. She was feeling dishonest having them conduct tests that she knew she wasn't going to pass. She felt her omission of being upfront about her affliction was still a lie. She liked Martin too much to lie to him. Before they scheduled it, she pulled Martin aside and shared part of her dark secret with him. Which prompted him to immediately set up a pyrokinetic test.

The testing resulted in the use of a fire extinguisher, but she passed the test with flying colors. She was still afraid of this thing inside her, but now she knew what it was. There was hope in knowing there were people there to help her. There was hope knowing that Martin was there to help her and explain it to her.

She cleared from her daydream and stopped brushing her hair. She looked at the few boxes she had packed for her move tomorrow. For the first time, she was confident in her decisions. Martin had been there to show the way. And now, he was there to love her. She had renewed her resolve to control this. With Martin by her side, she knew anything, and everything was possible.

Chapter Eight
Not So Secret Love

The PSI Department was quiet late at night. Martin was the only person still working. He had been sitting at his desk for over an hour writing an entry in his personal journal. He kept these notes separate from the other research files since they contained his private thoughts and not just scientific data. These entries allowed him to relate his data and research in a more personal format. He could organize his thoughts on the paper by writing down his hopes, frustrations, discoveries, and failings. All from a human perspective. Maybe, one day, he would publish this "diary" to accompany his scientific findings. But for now, its purpose served only him.

"September 23, 1962.

I don't know where to start. The PSI Department has been tremendously busy. With new equipment, subjects, and data coming in every week, we have made some amazing discoveries. And now with Watson, Crick, and Wilkins getting the Nobel Prize for their work in DNA, a whole new avenue of possibilities is opening up to us. Using this new information in conjunction with what we are discovering about the unique chemical and hormonal makeup of the subjects with special abilities, brings a greater understanding of what gives these individuals their gifts. It seems that the data is leading us to the conclusion that these abilities are passed down from the parents and inherited by their children. Certain abilities may be more prominent in certain lineages, or even exclusive to it. Possibly skipping generations, in the same family tree, by remaining inactive. Only time, and further testing, will tell.

Although, it looks like the fates may be smiling on us in proving this theory. Two of our test subjects, Joseph Zanetti (subject #T-264) and Patricia Romano (subject #E-252), have recently announced their engagement. A while back, I overheard Joe asking a technician about Patty if she was single or seeing anyone. I figured he would need a better opportunity to speak to her, so I scheduled their testing times to coincide so they could cross paths more often. I hoped this would help further their romantic interests in each other, and it did. They plan on getting married at the end of December. I am very interested to see if any of their children will show signs of having either of their abilities. I am sure Dr. Burton would disapprove of my influence in getting them together, though I really don't see the harm in it. I will need to make sure that if/when they leave the PSI Department, we are able to keep track of them. A protocol should be set in place to keep track of all current and future test subjects. I will have to develop that system immediately.

On a more personal note, things have been going great with Janet. I resisted my desires for her as long as I could. But I find her so fascinating in so many ways that I had to know her as more than just a case study. I made up additional tests just so I could spend more time with her. While running these tests, I discovered more intimate details about her. Janet is a gentle soul. She speaks softly, has a habit of biting her lower lip when embarrassed, and tends to play with her long brown hair when she is nervous. She is also the most powerful pyrokinetic I have ever met.

I read the detailed information about her background and the personality profile in her file. All of that information doesn't convey how afraid she is of her ability. She lives in constant fear that she might hurt someone by losing control of this fire that seems to constantly live inside of her. For someone so loving and delicate to possess something so destructive... it's an enormous burden to bear. Janet has spent most of her life keeping her guard up and staying in constant control of her emotions. Getting her to open up and share her thoughts with me is yet another benefit of the extra time spent together from the additional tests. And the more time I spend with her, the more I realize just how deeply in love I am."

Martin closed his journal, smiling to himself. Just the thought of Janet Talbot warmed his heart and elicited a smile. He knew better than anyone that he shouldn't be pursuing her. He had known this the first time he asked to see her outside of a lab setting back in April. He had known these feelings were not appropriate the first time they held hands in the movie theater and the first time he kissed her on the dimly lit front porch of her home. He suppressed the conflicting feelings and allowed himself to only feel his love for her.

As he sat at his desk and reflected on his time with her, he began to think maybe Joe and Patty had the right idea. Rules be damned! Who better to love and care for Janet than a man who could understand her like no one else would? Why should they be denied? She wasn't his student. He wasn't her teacher. The rules forbidding the staff and subjects to socialize were in place to stop the possibility of emotional involvement tainting the testing results. Those rules were to prevent the hurt feelings from failed romances from spilling over into the labs. His love… their love, was real. What if they could get married before anyone was the wiser? Would it be too late for anyone to try and stop them from being together?

Unfortunately, he wasn't in a position to immediately purchase them a home to move into. He had moved out of student housing when he graduated and found himself a nice apartment not too far from the university. It only had one bedroom and one bathroom, but the living room and kitchen were both quite large. The place had always been suitable for just him. Now he began to question if it would be enough for the two of them. And who knows how long until it might be the three of them? He wasn't sure if he made the type of money needed to start looking for a home. Frankly, he wasn't sure if he made the amount of money he needed to buy her a wedding ring.

He glanced at his watch. It was too late to try and find a ring at this time of night. The first thing he would do in the morning would be to find the perfect ring to propose with. At dinner, tomorrow night, that's when he would do it. Then they could set a date. As long as she says yes.

"She will say yes, right?" he thought to himself. "We haven't even been dating for six months yet. Am I being logical about this? Have I thought this out?"

He sat silently now. No smile. Would scientific reasoning give him the answer to this question? Or an answer to the question he wanted to ask her?

"I know my heart," he now thought. "I know how I feel about her. And I am sure she feels the same way about me. If I want to guarantee that we can stay together, despite the PSI Department's rules, then we must be married soon."

Martin stood up from his desk. He moved with a purpose now. As he gathered up his belongings his mind was racing with a "to-do" list that must be completed for tomorrow to go according to plan. A ring, dinner reservations, flowers. He had to be sure that Janet's schedule was free as well.

Martin held his briefcase, filled with papers, in his grip as he took his coat off the hook on the wall. He draped it over his arm so he could close and lock his office door. He paused for a moment, attempting to go over his mental checklist of making sure everything was safely locked up. Everything seemed in order, so he made his way to exit the building.

He was so deep in thought that he almost didn't hear one of the members of the cleaning crew say goodnight to him as he passed by. He gave a nod and a wave as he exited the building, briefly catching a glimpse of his reflection in the glass door. He saw that he was smiling.

"Yes. I am doing the right thing."

Chapter Nine
Relationships

Christmas, 1962. Against his professional judgment, Dr. Burton attended the wedding and reception of Joe Zanetti to Patty Romano.

There had been some objections from the families of the bride and groom about having the wedding on Christmas. But they figured this was the only way to be able to get all of the members of both sides of the family together at the same time.

The wedding was very traditional. The bride was in a modest white dress. It had a scoop neckline that barely exposed her clavicle and short sleeves that just grazed her elbows. Her mother wanted her in a more elegant design, but Patty preferred simpler silhouettes. She made a slight compromise when she chose a dress that had a lace overlay and small pearl-like beading along the neckline. She decided on a small veil, which covered the back of her head and the base of her neck. It was held in place by a pearl-beaded comb, which was nestled into the top of her dark-haired French twist. There had been some whispering among the groom's family about her calf-length dress. Which they thought was exposing too much skin.

Joe was the typical nervous groom. He stood at the end of the aisle, wringing his hands, as he waited for his bride to make her way to him. He was in the traditional black tuxedo, with a large black bowtie, that he occasionally tugged and adjusted. But all of his fidgetings stopped when he saw her. He was going to marry the girl of his dreams.

After the ceremony, the congregation moved to the home of one of Joe's wealthier uncles. The man wasn't married and had a zest for life and an appreciation for young love. It was his wedding gift to the newlyweds to supply the food for the party held at his rather large estate. He had enough property to comfortably accommodate all of the wedding party and their guests. Trays of homemade food were paraded out, along with an astonishing amount of liquor. Everyone celebrated and toasted the newly married couple.

Even though the large families of both the groom and bride had made Dr. Burton feel welcome, he still felt oddly out of place. He was uneasy, like a secret observer who had been discovered by the people he was studying, and yet the subjects still weren't fully aware that they were being observed. He continued to smile and attempted to interact with these people, despite his odd sense of detachment. All the while, he wondered, if any of the family members in attendance had special abilities like the bride and groom.

Most of the family members believed Joe and Patty had originally met by taking similar classes at the college. Only select members of the immediate families knew the truth about their abilities and the studies they were participating in. They understood why Dr. Burton was thanked in a toast by the groom for introducing them. However, Dr. Burton did find it odd when Patty privately thanked him for scheduling her sessions so close to Joe's. A fact he was previously unaware of.

"If he didn't keep running into me," Patty said to Dr. Burton, "I don't think he would have ever asked me out. I could see the way he watched me, and of course, I could sense his feelings. But if he didn't have those multiple opportunities, I don't think he would have gained the courage to speak to me." She chuckled a little at how shy Joe was.

Even Patty's mother approached him to thank him for helping her daughter. "She's never been so happy and…" she lowered her voice to a whisper, "…so in control of her 'gift.'"

Indeed, Patty had a rough childhood due to not being able to discern her emotions from the emotions of those around her. Patty had empathic abilities. She could feel the emotions of people in her proximity. At times, she could be overwhelmed by them and experience them as her own. If she hadn't found the PSI Department, she would have led a life of isolation or might have been misdiagnosed as having a mental disorder. Now she was in control of her "gift." She could tell when the feelings of others were creeping into her mind and she was able to block them out. She was able to feel the emotions of her wedding guests. She could sense the joy and happiness for her. She could also pick up on her Cousin Gina's jealousy for not getting married before her. Unlike before, she was able to keep these emotions from overwhelming her. She could even ease Gina's jealousy a bit. If she wanted to.

When it seemed that this celebration would continue into the late evening hours, Dr. Burton decided it was best for him to leave. He wanted to make his way to the groom and bride and thank them for including him before making his exit.

"It was a beautiful ceremony," he addressed Joe and Patty together, "and I am so very thrilled for both of you. But, I'm afraid I can't keep up with this party, so I must say goodnight."

"Thank you so much for coming, Dr. Burton. It really means a lot to both of us," Joe said as he gave him a hearty handshake.

"I am very honored to have been invited," Dr. Burton said. "And not to put a damper on your celebration, but I would be remiss if I did not remind you both on what the effects of too much alcohol can have with your," he cleared his throat, "conditions."

"No need to worry," Patty assured him. "I've limited myself to the one glass of champagne. More than that tends to give me a headache anyway."

They thanked him again for all he had done for them. Patty gave him a small thank-you kiss on the cheek before they returned to the crowd.

Dr. Burton said the rest of his goodbyes as he worked his way to exit the home. It was an odd mix of Christmas decorations and wedding decorations. But very festive, nonetheless. Before he reached the door to the front driveway, he ran into the man who financed the joyous event, Joe's Uncle Marcello.

"Hey there, Burton!" Marcello shouted with a wide smile and outstretched arms.

"Mr. Zanetti," Dr. Burton held out his right hand to greet him. "Thank you for hosting this wonderful evening. You have a very lovely home."

"You are always welcome in my home," he said, with some of his Italian accent coming through. "I know all you have done to help my favorite nephew and his new bride. He had a lot of difficult years growing up. But I knew he was a special boy. I knew he was very special, indeed." He said with a wink.

"He is, indeed, a remarkable young man," Dr. Burton replied.

"No, no," Marcello said, as he put his hand on Dr. Burton's shoulder and leaned in closer. "I know about how he is special. I have always known since he was a little boy." He leaned in closer and lowered his voice. "He can hear what you think. Made surprises and playing poker very difficult with that boy."

They both laughed at that. Even though Dr. Burton was confident that Marcello was completely aware of Joe's secret ability, he was still uneasy discussing it in public.

"No need to worry, Burton. You keep his secret safe and I keep his secret safe, always. I am just thankful that he met this wonderful girl who makes him so happy. I think she is special too? No, no. Don't tell me. I'm not asking." He placed both hands on each of Dr. Burton's shoulders and stood back. "Yes, you are a good man."

Marcello gave Dr. Burton a solid pat on the shoulders, exclaimed a cheerful Italian word that wasn't familiar and left to rejoin the party. Dr. Burton took this as his opportunity to leave.

He was deep in thought as he drove home. He kept the radio off, preferring the silence as he drove. He kept his eyes focused on the road, being mindful of the snow that covered the ground outside. Unlike most people, he didn't mind driving in the snow. The sight of white coating the sides of the roads was preferable to the usual scenery. The light dusting of snow that fell in the path of his headlights and landed on his windshield added some sort of peace to his drive.

He thought about the comment Patty made to him about scheduling the sessions in conjunction with Joe's. He supposed it could just be a coincidence. But that seemed to happening a lot lately. A lot of "coincidences."

He still had not confronted Martin about his supposed relationship with Janet Talbot. He wasn't sure as to exactly why he hadn't brought it up. It wasn't in his nature to bring up confrontation. He knew that this was something that could affect the progress of the department if the relationship ended badly. Not having had the best luck in his own romantic relationships, it was difficult for him to be optimistic in predicting how most relationships would go.

Dr. Burton had a great deal of care and respect for Martin. He knew how much the young man had given up to graduate college, become a doctor, and already dedicated so much of his life to everything leading up to the PSI Department. Including all the time he was currently putting in, as well. Dr. Burton couldn't help but reflect on his past relationships, and how they had failed because he always put work first. He knew Martin was busy with his work. He seemed to always be there, either in the labs or in his office. How could he find the time to even have a relationship? Or was it just that managing time between work and living was a foreign concept to Dr. Burton? There were so many things he had missed out on, and he didn't want those regrets to be passed on to Martin.

He was sure that Martin had to know the repercussions of his actions. And if he does know, then could he truly be in love with this girl, Janet Talbot? Dr. Burton knew the name, as he made it a point to meet each subject in person and be at least casually familiar with every subject's file. He wasn't sure he had been a part of any of her sessions for quite some time. Another coincidence? One of the methods used in the testing process was to occasionally change the technicians in charge of the sessions. He hoped this would give fresh perspectives on each case, and apply cross-training in each of the types of psychic abilities. As of late, he had been less hands-on with the personal workings of the department and further involved with what would be considered the "business and paperwork" end of it. He had been getting more and more pressure from the university's board of directors. They wanted him to produce documented proof of the results he was achieving and the medical implications of the research at the PSI Department, or threats of cutting their funding would be imminent. The board wanted their medical center to have the prestige of unique and groundbreaking findings, and have that translate into more money for the university.

He pulled up to his home and parked the car. His home was small and modest. Smaller than Carol's house. He bought a smaller home because he didn't require much. It had two small bedrooms, one of which was used as his office. There was only one bathroom, situated evenly between the two rooms. It wasn't much, but it was home.

The cold winter air enveloped him as he stepped out of the car. The night was very quiet, except for the crunching sound of snow under his feet. He removed his glasses and looked up at the moon. It was hidden occasionally by the passing clouds, but still shining very bright. A small snowflake landed on his eyelash. He brushed the snowflake from his eye, put his glasses back on, and wondered if this meant a heavier snowfall was on the way.

On his walk to the entrance of his home, he blew a bit of hot breath from his mouth, noticing how visible it was in the chilled air, illuminated by the Christmas lights on his neighbor's house.

Even as he put his key in the lock to open the front door he was still debating on how to handle the possible relationship between Martin and Janet.

"For now," he thought to himself, "I will just wait and observe until I am sure of the situation. Martin has had good judgment in the past, perhaps I should trust his judgment on this as well."

He went inside and closed and locked the front door behind him. He hung his overcoat and suit jacket in the closet next to the front door. He was conscious of keeping his home tidy, since he lived alone there was no one to clean up after him except himself. He didn't mind the solitude, most of the time. His home was adequate for his needs. He didn't spend money on lavish decorations. He never had company over or anyone he needed to impress. But that didn't mean he would not keep his home nice and clean. It was all part of his innate need to have order and structure in his environment.

The lack of decorations carried through the Christmas season as well. He didn't have a Christmas tree or hang any stockings or mistletoe. He didn't feel the need to put on a show for the holiday if he was going to be the only person there to see it. He felt he could live without it.

However, he did enjoy taking the occasional stroll through the neighborhood to take in the sights of how the other homes were decorated. Seeing some of the Christmas trees through the windows of some of these homes would bring him both joy and sadness. The twinkling lights were almost hypnotic, taking him back to his childhood and how he spent Christmas with his family.

He remembered one particular Christmas when he was very young. He knew he was only 9 years old because he remembered it so clearly. His grandmother was still alive at the time and was staying with his family for Christmas. She was sitting in one of the two new chairs his mother had purchased as an early Christmas present for "the family." In truth, it was to satisfy her new fascination with furniture that had an Asian flare to it, and she was systematically redecorating the whole house in this fashion.

The armchairs were a darker hue of golden yellow, with a very slight silky sheen to them. There was a pattern of white orchids and vague Asian symbols that ran down the middle of the back of the chair and the seat. Dark wood piping framed the chair across the top and through the center of the arms, matching the dark wooden legs underneath.

"These chairs are as comfortable as they are attractive," his grandmother said as she beckoned him to approach her. "Which is to say, they are not. Not at all."

She continued to sit on the chair though, holding tightly to her small glass of whiskey and ice. She would sip it occasionally, careful not to smear her lipstick. (As much as that was possible.)

"Ross, my best boy, come to me. I want to talk with you. I want to talk out loud."

The young boy watched her from across the room. He looked at her, lovingly, through his small round glasses. He was glad she had complimented him on his fancy Christmas attire when she had first arrived. The wool dress pants, a pattern of tan and brown plaid, which were a bit itchy, were cuffed just below his knees, barely touching his knee-high socks. The matching jacket was itchy as well. Luckily, he was only required to wear the jacket inside his parents' house if nonrelated company were present. His white dress shirt was kept buttoned up tight around his neck, held in place with a dark brown silk tie. An accessory he did not enjoy having to keep on.

He went to her, and stood by the chair, in front of her. She had kind eyes. An astonishing light blue. Unlike anyone in his family. Her hair was a mixture of blonde and grey and white, kept in a shorter style, freshly washed and curled at the beauty parlor the day before. She was always well dressed and diligent in being properly put together. Her smart dress and jacket were clean and pressed. She chose darker, muted shades to wear. A deep, dusty teal for this Christmas gathering. She always had her hat, gloves, shoes, and handbag coordinated with her outfit as well. Despite how the majority of the family viewed her, due to her rambling outbursts and drinking, she was a woman of class from a well-to-do family.

She reached up and touched his face. Her hands were aged but soft to the touch. The tip of her mauve polished nail touched the dimple in his cheek as she looked into his eyes.

"You are such a quiet boy," she said to him. Her words were slightly slurred from the whiskey. "You take after your father's family it seems. Smart and sane. So very smart. Lucky enough for you, so very quiet too," she then used the same nail to gently tap him on the scalp as she smiled. "One of the reasons you are my best boy."

He could smell the whiskey on her breath as she spoke. It didn't bother him. He considered it to be her signature scent. Almost like a favorite perfume. It was comforting to him as it always reminded him of her. She held his hands and pulled him closer to her.

"I will tell you a secret, my love. I am not mad like they say about me. Oh, I know what they say. The breeze tells me. It steals their words away and brings them to me. It tells me all the secrets people try to keep hidden. All the time. All at once, sometimes. A glass of rye helps, occasionally. I suppose we could say it's my medicine. My medicine to quiet down the whispering breeze. But it never whispers your secrets. You have no secrets about me, do you?" She spoke with a gentle smile. She couldn't make him understand something she didn't understand herself.

"No, ma'am. I know you aren't mad. I believe the wind talks to you."

"It's good to hear it out loud. You're such a smart boy, maybe when you're older you will be able to help your dear grandmother. You'll learn how to quiet the whispering devils."

She took another sip of her whiskey and gazed at her grandson with pride. She didn't know why his secret voice was silent to her. Over the years more and more whispers became known to her. For most of her life, it had been just hints of words here and there. A clue as to what someone was thinking, being gently placed on the edge of her ear. Now, as she aged, complete sentences were shoved into the base of her skull. She wasn't sure if the whiskey dulled them down, or if it helped her to just not notice. But she knew it was taking more and more whiskey to make it effective.

"Why don't you go and play and leave me to enjoy my 'medicine'," she said to the young boy. "Oh, but before you go, one last secret that I know. And it's about you." She gestured to him to lean in close so she could whisper it into his ear as it had been whispered into hers. "You're getting a bike for Christmas. Shhh, don't tell."

That was the last Christmas he would spend with her. As the years progressed, her alcoholism became worse. As would her violent outbursts. Dr. Burton would never be sure if her doctor's diagnosis of senile dementia was accurate or not. She might have developed the condition and that was what spiraled her abilities out of control, leading her family to have her institutionalized until her mind eventually faded away. Soon followed by her death.

That last Christmas with her is what led him down his academic path. He didn't know that it would also involve his son. He then realized that he didn't have many memories of Christmases with Carol and Paul. They had separated when Paul was so young, and there was always his research to keep him occupied.

The bitter sting of the holidays was felt the most when he became aware that there would not be a phone call from Paul. There probably wouldn't be an invite to his son's joyous Christmas wedding someday either. Or a wedding any day. It did hurt him that his son was the way he was towards him, but it hurt him more to know that Paul treated his mother in the same fashion.

"A hot cup of tea would be good," he thought to himself.

He went into the kitchen, which was smaller than most newer kitchens. A soft butter yellow was painted on the walls. The oak cabinets were painted white. He flipped on the overhead lights, which added to the warm hue of the already yellow walls. He opened one of the cabinet doors and retrieved a mug from inside. It was a plain beige mug. No "World's Best Dad" or "#1 Father" emblazoned across the front of it. He had never received anything like that from Paul. Was it a side effect of Paul's ability that kept him distant? Or was he just not a good enough father to get such gifts from his son?

He placed the kettle on the stove and set it to boil the water. As the flame heated it, he found where he kept his tea and placed a tea bag in the plain beige mug.

"Perhaps my intelligence is my special ability," he wondered. "And my lack of paternal instinct is a side effect of it? Perhaps it's not something I could have avoided."

The whistling kettle brought him back to the present. He used a towel to grab onto the hot kettle handle and pour the boiling water into the plain beige mug. He stared at it for a moment. He wondered if Carol had the same feelings of doubt and failure that he was experiencing.

He took his mug of tea into the living room and placed it on the small table next to the armchair. The phone sat on top of the table, next to where he placed his mug.

Dr. Burton picked up the telephone receiver and dialed Carol's phone number. He wasn't sure what he was going to say to her, aside from "Merry Christmas." He just felt like she may need a friendly phone call and some kind words. Maybe he was the one who needed it.

The phone on the other end of the line continued to ring. It appeared Carol was not home.

"Perhaps she was at a holiday party or a neighbor's house," he thought. "Maybe a Christmas date?"

He would try calling her again tomorrow.

He sipped his tea and began to ponder the mysteries of the holidays. He couldn't understand why the holiday season would bring up so many reflections on your past, and all the emotional baggage that went with it. He wondered if it was seeing how other families interacted that made him question the choices that led him to his current position. Though he was sure others had these thoughts as well. He also wondered if it was just all the snow and gloomy weather that exacerbated these types of feelings.

It was getting late. He decided he would make himself one more hot mug of tea and then head to bed.

Chapter Ten
A Renewed Interest

D r. Burton's alarm clock woke him from a deep sleep. He was still getting back into the habit of getting up so early. He knew it was necessary, but that fact didn't make it any more enjoyable.

He went through his morning routine of showering and shaving. He had already decided on what clothes to wear while he was brushing his teeth. Not that he deviated from his normal format of dress slacks, button-up cotton shirt, and the cardigan sweater over it. His white lab coat was still in his office at the university. Leaving it there meant he wouldn't be constantly forgetting it at home. While his mind was continuously multitasking on ways to efficiently make use of his time, it meant he would occasionally skip over the minor details of remembering to grab his coat or keys.

Dr. Burton arrived at the labs just before 8 a.m. He had already had his cup of coffee at home while he had been getting dressed and ready for the day. But he decided to have a second cup when he got to his office. One of his New Year's resolutions had been to be in the office earlier so he could go over the day's schedules and session appointments. It was a resolution he had kept for the first 3 weeks into the new year so far. As he looked over the scheduled lab times, he noticed that Janet Talbot was to be in for testing at 10 a.m. and Dr. Sellers was the technician overseeing the testing. Dr. Burton would make sure he would be available to sit in on this session and observe the procedures.

He pulled the necessary files and data to make sure he was up to date on all the testing that had been done so far. The data was quite amazing. A tremendous amount of progress had been accomplished with Janet's abilities and a lot of data to show the connection between the control of her pyrokinetic abilities and her emotions. There was even data on the objects she was testing her abilities on and how they were being affected by them. Those lab tests consisted of how and to what degree the combustion of the objects took place. The chemical analysis comparing the objects before and after Janet used her abilities on them had some very interesting results.

As he continued to read, he was stunned by just how little he knew about Janet's progress. Her abilities and control had advanced so far that she had been able to cause a cinder block to heat up and explode. The data concluded that her abilities were affecting the objects down to a molecular level. The technician who signed off on these findings was predominately Dr. Sellers.

He reviewed the testing schedules for the rest of the day. Making notations of the times and in which lab locations they would be held. He wanted to make sure his day was planned out accordingly. Part of this New Year resolution was to be more visible and accessible to the staff and patients of the department. He had a sense of protectiveness towards many of them and wanted to reassure them that he was still very much invested in their futures.

He also wanted to be sure to make the extra effort to be more sociable with the other doctors in the medical center. He was more aware of how much of a political game, within the workings of the university, was a part of securing funding and keeping an eye on those who would gladly scoop up your assets.

After a quick tour of the nurses' station, where they would have all of their test subjects sign in and fill out all of the appropriate paperwork, he decided he had time to leave the confines of the medical center and pop outside for a quick breath of fresh air. He knew it would be cold, but didn't plan on being outside long enough to require going back to his office for his coat. The layering from his lab coat and cardigan would be sufficient.

It was indeed very brisk outside. The sun was shining through the passing winter clouds. He watched the students making their way past the courtyard to the outlying buildings where their classes would be held. Some shuffling along, bundled up in winter coats, attempting to wake up. While others, obviously running late, rushed past them in hopes of making it to their class on time.

A few "good mornings" were exchanged as he took in the crisp morning air. Even though he had plenty of time until the scheduled testing in Martin's lab, he felt as if his detour outside was his way of stalling a situation that might result in a confrontation. He was sure that he wasn't going to walk in on some inappropriate use of lab time and resources for some sordid rendezvous. But if he was made aware of their relationship, would he press the issue and hold Martin accountable? He couldn't be sure of what action he would take until he faced it. This was one event he was not able to foresee. Nor, did he want to.

It was getting noticeably cold now, so he headed back inside. There was still enough time to occupy himself with further distractions.

"Perhaps another cup of coffee," he thought to himself. "Then, the testing lab for the possible telekinetic young man. That should get out by the time Martin is ready to begin testing for Ms. Talbot."

Dr. Burton arrived at Martin's testing lab at 10 a.m. Martin was already there setting up for the session. He was moving tables and stools around, and setting out the clipboards with the proper paperwork attached to them. He was whistling and humming a tune as he did all of this. He was smiling and appeared to be in a very good mood. At first glance, Dr. Burton didn't realize this was Martin because his lab coat was draped across a nearby stool.

"Good morning, Dr. Burton," Martin said. "I didn't realize you were in today."

"Good morning to you, Dr. Sellers. Yes, I decided I needed to renew my interest in all facets of the Department. I seemed to have gotten myself stuck behind a desk and thought I should remedy that. All part of my New Year's resolution. You don't mind if I sit in on your session with Miss Talbot do you?"

"Of course not, sir," Martin replied. He could feel a change in how Dr. Burton was addressing him. The tone and body language were utterly professional. He made a quick move to the stool that his lab coat was on and retrieved it. It seemed proper protocol needed to be observed and that meant getting his lab coat on fast. He wondered if Dr. Burton was here to sit in on this session just because it happened to be occurring at this point, or was he here specifically for his session with Janet?

That question would have to wait because Janet had just walked into the lab. She was the very definition of a beautiful young woman. Long, dark brown hair that had a soft wave in it. She kept it pulled away from her face, secured by a navy blue ribbon that laid across the top of her head. Her walk was accentuated by her tight fitted skirt, the same navy blue as her ribbon, and beige sweater that tapered in at her thin waist. She carried her dark brown winter coat on her right arm, set a top of the strap of her purse.

"Dr. Burton!" she said with delight. "It's been quite a while since I last saw you. Are you going to be staying for my session?" She walked towards Dr. Burton, her brown eyes sparkling as she stuffed something in her pocketbook, and shifted it to her left hand so she could extend her right hand out to shake his.

"Yes, Miss Talbot, I am. I hope you are alright with that."

"I am very glad to hear it. I can't wait to show you all the progress I've made. I think you will be very pleased." She smiled at him, her lips lightly coated with a red lipstick that made her teeth appear even more gleaming white.

"I'm sure I will be. Just go on with your session as normal. Pretend that I am not even here," he said and glanced over at Martin. "I do not wish to interrupt your plans."

Once the room was all set, Janet sat on a metal stool facing the far end of the lab where three thin sheet metal walls partially enclosed another metal stool. Fire extinguishers sat next to each side of the plain gray walls, and other fire extinguishers were placed throughout the lab. A necessary safety precaution, to be sure. Dr. Burton noticed some scorch marks on the sheet metal around the metal stool and wondered how many times the extinguishers had been needed.

"Alright Janet…" Martin quickly corrected himself, "Miss Talbot, let's start with a simple warm-up exercise."

He walked up to the empty metal stool and placed a small square block of wood on it. A simple piece of white pine that looked like an 8-inch cube. Most likely a scrap piece from a woodworking class.

As he walked back toward her he said, "Now start with the top of the block and slowly work your way down to the base. Without it catching fire."

Janet sat on the metal stool with perfect posture. Back straight, knees together, with her hands gently resting in her lap. She took a couple of deep breaths and narrowed her eyes slightly. Concentrating all her energy on the top of the wood block.

Dr. Burton watched as the top of the block slowly began to darken and a small trail of smoke began to appear. He was fascinated by the process. The dark area grew larger and then began to glow with the first embers appearing in the wood. Martin moved from behind Janet and walked over to some switches on the wall. He flipped one on and an exhaust fan above the test area began to hum, sucking the smoke out of the room.

"Amazing." Dr. Burton said in a low tone. But loud enough for Janet to hear.

She smiled with a sense of pride for having her progress noticed by Dr. Burton. This sense of accomplishment allowed her concentration to wane for a moment and the top of the wood burst into flames.

"Janet, concentrate!" Martin shouted to shock her back to the task at hand. "Bring the flame down and regain control of what you are doing."

She shifted on the stool to regain her composure. This time, with her back still straight, she gripped the sides of the seat and narrowed her eyes again. She focused on the flame that danced on the top of the wood block and willed it to diminish in size. She pulled its power back into herself and the flame grew smaller.

"Now darken the block all the way to the bottom, without it catching fire and without heating the stool," Martin said.

The two men watched as this amazing girl made the blackened area creep down the block of wood. An occasional flame would jump out but quickly disappeared each time. When the whole block had a completely charred appearance, Janet took a final deep breath, reached out to the wood cube with her mind, and pulled the heat from it.

"Go ahead, Dr. Burton, touch it," she said.

Dr. Burton paused for a moment. Considering her request, he saw that no smoke was coming off of the wood block. Even as he walked towards it, he could not feel any heat emanating from it. There was a faint scent of smoke in the air, but no other signs of a fire. Sure enough, he picked up the block and felt that it was cool to the touch. As if it had been charred hours ago.

"Simply amazing," Dr. Burton said as he held the block in his hand. "I had no idea that you could pull the heat back as well as send it out."

"A talent we discovered and cultivated as a result of having to disconnect the fire alarms," Martin said as he walked back to Dr. Burton and Janet.

"Disconnect the fire alarms? Do you think that is wise Dr. Sellers?"

"They are only disconnected in this lab, sir. It was necessary. Every time Miss Talbot was able to cause combustion the alarms would go off and our sessions would be interrupted. Thus all the fire extinguishers around the lab, just in case."

"And what of any of the others with pyrokinetic abilities? Are they on par with Miss Talbot, to be tested in an environment with no safety protocols?" He was obviously a little upset that this had been done without notifying him of the changes.

"There is only one other confirmed pyrokinetic at this time. He hasn't shown to have the amount of power that Miss Talbot has." Martin stood by Janet's side, placing one hand on her shoulder. "Sir, if you will just place the block back on the stool, please. We have another demonstration to show you. Now, just stand back here with me please."

Then Dr. Burton set the wood block back on the top of the stool, walked back to Martin, and was handed a pair of safety goggles.

"If you will put these on please," Martin requested. "Safety first. Now Miss Talbot, if you will dispose of the block as quickly as you possibly can."

Janet again readjusted herself on the stool. She clenched both hands into tight fists and drew in a deep breath. Martin took hold of Dr. Burton's arm and gently pulled him further behind Janet. Dr. Burton could tell this was another safety precaution.

Although the buildup only took seconds, the anticipation of it felt like forever. Janet summoned all her energies to build up inside her. Forcing it to fold in on itself inside her. Each fold making it condense into a tighter bundle of energy. The energy was spiraling inside her and threatening to break free. There was a slight increase in the temperature around her as well. Just before she thought she would no longer be able to hold it in, she narrowed her vision and forced all her power upon the wood cube. The goal was not to explode it, but to turn it to ash as fast as she could. And she did.

The cube burst into flames and roared. The heat given off was intense, as was Janet's level of concentration. It blazed so brightly, and burned so quickly, as if it were made of tissue paper. In less than a minute the cube had been reduced to a pile of ash. When it was all over, there was no flame left lingering. Just a small plume of smoke rising from the ashes into the exhaust vents.

"Good work, Miss Talbot," Martin spoke. "I'll just open a window and let some of this excess smoke and heat out." He crossed the room to open two of the large windows. "One of the reasons I chose this room is that it is on the third floor. No one to spy in the windows during sessions, no one above us to worry about if a fire gets out of hand, and the large windows for ventilation."

Dr. Burton heard Martin's words as he walked up to the pile of ash on top of the metal stool. He removed a pen from his lab coat pocket and sifted through the ashes. There was no trace of the wood. No chunks, pieces, or even a splinter was left. It had been utterly consumed by the fire.

Dr. Burton adjusted his glasses and turned around to face Janet as she spoke.

"Can you believe the progress I've made Dr. Burton? Dr. Sellers has been so patient and methodical with our sessions that I know how to control it now. Even the fires I would start in my sleep from having nightmares have stopped." Her voice was excited and filled with happiness.

"This is indeed fantastic news Miss Talbot. Perhaps Dr. Sellers' techniques can be applied to all of those with special abilities, as well as future pyrokinetics we may encounter. I would very much like to see detailed reports on the progression of these sessions. Personal notes, as well, if you have any. Maybe we could establish a syllabus to follow for each program."

"That is a good idea," agreed Martin. But he felt like Dr. Burton was testing him somehow. Like he was double-checking his work to make sure actual sessions had taken place.

"I look forward to reading it. Until then, continue with the good work." Dr. Burton nodded and smiled to Martin and Janet, and turned and left the room.

They both waited until they were sure he had left the room and the door was closed before they spoke to each other.

"Somehow his tone didn't match his words," Janet said.

"How do you mean?" asked Martin.

"I don't have to be in the telepath program to tell he was in here checking up on us, Martin. He knows about us. I'm sure of it. I don't think he saw me put my engagement ring in my pocketbook, but I don't think it matters."

"I thought we agreed that you weren't going to wear that on campus. Well, he didn't say anything if he suspects it. And besides, he was so focused and impressed by your progress... the bottom line is all that matters to him. We got results, that's all he ultimately cares about."

Janet placed her delicate hand on the side of Martin's cheek. "That isn't all he cares about, Martin. He cares for you as well. He respects you a great deal, and I think if he knew how happy we are, he would give us his blessing. I know how important he is to you."

"Just a few more weeks," Martin told her. "We'll be married, he'll see that we're serious about this relationship and won't be able to question our commitment to each other."

She leaned in close and gave him a quick kiss on his lips. She gave a little chuckle as she used her thumb to wipe the residue of lipstick she had left behind on his bottom lip.

"Now THAT would have given us away for sure."

Dr. Burton spent the next few hours looking in on the other sessions taking place. He monitored the testing and reviewed the results. Comparing the scientific data to the physical and mental well-being of the subjects. Even though many of the subjects had progressed in controlling their abilities and overcoming their fears, they all paled in comparison to the demonstration he had witnessed by Janet Talbot. He had noticed Martin calling her by her first name and then correcting himself. He could feel how they were trying to keep the utmost level of professionalism for his benefit. And as much as it angered him that a rule had been broken, he couldn't argue with the results.

If the relationship was the motivation behind the amazing results that were achieved, then who was he to question what they shared? He had never known Martin Sellers to be frivolous with the emotions of others. Perhaps this was something that was meant to be.

Again, he decided to ponder on this situation a bit longer. Or stall making any movement on it.

The whole department was alive with action by this point of the day. The one-on-one sessions were in full swing, apparent from the "Testing in Progress" signs on the doors. They became a requirement after one of the technicians had interrupted a session with a telekinetic and startled the subject so suddenly that it caused a flux in the subject's concentration. The result was the levitating pencil flying across the room and lodging into the technician's right arm. Nothing too serious, but a lesson well learned.

Dr. Burton continued his rounds into the medical labs, weaving a slow path back to his office. The testing on the different hormones and genetic codes of those with abilities had been stepped up considerably.

Every advancement in science was being sought after and applied to the studies being done at the PSI Department. They were coming closer and closer to understanding the cause, effect, and very nature of these rare gifts.

He ended his day back where it began, in his office. This renewed interest in all the workings of the department made him realize just how much he had let slip away. For so long he had been wrapped up in faculty meetings, securing funding and grants, and the paperwork that goes with it. Now it seemed, in his absence, these tremendous advances had been made. Would these still have occurred if he had been more involved? Had he been holding the advancements back with his outdated notions of scientific methods?

He set these questions, and the accompanying guilt, aside as he looked over the schedules of tests and sessions. He could see a pattern emerging. Certain subjects had similar appointment times. Others had even been paired together into the same session. What was the reason for this? Was there truly something to be gained by having a telekinetic and an empath paired together in the same session? Was Martin responsible for this scheduling, or was this another coincidence? He searched for the data on such pairings. Apparently, the empath was being used to gauge the emotional level of the telekinetic. Having the empath monitor their emotional responses along with electronic equipment, was a way to create a baseline on the empath's ability as well. Another report said this was also to use various emotional outputs to influence the concentration of the telekinetic subject. Other pairings were just as interesting and yielded different levels of results. Some subjects were being kept together, while others were being rotated. What prompted this course of action?

Chapter Eleven
A Burning Love

Janet had spent the early morning hours fixing her hair and carefully picking out her clothes. She wanted to be ready to go when Martin showed up.

She sat in front of her mirror, trying to keep one curl of hair tucked behind her ear. She looked at herself in the mirror and her mind began to drift. She knew how much she loved him, and was sure he felt the same way. That love gave her comfort, but she also wondered if it would be enough.

Janet thought back to her parents' relationship. They had come from very different upbringings. Her father's family had money. He had grown up in a large home, vacationed at a summer estate, and attended a very elite private school. Her mother's family were typical working-class folks. She had gone to a public school and had dropped out before finishing high school to get a job and help her family pay bills.

Her mother had been working in a diner when she met Janet's father. He instantly became smitten with the raven-haired waitress and made it a point to eat at that diner every day so he could see her. Even though she very much liked his classic Hollywood leading-man features, she had denied his requests for a date numerous times. She would tell him that she knew the only thing a rich boy like him would want from a girl like her was something she wasn't going to give him.

He continued to pursue her. Bringing her gifts, and continuously asking her on dates. He was persistent, and it eventually paid off. Her mother finally, reluctantly, accepted.

The courtship didn't take long. Her father knew he was in love with the beautiful waitress and wanted to give her anything she desired. His promises of security and devotion were enough to get her to accept his marriage proposal. Despite the objections from his family.

He moved them into a spacious home. It had been built with a growing family in mind. Four large bedrooms, 3 bathrooms, and a kitchen that would be the envy of a professional chef. A grand dining room and a living room with vaulted ceilings, perfect for entertaining. In the backyard there was a swimming pool and surrounding land big enough for a swing set and for kids to run and play. It was the ideal home for the picture-perfect American family.

Soon after they married, her mother became pregnant. But before her second trimester, she lost the baby. A boy. Two more times they tried, and both times she miscarried. Each time it was a boy. The tragedies were a strain on the marriage. Fighting and blame had become more common between them. The topic of divorce had been brought up, but before they could pursue that option, they discovered she was pregnant again. This time, Janet would be born.

They stayed together until Janet was 7 years old. Her father showered her with love and attention. But it always seemed her mother secretly resented her. She blamed Janet's birth for keeping her trapped in her marriage. A week before Janet's 8th birthday, her mother left.

She had left a note for Janet's father. Janet never discovered what the note said. She never knew if it contained remorse or regret in her decision to leave her daughter behind. Never to see her again. The pain of trying to process the fact that her mother left, and was not coming back, a week before her birthday, was too much for her to handle.

Her father sat next to her on her bed. His suit jacket always made him appear very broad-shouldered to the little girl. He couldn't look her in the eyes as he tried to explain to her that her mom had left them both. His words were gentle as he tried to explain this abandonment in the kindest way possible. He wouldn't speak ill of her mother, even though his heart was broken. Little Janet exploded in a fit of tears and screaming. She screamed out how much she hated her mother, and tore the covers from her bed and flung them across the room. They landed in a heap and began to smolder. A small trail of smoke rose from them.

She sprang from her bed and ran across her room. A panic took hold of her as she searched for either a way out or something to take her anger out on. She pounded her small fists against her closet door, leaving small charred prints and bubbling paint where she had touched. The whole environment of this little girl's room was feeling the rage and betrayal she was going through.

Her father stood in the room, watching the crazed child, stunned at the wake of the destruction she was causing. He tried to calm her, but it was more difficult than he first thought. When he went to grab her, his hands burned. He felt the sensation of reaching into a hot oven. The very air around her was burning hot. Yet, she did not seem affected by it. He saw the sheets smoldering on the floor, the scorch marks on the closet door, and now small footprint-sized burns on the carpet. He knew she was doing this. He feared she would be the next thing to be set on fire.

There had to be a way to snap her out of it. He removed his jacket, quickly wrapped her in it, scooped her up into his arms, and ran as fast as he could through their house to their back yard. He hoped he could make it to their swimming pool before either of them was too badly burned.

He could feel the heat boring its way through the jacket, through his shirt, and onto his skin. He could smell the fibers of the jacket burn as the invisible heat began to crisp them. If it had been anything else generating this heat, he would have been holding it away from his body. But it was his daughter, and instinct had him holding her close to his chest as he dashed to the pool.

He clutched her tight as he leaped into the swimming pool. They both plunged underwater in a great big splash. He immediately brought her to the surface and pulled the jacket back from her face. She was stunned, crying, but no longer warm.

She looked at her father's red face. He looked sun burned. His shirt had a large burn hole in the front, exposing his bright red chest. She reached out and gently touched his face. She wasn't sure what had happened. He could see the confused fear in her eyes.

"I'm alright. We are going to be alright," he said to her. He was looking right into her eyes. Even though there was pain in his eyes, he forced a small smile on his face to try and reassure her.

As the years moved forward his family would constantly remind her of her mother's abandonment and that her father was a saint in their eyes for taking care of her on his own. When he and Janet moved away, around the time she turned 12 years old, she never saw much of that family again. That side of the family spent years trying to keep up a façade of wealth and privilege, even though they were all spending frivolously and burning through the money at an alarming rate. Because he was a successful businessman, he would send money to his family, whenever asked, to try and keep the peace and harmony within the family. He kept Janet free from negative influences as much as he could. He knew her curse was tied to her emotional state and the influences of her environment.

He never remarried. He was always completely devoted to Janet. After she graduated from high school, he was reluctant to allow her to leave home to attend college but had faith in her to be in control of her burden, and to make the right decisions in her life.

She was missing him so very much on this particular morning and wished he could be with her today. But he was now living in Florida. He had moved there to care for his elderly mother soon after Janet moved into the dormitory. The old woman may not have always been kind to him, or his siblings, but his sense of duty to his family obligated him to step up when no one else would. He used what was left of his savings to make sure the remainder of his mother's life was comfortable.

His role as caretaker didn't last very long, as his mother passed away rather quickly after his arrival. There wasn't a funeral, as most of her money had been used to take care of her prior to his moving there, and a large sum of his money had been used up to pay for her medical bills. After he had settled her estate, and divided up what was left amongst his greedy siblings, he decided to continue to live in Florida.

"Janet, honey," he said over the phone, "I've decided to stay in Florida and continue living in Grandma's house. I've met someone here, a lovely woman named Mary Jo."

"Oh, Daddy! That's fantastic. I am so happy for you. Speaking of special someones, I've met someone as well. His name is Martin Sellers. I wish you could meet him."

"Well, there was a little bit of money left from Grandma's estate. I was thinking of coming for a visit. How about for Christmas?"

"I would love that, Daddy. I can't imagine spending a Christmas without seeing you."

"I'm going to stay at the Cline's house. You remember them? Our old neighbors. They've extended an invitation, and that'd save me from having to pay for a hotel."

"I can't wait to see you! Let me know when you get your airplane reservation. I want to make sure I can spend as much time with you as possible. And for you to meet Martin too!"

When he arrived, 2 days before Christmas, he treated Janet and Martin to what would end up being a celebratory dinner. It wasn't a fancy restaurant by any means. Just a simple pizza parlor. They all talked, discussing current events, work, and other pleasantries. Most of the questions were directed to Martin by her father.

When the dessert arrived, a plate of 3 cannolis, Martin decided it was time for him to ask a question.

"Sir," Martin addressed Janet's father, "now that you've had a chance to meet me, I wanted to ask you something. Something very important."

"Go ahead, son. Ask away," he said with a stern look on his chiseled face. He sat back in his chair and folded his arms.

"Well, sir," Martin paused and nervously swallowed. "I've asked your daughter to marry me, and she said 'yes.' I would very much like your blessing to, uh… marry her."

He unfolded his arms and leaned into the table. He stared Martin directly in the eyes.

"Unfortunately, I've only known you for a couple of hours. And now you are asking me for permission to marry my daughter. Is that correct?"

"Yes sir."

"All I can say to that, is I hope this means I get the opportunity to get to know you better in the future. You seem like an upstanding young man and my Janet seems very fond of you."

"I love him, Daddy," Janet said, as she took ahold of his hand on top of the table.

"In that case, how can I say no?"

He reached across the table to shake Martin's hand.

"Welcome to the family, son!"

After finishing their desserts, they spent the evening talking as they took her father on a tour of the campus and medical center. The next few days were spent celebrating Christmas and having her father get to know Martin better. He told Janet, before he left to return to Florida, that he was happy for her and confident in her making the right choices. He also told her that he was very proud of her.

Janet blinked herself out of her daze and finished getting dressed. After she checked herself one last time in the mirror, she headed outside to meet Martin.

He had just pulled up when she came out. He jumped out of the car and ran to the other side to open the door for her. She paused before getting into the car. She wanted to take a moment to look at him. To look into his eyes. She smiled, touching the side of his face, and leaned in and kissed him. He stood there, holding the door open with a smile across his face as she got into the car.

They had only been driving for a few minutes when Martin nervously broke the silence.

"I know you said that you were okay with this Janet, but I just want to make sure this is what you want before we go through with it."

"Martin, I love you. As long as we are together, that's all that matters to me. I don't need a big fancy wedding. I don't have a mother and I don't have any siblings. My father respects you, knows I love you, and wishes he could be here. But he can't afford to travel right now. You are all that I need."

Martin glanced over at Janet as he continued the drive to the court house. She was stunning. He reached over and gently touched her cheek. She had her hair all swept up in curls on the top of her head. Held in place with hidden hair pins and a large pearled comb. One tendril of hair had fallen free and she shyly tucked it behind her ear as she closed her eyes and rested her cheek against his warm hand.

He parked the car and they made their way into the court house. Even though they made the effort to get there early in the morning, they still expected somewhat of a wait. It may not have been the most romantic setting, but at least it was on Valentine's Day. Being short on time and cash, they couldn't dress as the traditional bride and groom. He wore a modest charcoal grey suit, and she wore a one-piece white dress. It stopped just short of her knees and had short sleeves. The air was crisp and cool that morning, so she finished off her wedding dress with a matching white wrap, instead of a veil.

They waited in line, filled out the appropriate paper work, and then sat patiently for their turn to be married. Even though they were both silent, they could each feel and understand the love felt by the other. Sitting on the wooden bench outside the judge's chamber doors, holding hands, Janet leaned in and rested her head on his shoulder. She was at ease with their decision. Excited, to be sure, but not nervous.

The event was not a blur, but rather in slow motion. They walked into the judge's chambers, facing each other. Martin stared into her beautiful brown eyes as the judge spoke, it all seemed to be happening at half the speed. All he wanted to focus on was her eyes.

"Dr. Sellers," the judge spoke and snapped him back to reality. "One more time. Do you Martin, take Janet to be your lawful wedded wife?"

"I do."

"And do you Janet, take Martin to be your lawful wedded husband?"

"I do."

"Then by the power vested in me by the state of Connecticut, I now pronounce you man and wife. You may kiss your bride."

He took her delicate face in his hands, paused a moment to look into her eyes once again, whispered, "I love you," and kissed her.

They raced back to the campus, cleared out the rest of her things from student housing, and took them to his apartment. Luckily, most of the things she needed were already at his place, but moving the rest made it all the more official.

Janet was carrying the last box up to his apartment, a small box containing some paper work and photographs. Martin, already inside the apartment, stopped her just before she entered.

"Hold on there a minute. I didn't get to carry you across the threshold." He seemed slightly out of breath.

"Martin, don't be silly. I've been here a hundred times. I helped move my things in…"

"That doesn't matter," he said. He scooped her up into his arms, box and all, and proceeded to walk into the apartment. "Welcome to our home, Mrs. Sellers."

"I can't think of anywhere I would rather be," she replied. Her arm was draped lightly around his neck, the other arm was cradling the box in her lap. She could feel he had a firm hold of her.

"Well," he said, "I can think of *one* place." He slyly smiled at her and kicked the front door closed behind them. She let the box fall to the floor, making a thud as it landed.

Martin carried her to the bedroom, where candles were lit and rose petals were scattered on the bed. He held her for a moment longer while she looked around the room, stunned by the scene.

"When did you do all of this?"

"When you made that last trip down to grab that box. I had to work fast, but I hope you like it."

"No wonder you were winded. Martin, I love it. I love you."

He carried her to the side of the bed and gently laid her down. She kept her arms wrapped around his neck and pulled him down to her. Their lips touched and both could feel the love felt by the other. Even though this wouldn't be their first time making love, this time was different. It was special.

He unfastened the buttons on the back of her dress, kissing her the whole time. He slowly slid it off her shoulders, kissing her flesh as it became exposed. His hands worked without the need of his eyes to guide them. Slipping off each layer of clothing until she lay before him surrounded only by rose petals and the soft light of the candles.

Her body was perfection to him. She was fit and toned and had all the curves of a woman. A moment of self-doubt crept into his mind. How could such a beautiful creature love him? How could he deserve her?

Martin couldn't see himself as she did. She could see past the baggy lab coat he wore every day. Past the dress pants and oxford shirts he wore. She had always known underneath all of that, he was lean and masculine. She unbuttoned his shirt and pulled it down off his arms. He pulled his undershirt over his head revealing the flat stomach she loved so much. She reached up to touch it as he unbuckled his belt and unbuttoned his pants. It was like seeing him for the first time. She recognized how uncomfortable he was with his naked body.

He hovered over her, gently kissing her lips, her chin, and her breasts. They were living only for this moment. The outside world was gone. No worries about hiding their love or being discovered. No pressure of lab results. Only them. Only now.

Their passion was intense. Each of them wanting to satisfy the other. No words were spoken as they each took turns exploring the other's body before they made love. Their bodies fit together like perfectly matched puzzle pieces. There were no clumsy movements. No awkwardness of repositioning or fumbling hands. Time had stood still for them. They were focused on each other and lost in the heat of passion.

Janet's passion had created a heat of its own. Neither of them noticed how quickly the candles were melting. Or that the rose petals had started to whither and brown. Janet's abilities were tied to her emotions. Unbeknownst to them, her excitement had begun to affect the room around them. Martin hadn't realized that his sweat wasn't just from physical exertion, but that the room was quickly becoming a dry sauna. Even more so, a tinder box.

"Oh my God, Janet!" Martin shouted.

"Yes! Oh yes, Martin!"

"No, Janet, the room! You are lighting the room on fire!"

Martin sprang from the bed and headed out of the room to search for the fire extinguisher. The base of the curtains had indeed burst into flames and were quickly spreading. Martin was frantically trying to gain access to the hall closet, knowing he had stashed fire extinguishers there for just this type of emergency. But the extra boxes from the move had made it more difficult to retrieve them. They were stacked in front of the door to the hall closet. He worked frantically to shove them away from the door. He tried to open the closed door, but the boxes were still too close to allow him enough access to reach inside. He pushed and shoved the door, trying to widen the opening into the closet.

Janet was still sitting on the bed. She was both frightened and embarrassed that she had so mindlessly caused this.

"No," she thought, "I will not let this happen."

She looked at the fire climbing the curtains and spreading now across the carpet. She noticed some of the rose petals were smoldering too, threatening to light the bed on fire as well. She pulled herself up on her knees, closed her eyes, and held her hands out to her sides. Feeling the heat in the room, she pictured herself drawing the heat into her body. Willing the flames and the heat to be reclaimed by her body and smother the fires in the room.

Her dewy skin was illuminated by the light of the flames. She could feel the movement of her hair, reacting to the bursts of heat being put off by the fires. She could feel the air on her skin, exposed by her nudity. She repressed her feelings of vulnerability and concentrated on feeling the heat within the room.

She had put out small fires this way before in the lab. Martin speculated she was either slowing down the chemical process that caused the combustion or separating the oxygen away from the fire and putting it out. The scientific reason always confused her. So, she would just visualize in her mind that she was drawing the heat back to her. She had only done this on single targets, never a whole room.

Janet continued concentrating. Willing herself to feel the temperature in the room get cooler. Knowing she was putting out the fires and cooling the embers of what had been burned. She opened her eyes to verify what her mind's vision already told her was true. The room, now only lit by the one candle that had not completely melted, was smoky but with no signs of any fire.

Martin came dashing back into the room with the fire extinguisher ready. He stood in the doorway, eyes darting around the room searching for the fire. In his panicked state, he turned the fire extinguisher on the only flame he saw in the room. The one lone candle. Puzzled, he looked at Janet.

"What happened to the fire? Did you put it out?" His eyes were still searching the room.

"Yes. It seems all your training paid off." Janet said with a smile, but her eyes were beginning to tear up. "I almost burned down your home! I could have…" she could barely speak as the tears began to flow, "I could have burned you."

"Janet, darling," Martin set down the fire extinguisher and came to her on the bed. "Actually, you almost burned down OUR home." He could see his attempt at a joke was not being well received. "Everything is fine. It was an accident. No one was hurt." He gently held her face and lifted her chin to look her in the face. He could see the sparkle of tears streaming down her cheeks.

"Martin this isn't a common accident. This wasn't me burning the toast or vacuuming up a sock. I lit the room on fire! I caused a fire. Because I love you so much I lost control!"

"And you put it out. On your own." He was trying to comfort her. Not only because seeing her in pain like this caused him pain, but because her distress was causing the temperature in the room to rise again. If she became aware of it, it might frighten her even more.

"Janet, look at me. I love you. This little accident is nothing. If it's not enough to scare me, then you shouldn't worry either." He smiled at her, "We'll just make sure that the next time we are both naked we have the fire extinguisher handy."

They both chuckled lightly at his comment. "And besides," he continued, "you hated those curtains."

They laughed together and broke the tension. Martin could feel the temperature returning to normal. He glanced around the room at the charred remains of the curtains and carpet. He thought it best to get Janet into another room and distract her from what had happened.

"Why don't you go shower and we'll go out for a proper honeymoon dinner," he said to her.

"You don't want me to cook you dinner?" Janet asked him. "Are you afraid I'll burn it?" It took a moment for Martin to realize Janet was making a joke. She laughed at how nervous he appeared for a moment.

"Well, seeing as how we're both still naked…" she winked at him. She stood up from the bed and seductively walked into the bathroom and turned on the shower.

He jumped from the bed and chased her into the bathroom and then into the shower. He kept his thoughts to himself on how it might be safer for them to be together under the running water.

Chapter Twelve
October 1964

The seasons of 1963 rolled by in normal fashion. When Dr. Burton was told by Martin that he and Janet had been married, he responded to the news with quiet contemplation. He wasn't happy with the confirmation of what he had suspected, and that he had failed to confront Martin about it. But, he wasn't truly angry about it either. Martin wasn't formally considered an educator at the university, so Janet was not technically one of his students. The situation was both wrong and tolerable at the same time.

As time passed, and Dr. Burton spent time with the two of them outside of the university setting, he got to see their dynamic as a married couple. It was beautiful to him. Janet seamlessly became the daughter-in-law he knew he would never have. On the eve of ringing in 1964, he toasted Martin and Janet to the New Year bringing wondrous discoveries, as well as his blessings towards their marriage.

Just as in the year prior, 1964 continued in a forward progression for the PSI Department. A few new subjects had been discovered and research on them ran alongside the subjects who were continuing to discover new insight into what their abilities meant.

Not all of the past subjects stayed with the department. There were the ones who had been students at the university and left once they had graduated. Others would just leave. Feeling they had achieved as much as they could.

One subject left under more suspicious circumstances. His room in student housing had been cleared out, with only a note stating he preferred to backpack across Europe, never to be seen again. The rumor was that he had a back-room gambling problem and owed money to the wrong type of people.

Then there was the couple who fell in love, got married, and left to start a family. Joe and Patty Zanetti. It was later discovered that their romance was not an isolated incident. Other subjects found comfort, friendship, and love in discovering this rare thing they had in common. Though, Joe and Patty were the first to conceive a child.

1964 was unfolding to show the promise of progress. New technology was allowing for different methods of measuring the effects of various abilities. New papers were being submitted and published, even though they were still being met with a great deal of skepticism. But it was succeeding in opening opportunities to bring in new doctors, scientists, and experts in different fields. Some of the past subjects were staying on to assist by applying the knowledge they acquired with their various educational degrees. Others filled in office duties or in whatever capacity they felt they could be helpful. Others, who had left, would stop by for no other reason than just to visit.

It was on one bright afternoon that Dr. Burton barely heard the knock at his office door. He had been so deep in thought reading over his case files that he was almost oblivious to the world around him.

"Uh, yes. I'm here, come in," he shouted to the mystery visitor knocking on his door.

"Hello. Dr. Burton?" a man said, peeking his head into the office as he opened the door. "I hope I'm not disturbing you."

"Oh, hello Joe! No, not at all. I haven't seen you since your wedding. How are you and Patricia doing?" He came from behind his desk to greet Joe Zanetti as he opened the office door.

Joe looked the same. His broad smile and kind eyes always put everyone at ease. He was the type of handsome Italian man who made friends wherever he went.

But Joe didn't come alone.

"We are doing well Dr. Burton. I want to introduce you to my son, Robert."

Joe entered the office, hunched over, holding the hand of a little boy, who was taking very small steps. He was the spitting image of his father. His brown hair was perfectly combed away from his face as if to force you to notice his large brown eyes and tiny full lips. He had on a light blue pull over shirt with dark blue short pants and tiny white shoes.

"Well, hello there, Robert," Dr. Burton said as he kneeled to the boy. The child did not seem too excited to meet someone new but was not afraid of the encounter either.

Dr. Burton thought to himself, "I wonder if the boy has any abilities like his parents?"

"We haven't noticed anything yet." Joe immediately bit down on his lips as soon as he realized he had responded to Dr. Burton's unasked question.

"Now Joe, you know it isn't polite to listen in on someone's thoughts like that," he said with a smile.

"I'm sorry Dr. Burton. Between work and the baby, I have been a little out of practice. Sometimes it just slips past me. And I could practically read it on your face. Do you think it's possible that he will have any special gifts?"

"I think he might be too young to determine if there are any abilities present. But anything is possible."

"That was one of the reasons I stopped by. I didn't know if some sort of test to detect it had been invented yet. The other reason I came by is that Patty and I would both like to come back and resume our sessions. Especially Patty." Joe paused a moment and lowered his voice slightly as if to hide it from his son. "Ever since Robert was born, Patty has been having difficulties with her abilities."

Joe lifted up his son and placed him in one of the chairs next to him, facing Dr. Burton's desk.

"How exactly, Joe? What kind of problems?"

"Well, she has always been very in touch with her empathic abilities. Tuned into the emotions and attitudes of the people around her. Now it seems she's picking up even more on residual feelings that are left behind. I mean, she can go into an empty room and pick out the feelings of the people who aren't even in there anymore."

"That is very interesting. Like a form of empathic psychometry."

"Empathic psychometry?" Joe asked, raising his eyebrows to a term he'd never heard before.

"Well, regular psychometry is the ability to pick up psychic vibrations, sometimes psychic visions, off objects. Usually from objects that hold some sort of sentimental value. Objects that are consistently used or kept in possession by the same person for an extended amount of time. It's almost like the owner's psychic 'scent' is left on the object. She could be sensitive to picking up a type of 'emotional scent' that is left behind. Is she unable to block it out when these episodes happen?"

"Occasionally. But there's more," Joe paused to look at his son and make sure he wasn't comprehending the topic of conversation. "She can impose her emotions onto others now. I know you had empaths here who could already do that, but Patty never could. Now she can."

"This is an interesting development." The doctor had his eyes focused on little Robert. "And you say this began after your son was born?"

"Yes. Well, not immediately. And not all at once. I suppose we first started noticing it a few months after he was born."

"How old is he now?"

"He'll be a year old next week. Is he doing this to her?"

"I can't be sure. It could be the result of hormonal changes from having a baby. Or perhaps just the natural progression of her abilities. We have always speculated that, with all of the various abilities, they are like any natural talent. That with continuous use and practice you gain more control and mastery over them. Some find that their talents grow stronger and continue to evolve. While others gain better control. But, we assumed that some were just naturally stronger in certain areas than others. She may have had the ability to do this all along but just never tapped into it. Why don't we schedule you and Patty to come back in for some testing?" He was speaking to Joe but had turned his attention to Robert, who was now looking back up at him.

"I'll set it up before we leave. Thank you, Dr. Burton. I knew we could count on you for help."

"Of course, Joe. Once you are part of this family, you are always a part of it. And you will always be welcomed back."

They continued to chat and catch up on the events of their lives. Joe let Dr. Burton know that Uncle Marcello sent his greeting and well wishes.

"He respects you a lot," Joe told him. "He wanted me to be sure that I told you hello for him."

"I appreciate that. He seems to respect you a great deal as well. I was a bit surprised that he was fully aware of your abilities. Even though he said he would continue to keep that knowledge a secret."

"Uncle Marcello has never made it a secret that I'm his favorite nephew. Back when I first came here and saw I wasn't alone and how many different types of special people there are, I wondered if he may have secret abilities as well. But if he does, I don't think he would ever let it be discovered. Not by this facility or by any family members."

"That is always a possibility. Which might make it even more plausible that young Robert here would have abilities as well." Dr.

Burton looked down again at the patient little boy who sat silently looking up, back and forth, between the two men.

"Frankly, between you and me, I think Uncle Marcello has other big secrets he prefers the family not to discover," Joe said with a wink. "If you get what I mean."

Dr. Burton was silent for a moment, wondering what Joe meant by his statement.

"I'm afraid I don't know," he said puzzled.

"Uh, he's never been married. He is very affectionate. I don't think his instance on making sure I conveyed his well wishes to you was on a purely platonic level." Joe raised one eyebrow hoping this would get his point across.

"Oh," said Dr. Burton, momentarily not grasping what the point was. "Oh!" he exclaimed. "Oh, uh… yes. I see. Well," he was quite flustered at this point, "as flattering as that may be, I'm afraid he would be wasting such attentions on me. If that is indeed the case."

"I guessed as much, but I'll be sure to let him know," Joe chuckled. "Thank you again, Dr. Burton. I'll be in touch soon."

"Of course, Joe." He was still a bit flustered.

Joe picked up little Robert from the chair and held him on his left hip. He shook Dr. Burton's hand. Dr. Burton attempted to shake Robert's hand, but the little boy preferred to shyly bury his face into his father's chest.

He directed Joe where to go to set up the appointments, and told him to be sure to inform them that he was being sent directly by Dr. Burton. He closed the office door as Joe and his son left, speculating on what would cause a shift in Patty's abilities. Perhaps a review of her file might have some answers.

He did a quick search through the file cabinet in his office for Patty's file. But it wasn't there. He had to assume that she had been gone long enough that her file would have been archived with those of other subjects who were no longer actively participating in research and testing.

It would be easy enough to retrieve her file. The room where all of the past subjects' information was kept was just down the hall from his office. It seemed like perfect timing, as he felt the need to stretch his legs a bit and take a walk to clear his head.

It seemed to be a bit quieter on this day. Not as many people wandering the halls as usual. Perhaps it was later in the day than he had realized. Keeping track of time wasn't one of his strongest qualities.

Dr. Burton used his key to enter the small room containing all of the filing cabinets. Here is where they kept all of the information on the subjects. Including their backgrounds, their evaluations, and the results of all of their tests. He went to the file cabinet that should contain Patty's case study, along with her alphabetical peers. He fingered through the tops of the files, searching for the one that had the label he was looking for. Luckily, the filing system was very efficient, and he had no difficulty locating her file.

Once he retrieved it, he made his way back to his office. Stopping only briefly to relock the door to the small room.

He returned to his office, closed the door behind him, and set the file on top of his desk. There was a coffee mug on his desk as well. He sipped the coffee. It had gone cold quite some time ago. He thought about going back out to get a fresh cup but then thought better of it as it was fairly late in the day. He had enough problems getting to sleep at night.

He settled into his chair and opened her file.

File #E-252: Patricia Romano

Case Summary:

Patricia "Patty" Romano came to the PSI Department as a volunteer for group studies. She was initially believed to have faint telepathic abilities. Passing some of the tests for telepathy, but failing many others. More extensive testing showed she is an Empath. Her abilities are not as strong or fine-tuned as some of the other subjects in the Empath category, but her results are very consistent.

Patricia's abilities had drawn her to classes and interests dealing with psychiatry and counseling. Her empathic abilities allow her to sense another person's emotions and feelings. Like most empaths, she is naturally intuitive in relating to others and commonly seeks ways to help them deal with turmoil and uneasiness. Thus, calming the conflict they feel as a result of her empathic abilities.

She had originally had problems with taking these foreign emotions in and attaching them to herself. This would cause her to feel another person's happiness, fear, sadness, etc. as her own feelings. Without having an understanding of her abilities this had caused her great confusion.

Unlike a couple of the other empaths, she cannot project her emotions onto others, causing them to experience emotions that are not their own. Also, unlike most of the other empathic cases, she is very capable of detecting the deep, usually hidden emotions and intentions of others.

When tested, she was able to detect when a subject was lying to her or exhibiting false emotions (even to the smallest extent of bluffing while playing a card game).

It would appear she had become so adept at suppressing her own emotions that it allowed her to automatically detect deeper emotions in others, more so than most other empaths can detect.

Update:

Her testing seems to have reached a plateau. In an effort to push her past this point, she will be paired up with other test subjects in an attempt to use her ability as a monitor on how the other subjects' emotional states vary as they are being tested.

See attached files for the results of blood panels and physiology tests.

Update:

Patricia has canceled any further studies with the PSI Department. She has obtained her degree and is leaving the college. Her testing with the Department has not shown any changes or progression in more than 6 months. All results show her abilities have progressed to their full potential and have not expanded with continued practice or testing.

He thumbed through the other papers containing the information on her testing sessions. Comparing her starting results to the results of her last testing. By all accounts, it looked as if she had progressed as far as she could.

Dr. Burton took a separate sheet of paper and wrote on it what Joe had described to him of how Patty's abilities had changed. He added it to the file, closed it, and set it on his desk. He would keep it handy for when they returned.

He was already trying to speculate on what would cause a flux in her empathic talents. A hormonal change from having a baby? Any other shock to her system from having a baby? An outside influence perhaps? Was it the baby, Robert, who was directly affecting her? Was he developing abilities already? He could only hope her return would lead them to find an answer.

Another question bothered him. He felt frustrated because he knew this other question may not be a question he would ever find an answer to.

"Why would Joe's uncle think I was a homosexual?"

He understood he had been out of the dating game for quite a while, but he wasn't aware of any of his actions that may lead someone to question his sexuality.

"That was what Joe was referring to," he thought to himself. "Wasn't it?"

Someone was knocking on his office door again. Only this time he wasn't so deep in thought to not notice it.

"Hey, Dr. Burton, you in there?" asked the voice on the other side of the door.

"Yes, Dr. Sellers. Come in."

"I just wanted to let you know that I am heading home. I've left some of my paperwork to be done by the lab assistants."

"That is quite alright. I imagine Janet needs you at home a bit more these days. She should be ready to deliver the baby anytime now."

"That's why I want to get home. I could become a father at any time now," Martin chuckled. "And if I'm not there when it happens all hell will break loose. And with Janet, well, that could be quite literal."

"Indeed. I certainly hope she has been practicing her breathing to help her remain focused. I would hate for you to miss the birth of your child because you had to prevent the hospital from burning down." Although Dr. Burton meant it as a joke, it did have a certain sour truth to it.

"Yes, we've been practicing." There was awkwardness now. As if the reasons for Dr. Burton's original disapproval of Martin and Janet being together were now becoming apparent. However, who better to coach her through this process than Martin?

"You know, Martin, the facilities here could be used for the delivery if need be."

"I know, and I even suggested that to Janet. But she thinks she can handle it, and wants the normalcy of a regular hospital. Without the chance of my colleagues being present. She said that giving birth here would feel like she was giving birth to a science experiment." They both chuckled.

"Get going then," Dr. Burton said with a smile, trying to defuse the tension. "Let me know if there is anything I can do. And send my regards to Janet."

"Thank you, sir. Have a good night."

It would be another birth connected to the PSI Department. Yes, birth was part of the natural order of life, but there seemed to be a fair amount of people connected with the program who were having children lately. Two subjects who married last year had just become parents of twin boys. One female subject, who married someone not connected to the department or its tests, recently gave birth to a girl. The increasing number of children had even prompted a discussion on adding some sort of childcare facility to the building. This would allow the staff and subjects of the PSI Department to continue with their testing while their children were taken care of close by. It could also be available to all of the staff of the university medical center.

Dr. Burton paused on this thought. The thought of those with children outside of his department. Perhaps this next generation wasn't something out of the ordinary. Maybe he was just hyper-focused on it because of the impending birth of Martin and Janet's baby. Maybe it had just caused him to be more aware of something that had been happening all along.

The next day, Janet went into labor. The ride to the hospital was typical for expecting parents. Martin was frantic, making sure they had her bags and followed the correct path to the hospital. She kept reassuring him on the drive that she was fine and to slow down. But that didn't stop him from asking her how she was doing every 15 seconds.

They arrived at the hospital and she was admitted with no problem. The contractions and labor kicked into full swing once they had settled into the hospital room. The doctors speculated that this would not be a long labor and the baby would be arriving rather quickly.

The attending nurse attempted to escort Martin to the waiting lounge, but he wouldn't hear of it. He continually reminded her that he was a doctor himself, and needed to be in the delivery room with her. Janet was aware of his arguing with the nurse and convinced her doctor to allow him to be in the delivery room with her. He reluctantly agreed to her request.

Janet had to split her focus between breathing, pushing, and not allowing the discomfort of labor to let the heat escape from her body. The only indication that she had let her concentration slip was when one of the doctors asked if the room felt warm to anyone else.

It didn't take long until they were welcoming a healthy baby girl, Margaret, into the world. When all the commotion had settled down, the baby was cleaned up and brought to Janet in her hospital room. She held the baby close to her, loving her more than she had ever loved anything before. Martin sat on the bed next to Janet. Still attempting to comprehend that he had a daughter. Their family was complete now. Even as a newborn, she had her mother's features to go with the dusting of chocolate brown hair on her tiny head.

"Beautiful," he said, "just like her mother."

They looked at each other with love and pride over what they had created together. This wonderful baby girl was the representation of the bond Martin and Janet shared. Martin had his arm around Janet while she held Margaret. Silently, they both wondered if she would take after her father or would she be gifted like her mother.

Chapter Thirteen
Control Issues

June 1966

"You had no right giving my child a vaccine without consulting with me first!"

A woman was shouting outside of the childcare room at the PSI Department. The volume of her voice had drawn a small crowd. The woman stood, holding her crying 5-year-old son, as she yelled at the male lab technician.

"There is no reason to get upset. It was a simple vaccine," said the man in the white lab coat. "It's to keep him and the other children safe from passing around diseases." The male technician tried to calmly explain to the woman. "I swear it won't hurt him. He's just crying from getting the shot. That's all." His voice quivered and a bead of sweat ran down his temple.

"I never told you it was okay to give him anything," she said through clenched teeth. As she held her son with one arm and grabbed the front of the technician's white lab coat with the other.

"Judith, calm down," said a beautiful, red-haired woman who had just walked upon the scene. She placed her hand on the mother's shoulder as she spoke. "There is nothing to be upset about. See, little Steven has stopped crying," she spoke in a soft, calming tone, looking into the mother's eyes.

Just then Martin approached the crowd to see what the fuss was about. He pushed his way through the small crowd of observers to the mother, the red-haired woman, and the technician.

"What is the problem here?" asked Martin.

"Sir, I was simply following procedure," began the technician, "and the boy started screaming when I gave him his shot. His mother heard him and rushed in. She is getting upset over nothing."

Martin took a quick look at the crowd that was hovering around watching the events unfold. He glanced quickly at the red-haired woman who had calmed the angry mother. She caught Martin's glance and nodded a silent reply back to him. She surveyed the crowd and paused for a brief moment. A wave of disinterest washed over the spectators and they began to disperse. She then turned her attention back to the mother, who was still holding tightly to her child.

"Judith," Martin began to speak to the mother, "I apologize if there was some confusion as to the permission of administering the vaccines to your son. It is routine, and normally we have the consent from the parents of any child who is left in the care of our facility. Informing you of this must have been some sort of clerical error."

"Um… yes… of course," the mother spoke as if slightly intoxicated. "Everything is fine now, isn't it? I suppose there was no reason to be so upset. Everything seems so much better now."

"Yes, all better. Why don't you take Steven home? Or better yet, stop for some ice cream first," Martin said to her with a smile and a gentle pat on her shoulder.

She slowly set her son down, still holding his hand. They both had a pleasing smile on their faces as they turned and made their way to exit the building.

"Katherine. George," Martin spoke in a low, but pleasant tone, "would you both come to my office, please?"

He led them down the hallway, a short distance from where the commotion had taken place. Martin opened his office door and allowed the other two people to enter before him. First was Katherine. She was the red-haired woman who had calmed the angry mother and dispersed the gawking crowd. She walked with perfect posture. She almost seemed to glide with each step. It would have been a difficult task for any other woman to wear a black skirt as tight as the one she had on, but not for her. She had an aloofness about her. A coldness that would suggest a lack of emotion. She did not wear a lab coat, but she did have an identification badge that marked her as a staff member. It was clipped to the collar of her deep green blouse.

The man who followed after her was George. His lab coat looked like it was a size too large for his body. And even though he was clean and properly dressed, he always appeared as though he had dressed in a hurry. Like someone who was perpetually late for work. Even though he had been at the PSI Department for a couple of years now, he still had an awkwardness about him that would make you think he was new to the job. He was seen constantly searching for misplaced pens and files and rarely stood still due to some sort of ever-present nervous energy.

Martin entered the office last and closed the door behind him. He crossed the room and stood behind his desk to face the other two. He stood silent for a moment.

"What the hell was all that?" Martin spoke, but not to either one specifically.

"We obviously had a little problem when getting a sample from Steven." It was Katherine who spoke first. "I had no problem keeping the kids calm as we took samples from the first group, but then Dr. Burton showed up. You said you didn't want him to know about this, so I had to 'persuade' him that he was tired and to head back to his office and take a nap. Only every time he got more than 20 feet away from me, my influence would wear off. He wouldn't leave. So, I had to walk him back to his office and wait until I could get him to fall asleep."

"He's resistant to your empathic abilities? Probably from years of exposure to his son's abilities," Martin explained. Then he turned his attention to George. "And without Katherine there to keep the children from experiencing fear, you tried to continue taking samples on your own?"

"Yes sir. I mean, I didn't think that it was necessary to wait for her to return to continue. I'm sorry I…"

"You idiot! Do you realize what could have happened? A room full of scared, screaming children who are afraid of needles and from having blood drawn? Those samples could be the key to detecting the next generation of those with abilities. I can't have it all ruined because you aren't patient enough to wait for your partner to come back."

Katherine stared intently at Martin. Watching him scold George as he attempted to apologize.

"Please sir, let me just say how sorry I am this happened. I promise it won't…" but Martin interrupted before George could finish.

"No! It has taken me years to hand-pick those I can trust and those who have the abilities and are capable of keeping this research expanding. I cannot imagine it all being jeopardized by someone being impatient."

"I just wanted to finish taking the samples as quickly as possible, in case Dr. Burton came back," George stammered out.

"I know you did George. I'm sorry I got angry with you." Martin was shocked at how angry he had become. He couldn't explain why he was so aggressively focused on his research lately. "Let's just stop all sample gathering for now. At least until we are sure this mess is all cleaned up. Give me what samples you have George, and then why don't you just head home for the day. And we'll start fresh tomorrow. Alright?"

"Yes sir," he said. Reaching into his lab coat pockets and handing over the several small vials of blood they were able to obtain from the other children. Once he had given them all to Martin, George apologized again and left the office.

"Dr. Sellers," Katherine addressed Martin. "George has been acting a bit more… how should I say this…nervous, than usual. Might I suggest that we keep an eye on him?" She was very focused on Martin.

He knew she was right in suggesting this. He had a feeling that George was against him. A feeling that George was hiding a secret agenda from him.

"Katherine, I need you to get Oliver and follow George. Have Oliver read his thoughts. See if he plans on turning on us."

"And if he is?" she asked. All while keeping her full attention on Martin.

"Then have Oliver do whatever is necessary to make sure he doesn't. Short of killing him. I don't think it will come to that."

"You know how Oliver can get, Dr. Sellers. He'll probably try to tell me George is going to betray you just so he can fry his brain and make him retarded."

"Then lucky for us you can sense if he is lying or not," Martin said to her. He felt that he could trust Katherine completely. "If George decides to try and sabotage my work, then use your influence and Oliver's telepathy to give him some sort of post-hypnotic suggestion that will cause overwhelming fear if he tries to expose us."

"That's an interesting combination of our abilities. I hadn't thought of trying something like that. I guess that's why you are in charge." She slyly smiled at him. Giving him full credit for coming up with this plan of action.

Katherine gave a small nod and left his office. Martin stood at his desk for a moment. He realized his thirst for answers was overwhelming, but he couldn't help himself. He had been dispatching members of his staff, who were almost like his own secret enforcers, to gather information and enforce his directives. It was something that, previously, was not in his normal character. But, it seemed like it was what he had to do to keep anything from stopping him from obtaining his goals.

The events of the day settled and passed. Martin was the only one in the lab late that night. The air was still and quiet, which is what he needed. He was analyzing the new blood samples and needed to work in secret. He sat at the tall metal table, looking into the microscope, studying the fascinating micro-universe carefully, and making notes in the file next to him. Even though the lab was kept at a very cool temperature, his white lab coat was sufficient to keep him comfortable.

His research had grown by leaps and bounds. The information available to him wasn't even known to the general science community. He had to carefully balance how he presented his findings and what he would keep secret. If he had to explain how he came to his conclusions it could risk exposing the methods he used to obtain his data. His work, and probably all of the PSI Department, would be shut down.

How did it all start to spin out of control?

Paul. It all started with Paul Burton. He had approached Martin one night, working late in the lab, much like he was now. Who would have guessed that two men who hated each other so much could benefit from working together?

It was just after Martin's daughter, Margaret, was born, that Paul showed up at the PSI Department labs, accompanied by Katherine. He said he had some information that could catapult the PSI Department to the front of the science community. But, the way this information had been obtained, and even the application of what it entailed, was not totally ethical. Paul knew his father would never approve of such practices, but Martin Sellers might. Yes, he knew Martin had a thirst for knowledge and that the ends justify the means.

The whole time Paul laid this all out for Martin, Katherine just stood next to Paul, silently focused on Martin. The information Paul provided did prove to be most valuable.

Information on gene mapping, RNA, DNA, and all of the information that scientists were keeping to themselves. Each of them wanted to be the first to uncover the mysteries of the universe so they refused to share their information with each other.

But Paul didn't have to ask to have such things shared with him. He took from their minds whatever he wanted. Whatever he needed. He knew Martin would be interested in this new science. So he gave a small sample of what he learned to Martin. These new findings were like a drug to Martin, and he had to have more.

Even though Paul may not understand all the things he'd gather from the various scientists, he would still pluck it from their minds, and deliver it to Martin. Paul was an excellent and very experienced thief. He had spent his whole academic career jumping into the most brilliant minds and taking the information he needed. He continued this trend in his professional life. It had made him very rich, but it still wasn't enough. So why would he betray his father's values and dare to approach Martin with this?

Power. Plain and simple. Paul couldn't get enough.

Was he motivated by the need for approval from his father? Was his plan to build up Martin and then set him up for failure? Maybe originally. But now it was just the lust for more power and control. He knew what the PSI Department could become in the right hands. His father wasn't the right one. His morals and old-fashioned way of thinking would hinder the growth of the PSI Department for generations. Paul wasn't the right one. He could get the information but didn't know what it all meant or how to apply it correctly. Nor, did he have any interest in learning what it all meant. Dr. Martin Sellers was the right one. He had the drive, and the knowledge to run with what Paul would give him. Yes, he could be controlled with the promise of more knowledge, just like Paul wanted. With Paul's money and connections, he could see himself using the PSI Department to further his reach, influence, and power even more.

"Congratulations on your new daughter," Paul had said when he approached Martin just a week after her birth. He was dressed in a finely tailored suit. A dark blue, or black. It was hard to tell from the lighting in the lab and Martin's eyes were already tired. He walked toward Martin, with a tan overcoat hanging over one arm and that Cheshire grin on his face.

"Thank you, Paul," Martin replied, careful to keep his thoughts silent or guarded. While also carefully keeping an eye on the red-haired woman who walked in with him.

"I suppose congratulations are also in order on the work you have done with your wife. Quite a feat for her to give birth and not start any fires. That must have been exhausting for her to have been that focused the whole time." There was a definite lack of sincerity in his tone.

"It was. Enough small talk, Paul. What do you want?"

"Cut right to the chase. I always liked that about you, Martin. And you needn't keep humming in your thoughts. If I want to pry past that, I can. I've come waving a white flag, Martin. A truce. I think I have something we can both benefit from."

Paul walked around to the other side of the lab and glanced carefully at the top of the table. He ran two fingers across the table's surface, rubbed them with his thumb, and examined them before placing his coat on top of it. He then sat on the stool across the table from Martin. The pretty, red-haired woman had followed Paul around the table and stood just behind his left shoulder. Her eyes fixed on Martin the entire time.

"You see, Martin, I have access to many different types of people in my line work. Captains of industry, artists," he paused for a second, "and scientists." His wicked smirk crept back into his lips.

"How very interesting for you, Paul. What does this have to do with me?"

"As smart as I may be, Martin, I just don't have the wherewithal to know what to do with information on things like 'gene mapping.' Does that mean something to you?"

Paul could see he had piqued Martin's interest. And that momentary slip, just a split second of letting his guard down, was all that the red-haired woman needed. She could feed his desire for knowledge.

"Sometimes I come across this information. Just floating around in these men's thoughts. They get to keep the information. I'm just making a, shall we say, mental copy of it. And because I have no problem gaining access to men in this profession, I tend to have an abundance of information that I could pass on to someone. But with whom should I share it?" Again he paused and looked around the lab. "I don't suppose you keep any wine handy? No?"

The red-haired woman was still focused on Martin. She could tell the question about wine would not distract him from the topic at hand. He wanted to know what Paul knew.

"I, of course, do not have the understanding of such things," Paul said as he put his hands on top of the table, fingers intertwined. "But you do. Occasionally, I would recognize items that might be applied to my father's work. Many times, information from one mind could lead me to gather even greater information from someone else's mind. I do come across it quite a bit. I'm sure if you were to properly apply all of my findings, you could really turn this little school project of yours into something worldwide. Quite the legacy for a father to leave his daughter. Wouldn't you say?"

Martin listened to what Paul was saying, and although he was aware of the woman standing next to him, he was only able to stay focused on what Paul was saying. He was only able to momentarily shift his gaze to her.

"Oh," Paul exclaimed, "how rude of me! This is my companion, Katherine O'Bannon. Katherine, this is Mr. Martin Sellers."

She stepped forward and extended her hand. "Pleasure to meet you," she said. Though her tone was neither friendly nor cold. She was simply making a statement. Unlike her single step forward, in which her hips swayed with a quiet sensuality.

"Dr. Martin Sellers," Martin corrected Paul as he stood up to shake her hand.

"Of course, Dr. Sellers. My mistake," Paul corrected himself with an obvious insincerity.

It was apparent that the mistake was intentional, but Martin wasn't too concerned with it. Which was odd in itself, as that type of behavior normally set him on edge. In this moment, he was content with ignoring it.

Katherine released Martin's hand and slinked back to her spot just behind Paul. Martin retook his seat, oddly prepared to listen to what Paul had to say.

"Are you ready for verification that I can deliver on what I'm claiming?" Paul's question to Martin seemed very much like a question posed as an agreement to a deal being struck.

Martin felt hungry for this information. His desire for it was borderline obsession. His heartbeats had increased. He was eager to know if this was true. If this way of obtaining information was possible. The possibility of it was so overwhelming that he wasn't concerned with the ethical repercussions of it. The result of getting this information was all he wanted.

"What do I have to do?" Martin asked.

Paul leaned in a little further on the table. He reached out to Martin's mind with his own and found that Martin was very receptive to him having access.

Martin could feel the familiar electric tingle at the base of his skull. He knew Paul was in his head now. There was nothing for him to do but to receive the information as easily as recalling a recent memory. He could see everything Paul had promised, written in a notebook in his mind. As if he was remembering information he had written down himself. There was more. Writing on a chalkboard that was in a lab setting that was foreign to Martin, yet now it seemed vaguely familiar too. It all made sense to him, even though he hadn't come up with the information on his own.

After verifying the information Paul was offering was real, they sealed the deal. It was a slippery slope down a dark path from there. Not only could Paul spy into the minds of these most accomplished scientists, but if he could get them in close proximity to Martin, he could relay the information directly to Martin's mind.

It wasn't a difficult task to get Paul into any medical conference that Martin could attend. All Paul had to do was scan the minds in the room, looking for traces of specific key phrases, markers, or formulas that would be related to the work done at the PSI Department. He could then act as a conduit between the source mind and Martin's mind. The flood of information would unfold into Martin's head as if he were recalling his own memories. He could get information, firsthand, that answered so many questions, completed so many equations and possibly advance his work by years. Paul would attend these functions with his assistant, Katherine O'Bannon.

It had even been commented to Martin that the stunning redhead seemed to have somewhat of a crush on him. Seeing as she was always so intently focused on him.

Paul also convinced Martin to agree that Katherine would be hired on to the staff at the PSI Department, and she would assist him in whatever means she could. She could also set up the meetings between him and Paul without anyone finding out. Martin felt shame, somewhere deep inside, about this agreement with Paul, but his consuming thirst for knowledge forced him to go against his better judgment.

Martin just kept telling himself that in the end, it would all be worth it. Katherine would tell him it would all be worth it. Sacrifices had to be made. Just moral sacrifices at this point. Luckily, that had been all.

It had continued this way, without incident, until today. The morning seemed so long ago. Now, at nighttime, he sat in the lab, alone. He was studying the samples of blood he had stolen from the children.

"Stolen," he thought to himself. "Like some kind of monster in a scary childhood bedtime story." No sooner did he think it, and the thought was gone. He would continue analyzing his work.

All the children involved with the PSI Department had samples taken. Comparisons would be made from those who had one parent with abilities, to those with both parents being gifted. Even his daughter was among those who were cataloged. Unknown to Janet. There was nothing conclusive yet. Margaret was too young to display any kind of abilities.

Now they were taking samples of all the kids who were in the Department's Day Care Center. Children whose parents weren't part of the program, but who simply worked at the university. He hoped this would give them a broader database to make comparisons between.

The research would have to continue. Luckily, Martin did have his secret help. He had established a small, trusted group who could help him keep control of the projects and further all the findings that Paul provided. Although he did wonder, in private, just how loyal some of them were. There were a few that he wasn't sure what their motivation was. And those few seemed to gravitate his thoughts towards Paul.

"Enough distractions," he thought to himself. He rubbed his eyes, adjusted his grip on his pen, and leaned down to the microscope again. Only looking up to make the occasional notation on the files he kept next to the microscope. The work would continue, but he would attempt to be mindful of the other workings going on around him. He must not lose control of the PSI Department.

Chapter Fourteen
Katherine's Tale

"Mister Burton," a female voice said coming out of the large speaker on top of the desk.

Paul leaned forward, seated in his large leather chair behind his grand, highly polished, cherry wood desk. He flipped a small switch on the speaker box and replied, "Yes, Miss Baker."

"There is a Katherine O'Bannon here to see you."

"Thank you, Miss Baker. Show her in please."

Paul Burton sat behind his enormous oak desk. There was a full window taking up almost the entire wall behind him, giving a fantastic view of the city below from the 28th floor. Even though the window was fully exposed with the curtains drawn back, it was an overcast day out so the office was fairly dim. The darkness of this space was not just from the lack of natural light coming in the window, but also from the dark décor of the room itself. The walls to his left and right were both dark wood paneling. He hadn't guessed at the type of wood, the specifics of such things were not important to him. Two large, dark maroon leather chairs sat across from him, facing his desk. There was an odd-shaped wooden sculpture that Paul acquired in Africa, which sat near the wall to the left of his desk. A large area rug that ran underneath the twin maroon chairs, all the way to the office door, was festooned in beige and dark brown fleur-de-lis patterns. With all of the rich brown tones, supple leather, and polished wood finishes, the office had a very regal, yet very dark, feel to it.

Miss Baker opened the large pair of double doors and stepped into the office, leading the way for Katherine O'Bannon.

Once Katherine had entered the dimly lit room, Miss Baker asked, "Is there anything else Mr. Burton?" She stood patiently, hands clasped together at her torso, until he answered her. She had a polite face and greying hair neatly fashioned into a bun on the top of her head.

"No, Miss Baker. That will be all for now. Thank you."

Miss Baker exited the office, closing the double doors behind her.

Katherine approached the desk. The plush rug gave slightly underneath her step, making it slightly difficult to walk on in her high heels. But she still managed to walk with her perfect posture and grace.

"Please Katherine, have a seat," Paul said gesturing to one of the maroon leather chairs in front of him. It was a polite gesture, even though he remained seated the whole time. He sat back and took in the entirety of her outfit. "I do love it when a beautiful red-haired woman wears such a deep shade of green, like the one you have on today. It's very striking on you."

"Thank you Mr. Burton," Katherine said as she took a seat. She touched the front of her dark green silk blouse as if to affirm that she indeed had on the color Paul had described. She sat near the front of her chair, her back poised, and her knees together. She kept both feet off to one side, the proper way for her to be seated when wearing a skirt.

"I assume you are here to give me an update on what is happening in the labs?"

"I am," she started. She realized that with the window positioned behind him, it made it difficult for her to see his features clearly. Particularly his eyes. "There are just a few incidents that I thought needed to be brought to your attention. First is the continuing manipulation of your father."

"Is he still resistant to your influences?"

"A bit. But don't underestimate me," she said with a grin. "I can handle him. I just thought you should know just how much influencing Dr. Sellers has me doing."

"Are you being instructed to use your influence outside of the program?"

"No, it's just that I…"

"Then I don't care. Continue as Martin instructs you. And continue with Martin as I have instructed you. Was there something else or did you purposely come to waste my time?"

Katherine readjusted her posture. She drew a deep breath and made sure she was sitting up straight. She would not let this man intimidate her. No one would ever intimidate her again.

Paul was well aware of Katherine O'Bannon's background. She was very accomplished at controlling her empathic abilities. Able to force emotions and feelings onto those around her. Although she had not always been so capable of wielding her abilities with such expertise.

She was the middle child of three female children of an Irish family living in New York. Her mother's parents had immigrated to America when her mother was a baby. Her father had come directly from Ireland when he became an adult. They lived in a modest brownstone, her father worked construction, and her mother tended to the home and children. Her father worked long hours at a very hard, physical job. When he would come home from those grueling days of work, he would drink to unwind. Unknown to any of them, this left him susceptible to Katherine's newly developing abilities.

His drinking began to increase around the time she was 12 years old. It would bring out his loud and aggressive tendencies, which would frighten young Katherine. Her empathic abilities would then project her emotion of fear onto her drunken father. Without knowing why, he would then become afraid of everything around him, including Katherine. The shock of being afraid of his beautiful red-haired daughter caused him to flee from her and seek shelter anywhere away from her. Then, once out of the range of her influence, he would go into a rage from the shame of being afraid of a little girl. If he approached her in this rage it would only serve to scare her further. She would then, unknowingly, project her fear back at him again.

This cycle would continue until he would finally seek refuge in a bar down the street. Only coming home to pass out in his bedroom from a mix of exhaustion and alcohol. Eventually, passing out no longer pacified him. He would awake the next day, recalling his fear and the rage would still be present, even when he wasn't drinking. Without the alcohol in his system to leave his mind susceptible to her untrained ability, he was able to get close to her and take his rage out on her by beating her. His mind was focused on the anger. Her mind was disoriented from being beaten. He would shout at her that she was sent by the devil and given the face of an angel to deceive them. Soon her constant fear of him stayed near her like a haze. And the haze would grow thicker and stronger. Making him feel her fear as well. As always, once out of her range, it would anger him more.

The abuse continued. One of the nights when he drank and her fear kept him from getting close to her, he took out his anger on her sisters and her mother. Her fear began to change. Eventually, it started to turn to resentment. Only causing him to resent her, and soon all those around him, for ruining his life. He would shout that he blamed her mother for bringing this demon child into the world.

One evening, as she lay in her bed in the room she shared with her two other sisters, she was curled up with blankets around her as she listened to her father beat her mother in the next room. She heard the pleas and cries from her mother to stop. But he continued. The walls shook with a loud thud. She knew it was their oak dresser that was banging against the wall from her mother being thrown against it. She heard the sound of glass shattering on the floor. Most likely one or more of the picture frames that sat on top of the dresser.

There was suddenly another person screaming for him to stop. Katherine hadn't noticed her older sister had left their room. She had gone to try to stop their father. It didn't work, he only turned his attention to her.

He grabbed her sister by her hair and dragged her back to her bedroom. Bursting through the door and flipping on the light. Katherine jumped from her bed to her younger sister's bed and huddled next to her. He still held tight to her older sister's hair as he screamed at the girls. Her sister clutched at his hands, trying to release the hold he had on her hair. She cried and screamed for him to let her go. But he held her hair tight as he made his way towards Katherine and her little sister.

Behind him, propping herself against the doorframe, was Katherine's mother. Her face was bloody and already swollen with injuries.

"Stop," her mother could barely say. "You leave them be." She could hardly stand. She attempted to slow him down by reaching out and grabbing ahold of his shirt. He easily pulled himself free and smacked her to the ground with his free hand. She would not be able to protect them.

His rage was out of control. He threw the oldest sister to the floor. Katherine's fear could not reach into his mind. She wasn't strong enough to hold her little sister when he grabbed her and pulled her away. She wasn't fast enough to evade his grasp when he grabbed Katherine and threw her into the corner.

He came at her. His face was red and flecks of spit came from his mouth as he screamed at her, calling her an abomination and questioning if she was even his daughter. She wasn't just frightened, she was terrified. She began to panic and wanted nothing more than to flee but this beast of a man blocked her path.

Escape. Flee. GET AWAY! The dire and overwhelming need to flee for her life was all she could feel as he grabbed her by the shoulders and lifted her off of the floor. She was face to face with him, unsure what he was going to do next.

She locked eyes with him and felt her mind connect to his. Like a small white flash in her brain, she felt it. She felt herself push all her terrified fear right at her father. He felt it too.

Escape. Flee. GET AWAY!

"Demon! Demon child," he screamed! He let go of her and she dropped to the floor. Her legs buckled beneath her. Then he suddenly turned and bolted for the window. As if he were on fire, with arms flailing, beating at some invisible flame that consumed his body, he jumped at the window. The glass shattered and he went right through the third-story bedroom window.

Katherine and her sisters ran to the window. They peered from the broken glass and saw him lying in the street. He was barely moving. He began crawling in the street using his one functioning arm, dragging his legs behind him, still trying to get away from the house. The street was dark, and his body was barely visible. Only the slow movement and the wetness from the blood separated him from the blackness of the street. Through the pain of his broken body, his fear still compelled him to flee from his home.

He was rushed to the hospital, but he didn't live through the night. The injuries from the fall and massive blood loss caused his death. Mental instability caused by alcohol abuse had been used to explain his mood swings and cause of death.

Katherine, her mother, and her sisters then moved in with her grandparents. From then on, deep in her heart, she knew what she had done. But she kept it secret. She would keep herself guarded and in her mind she pictured herself as an ice statue. She would have no emotions of her own for fear of what it might do to others. Her family thought the death of her father was what caused her to emotionally shut down and separate herself from others. Constantly keeping herself isolated and not allowing herself to form any relationships. That is until Paul and the men in the dark blue suits found her and taught her how to control her gift.

Katherine now sat in Paul's lavish office. She made sure to keep her composure, no matter how he tried to goad her.

"Mr. Burton, you chose me to be your eyes and ears at PSI Department for a reason," she said to Paul. "I am also here to let you know the progress Dr. Sellers has achieved with the information you've supplied to him. That, and the schedule for the visiting scientist coming at the end of the month. I wouldn't consider that a waste of your time."

"Very good Katherine. Oh, and what was the outcome of the incident with George? Has he been dealt with?"

She was slightly shocked. How did he know about what happened when George botched taking blood samples from the children? There had to be someone else reporting to him. Maybe more than one other person.

"He won't be a problem. I took Oliver to have a 'conversation' with him."

"Excellent. No need to try and hide your surprise at my knowing this Katherine. You are not my only set of eyes and ears," he said with a smirk. "I'd like you to continue influencing Martin's hunger for more knowledge. Adding some pride and paranoia seems to be working for keeping him under control. We have a schedule to keep and I need you to keep him focused, obtaining more information, and getting results."

"If you don't mind me asking. How long do you plan on keeping this going? How long do you think we can keep this up without it all falling apart?"

"I think we'll keep this going until Martin Sellers is no longer useful, or until he self-destructs. Preferably, I'd like those to happen at about the same time. Since that time doesn't seem to be approaching anytime soon, I need you to continue doing what you are told so he'll continue doing what we need. Do you think you can handle that?" There was a bit of a condescending sting to his words. He didn't like to be questioned.

"Yes, I think I can handle that," she replied.

"Good, see that you do. You can leave a detailed schedule of who is planning on visiting the Department with Miss Baker. She'll coordinate it with my schedule. You can leave when you finish with that."

Paul turned his chair around, away from Katherine, to gaze at the city view. A blatant action to signify her dismissal from his presence.

She may have found him irritating but knew better than to think about it while so physically close to him. As soon as she left his office he buzzed his secretary.

"Miss Baker, when you finish with Ms. O'Bannon could you please get me Agent Brown on the line."

"Yes sir, Mr. Burton," said Miss Baker's voice from the speaker box.

Paul stared at the clouds rolling by. His mind wasn't on the weather outside, but on what his next move would be. No one had his vision. He didn't simply want control of the PSI Department and to ruin Martin Sellers. This was just a stepping stone. Or rather, a chess piece. Just one piece that was going to lead him to rule over the entire chessboard.

After a few moments, Miss Baker buzzed Paul back, "I have Agent Brown holding on the line for you, sir."

Paul picked up the receiver, "Agent Brown, everything is running on schedule. Yes, I believe I will have some very useful information for you very soon. All of which can be implemented within your facility."

Chapter Fifteen
A Display of Talent

Dr. Ross Burton was sitting quietly in his office. Seated behind his desk with his hands folded in his lap. He sat there, staring at the wall on the other side of the room, seemingly unaware of his surroundings. Almost in a trance. Until his phone rang and he was shocked back into reality.

He was slightly disoriented. He looked around the office as the phone continued to ring on his desk. It appeared to be late afternoon judging by how the sun was coming through his office window. He wondered how long he had been sitting there. And what exactly had he been doing before the phone rang and woke him from his daydream? Had he been daydreaming?

"Uh… Hello? This is Dr. Burton speaking," he said into the phone receiver.

"Dr. Burton," responded a female voice on the other end. "This is Caroline White, I just wanted to be sure to thank you again before we left for California. You and your program have been such a tremendous help to William and me. Even though we are moving away, you will always be in our thoughts and have our thanks for helping us lead normal lives."

"No thanks are needed, Caroline. I am indebted to you for contributing your time and abilities to help further our research and being able to help others. You will both be greatly missed."

"I just feel like we owe so much to you. PSI Department isn't just the place where we gained control of our gifts, but it's where William and I met. And if not for that, we wouldn't have our beautiful daughter. I hope we get the opportunity to come and visit you again someday."

"I hope so as well. Who knows, if your daughter shows any signs of having similar gifts, maybe you'll come to see us again."

"That's funny, Dr. Sellers said the exact same thing when I called him 5 minutes ago. Are you sure you two don't have any special abilities?" She chuckled on the other end of the phone. "And I couldn't think of a better place to bring her if she does."

They said their goodbyes and Dr. Burton hung up the phone. He looked around the office, prepared to go back to whatever it was he was doing before the phone rang, but he couldn't recall what that was. How long had he been sitting and staring at the wall?

He could remember beginning the day at home. Driving to the university. Making the rounds to the labs to check on various projects and subjects. Then the phone rang.

"Am I experiencing blackouts?" he wondered.

He sat quietly, this time pondering where the missing time was going. If it was a medical condition or … No, he couldn't think that there was something, or someone, behind this odd occurrence. This one occurrence. Or had it happened before?

Yes. He could vaguely recall other missing points in time. However, he was barely able to pinpoint when they occurred. Almost as if the memories were just out of his reach.

He began to recall recently arriving home, but not remembering the drive home. Or returning to his office from making his rounds, but not remember seeing or talking to anyone. Was there an outside influence to blame this on? If so, who could be behind such an act?

He stood up and grabbed his lab coat off the back of his chair. He put it on over his cardigan as he left his office and locked the door behind him. He made his way towards Martin's office. If someone was behind this then they would discover who.

When he got to the door of Martin's office he paused. He wanted to knock but felt as if he might be disturbing him. He didn't want to disturb him, so he couldn't knock on his door.

"Hello, Dr. Burton," said a young man wearing one of the Department's white lab coats. "Are you looking for Dr. Sellers?"

"Oh…uh, yes," Dr. Burton stumbled on his words for a moment. His mind was foggy again, but not as bad as before. "I thought I needed to talk to him, but I don't want to disturb him."

"You wouldn't be disturbing him. He's not in his office."

"You don't say," he said and could feel the fog lifting from his mind. "Do you happen to know where I might find him?"

"I believe he's just started some testing with a subject in Lab 4."

"Thank you very much…uh, Dan…is it?"

"Don, sir. No problem at all."

"Don! Yes, of course. Don. I'm sorry about that. Thank you."

Dr. Burton found Martin in the testing lab where Don said he would be. He was working with a young boy with telekinetic abilities and a lab assistant. Dr. Burton didn't recognize the boy, who couldn't have been more than 10 years old. He was obviously too young to be one of the college students who were discovered by tests or recruited by signing up for research studies. His parents might have come to the PSI Department already knowing he was gifted and looking for answers about his gifts. A scenario that wasn't completely common, but not as rare as it used to be.

Martin had the boy sitting on one of the metal lab stools. He had various wires stuck to his head connecting him to the Electroencephalography machine. It would monitor and measure his brain waves as he used his ability.

He was concentrating on holding a cinder block in midair approximately 10 feet away. There was nothing above it or below it. It seemed to float with barely any movement as if frozen in place. Martin noticed Dr. Burton quietly sneaking into the lab. He smiled at him and acknowledged his presence and approached him.

"Hello," Martin whispered, extending his hand to shake. "Thomas here is a very remarkable telekinetic."

"Indeed," Dr. Burton whispered back, being sure not to disrupt the boy's concentration.

"As you know," Martin started, "most subjects displaying telekinetic abilities can move objects from one spot to another with no problem. Now moving the objects and holding those objects in a specific location has been a more difficult task. Up until now, the heaviest object any of them has been able to handle with this much control has been a textbook."

"Amazing! And this boy has been able to manipulate this cinder block with the same amount of ease as a book?"

"The cinder block isn't his best effort. This is just the warm-up, Doctor," Martin said with a smile. "Thomas," he now said in full voice, addressing the young man.

The boy turned around to face both Dr. Burton and Martin. The cinder block wavered a bit but did not cease hovering in place. He had large, bright blue eyes and copper-red hair. A smattering of freckles decorated his fair-skinned emotionless face. Even though he was looking at both men, it was apparent that his concentration was still on the floating cinder block.

"This is Dr. Burton," Martin announced to Thomas. "He founded the PSI Department. I would like him to see a demonstration of your abilities. Would you please gently set the block down?"

Thomas didn't say a word and turned back around to face the cinder block. As he turned his head towards a nearby table, the block floated towards it and slowly settled on top of it. It made a light scratching sound as its full weight rested on the stainless steel lab table. He turned around to face the two men again. A lab assistant, silent in the background, busily scribbled notes of the event onto his clipboard. Even though Thomas was no longer concentrating on keeping the block afloat, his expression hadn't changed. It seemed a mix of contempt and boredom.

"I'm sorry Thomas," Martin began, "I should have been more specific. I wanted you to set the block down in the position it was when we began."

Thomas's eyes narrowed slightly and his head tilted to one side, betraying a bit of his sour attitude. He still hadn't spoken a word. This time he didn't turn around. The cinder block rose off the table and began its midair journey back to where it was hovering when Dr. Burton first entered the room.

"Now, place it as it was when we first started our session," said Martin.

Thomas's face changed slightly at this point. His brow creased and his lips pursed a little. It was obvious his concentration was increasing and he was visibly frustrated. He then turned back around to face the floating cinder block and table.

The machine keeping track of his brain wave activity began to hum a bit more as it scratched jagged lines to indicate an increased flux in activity. The lab assistant took notice of this and began noting the results on his clipboard.

The cinder block stayed in the same spot, barely moving. Then the stainless steel table rattled and quickly slid across the floor. Stopping directly under the block.

"Remarkable," Dr. Burton uttered under his breath.

The cinder block came down with a bang on top of the metal table as if the invisible strings that held it in the air had been cut.

"Gently, Thomas! I said gently."

The young boy turned once more to face the men, only this time his face plainly had a look of contempt on it. The lab assistant continued to transcribe notes onto the clipboard as he approached Martin.

"Thomas, why don't we take a 10-minute break," said Martin. "Go get something to drink and get some air while I bring Dr. Burton up to date on your progress."

Thomas didn't respond with any words. He sat still while the lab assistant unhooked all of the wires. When he was completely free he stood up from the stool and fixed his hair. He walked with the lab assistant past the two doctors, out of the lab, and into the hallway.

"A remarkable young man Dr. Sellers," said Dr. Burton. "I don't think we have seen a telekinetic with that degree of control. And to be able to manipulate two objects at the same time!"

"You are correct. But he is even better than what you've witnessed today. As you no doubt noticed, he has a bit of an attitude problem."

"I wasn't sure at first by his silence if it was attitude or ailment. Typical in boys his age, if not a bit extreme. Paul had very much the same characteristics at his age."

"I'm beginning to think that is something that comes with having abilities to this degree. That cinder block crashing down was not by accident, it was by choice." Martin spoke as he retrieved the clipboard off of a table and they walked towards exiting the lab.

"May I have a look at his file," Dr. Burton asked.

"Of course," Martin responded as he handed him the clipboard with the file on it.

Dr. Burton began reading through the file and was amazed at the documented results. Martin looked over Dr. Burton's shoulder to comment on the sections he was reading over.

"You see here," he pointed out a particular section, "we discovered that Thomas can continue to manipulate the object even when not looking at it. And then at this point, we found he can reconnect to the last object he had under his control, even if he isn't looking at it."

"Yes. Just as he did with the cinder block after he set it down the first time. Extraordinary."

"None of the other telekinetic subjects, so far, have been able to control any objects unless it's in their line of sight. Granted, he has to see the object first in order to gain initial control over it. But after that, he can regain control over it even after releasing it. It's like this boy's mind remembers the last object it touched and holds it in his mind's eye somehow."

"Has he shown any telepathic abilities as well?"

"No. I thought the same thing. But as of yet, we still haven't encountered anyone with two abilities."

"Well this is interesting," said Dr. Burton as he continued to read the file. "I did not realize that this young man is Katherine O'Bannon's nephew!"

"He is. That is how he came to us. Katherine's sister was having difficulty dealing with his abilities and his attitude problems. We are hoping that by helping him control one, he will also be able to control the other."

"Has Katherine or her sister shown any signs of having abilities?" Dr. Burton asked.

"No. Neither one of them has." Martin knew he was lying, but felt compelled to avoid telling Dr. Burton the truth. "In fact, Katherine said that her nephew is why she initially came here. She was hoping this would be the answer to why he was different. And now that she knows why, she's even dryly joked that if she'd had abilities she might have been able to deal with him on her own."

"That's interesting. I always felt that with how detached she seems to be..." Dr. Burton trailed off, slightly losing his train of thought. "Then perhaps we should look into his mental well-being a bit closer. It must be noted that he is a young boy and not just a test subject. Especially being so young."

Martin raised his eyebrow slightly at this comment. Was this statement some hint at the guilt that Dr. Burton felt for not being able to grant his son a normal childhood?

"What are you suggesting, Doctor?"

"I'm not sure. I don't know if we are ready to try testing outside of the safety of this building, and yet I feel this boy would benefit greatly from being able to get some outdoor activity while practicing his talents. I've always preferred physical activity over psychological therapy." Dr. Burton said, raising his eyebrow.

"That's not a bad idea. There is a park about 4 miles from here that shouldn't have nearly as many people around as the campus grounds. I could take a couple of extra assistants with me and see how Thomas does in a different environment."

"I am intrigued by this idea. But still a bit nervous as well." Dr. Burton pondered the idea for a moment. "I would be more likely to approve this plan if you could give me a project outline for it first. I would like to know the specifics of what testing you will be doing, how you will be going about it, and who you will be taking with you to assist. You'll want assistants who are very observant, as you won't have the machines for readouts. We need to make sure all safety precautions are in place."

"That all sounds reasonable to me. I'll work out the details today and have the proposal to you by tomorrow. Maybe we can get this going before the end of the week." Martin was pleased with this change of attitude in Dr. Burton. It seemed a great step forward in another phase to expand the PSI Department.

"Very good. I'll leave you to continue your work, Dr. Sellers."

He congratulated Martin on his progress one more time before leaving. He walked the halls of this wonderful facility he created, observing all that was going on. Watching technicians with their clipboards and charts, noting their progress and failures on them. Even though they had made great discoveries and helped many people here, there was pressure from the University's board of directors to produce something tangible from all these tests. Simply proving these people existed wasn't enough anymore. They were asking questions such as, "Can these abilities be used to cure diseases?" "What are the medical applications of such abilities?" and "How is this research going to make the University money?" It always seemed to come down to money. Needing more and making more.

They couldn't deny the new connections that were made and the notoriety the university's medical center was receiving because of the PSI Department. Other programs in the university's medical center benefited from the visiting scientists and doctors. A majority showed great interest in scheduling time to tour the PSI Department. Even if their specialty didn't seem directly related to the department's purpose. However, the university did acknowledge that it was getting more exposure because of their research. But it still wasn't enough.

Dr. Burton knew that unless they could produce results that could be considered beneficial to the medical community, it would only be a matter of time before the funds ran out and the PSI Department would be closed. All he could do was continue with his dream and hope that such a discovery would be made.

He had returned to his office at the end of the day. He set the files he was carrying onto the top of his desk and removed his lab coat. He placed the coat on a coat hook on the wall next to his desk and then sat in his chair.

It felt good to sit down. He looked over the files that lay before him. He picked one out of the stack and began to read its contents.

File #E-252: Patricia Romano-Zanetti
Update:
Subject has returned to resume testing. Concerns over an inconsistent shift in abilities performance.

The empathic abilities of Patricia seem to fluctuate after having given birth to her son, Robert, 3 years ago. The data collected from her tests (ref. blood work/hormone levels vs. empathic trials) all suggest that she has undergone a chemical imbalance that has affected how her abilities work. Charting her hormone levels, stress levels, and environmental influences with her increased or decreased control of her empathic abilities has led to this possible conclusion. It has been especially noted that she has a greater empathic influence on those around her when there is a concern for her son's safety.

Patricia's body is able to tap into the primal maternal instincts needed to elevate this chemical imbalance and increase the potency of her influence as a defense mechanism. This data has been forwarded to the Bio-Chemical Lab to be studied and considered for applications.
Update:
As of the update of this file, Patricia has decided to decrease the number of sessions at the PSI Department, return to life as a "normal" private citizen, and attempt to handle any future incidences on her own.

He closed the file with a small smile on his face. There was a slight hint of disappointment at not being able to help Patty more, but he was grateful that she was back in touch. Joe and Patty did have a special place in his heart.

"It's getting a bit late," he thought to himself. "I suppose I can go over the rest of these tomorrow."

He placed the files into the top drawer in his desk. He made sure he had his briefcase and his car keys before shutting off the lights, exiting his office, and locking the door behind him.

Martin was excited to be arriving home. He pulled into his parking space in front of his apartment building and shut off the car's engine.

He glanced down at his watch as he gathered his briefcase and coat off of the passenger seat.

"Home in time for dinner," he thought to himself.

It was a short walk from his parking space to the door that led to the lobby of the building. That was a blessing during the winter or rain storms. Once he was inside, he only had to walk across the small 20-foot lobby to the elevators.

Martin pushed the arrow up button to call the elevator down. While he waited he looked around the lobby. There was no one around at that moment. It was silent, except for the sound of the approaching elevator. Even though he liked this apartment, as it was much nicer and much bigger than the previous one he had shared with Janet, he wished he had been able to move his family into a proper home with a yard. He wanted to be able to do more than provide just the necessities for his family.

Martin could see his dream house in his head. The picturesque home with a sprawling green lawn, shutters on the windows, and a swimming pool. A white picket fence. He wanted his little girl to have a swing set in the backyard. In his mind, he could hear her laughing on the swing. Maybe there was even a golden retriever running around and barking.

The ringing bell announcing the elevator's arrival brought him back to reality. The doors slid open and he stepped inside. He maneuvered holding his coat so he could press the number 5 button. The doors closed and the elevator climbed upward.

When the doors opened again he exited into the 5th floor hallway. There were only 8 apartments on each floor. Four to the left and four to the right. His apartment was the last one on the left. He could smell Janet's wonderful cooking as he got closer to his door.

"Honey, I'm home," he shouted as he entered the apartment.

"Hi sweetheart," Janet said to him. She leaned in and kissed him as she took his coat and briefcase from him. "We've got about 10 minutes before dinner is ready."

"It smells delicious," he said as he watched her hang up his coat and place his briefcase into the coat closet. "I have some exciting news."

"Oh? It must be something good, judging by your mood. What is it?"

"I've made some tremendous progress with Thomas. You know, the telekinetic boy. Well, Dr. Burton was able to witness it first-hand today. He was so impressed by how advanced Thomas is compared to other telekinetics that he is going to allow me to conduct testing outside of the lab"

"That is exciting news. But do you think it's safe?"

There was something odd about having his work questioned. Almost like a trigger had gone off in his mind and was suddenly making him upset. He had never been bothered by Janet's inquiries about his work or offering constructive criticism. Lately, something had changed in him.

"Of course it will be safe!" He snapped at her. "This is MY work. MY research. Of course, I'll make sure it's protected and safe."

They were both silent as they stared at each other. The look on Janet's face was both surprised and annoyed at his tone towards her. He could see it in her eyes and he was immediately aware of who he was talking to.

"Janet, darling," his tone was soft and apologetic. "I'm sorry. I'm so sorry. I didn't mean to be so short with you like that. I guess I'm just tired. I'm sorry."

"It's ok," she said as she gently reached up and touched his face. "I know how much your work means to you. And I know how much time you put into the department."

She leaned in and gave him a soft kiss. He wrapped his arms around her, to hold her for a moment longer. Her touch brought a calmness to him and allowed him to relax in a way that was only possible in his home.

"I love you, Martin. But speak to me in that tone again and I'll singe off your eyebrows." She pulled away from him with a smile and a wink. "Now go wash your hands, and make sure Margaret has washed hers too, please. I'll have dinner on the table by the time you're both done."

Martin walked down the short hallway to Margaret's room. He found her setting up a small table for what appeared to be a tea party with a baby doll, a stuffed toy elephant, and a plush teddy bear.

"Hi, princess," he said to her and he entered the room and knelt down to kiss her forehead.

She looked up at him and smiled. "Hi Daddy," she said back to him.

"Are you having a tea party with your friends? You'll have to put it on hold for a bit. It's time to wash your hands and get ready for dinner.

Alright?"

"Alright, Daddy," she said in her tiny voice.

He stood in her doorway, waiting for her as she situated her imaginary friends into comfortable positions. She was very meticulous in putting them each in just the right pose, to wait for her until she returned after her dinner.

Martin lifted her and carried her to the bathroom, kissing her cheeks repeatedly as she giggled and squealed to his affection. He held her up to the sink so she could properly wash her hands. When she finished, he handed her a small towel to dry her hands with and then washed his own hands.

As promised, dinner was on the table and waiting for them when they returned.

Chapter Sixteen
A Day in the Park

A week had passed since Dr. Burton had approved Martin's request for testing Thomas in an open environment. It had taken almost a full week of scouting locations to find one that would serve his needs. Most of the parks and open areas had too much public traffic present. There would be no sense of privacy for them to conduct their experiments.

The day came when Martin happened upon an old community park. The grounds were in pretty decent shape, though it was apparent that this park got much of its use and attention during holiday weekends and school breaks during the summer. Much of the greenery was overgrown and in need of some landscaping attention. It had a wide-open field that was surrounded by large trees and shrubbery on 3 sides. The fourth side was a wide open pathway that led to the parking lot. It had plenty of room while still maintaining a semi-private atmosphere. This would be the place.

Martin scheduled with Katherine for Thomas to meet him at the university parking lot at 10 a.m. where he would have the use of a van to transport them, and 2 Department lab assistants, to the park. Being anxious to begin the day, Martin had already had his coffee and loaded the van up with various equipment before the others had arrived. Even though he had plotted out an itinerary for how the experiments would go, he was constantly revising them in his head as he drove them all to the park.

Martin parked the van in one of the dozen, or so, parking spaces. All of which were vacant. He was relieved that there were no other cars in sight. And with a direct line of sight to the parking spaces, they would notice very easily if anyone else pulled into a parking space. It wasn't a weekend, so the park appeared to be completely deserted.

It was a nice day out. Not too sunny, but slightly overcast. A good thing since Thomas was so fair-skinned and likely to get a sunburn on a bright sunny day. Martin turned around in the driver's seat so he could address the other 3 passengers in the van.

"Alright everyone, we're here," he said. "Thomas if you will grab that sack next to you, please. Greg, Elizabeth," he addressed the two assistants who were seated in the back of the van, "I'm going to have you observe us from here for a bit. Just stay near the van so you can see us and keep an eye out for anyone nearby."

"Yes, Dr. Sellers," said Greg.

Thomas got out of the van dragging the large sack behind him. It was one of the laundry bags they used in the lab, with the drawstring closure on top. Only this one didn't contain lab coats and sheets. Thomas guessed it contained various sizes of balls. Soccer ball, basketball, baseballs, and maybe a baseball bat. Although he would not let it show in his expression, he was very excited to know what was inside the large sack.

Martin helped Thomas carry the sack as they walked down a small slope from where the van was parked to the open grassy field. He opened the sack and pulled out one of the objects inside. A large red ball. Thomas recognized it as the kind they used for playing dodgeball at school. He didn't like dodgeball.

"Alright Thomas," Martin began, "let's toss this ball back and forth. Of course, after you catch it, I'd like you to toss it back without using your hands. Understand? Think you can do that?"

"I think I can manage that," Thomas replied. Apparently annoyed at having his talents underestimated.

"I know you are capable of more," Martin said, putting his hand on Thomas' shoulder. "This is just the starting point. The warm-up. We'll get to the challenging part soon enough."

Martin held the ball and walked about 30 feet away from Thomas, back towards the parking lot. "You ready?" he shouted to the boy and tossed the ball to him.

Thomas caught the ball with his hands, with an obvious awkwardness, and held it for a second. He was a little surprised that he was able to catch it on the first toss. He gripped the large red rubber ball in both hands and held it out in front of him. He then opened his hands and let the ball hover in place. His mind gripped the ball now. Like invisible hands holding it steady in front of him. In his mind, he coiled one of the invisible hands back and released it on the ball. It made an echoing sound inside the ball, signaling that something solid, did in fact, strike it and sent it flying past Martin.

"Thomas! This was supposed to be a game of catch, not fetch!"

As Martin ran for the bouncing ball, it stopped mid-bounce and floated to him. When he reached out and took the ball, he could feel the energy surrounding it. He could feel it when it had been released into his possession. Almost as if the ball was weightless when he first touched it.

"Let's try this again," he shouted to Thomas as he threw the ball back to the boy. Martin decided to increase the distance between them, hoping this would lessen the odds of having to chase after the ball again. Martin tossed the ball.

Thomas caught the ball and held it to his chest. Again, he held it out for a second, released it, and sent it directly to Martin. Martin caught it and tossed it right back to him.

The game continued in this manner for a few minutes, until Thomas decided to change it up a little. Upon sending it back to Martin, he stopped it short of its target and it began orbiting around Martin instead. Taking the opportunity to keep the mood light, Martin began chasing it in a most comical fashion. Thomas giggled at the spectacle. It was probably the first time Martin had seen a genuine smile on Thomas' face.

When Martin finally caught a hold of the floating ball he issued a new challenge to Thomas. "Ok then, hotshot. This time catch the ball and send it back without any use of your hands."

"Easy enough," thought Thomas. It was a fairly simple task for him.

As the ball came soaring at him, he could feel his mind lock onto it. He stopped it about 4 feet away and slowly brought it close to him. Having the ball hold its position in front of him, just as before, and then sending it back from where it came.

Martin caught the ball. Impressed with the boy's skills. He turned to the van and saw his assistants chatting and taking notes on the events. This boy was indeed talented, and in this setting, he seemed more relaxed and was treating this as a game instead of a scientific study.

"You are doing remarkable Thomas," Martin exclaimed to the young boy. He saw Thomas standing there, hands at his sides, with a slightly playful smirk on his face and concentration in his eyes. That's when the noise of something dragging caught Martin's attention.

It was the sack next to him. It was sliding across the grass as the back end of it began to lift into the air. Thomas meant to dump out all the balls inside of it. The sack rose and the drawstring came loose, releasing all its contents onto the grass next to Martin.

"I'm not picking all of this up," Martin shouted in a playful tone.

"You don't need to, sir," Thomas shouted back.

Both of the assistants left the van and walked down the slope towards Martin. They all stood in disbelief as another soccer ball, a basketball, 3 tennis balls, a Frisbee disk, and a baseball bat began to rise off the ground and spiral around them. Martin still held the original red ball in his hands but he could feel a gentle tug on it. He lightened his hold on the ball and it slowly pulled away and joined the others.

"Thomas, this is incredible! How are you able to handle so many objects at once?"

Thomas simply smiled. Pleased that he had impressed them and pleased with himself. Though he didn't want them to know just how difficult it was to keep this level of concentration up. In his mind, he was not just using the 2 invisible hands to manipulate the objects anymore. Now he was imagining 8 of them.

His concentration broke when the sounds of loud laughter and voices came from the distance behind him. The objects all dropped out of the air. Including the baseball bat, which struck Greg on the head with a loud thud. He dropped to his knees, stunned by the sudden blow.

"Greg, are you ok?" Asked Martin. "Elizabeth help me get him up and to the van. If we are going to have an audience now, then it's time for us to go." He and Elizabeth got on either side of Greg, propped him up, and began walking him back up to the van. "Thomas," Martin shouted, "time to go!"

Thomas went to where all the balls had dropped and began to manually put them all back into the sack. He felt so angry that he let his concentration slip. He was more upset that he lost control, not that Greg got hit with the bat. It hadn't even concerned him, frankly. He was so busy scolding himself as he collected the balls that he didn't hear the approach of the people behind him.

"Hey kid, what are you doing?" asked a disheveled young man.

He had long wild hair, whiskers on his face, and his eyes were glassed over. The same starry-eyed look was matched on all three of his companions. All of their clothes were once brightly colored patterns but were faded and dirty now. None of them were wearing shoes. They each seemed to sway slightly, unable to stand straight and still. The young man who spoke wore an open fringed suede vest that exposed his bare chest. He watched Thomas with some fascination. His eyes darted from Thomas to the red ball next to him, and then back to Thomas.

"You playing some kind of game here, kid?" the stoned man asked. His speech was slurred, sounding like a warped record.

"No," Thomas replied very quietly. He did not want to look up at the strange man or his friends.

Martin had just gotten Greg into the van when he turned and saw Thomas and the men in the distance. He had a bad feeling about this. He saw the man, talking to Thomas, bend down and pick up the red ball. Even from the van Martin could see the man's unruly hair fall in his face as he bent over.

"You playing dodgeball kid? Wanna play dodgeball?" His voice spiked up at the end as he flipped his hair away from his face. His friends, stood next to him, giggling and snickering at this odd exchange. He had a crazed look in his eyes. "I'll give you a 5-second count before I throw it. Go. GO. GO!" he shouted at Thomas.

Thomas sprang to his feet and turned towards the van. The man's friends began laughing like hyenas behind him. Out of the corner of his eye, Thomas saw the man pull back his hand holding the red ball. He had to run for the van.

"ONE," shouted the crazed man, "two…" and he threw the ball as hard as he could at Thomas.

It struck him in the back, sending him face-first into the grass. He heard the familiar echo the ball made as it hit him and bounced off his back. He was stunned, but he was already trying to force himself to his feet when he saw that Martin was running towards him.

Everything was happening so fast that it appeared to Thomas that Martin was running in slow motion. His white lab coat billowed behind him as he dashed towards Thomas. Thomas turned his head back to see if the man was chasing after him. The force of the impact had sent the red rubber ball bouncing back to the man and his friends.

"That wasn't fair o' me little man" slurred the man. "I'll give ya another chance." He picked up the ball and coiled his arm back. As he did this he also began to close the distance between them. Thomas knew that this man, no matter what chemicals were in his system, would not miss a shot at such a close distance. He also knew he would be aiming for his head this time.

Thomas stood and turned to face him just as the ball was released and was racing towards his face. It stopped just inches from Thomas' nose. It stayed there as if frozen in time. It didn't rotate, it didn't waiver in its position at all. Then its perfect roundness became egg-shaped as Thomas grasped it with the invisible hand from his mind and squeezed it. His anger fueled his telekinetic power now. Not the desire to please Martin, as it had earlier.

"I…. HATE… dodge ball," he said through clenched teeth.

The ball flattened with a loud "POP," but its deflated shell still floated in place.

"What the hell man?" said one of the man's friends. Still trying to focus on the now deflated ball through blinking eyes and unsteady legs.

Martin reached Thomas and gripped his shoulder. "Come on Thomas. Let's go. You can't do this here."

"Can't I?" he said in quiet defiance. His eyes were still focused on the hovering deflated ball. Its shape now very disk-like.

The red piece of rubber flew at the crazed man and smacked him in the face. He screamed and held his hands up to attempt to protect his face. The angry, deflated ball continued to slap at his hands and face. It then broadened its arc to slap his friends as well.

"Thomas!" Martin shook him gently by the shoulder. "You must not do this. They are obviously under the influence of drugs and we cannot have you involved in any type of incident. We must go."

Thomas turned to look at Martin. It was not anger he saw in the doctor's eyes, but concern. The sting of the ball on his back, the scariness of these men, all came rushing to him now. Thomas began to cry. He leaned on Martin as he was led back to the waiting van. Elizabeth had raced back to gather up the rest of the balls after she had Greg situated in the van. She flung the sack over her shoulder and ran back to the van.

The mysterious attacker had ceased its assault on the stoned men. The rubber shell stopped its flailing attack and dropped to the ground. They slowly lowered their hands and stared in a daze at their lifeless assailant. They used their bare feet to poke at the deflated ball, wondering if it was going to spring back to life. They were so focused on it (and under the influence of whatever drugs they had taken), that they hadn't noticed that Martin and Thomas had safely made it to the van.

Thomas sat in the back of the van, looking out the back window. He dried his eyes on his sleeve and tried to regain his composure. He could see the men still standing in the field, now watching them as the van pulled out of the parking space and began to turn to exit the park. The crazed man saw the van and waved his middle finger up at them.

Just as the van rounded the corner, Thomas heard the man scream in the distance. It was the kind of scream a man would make if his hand had suddenly been broken. Not just broken, but crushed in the palm of a giant hand as it made a fist around it.

Thomas turned around to face the front of the van. Martin could see him in the rearview mirror.

"Are you ok Thomas?"

"Yes sir," he said. "I think I'm ok now."

They returned to the parking lot in front of the University Medical Center that housed the PSI Department. After Martin parked the van and shut off the engine he turned to face his passengers. He sat in silence for a moment, carefully choosing his words before he spoke.

"I think we are all aware of the magnitude of what happened today." Martin's eyes went to each passenger as he spoke. "Thomas made amazing progress today and I don't want that to get overshadowed by the incident with those men."

"Dr. Sellers," Greg said as he continued to rub the bump on the top of his head, "are you asking us lie to about what happened?"

"Not exactly, Greg. I simply want to omit it from the notes on Thomas's session."

"I agree," said Elizabeth. "What happened with those men in the park shouldn't be a factor in continuing any further experiments outside of the lab. Not only was Thomas able to apply his abilities in an entirely new fashion, he enjoyed the session… well, until… Which is a benefit in itself." Her expression became more serious, "I just don't know if trying to keep secrets in a place where your mind can be read is the safest thing though. I don't want to lose my job here."

"I do not believe we need to worry about that as much as you think," assured Martin. "I don't think any of the telepaths will look for this particular secret unless we give them a reason. We are to simply focus on the positive outcome of today and ignore the rest."

They all exited the van, and Greg and Elizabeth took the sack of balls and clipboards back to the PSI Department. Martin paused for a moment to talk to Thomas as the others walked out of sight.

"Thomas, I want to be sure you are alright?" he asked as he knelt to be level with the young boy.

Thomas looked into the doctor's eyes, not needing to be empathic to read the genuine concern behind them. This made him realize something.

"My Aunt Katherine will know something is wrong. She will be able to sense it from me."

"Thomas, I am not going to ask you to lie. You know your aunt better than I do and you know how she will react to finding out what happened. You must do what you think is right."

"I want to tell you something, Dr. Sellers," Thomas said, still looking directly into his eyes. "I'm just afraid. I don't want to upset my aunt or get her into any trouble. But you said I have to do what is right."

"Of course, Thomas. What is it? You can tell me. I will do my best to help you, however I can."

The boy's eyes looked away in shame as if he were confessing a betrayal of sorts. He was conflicted about keeping secrets from this man or possibly betraying his aunt.

"I don't want my aunt to know what happened because I'm afraid of who she'll tell, or that they will find out."

"Who? Dr. Burton? You let me worry about that Thomas."

"No, sir. The man in the fancy office building and the men he works for."

"What man? Thomas, I don't understand. Are they men here at the Department?"

"No, sir. The men who originally wanted to take me away. The men who took me to the man in the fancy office. He told them that Aunt Katherine could bring me here. That it would make the expansion easier."

"I am confused, Thomas. Where is this office? Do you know the man's name?"

"He tried to make me forget. Forget about him and the other place they took me. But I didn't forget all of it. Not completely. I can't picture their faces or even what they were wearing. But I do remember the name Paul."

Chapter Seventeen
Confession of a Traitor

For anyone witnessing the events that were about to take place, it might look as if a beautiful, young, red-headed woman was about to be assaulted in the parking lot on the way to her car. A dark, moonless night, in a dimly lit parking lot. Her high-heeled shoes clicking on the asphalt were the only sound. The shadow of a man approaching quietly behind her. He wasn't going to let her know he was there until it would be too late for her. Anyone watching could have shouted to her to look out. Unfortunately for her, there was no one around to witness it.

Just as she unlocked her car door and began to open it, a man's hand pushed past her and slammed it shut again. She froze, shocked by the action that had taken place. The man's hands quickly gripped her by the shoulders and spun her around to face her assailant. She was shocked to be looking at Martin Sellers.

"Dr. Sellers, what are you…."

"Shut up, Katherine!" he spat at her. Shaking her by the shoulders again. Causing her hair to fall around her face. "I need answers from you, and you aren't going to use any of your empathic talents on me!"

"Dr. Sellers, I don't understand! What are you talking about?"

"I'll ask the questions!" he shouted. Shaking her again. He continued to push her back and shout to keep her from being able to focus long enough to use her abilities. "How are you connected to Paul Burton? Answer me!"

"I don't know what you are talking about." She was trying to connect with his mind and force some emotion of fear or distress on him. But he kept jostling her around and she found it too difficult to do.

"Stop lying to me, Katherine! I trusted you! Tell me why you are working with Paul Burton. NOW!" He continued to shout his demand at her, over and over, hoping it would break her down.

"I had to!" she shouted at him, trying to break free from his grip.

"It was the only way to get Thomas out of there. Away from them. You don't know what it was like there! I don't know what they would have turned him into."

"Who? Who would have turned him into what?" He shook her again.

"Stop. Please stop," she begged. "I can't tell you. God, they'll probably kill me now just for saying this much!" She began to cry and dropped to the ground.

"No more games, no more lies, Katherine. You need to tell me everything you know. I won't be able to help you or Thomas, unless you come clean right now."

She continued to sit next to her car, sobbing. Muttering under her breath, "So much bigger than you know."

He helped her to stand and then looked her in the eyes and said, "Thomas trusts me. I need you to trust me now as well. Tell me all you know and maybe I can help you."

"Knowing it all won't matter," she said. "I'll tell you, but you won't be able to do anything."

He let her gather herself up, and they took her car to someplace they could talk. Someplace public where they would both feel a bit safer.

They sat across from each other in a booth at a diner on the far side of town. Knowing that being seen together at the diner near the campus wasn't such a good idea. They each only ordered a cup of coffee. They sat in silence for a while. Although her posture was as perfect as ever, her face wasn't emotionless. Martin could see and feel the anxious fear coming off of Katherine. Even though she was not consciously projecting it onto him, it could still be felt.

"Not long after my father died," she began, "and we had moved in with my grandparents, my mother was approached by some men who said they were from the government. They had suspected that my father's death was not caused by mental illness or drinking. They said they knew about my special gifts and that unless I was handed over to them, my whole family would be taken away, quarantined, studied, and eventually tried for my father's murder."

"Are you telling me the government essentially kidnapped you from your family?"

"Yes."

"Where did they take you?"

"Not to just one place. They have bases set up all over the country.

Maybe even outside of America. I don't know for certain. I was sent to 3 different facilities. But I had met others who had been to more than I had."

Martin was stunned. He was hearing for the first time that the U.S. Government had its version of the PSI Department up and running, and had more than just one operational facility. How had this been kept a secret from them for so long?

"A number of years ago," Katherine continued, "Paul had been approached by two agents, who had also contacted Dr. Burton, about joining the government programs. Dr. Burton had turned them down, of course, but Paul saw it as an opportunity. While promising them inside information on his father's progress, Paul read their thoughts and got inside information on their facilities and operations. He used them just as much as they thought they were using him."

"How did you get involved with Paul then?"

"He told the agents that he could get them more information and further their goals if he could place his own people into the PSI Department. That extracting the information on his own was becoming increasingly impossible. Which was a lie." She paused for a moment to sip her coffee and clear her throat. "He was well aware of their 'training' techniques and knew any of us there would have sold our souls to get out. Which, I suppose, is what I did."

"What exactly were you being trained for?"

"I don't have to be a telepath to see in your eyes that you already know the answer to that question. But I'll indulge you anyway. Living weapons and spies of all kinds. Tools to be used to gain control in whatever areas the government wanted. Their methods were harsh on some. Those who fought against the training were broken into submission. Others succumbed to brainwashing. Then you have the rare cases like Paul. He embraced their training. His abilities have grown to proportions you can't even fathom." She paused to take a sip of her coffee before continuing. "I purposely failed many of my tests so they could never gauge my true potential. Paul knew this when he reached out to my mind. He whispered in my thoughts about being free from that place. And all I would have to do is be his eyes and ears at the PSI Department."

"And you agreed to this? I don't fault you for wanting to get out of there, Katherine. Honestly, I don't. But why not just escape once you were out?"

"Because of Thomas. Paul promised that they would release him if I continued as he instructed. Which they did. If I refused to continue to help him… then he said he wouldn't be able to stop them from stealing Thomas away again and subjecting him to whatever 'training' they saw fit. Dr. Sellers, Thomas is an extremely powerful telekinetic. You have no idea what they had planned for him there. They test various ways to control and block abilities. Electro-shock, drugs, gas, chemical injections… and if they don't deem it effective, then they continue to raise the bar until they achieve the results they desire. He was only there a short while, and I fear it may have already done damage to him."

"I often wondered what contributed to his shifts in attitude and possible inner conflicts. Now it makes sense. No child should be subjected to whatever horrors they put upon him." He looked down into his coffee mug. The lights of the diner reflected in the dark liquid.

"There is nothing we can do, Doctor. If you confront Paul, he will know I told you and he will let them take Thomas."

"You can't expect me to simply ignore all of this information and allow him to continue to undermine all we are trying to accomplish at the Department? Maybe Dr. Burton will know what to do."

"He won't be of any help to you."

"What do you mean? Paul is his son. If anyone has a chance at getting through to him and showing him how wrong this is, it's him."

"You are wrong. Paul doesn't care about his father. All he cares about is power. And not just his telepathic abilities. The people he reports to aren't aware of what he's capable of now. Or what his true plans are," she paused again to sip her coffee. "Did you know that PSI Department is less than a year away from shutting down? Paul has been pulling the strings for years, Dr. Sellers. PSI Department has been gaining results unlike any of the government facilities, and they want what you have. Your techniques of working with us, helping us… You got results through cooperation while they operated with intimidation and torture. You have been able to process information and apply the research at a much faster pace than they had previously been able to. But soon they will be ready to take over and Paul is poised for that event. He's been working the Board of Directors into slowly pulling out their funding. It will leave the Department with no choice but to merge with the Government facilities or close down completely."

He sat quietly, thinking about this information. Paul had figured out all the moves in advance. Paul was aware that his father did not ever want the control of his research to fall into government hands. But if it came down to it, would he allow the PSI Department to be closed instead of merging? That loss of power would mean more control for Paul. All while supplying Dr. Sellers with sources of knowledge, making the Department all the more valuable to the Government. Would they allow the PSI Department to just close? Without its founders to run it properly, it would. Paul had indeed been playing both sides. Assuring himself a power position of his own.

Even though this was all very distressing information to be processing, Martin was feeling a great deal of calm. Almost an indifference to it all. He was beginning to not even care. All thanks to an extremely calm, extremely focused Katherine O'Bannon sitting across from him.

"I can't let you go rushing in and confront Paul on this. I'm sorry, I just can't." She focused harder, latching onto his emotions. "I know it won't hold you forever, but I have to stall you until I figure something out." She gave one last solid push into his brain. After one more sip of coffee, she left some money on the table, got up from the booth, and left the diner.

He sat there for 45 minutes. Not caring that it was getting late. Not feeling motivated to get up out of the booth and go home. He continued to sit until the waitress came to the table and told him he had to either order something or leave. He sighed and lazily exited the booth.

When Martin finally made it home it was well past midnight. He had sat in his car, in his parking space, for a solid 15 minutes before he slowly got out. He dragged his feet through the apartment building to the front door of the apartment he shared with his wife and daughter, unlocked it, and went inside. Barely closing the door behind him.

"Honey, is that you?" called Janet from their bedroom.

"Eh… huh? Yeah," he replied. Barely audible.

"Are you ok? You must be really tired," she said as she approached him.

"Yeah, I guess. Tired."

She took hold of his hand and pulled him to the bedroom. He just stood there in a daze, not motivated enough to undress himself. So she did it for him and put him to bed. He turned to his side and went right to sleep.

"Poor guy," she thought to herself, "he must be exhausted."

Martin slept soundly that night and all the next day. He lacked any desire to get out of bed and engage in his life. Janet was worried about him.

"Hello, Dr. Burton," she spoke into the telephone receiver, "it's Janet. Something is wrong with Martin. He's been in bed for almost 2 solid days now. I thought maybe he was just tired, or not feeling well. But I think it may be depression or something worse. Maybe something from the lab?"

"What do you mean," asked Dr. Burton.

"Ever since he got home late from work the other night he's been in bed. He doesn't want to eat or drink or talk or… or… anything."

"Is he ill? Has he been showing any signs that he…"

"No. No fever. No coughing or sneezing or anything. He just lays there. It's as if he's in a coma, but he wakes up now and then. He'll mumble something incoherent, and then go back to sleep. I don't know what to do."

"Let me make a quick phone call and I'll come right over," responded the voice on the other end of the phone.

Less than two hours later there was a knock at Janet Sellers' front door. She opened it expecting only to see Dr. Burton, but he had someone with him.

"Janet, good to see you, my dear. I believe you know Patricia Zanetti."

"Patty! Hi, it's so good to see you again," Janet said, shaking Patty's hand. "I thought you had left the PSI Department."

"I did. But Dr. Burton called me and told me about Martin. He thought my empathic abilities might be of some help to determine what's wrong."

"I can't thank you enough for doing this," Janet said as she backed away from the front door to let them in. Even through her polite demeanor, Patty was able to feel the anxiety emanating from Janet. "He's back this way, in the bedroom."

Janet led them to the bedroom where Martin was still in bed. The curtains were drawn shut and he had the sheets pulled up around his head.

"He's been like this for two days now. I don't know what is wrong with him." The tone in Janet's voice made her concern apparent.

"Patricia," Dr. Burton began to ask, "Are you sensing anything from him?"

"Yes. But it's very odd. It's not just depression. Or a sense of being lethargic. There are a few emotions at work in him. All of them keeping him in the state of... well, I suppose I would call it overwhelming apathy."

"So he isn't ill?" Janet asked.

"Not physically. No. If I didn't know any better I would say these feelings were forced upon him. These aren't his," Patricia continued to stare down at Martin.

"How can you tell?" asked Dr. Burton. He had approached the side of the bed where Martin was lying. Bending forward as if studying him would give a clue as to what was happening.

"I can just sense that these are foreign in him. His aura... It's like seeing someone wearing a shirt that you know belongs to someone else because it's not their size or style. Only he can't take it off. It's stuck on him."

"Patricia," Dr. Burton turned from the bed to face her, "is there anything you can do to help him?"

"I'm not sure. I am trying to sense any of his own emotions. Maybe bringing them to the surface will force the others off of him somehow. A very talented empath did this to him."

As Patty concentrated on the barely conscious Martin, Dr. Burton gestured to Janet to go and bring Margaret into the room. He hoped that her presence in the room would stir some emotional response in Martin, and perhaps give Patty something which might strengthen her empathic abilities.

Janet carried their daughter into the dark bedroom. The little girl stirred in her mother's arms at the sight of her father, reaching out for him.

Patty twitched, "It's all just apathy. I'm not sensing anything else."

"Daddy," Margaret said as she touched the hair on her father's head.

"There he is," Patty said. "I think I found something."

The covers on the bed moved slightly at first, then rustled as the man underneath them sat up. Tears streamed down his face as he reached for his daughter and hugged her close.

"My fault," said Patty, "I may have overdosed him a bit on his joy. Hearing Margaret connected him with an emotional memory of when she was born. The intensity of it will wear off on its own."

"Why don't we go wait in the living room," said Dr. Burton. "We'll give him some time to wake up and get situated." He put his hand on Janet's shoulder, "Don't worry, we'll get to the bottom of this."

Dr. Burton and Patty made their way into the living room. They sat on the couch next to each other, both deep in thought about the recent event. They sat in silence for a few moments.

Patty turned to face Dr. Burton as she spoke. "I don't understand why someone would do that to him. Who would do that?"

"I don't know," Dr. Burton replied. His gaze was elsewhere. Staring blankly as if studying a diagram that was floating in the air before him.

"Dr. Burton," Patty said to him to get him to focus on her. "Dr. Burton, there's something you aren't telling me. Why would you think to call me tonight if you weren't sure what was going on?"

"I have my theories and suspicions, Patricia. I called on you because I had hoped that if there was any sort of psychic foul play at hand you would be able to detect it. And you did. I also called you specifically because you are no longer active with the PSI Department, and I trust you. So, if this is somehow connected with someone within the department, I don't need to worry about the guilty party knowing we've discovered their assault on Dr. Sellers. Or any other type of information leak."

"Of course, you can trust me. Do you really think that someone you work with did this to him on purpose?"

"Yes," Martin said as he walked into the living room. He was fully awake and dressed now. His hair was still a bit disheveled, but he was alert with a most determined scowl on his face. "It was Katherine."

An hour later, the four adults were sitting around the kitchen table in the Sellers' apartment. Martin recounted the events that led up to his now-cured condition. He was sure to omit the events that took place with Thomas in the park, but he told them about the information that led him to confront Katherine.

"Katherine made me not care about confronting Paul or telling you all of the things she had told me. I didn't care about anything. It was like being stuck down a well without the energy to climb out."

"Are you telling me that after everything you've done to help her," Janet spoke and was getting more upset with every word, "Katherine O'Bannon betrayed you and did this to you?"

"Is it getting hotter in here?" asked Patty.

"I'm sorry," said Janet. She closed her eyes and took deep breaths to cool her temper and the temperature of the room.

"I don't know what she would be able to accomplish in the two days that I've been out of commission. If she has had time to warn Paul, cover her tracks, or call in reinforcements?"

Dr. Burton sighed and shook his head. "Now that I think of it, I do not believe Katherine has been at the PSI Department in the last couple of days. And I do not think I have seen Thomas around either. I just assumed that if his sessions were with you they had been canceled due to your absence."

"If I may interrupt," said Patty, "but I believe she may have done more damage than you are aware of."

"How so, Patricia?" Dr. Burton asked while adjusting his spectacles.

"I can feel her influence deep into Dr. Sellers. I don't believe this was her first time playing with your emotions. Imprinting emotions leaves a psychic 'fingerprint' on you. I doubt if any of the telepaths would detect it. But I can sense it."

Martin sat frozen for a moment. He was scanning his memories to try and pinpoint when she could have manipulated him. Then it all began to unfold and make sense to him. From the very first moment he saw her, with Paul, she had been using her influence on him. The thirst for more knowledge, distrusting others, being paranoid about keeping his work secret, and the fits of anger. Even using Katherine to keep Dr. Burton under control. He wasn't using her, she had been using him. But he couldn't let the others know. Influenced or not, how could they ever trust him if they found out?

"Mark my words," Janet said in a calm and even tone, "I will make Katherine pay for this. No one attacks my family and gets away with it."

"Pardon my prying," Patricia interrupted, "but Dr. Sellers isn't the only one with her 'fingerprint' on him. I'm sorry, but my curiosity prompted me to take a look and I can tell she's worked her influence on you too." She was looking at Dr. Burton.

"I was afraid of that." Dr. Burton removed his glasses and took out a handkerchief to clean the lens. "I didn't know the 'who' or the 'how,' but I knew something was wrong. I had been experiencing blackouts, of sorts. Waking up in my office from a nap that I didn't remember going in there to take. Or just coming out of a daydream while sitting at my desk with no recollection of how long I had been sitting there." A look of disappointment and violation was displayed on his face.

"I can't tell you when or even what emotions she forced on you. But I can tell you that she has exerted a considerable amount of influence on you. I'm sorry." Patty reached over to Dr. Burton's arm to try and comfort him. "It's odd though. It's just kind of on the surface. Like a smudge. She wasn't able to get it to stick like she did on Dr. Sellers."

"There's no need for you to apologize, my dear. I am just stunned. I can't imagine why she would have needed to manipulate me." The doctor's voice trailed off. He was trying to recall all the blanks in his memory. And he wondered if there had been any other types of tampering with his mind that he was not aware of. The conversation continued and he was brought back to the situation at hand.

"The question now is," said Janet, "what are you going to do next?"

Martin looked at Dr. Burton. The final decision on what course of action they were going to take would have to be up to him. This was his life's work, after all, and it was his son who was at the center of it.

"It would seem my son has planned this all very carefully. And at this point in time, I do not know if confronting him will yield the outcome we desire or simply escalate how quickly we are defeated."

"Sir, you don't mean to just let him..." started Martin, but Dr. Burton cut him off before he could finish.

"Martin, I must not only take into consideration what will happen to the PSI Department, but what that outcome will mean to all those involved with it. There are so many who have come to us to try and find an understanding and control of their abilities." He looked at Janet and Patty. "And there are those, like Thomas, who have truly benefited from being in our care and not a clandestine agency. Regardless of the original reasons they were brought to us. I can't help but think of him, and any others that we don't even know about. All of those people are being experimented on in those other facilities. If we fail now, all of those in our care will fall prey to those monsters. We may never be able to help them, or any others, in the future."

They were all silently nodding in agreement. No one had any alternative plan to offer.

"For now," Dr. Burton continued, "we will continue with business as usual. I will think this through and try to figure out what will work best in the end."

They looked back and forth to each other. Hoping someone could offer up a plan, advice, or even words of encouragement.

Before they parted ways for the evening, they all decided that it would be best if they kept this information between the four of them. Although Patty could not promise that she could keep it from her telepath husband, they all knew he could be trusted as well. They all felt it was a race between making a decision on what was to be done or having it all play out as Paul had planned.

Chapter Eighteen
Search for a Solution

A week had passed since the incident at Martin's apartment. Dr. Burton sat at his desk in his office at home, transcribing his thoughts into his personal journal. He had hoped that putting these thoughts down on paper, as he so often did, would help him gain a better understanding of the situation and possible consequences of whatever decision he might make.

"I have been having numerous meetings and phone calls with various University directors and benefactors. Most of whom are happy, for the time being, with the direction the PSI Department is going and the progress we've made. It would appear that I have secured our funding for at least another year. Though, I'm afraid, Paul has gotten to more than a few of our supporters. I fear that the number of those who believe in our work will continue to dwindle each time until there are no alternative paths to seek.

There has been no progress in locating Katherine O'Bannon or her nephew, Thomas. Her apartment had been cleared out of all her possessions. A manner in which every trace of her living there had been removed leads me to believe that the government agency, which she feared so much, had discovered she was going to try to run. It reminded me of the empty homes of some of the first subjects I had contacted who had later disappeared as well. I have to wonder then, are they aware that we know Paul's plans and of their existence? If they don't know already, I'm sure it's just a matter of time.

I have managed to keep contact with my son limited to phone conversations. His telepathic abilities do not work through the phone lines. I am sure he would read my thoughts and know how aware we are of his intentions, immediately, if I were to meet with him face to face. I don't know how long I can put off seeing my son. And I don't know how long I should delay seeing him and letting him know I am aware of his underhanded plot against me and my work. I had hoped he would never be capable of such things.

I have tried to come at this problem from every angle. Each time it seems that I come to the same conclusion, that we will eventually be absorbed by whatever government agency my son is in league with. Even knowing this, I will continue to seek other avenues, hoping that something unknown to me will present itself. And, I hope, save us from something I fear could spiral into a most disastrous… …"

He stopped writing. There was no word for what he feared. Could this lead to a single event that would only affect him and the PSI Department? Or would it be something that could engulf the entire planet? His brilliant mind raced. Playing out possibilities where the government could harness the power and talents of these special people. They could be used to further the evolution of society. Expanding the understanding of cultures and erasing the conflicts between all people of the world. Ambassadors of peace, overseeing negotiations and treaty signings.

Or they could be used to spy on other nations. Gain secrets. Become powerful, undetectable weapons. What if the government lost control of these weapons? These people have minds of their own. Powerful minds. What if they revolted and seized the power for themselves? What would become of those without abilities?

He sat at his desk, removed his spectacles, and placed his face into his right hand.

"Oh Paul," he said to himself, "What have you done? What in the world have you…"

He paused and removed his hand from his face. "The world," he thought to himself. One of his eyebrows raised with the thought. "The whole wide world. With so many different people. All over the world."

He picked up the phone and dialed Martin's phone number. With every spin of the rotary dialer, he tried to think of what he would say.

"Hello, Martin? It's Ross." His voice was hurried and he didn't wait for Martin to respond. "I have been at this from every angle I can think of. I don't see how I can keep this going from where we are now. I also know it's only a matter of time before Paul confronts me and discovers everything we know. There is too much at risk, so I've come to a decision. I am going to leave…"

"What? No! Dr. Burton, you can't leave. That will just end it all that much faster. You can't give up!"

"No, Martin, let me finish. I am going to leave the state. Even travel outside of the country, if need be, to find help. Financial or otherwise. There must be a solution that I have not even considered. And I know that if I continue to look for it here Paul will eventually find us out."

"So you are going to leave? You can't just leave. How will we run things without you here? We can't ask you to give up your life here."

"Nobody has to ask anything of me. And I will be continuing my work. Just abroad. I need to find a way to sustain the PSI Department away from the University. And far enough out of the reach of that government agency. You are more than capable of running things in my absence. There is also the fact that I don't see Paul paying you a social visit anytime soon or having access into your mind."

"I suppose," Martin said. Remembering that Dr. Burton did not know about the secret agreement he had struck with Paul in exchange for all the stolen information he would obtain. "Don't you think they are aware that we know? If they did get ahold of Katherine, they must know what she told me. And if she was able to disappear, then they've surely noticed her absence and have to be suspicious. Why hasn't Paul made a move yet?"

"I'm not quite sure about that. I've wondered the same thing. Maybe they aren't ready to make their move against us yet. This isn't just storming in and snatching up one person. This is university paperwork and numbers of people involved. I'm sure it will take time, even after they've decided to pounce."

"How long will you be gone?"

"As long as it takes, I suppose. We know we have funding for at least one more year. If I can find a solution to this mess, one that will guarantee Paul cannot interfere, then I'll return as soon as I've discovered it. Then I can see my son and let him know I am aware of his deception." There was a second of silence as Dr. Burton was still formulating his plan of action. "And I suppose I will be leaving as soon as possible. Within the next few days, if not sooner. If I am able to secure transportation and accommodations sooner, then so be it."

Martin could hear the sting of hurt in the man's voice on the other end of the phone. Under the influence of Katherine, or not, he had to make amends for his part in all of this. "I will do my best to keep the department running the way you would have it."

"As you always have, my boy." Dr. Burton wasn't aware of how his words secretly shamed Martin. "Alright, I should go make arrangements. I have some former colleagues I can call on to start this journey. When I've departed, I won't call Paul until I've left, so he won't have a chance to see me off. I think that is best."

"What should I tell the staff or anyone else who asks?"

"Well, I suppose we could say I am on sabbatical for an undetermined amount of time. I will try and keep my position with the university for as long as possible. If they feel the need to remove me from the staff, you can take me on as an offsite consultant. If it comes to that."

"Sounds like a plan. I suppose this is goodbye until you get to wherever you may be going."

"I will call and check in with you when I get settled and hopefully have some information to share."

"Good luck, sir. Take care of yourself."

"Thank you, Martin. Keep an eye on things until I get back."

Martin hung up the phone just as Janet walked into the living room.

"Who was that on the phone?" She asked.

"Dr. Burton," Martin responded. "He'll be going out of town for a while."

"Oh? Where is he going?"

"I don't know," Martin raised both eyebrows as he answered.

"How long will he be gone?" Janet asked.

"I don't know," Martin repeated.

"Why is he leaving? And don't you say that you don't know," Janet said, playfully crossing her arms.

"He's going to try and find a way to save the PSI Department. And before you ask… No, I don't know how."

Janet slowly walked towards him, batting her eyes and smirking at him. "For a doctor, you don't know very much. What is it that you do know?"

"I know," he started as he put his arms around her waist and drew her into him. "I know that I have a very beautiful wife whom I love more than anything else in this world."

He leaned in and kissed her passionately.

She lightly touched the side of his face. She could feel the slightest of stubble on his jaw. "How about we head to bed and I'll show you something I know."

Chapter Nineteen
Long Distance

Paul Burton paced in his lavish office. The day-to-day events of his life were usually enough to keep him distracted from his obsession with the PSI Department. When he had received the phone call from his father, almost a year ago, that he was about to board an airplane for some sort of extended research trip, he thought it was his perfect chance to put his plans in motion.

Unfortunately, bureaucratic paperwork seemed to be something he hadn't counted on. The funding for the PSI Department was securely in place. Even if he used his talents to convince the university's board of directors to pull the funds out, there were signed contracts and legal paperwork that would halt that process and raise too much suspicion. Clauses and wording that made it apparent to him that someone had considered his motivations when drawing up the contracts.

The government agency was no help to him either. They continuously advised him to "stand down" when he voiced any eagerness to make a move. They were afraid of his actions drawing attention, and possible press coverage, to their intentions. He considered them cowards for even worrying about such things. They were too content working in the shadows. But, for now, he had to be their obedient dog on a very long leash.

He sat at his desk and glanced at his watch. He had been waiting for his father's scheduled phone call for over an hour. His patience was wearing thin.

"Mister Burton," said a voice from the speaker box that sat on his desk, "your father is on the line."

Paul did not bother to respond to Miss Baker. He snatched up the phone and pressed the button to connect to the call.

"Dad? Dad, where are you? You're late calling me."

"Hello," Dr. Burton shouted back from his end of the line. "Yes, I know. I'm sorry son. I had a hard time finding a working phone line."

"Where are you?"

"India. It's astonishing how many wonderful things there are to see here! I just met a man who can …" he was interrupted by Paul.

"When are you returning? You have been gone for almost a year! You have responsibilities here. Mother has been asking when you are returning. What am I supposed to tell her?"

"I've spoken to your mother throughout my journeys. She has been aware of my itinerary this past year."

"What about your work here? You can't just leave it all in the hands of Martin Sellers. Who knows what he's been doing there while you've been away? You may not have a workplace to come back to."

"I am well aware of what Dr. Sellers has been up to in my absence. I have been in contact with him as well. The PSI Department is doing quite well."

"Are you so sure, Father?" asked Paul. "Since Martin has made it a habit to avoid my phone calls and requests to meet in person, I've taken the liberty of contacting the Board of Directors for the University. As it turns out, PSI Department isn't doing so well," he had a tone of snide pleasure in his voice. "It seems they are going to stop funding your work. And because I don't want to see your life's work go down the drain, I have been looking for alternate sources of money for you. Maybe you could pass that on to Martin the next time you speak with him."

"Actually, Paul, he is aware of the funding situation. And I believe I have found an alternate source while on my travels."

Paul now suspected why his father had been gone so long. This sabbatical of his wasn't just to study the possibility of psychic phenomena in other parts of the world, but to find outside financial backers so his work could continue away from the confines of the university.

"Father," Paul started, "if you needed more funding, I told you my company has a list of various investors who are available. Heck, my firm could be one of those investors for you."

"Paul, I told you that I have no interest in receiving money or the pressures that go with that money, from any of the pharmaceutical companies that your firm represents. I don't want outside influences dictating the direction in which this research will grow."

After an awkward few seconds of silence, Paul stood at his desk and continued, "I think you are making a mistake. In fact, I know you are. You'll wish you had listened to me. You'll …"

"Sorry to cut you off son, but I think my time is up. I'll contact you again in 2 weeks. Take care." And just like that, the call was disconnected.

Paul was furious. He slammed the receiver down onto the cradle, causing the phone to ring slightly. He stood behind his desk, staring at the phone, fuming. "How dare he dismiss me," he thought. "I'm not a child anymore. He'll realize that when I take that stupid PSI Department away from him, dismantle it, and sell it off to the government, piece by piece."

He slowly sat down in his oversized dark leather chair. Plotting out his next move, and the possible next move after that. He was not prepared to lose this battle. He had been working on this for far too long. Moving all the pieces into place. Lining up his pawns, many unaware of his manipulations. He had felt that Martin Sellers was avoiding him, but now he knew for sure. Those actions would not go unpunished either. Without Katherine in place, he had lost a tremendous amount of control of what was happening at the PSI Department. They had done a complete sweep of their staff, structured security protocols, and schedules. No one was useful to him there. It was just tidbits of information that mostly amounted to gossip.

Paul pulled open one of the side drawers on his desk and removed a black folder that was held closed by an elastic tie. He removed the tie and opened the folder. He flipped to a page that contained a list of names and numbers. Some of which had handwritten notations next to them. He scanned down the list of names until he found the one he had been looking for. Keeping his finger next to the name, he picked up the phone with his free hand and dialed the number next to the name.

"Hello? Is this Agent Coleman?" Paul asked. "You're Agent Brown's replacement in that department correct? Excellent. We need to set up a meeting as soon as possible. The situation with PSI Department is changing and we need to rethink our strategy. Tomorrow will be fine. I'll expect a car at 2."

He hung up the phone and sat back in his chair. His thoughts were spinning, planning out his meeting for tomorrow. He couldn't count on manipulating the new agent with his telepathic talents. Paul was sure the government had wised up enough not to send someone too susceptible to such abilities. Or at least not sending someone with as much authority as Agent Brown had.

Manipulating Agent Brown had given Paul almost a direct line to the top, and a much easier time getting what he wanted. When he had been notified that Agent Brown would no longer be his liaison, he could only speculate that they had discovered that Agent Brown had been compromised. He figured this new agent would take more work. Though, if he played it right, maybe it would get him into the government's head facility. A meeting with whoever was at the very top. Maybe he would get the opportunity to take control right at the source. If only it would be that easy.

Paul smiled to himself. Fate had given him this wondrous talent. Not just telepathy, but his knack for knowing when to use it and how to apply it to get the most out of any situation. He prided himself on his gift for strategizing. What seemed like a complicated corporate takeover to someone else, was a simple game of cat and mouse to him. He was confident that no matter how this meeting went tomorrow, he would end up on top. As usual.

It was almost 5:30 p.m. when the phone on Martin's desk began to ring. Luckily, he was just walking into his office after the second ring. There was a significant amount of static on the line, making it difficult to hear the voice coming through.

"Dr. Burton? Is that you?" Martin shouted into the phone. "I can barely hear you."

"Yes… hello. I'm sorry, I'm in India and I'm afraid the connection is not so good this time," Dr. Burton shouted back.

"It's great to hear from you. How goes the search? Having any luck?"

"On many counts. I have seen some marvelous examples of others with abilities. It truly is a worldwide phenomenon. Why, just yesterday, here in India, I found a boy who can levitate himself using telekinesis. I dare to guess that this is how those classic stories of flying carpets may have started." He chuckled loudly at the possibility that there might be truth in that guess.

"That is wonderful news! While our research has been going well here, I'm afraid we are running out of time as far as the money is concerned. If I didn't know any better, I'd guess your son had something to do with it. I don't know how much longer I can avoid him."

"So I've heard. I just got off the phone with him. I believe he is quite angry with the news that I may have found a way for us to become a self-contained PSI Department away from the university."

"Now THAT is great news! Wait, Paul knows? You told him why you've been gone?"

"Not in so many words, but I think he guessed as much from this last conversation. I don't think he's going to sit still any longer. I have a few more loose ends to tie up here to secure our future and then I am coming straight home. Martin," the phone call started to break up a bit, "this may be the big break we've been waiting for."

The line went dead. The connection had been lost. But no matter, Martin got the good news he needed. He knew if there was any additional information he needed, Dr. Burton would call back. If not, the next phone call would be to let him know when his plane would be arriving home.

Martin sat back at his desk. Able to breathe a sigh of relief. There was a light at the end of the tunnel now. He had been worried that he wouldn't hear from Dr. Burton before the funding would be cut off, the university would throw them out, and without a base of operations, all those people they were trying to help would have no place to go. Giving Paul the perfect opportunity to scoop them up and deliver them right to whatever clandestine agency he was working for.

Now there was hope. He stood up and grabbed his jacket. There was no other work to be done today, he was only waiting around for that phone call. He could head home and share the good news with Janet. He would enjoy a happy night at home with his beautiful wife and daughter.

"Hello? Hello, Martin?" Dr. Burton shouted into the phone. "Are you still there?"

The line had gone dead. Dr. Burton looked at the receiver and placed it back on the cradle. He then removed a handkerchief from his pocket and dabbed the sweat from his forehead.

Dr. Burton had been traveling across the globe searching for the answer that would save his life's work from being taken out of his control. The journey so far had been fantastic.

He had forgotten how much he enjoyed traveling. He was reminded of his time spent studying abroad. Meeting various people from many different cultures. He quickly remembered some of the things he learned, like the respect and manners expected from him in foreign lands. He also remembered the many friends he had made. Some of whom were interested in the scientific fields related to his area of research. Those were the people he called on for help now.

He had already traveled through England and Scotland. Finding a few different accounts of gifted individuals, and securing funding from one source. He had to keep reminding himself of the purpose of this expedition, and not lose himself in the hunt for discovering more unique subjects.

He was finding, though, that trying to track down these individuals often led to the possibility of gaining financial support for his research back home. As was the case with his time in England.

Other destinations didn't fare as well. Italy was very closed off to him when it came to trying to find anyone with special talents. The families there tried very hard to keep those secrets well-guarded and didn't look too kindly on Dr. Burton trying to put his nose into their personal affairs.

His time in France did not go much better. When he discovered an empathic boy, one who appeared would benefit greatly from his research and help, the parents dismissed him almost immediately. They were not convinced that an American would be any better suited to assist their son than any French scientist might be. They certainly were not going to take their son to America for "treatment."

Luckily, not all roads ended in a similar fashion. Dr. Burton was welcomed and listened to in Spain. He found doctors interested in his research in Sweden. Some expressed a great deal of interest in making the journey to America to be part of the scientific discovery in a way that could link funding and benefit both parties. He had also reconnected with an old colleague in Germany. He was a doctor specializing in Neuroscience who had already heard of Dr. Burton's accomplishments with the PSI Department.

Dr. Burton was quickly reminded of the timeline he was working against when his German colleague told him that he had been to America a couple of years back, and had met Paul Burton.

"Is he your son, no?" he asked with a very thick accent. "He said he wasn't a doctor, that it was a hobby of his. Seemed like a bright young man."

Despite learning about Paul's involvement, he had a great sense of hope. He found strength in discovering others with his thirst for knowledge (especially when they had money to back up their convictions). Seeing, firsthand, how global this phenomenon was, he knew he wasn't going to let anything stop the momentum of his research.

He decided that India would be his last stop. He had a couple more leads to follow through on and some meetings already scheduled for the next few days. If everything went according to plan, he would be able to fly home before the end of next week.

He headed into the lobby of the hotel he was staying in, very aware that it wasn't much cooler inside than it was outside. He wasn't missing his cardigan at the moment. After checking the front desk for any messages, he made his way upstairs to his room hoping to take a nap and pass the time until sunset and cooler temperatures.

Chapter Twenty
Global Trust Insurance

The long black limousine arrived after 2 p.m. 6 minutes late to pick Paul up. As punishment, Paul made the chorus of "Respect," by Aretha Franklin, stick in the driver's head for the duration of the car ride. Which was almost an hour-long journey to the office of Agent Coleman. If Paul thought his influence was wearing off on the driver, he would simply inject the chorus "R-E-S-P-E-C-T. Find out what it means to me…" into his head and that would start the process all over again.

"You ever get a song stuck in your head?" the driver looked into the rearview mirror and asked Paul. "And just when you forget about it, it comes back?"

"No," replied Paul. "I can't say that I have." As he pushed the button to raise the partition window between them. Even when he didn't have the money and position, his powers afforded him a sense of entitlement and arrogance. The money just helped make it look more appropriate.

Paul had already glanced into the driver's mind. He was just a driver. He wasn't informed of the details of who had hired him. He was just aware of the pick-up and drop-off times and destinations. His mind was very boring to Paul.

The limo ride was slightly longer than he expected. It wasn't traveling to the same offices where the meetings with Agent Brown took place. This was someplace new.

The driver pulled the limo up to the front of the building. He put the car in park but left the engine running. He got out and walked around the car to open up the rear passenger door to let Paul out.

Paul didn't say a word to the driver. He only smirked and lightly hummed the tune that had been haunting the poor driver for the past hour. It served two purposes: To place the song firmly in the driver's mind again and to cause confusion as to how his passenger would know the song in his head.

As the limo pulled away, Paul walked towards the office building. It was only 10 stories high with large, darkly tinted windows. The sign on the front of the building identified it as "Global Trust Insurance." The two glass doors, and all of the windows, in front were tinted dark enough to reflect the environment of the outside and obstruct any view of the inside. Paul didn't mind looking at his reflection as he walked towards the doors.

"Odd," he thought as he entered the building, "the lobby is simple enough. Why go through all the trouble to try and conceal it from being seen from the outside?" He also wondered why it felt like the pressure in his ears was changing. Almost a slight humming sound.

He approached the reception desk and informed the woman sitting behind it that he was there for a meeting with Agent Coleman. She was in her mid-20s, with wavy shoulder-length ash-blonde hair. A pretty enough woman, dressed in a professional light pink shirt. She asked Paul to have a seat in the waiting area and she would inform Agent Coleman he was there.

Waiting on other people was one of Paul's pet peeves. He detested having to sit and wait and flip through the idiotic magazines most places kept on display for visitors. He felt it was beneath him to read the trash that most of them contained.

"Why not read her mind instead," he thought to himself. "Let's see how much she knows about what's going on here."

He quickly realized that as he tried to reach out to her mind, he couldn't find it. He could see her sitting at the desk, but there was a static in the air that prevented him from locating her thoughts and hearing them. He stared at her from where he sat, trying to figure out if she was the one creating this annoying static. Now it seemed that this static noise was causing an odd sensation in his ears. Only it wasn't in his ears, it was actually in his mind.

He tried to broaden his search. He used his mind to try and scan the whole building. Again the static noise blocked him. He wasn't able to tell if it was only present in his surroundings or if it was throughout the entire building. This did not please Paul at all.

He calmed himself and began to concentrate. Determined to push through this fog, he thought to himself, "I don't think these people know who they are dealing with." And he began to push his mind out further into the building.

It was like being underwater. His mind was trying to "swim" from his area to the other floors of the building. He was only able to get vague impressions that there were other people in the building. He couldn't get a clear hold on their thoughts, or even tell how many people there were. It was obvious that this "static" was in place, somehow, to keep out abilities like his. Before he could focus on it anymore, the woman at the reception desk called to him.

"Mr. Burton, Agent Coleman is ready for you. Just take the elevator to the 5th floor. Someone will meet you there."

"Oh, he must have been mistaken," Paul said to the woman as he approached the desk. Even as he got closer to her, the ever-present static blocked him from her mind. "Could you ring Agent Coleman and let him know I made reservations for us to have lunch elsewhere?"

"No sir. You can take the elevators there," she pointed to them, still seated behind the desk, "and take them to the 5th floor where you will be escorted to Agent Coleman." She had a polite smile on her face.

Paul didn't respond to her. He only flashed her an irritated smirk and headed to the elevators. He pressed the button to call the elevator and felt like he was entering the lion's den. As he waited for the elevator, he wondered if the receptionist was aware of who he was and what he was capable of. He would figure a way around the static and wipe that smug smile off her face.

He took the elevator up to the 5th floor as directed. When the doors opened he was met by a young man in a suit. Much like the one Agent Brown wore, only slightly more up-to-date.

"If you will come with me, please," he said to Paul. "Agent Coleman's office is just down this hallway." The young man extended his arm, gesturing for Paul to exit the elevator and to follow him.

By all looks and appearances, this was a typical insurance office building. A large bullpen area with desks that had phones and typewriters on them. Closed office doors surrounded the main area, with a few people coming and going from them. People in proper suits and skirts bustling about doing some sort of busy work. Each one was blocked from Paul's mind by that damned static.

When they reached the door labeled "Agent Coleman," the young man opened the door and waved Paul into the room. Once Paul entered the office, the door was closed behind him.

"Mr. Burton, I'm Agent Coleman," said a man sitting behind a desk. He stood and extended his hand out to shake Paul's hand.

"So I gathered from the sign on the door," said Paul, who did not extend his hand out to meet Agent Coleman's.

Agent Coleman was younger than Agent Brown was when Paul had first met him. He wore the same style suit as the other men in the building, but he wore it with more authority. Despite his younger appearance, and the fact that his looks were softened by his lighter complexion and blonde hair, he was definitely one of the men in charge here.

"Well, I guess this means we skip the formalities and niceties and get right down to business." Agent Coleman used his extended hand to gesture to a chair for Paul to sit on. He then sat back down in his chair as he continued to speak. "I assume you are aware of the dampening field that prevents you from using your 'talents'? I'm sorry if this is the cause of your obvious irritation. Many of our subjects have described it as being stuck in a small box or even being blinded. It's just to ensure that you can't use your influence on anyone here. Sort of levels the playing field."

Paul wasn't pleased with Agent Coleman's description of the effect of this "dampening field." He did not feel trapped in a box or blind. The static was irritating, yes, but certainly not debilitating. It seemed he was more talented than what these people had previously encountered. Sometimes being underestimated is a good thing. Paul decided to play on that assumption.

"You can't imagine, Agent Coleman, how off-putting this feels. I suppose it would be like asking you to try and be calm while being tied and blindfolded at the same time. I feel as if you have cut off my arms. I'm curious how you are able to do this?"

"You don't need to concern yourself with the details. You called this meeting Mr. Burton. I hope you have a good reason and you aren't wasting my time."

Paul sat in the chair and crossed his legs. "As you know, Agent Coleman, my father has been away for almost a year now. He hasn't been on sabbatical. He has been looking for alternate funding to keep PSI Department running after the university pulls its funding and kicks him off campus."

"Yes. And?"

"Well, it appears my father might have found the funding he was looking for. I don't know the exact details of how and who, but if he has secured the money to continue the PSI Department, then your takeover will not happen as scheduled."

"That timetable is your schedule, Mr. Burton. We are perfectly satisfied to allow things to continue in the direction they are going."

"What? If none of this is of importance to you, then why even bother trying to position yourself to take over his project in the first place?"

"We are not just the U.S. government. We already have support and bases established in various U.S.-friendly countries around the world. When we think your father and his team have achieved all they can, and are no longer productive on their own, we will absorb them, and all of their research, into our program. To do so too early might hinder, or possibly completely halt, the discoveries they have yet to make."

"And how do you plan on doing that without my help?"

"The only help you have supplied us with is information. When we are ready to seize control of the PSI Department we will simply take it. This won't be a corporate merger. This will be a hostile takeover. With the full backing of the U.S. Government, we will simply go in and take up where they left off. If any of the staff wishes to stay on with us, they may. Or they can leave. We'll have all the information, so it won't matter."

Paul relaxed in his chair a bit. He had misread this man entirely. No matter how much authority he had in this building, he was clearly not a leader, and Paul could tell he was bluffing. At least, partly. He stared into Agent Coleman's blue eyes. He had been studying this man intently since he sat down, but he had also been trying to work his way past the static. Trying to get into this man's head. He wasn't getting any closer. He was still effectively blocked enough to not have any effect.

"It seems you have it all figured out then," said Paul. "I guess I will just continue my 'information gathering' mission. That is, as long as the deal I made with Agent Brown is still valid."

"Of course. The deal was you keep delivering and we don't bring you back to our facilities."

"Speaking of your facilities, may I ask how Katherine O'Bannon and her nephew, Thomas, are doing?"

"Thomas is secure in one of our training facilities. Katherine, I'm afraid has tried to escape numerous times, and has been resistant to behavior modification. She is… how should I put this, going through a more aggressive reconditioning program? We're hoping that she is salvageable. She has the kind of talent we don't want to lose."

"Indeed." Paul was well aware of what it meant to no longer have Katherine's talents at his disposal.

"Since you are already here," Agent Coleman said, "why don't we begin the next phase of what we have planned for you."

"Planned for me? I'm not quite sure I understand what 'plan' you are speaking of." Paul tensed up slightly. "I thought my duties to your agency were exactly what I have already been doing."

"You've been performing adequately, Paul. No reason to be worried. We just want to make sure that we are getting all the data as it becomes available. We've noticed that your father's facility has been able to keep ahead of our research by leaps and bounds. It appears having the cooperation of these freaks yields better results. Oh, no offense intended."

"None taken," Paul said through slightly clenched teeth.

"Although, they don't seem to be doing any of the more intrusive type of research we're doing here. It's just we've noticed that your fact-gathering and delivering isn't as timely as we would like."

"Well, I'm not the most welcome person in that building. I can't just waltz in and ask for the latest files of information. There are too many 'freaks' who are resistant to my abilities and are loyal to my father and Dr. Sellers. And upon losing Katherine, they've tightened up their security quite a bit. Unless you want to supply me with replacements for Katherine, I'll have to keep working with the limited number of people I can trust and you'll keep getting your precious data as it becomes available."

"We've anticipated that," Agent Coleman said as he opened a desk drawer and took out a file. "Here are your new contacts. I'm afraid we could only get two volunteers. Even those who have gone through considerable behavior modifications can't be trusted for this type of work. These two were already dedicated to our goals. Looks like you may have something in common with them."

Paul flipped open the file and thought to himself, "Let's hope we do have a common goal."

Agent Coleman stood from his chair and held out a business card for Paul to take. "This is your new contact information."

Paul took the card and looked down at it. It had the same insurance company logo as the front of the building. He looked back up to Agent Coleman.

"Yes, we keep the façade just in case the card gets misplaced or falls into the wrong hands. We aren't quite ready for the public to know about all of this."

"Well then," Paul put the card into his pocket, "it looks like I have everything I need. If there is nothing else?"

"I suppose that covers everything for now. I just want to remind you of something Mr. Burton," Agent Coleman walked around from behind the desk as Paul stood up. He looked Paul right into the eyes as he spoke. "I want you to remember that even though we may not have the ability to block you from using your talents outside of this building, we are more than capable of crippling you in other ways."

"And just what is that supposed to mean?" Paul stood his ground as Agent Coleman drew even closer to Paul. He wasn't going to allow this man to intimidate him. Paul refused to step back.

"We are aware of how much you value your wealth, your business, and your social stature. All things which would not be too difficult for us to take away. Just a reminder."

"No need for threats, Agent Coleman. This dog is quite aware of the leash he is on." Paul leaned slightly forward and stared him right back in the eyes as he spoke. Their faces just inches apart from each other. Yet, he was still no closer to reading his thoughts as he was when he first entered. "I can show myself out."

As Paul opened the door he was greeted by the same young man in the suit who had taken him to the office. Paul turned back around to give a deadpan look to Agent Coleman for not allowing him to leave unescorted.

"He's rather attractive," Paul thought to himself. "Hopefully, soon, I'll be able to make him MY pet on a leash." He turned his blank expression into a narrow-eyed smile and turned back to his escort.

He walked Paul back to the elevator and waited with him silently until it came.

The elevator made a nonstop journey down to the lobby. Paul exited the elevator, making the conscious decision to not even look at or acknowledge the receptionist. She was too busy flipping through a magazine to even notice him. He could see through the glass doors that the limousine was already waiting for him outside.

Paul left the building, stopping to look back before he got into the limousine. He studied the building for a moment, wondering where the dampening device might be located. Would it be on the roof dropping the static down like rain? In the center of the building creating a bubble around the structure? Or on the first floor or basement sending a signal upwards? There was no indication from looking at the outside of the building. He wondered: Was this something they were able to duplicate elsewhere?

Chapter Twenty-One
Homecoming

Martin watched through the airport window as the tall metal stairs were wheeled up to the airplane's door. The door opened and one by one the passengers filed out and carefully descended the stairs. There was a good amount of wind, which was evident to him by the women clutching their hats and trying to protect their hair.

Then he saw Dr. Burton appear in the doorway. Being gone almost a year had been kind to him. He still had on his signature cardigan and spectacles. But he was slightly tanner, thinner, and had a bit of a bounce in his step. Martin watched him navigate down the stairs, claim his one piece of luggage at the bottom of the stairs, and then walk towards the building. Martin moved from the window towards the door where the passengers entered the airport's lobby.

He could overhear the happy greetings from others who had been waiting for the passengers to arrive. A lot of "I missed you," "How was your trip?" and "How long was the flight?"

Dr. Burton entered the building, carrying a small briefcase and his one piece of luggage. He spotted Martin immediately. He set the luggage down and held out his right hand to greet Martin as he approached him.

"Dr. Burton," Martin said, clasping the man's hand in his own. "It's so good to finally have you back!"

"It is good to be back. I cannot wait to tell you of all my travels and adventures. So many wondrous places I've seen. But there truly is no place like home."

"Your trunk arrived two days ago. So if you have no other luggage to collect from the plane, I'll drive you home."

They walked side by side to Martin's car. Talking about the long plane ride and the bumpy landing caused by the wind. Once they reached Martin's car, they placed the luggage in the trunk, but Dr. Burton kept his briefcase with him.

During the car ride, Dr. Burton opened his briefcase, took out some papers, and read their contents to Martin. It was a detailed breakdown of the three main sources of funds he had secured while he was away. He was not just giving Martin the figures, but some of the back story of who was supplying the funds and why.

"The first, from England, I discovered from talking with a tavern owner. He told me of an English Lord who had been a steady patron for many years. This man, it seems, would drink heavily to drown out the 'voices' in his head. Many speculated that it was the result of some sort of trauma he had suffered in the war. The tavern owner told me that before this man would get too drunk, he would often perform bar tricks involving guessing numbers, colors, or secrets of the other bar patrons. A well-liked and good-natured fellow who seemed to be carrying a tremendous burden that no one was able to help him with. Unfortunately, he passed away just a few months before I arrived. But, fortunately, his widow was very receptive to my requests to talk and showed interest in my theories about the voices her late husband had been haunted by. Her wish is to make sure no one else has to live with the same pain as her husband. She was very eager to help fund our research. Luckily, she has a considerable amount of money to put towards our cause."

"That is amazing," said Martin. "Are you sure this lonely widow was only interested in your…eh hem, 'research'?" He smirked and nudged his elbow at the travel-weary man sitting next to him. He was trying to catch a glance at the paperwork but decided to keep his eyes on the road instead.

"Yes, well, I'm sure that was her only motivation." He blushed slightly. "While she was extremely hospitable, and generous, I can assure you nothing inappropriate occurred between us." He paused for a moment and then added, "But I can't say for sure what will happen when she comes to visit in the next year."

Both men chuckled, as this type of behavior was not in line with the type of proper etiquette that Dr. Burton usually followed. Martin had never known him to be the kiss-and-tell kind of man.

"The second is a very wealthy and influential family in Spain. They are a very established family that has a lot of interest in philanthropic endeavors. Explaining our research and goals to get them on board took a considerable amount of my time to secure. Even though I did not find any evidence of anyone having abilities in their immediate family, they were so amazed by our findings that they are very eager to see something good come of it.”

“So you don’t believe they have any alternative motives for backing us?”

“No. At least not on the surface. As with all of our research, findings, and dealings, we will release only the information we deem appropriate, and make that information available to them.”

Martin nodded his head in agreement and continued to drive. It seemed the re-exposure to the outside world and its many different people had expanded the doctor’s mind and caused him to lose a bit of his naiveté. He spoke with excitement in his tone. A new zest for continuing his work.

“And the last one is from India. Oh, Martin, what a magnificent place! These people are quite the opposite of what I had found in Spain. Virtually a whole family of gifted individuals!”

Martin had just reached a stop light and was able to turn his attention to the doctor. A look of excitement was on his face. The possibility of an entire family being gifted had never been fully explored.

“You heard me correctly. It appears that the abilities, as varied as they are, are hereditary in this family. Even extended family members possess them to various extents. From one end of the spectrum to the other. One child is such a powerful telepath that he is mute. He only communicates telepathically. Whereas another is such a low-level pyrokinetic that she only generates a warming ‘aura’ around her. She’s never been able to produce a fire.

“This family is a rarity, in both abilities and wealth, but have pledged tremendous funding if we can help some of their more challenged family members control their abilities. That seems to be the only ulterior motive behind their generosity.”

The light had turned to green and Martin resumed driving towards the doctor’s home. It felt as if a huge weight had been lifted off his shoulders. Things could continue forward, maybe even improve greatly with these new possibilities.

“Does this mean we can continue with our work at the PSI Department?”

“Martin,” Dr. Burton started as he put the papers back into his briefcase. “This may well be the beginning of something even greater. The family in Spain educated me on how we can expand our facilities on our own. Be in our own building, labs, research center…everything.”

“Sir? What about the university?”

“University be damned. I know I was resistant to breaking free of their hold in the past. I was a fool. And for that, Martin, I am sorry. I should have listened to you before. With these new avenues, we will be able to make great strides in the name of science, help those who need it, and be free to make our own choices without the outside influence of those who don’t even understand our work or our goals.”

“It all sounds wonderful, on paper. I just can’t help but think of what the price for this help might be. With the University we knew what to expect. Can we trust the sources of this generosity?”

“Martin, I’m sure there will be some issues to smooth over. There always are. Between the two of us, I am confident that we can handle it. That is if you are still on board?”

“Of course I am! I can’t think of any other thing I would rather be doing. I mean no disrespect if it sounds like I am questioning your decisions. I just want to make sure all our bases are covered.”

“I value all your input. Even if this isn’t the best decision, I am afraid it might be the only one left to make. With Paul manipulating the Board of Directors at the university, I don’t think we have too many options. That boat is sinking quickly and we have to jump ship before it’s too late.”

“Speaking of Paul…” Martin started to say.

“I don’t know yet how I will handle that,” Dr. Burton responded to Martin before he could ask his question. “I will have to see him face to face eventually. Quite soon, to be sure. I’m not sure I will be able to hide these thoughts from him. Even if I am successful in blocking him from reading my thoughts, doing so will alert him that I am making an effort to hide something from him. Have you discovered if anyone else has been spying for him?”

“So far, no. We don’t even have a handful of telepaths who can effectively read others with abilities. And even less that we can trust with the knowledge of why we need them to violate the privacy of others and secretly pry into their thoughts. It wasn’t something I was comfortable with exploring, so I’ve opted to restrict access to a lot of the files and information we have. It has been a constant rotation of the staff to make sure no one is in one position for an extended period of time. We are doing our best, but there is no way to know how effective it's been. And if we do discover a spy, I'm not sure I'd know what to do next."

"Then we do our best and deal with whatever situation comes as it arises. That said, it seems our first order of business will be to find a new place to relocate our life's work. It's time for the PSI Department to break away from Worthington University."

The car pulled into the driveway of Dr. Burton's home. Martin put the car in park and shut off the engine. He turned and looked at Dr. Burton and was glad to see his friend home safe and reinvigorated from his journeys.

"I suppose," Dr. Burton said, "this means we'll need a real-estate agent to start looking for places."

The two men got out and walked to the back of the car to retrieve Dr. Burton's luggage from the trunk.

"I think Janet has a friend who could help us," Martin said.

"That would be splendid. How are Janet and Margaret doing? Do you have a few moments to come inside and catch me up?"

"Sure, I do. Well, someone has been asking me for the past year when her 'Doctor Grandpa' is coming home."

"I have truly missed that little face. It is nice to finally be home."

The two men walked into Dr. Burton's house and spent the next 2 hours catching each other up on the events of the past year.

Chapter Twenty-Two
Center

The search for a new location took a little more time than expected. Dr. Burton and Dr. Sellers searched for a building that could house all the equipment and people they currently worked with, and have room to expand comfortably if that was in their future. They had broadened their search into New York and Boston. They had hoped to find one of the larger, older buildings that would fit their criteria. But they weren't having much luck.

"Maybe we are trying to stay too close to home," Dr. Sellers said one day.

"What do you mean?" asked Dr. Burton.

"Well, when you couldn't find the solution to our funding problem, you searched the world for an answer. And you found it. Maybe we need to think on a larger scale to find the solution for this problem as well."

"Relocate to another country? You think that's our only option?"

"No, sir. I think we should try taking a trip to the west coast. California may have the potential we are looking for."

"You may be right. Although, I'm not sure of how many of our subjects we'll retain if we were to relocate so far away from our starting point, but it may very well be worth looking into."

They planned a trip to California and left the following week. They met with a few different real estate agents and looked at various types of properties. Old office buildings and shopping centers, even an old grocery store. But nothing fit their criteria.

It appeared their trip to California wasn't going to yield the results they had hoped for. Although there was a fantastic piece of property that interested Martin greatly, Dr. Burton was not convinced that they could afford the building and all the costs to properly outfit it.

It seemed it was not the right time to move their research so far away.

When they had arrived home from their west coast trip, Dr. Burton received a phone call from Janet's real-estate friend about an older building in Greenwich, Connecticut. It had been used as a private hospital and was soon to be vacant. The whole facility was moving to a newly constructed building and the old property was up for sale. The agent also mentioned the possibility of finding a nice-sized home for Martin's family, but he preferred to concentrate on commercial properties first. Janet informed him that they could do both, as it was time to start planning their future as a family too. So the real estate agent called on some colleagues and split his time between the two property searches.

Dr. Burton, Martin, and the real estate agent drove to the former hospital to see if this prospective location would fit their requirements. There was some renovation that needed to be done, but the structure itself was in great shape. A fairly rectangular-shaped, 6-story tall building with evenly spaced windows along its front-facing wall. Each window had off-white trim around them which set off the red-brick face of the building. It had a very posh, medical look to it.

Once inside, they made their way through the building, checking the various rooms and offices. Many of the rooms could be converted to comfortable temporary housing for visiting patients. The space required for laboratories was already established, as were the offices. It had a large enough parking lot to accommodate the staff and all patients. Plus, it was surrounded by green grass and some mature trees. The simple changes needed to make it less of an old hospital and more of a new medical research center wouldn't be that difficult.

The deal was fast and the construction needed to make the building suit their needs would be done by the time everything was ready to be moved in. It was a solid month of preparation for the move. Organizing and boxing up files and equipment took the bulk of the time. All testing was stopped during this process of transition. They had to be sure to notify everyone of the location of the new building and when it would be open to continue their testing.

The timing for this move seemed like it couldn't have been planned any better because it was going very smoothly. As this was not just a move, but an expansion, a bigger staff would need to be brought on board. Thankfully, new doctors and scientists were not having to be sought out as much as anticipated. Word had gotten out in the scientific community about the PSI Department leaving the Worthington University grounds and going out on its own. More than a handful of prospective staff were very interested in the PSI Department's work and wanted to be a part of it. Dr. Burton had been receiving their letters requesting that he consider them for positions available at his new facility.

The university's board of directors hadn't stayed silent during the move. They threatened lawsuits over removing any equipment or university property. As well as "poaching" any doctors or staff to join their new venture. Dr. Burton, after reading over the contracts, and consulting legal counsel, concluded that new equipment would need to be purchased, but there were no clauses in place in any contracts that prevented anyone from joining the new facility.

Construction in the new building started a week after they finalized the sale. The renovations and improvements were going ahead of schedule. It seemed the old building had good bones and most of the work needed was cosmetic. As soon as construction on an area was complete, or near enough to completion to be safe, they would start moving in furniture, file cabinets, and all sorts of equipment.

Everyone helped in whatever area they were able to. Janet and Patty even pitched in by helping with the interior decorating. They wanted to make sure this new facility was professional, but also inviting. They didn't want it to resemble the cold, impersonal, hospital that it had been previously.

Dr. Burton stood in the elevator in the new building, patiently waiting for it to reach the top floor. He glanced around the inside of the newly renovated elevator. It was a smooth ride up to the 6th floor. Since the audio system had not been completed, there was no music in the elevator yet. He was alone with his thoughts as he was carried upwards, one floor after the next. He hoped that soon this place would be busy with people, and lonely elevator rides would just be a memory.

He initially thought the building might be too big. When he and Martin had first looked at the structure, he was sure that all the extra space would not be needed. However, Martin pointed out the possibilities of not only expanding the research labs but also building safe areas where they could test abilities. Areas with all of the proper insulation, padding, and fireproofing.

The extra space, and new equipment, also meant they could explore the various avenues of chemical and pharmaceutical applications. Dr. Burton had always been hesitant when it came to administering any sort of chemicals to control or lessen anyone's abilities. But, he was now learning that not all of those with these special gifts wanted to keep them. Some people may never be able to fully control them. He understood what those decisions could mean for the individual and those around them.

There was a small "ding" sound as the elevator reached the 6th floor. The doors slid open and he stepped out. This floor was designated to be mostly administrative offices and file storage. A few of his established staff members were walking about, setting up their offices and organizing the workspace.

He continued to the far end of the top floor. That was where the last two, and largest, offices were. Their doors, side by side, had nameplates on the front of them. "Dr. Ross Burton" and "Dr. Martin Sellers." His door was closed. His office was already set up and functional. All that was left to do was have the phone service activated. He noticed Martin's door was slightly open. He knocked lightly and pushed the door open further.

"Yes? Come in," said Martin. He was standing by a row of filing cabinets that covered one side wall. He was organizing and filing some paperwork into the metal cabinets.

"Good evening Martin. Almost ready for our grand opening?"

"Almost. I honestly didn't think I had this much organizing left to do. I guess the holidays set me back a bit more than I thought."

"Well, when you add the fact that you also had to pack up, move, and unpack your personal life as well. Although, with the amount of time you've been spending here, I assume that Janet is doing all the unpacking in the new house?"

"Yes, she is. And the decorating. And taking care of little Margaret. She has been incredible and supportive throughout this whole process. Especially with how frantic I've been. She deserves a medal."

"Frantic? How so? Now that you mention it, I suppose you have seemed a bit anxious for a while now."

Martin plopped down into the chair behind his desk. He set the last few files on top of his desk, rubbed his eyes and face with both hands, and sighed. "I was just really hoping to have everything in place and ready to go by the time the new year started. Having this place up and running would have been a great way to welcome in 1970. And now we are almost 3 weeks into it and still not ready."

Dr. Burton sat in the chair on the other side of the desk. He removed his spectacles and rubbed his own eyes with his thumb and index finger. He was tired as well. It was the first time that Martin had seen Dr. Burton as a 57-year-old man and not as the young teacher who had taught his favorite class at the university. It seemed like a lifetime ago.

"You mustn't be so hard on yourself," Dr. Burton said as he replaced his spectacles on his face. "The construction on the bottom three floors only finished a week ago. And we are still waiting on some of the lab equipment to be shipped in. These things, if they are to be done properly, take time. We must recognize that an amazing amount has been accomplished in an incredibly short amount of time."

"You're right. I know you're right. But I just can't help but feel like we should be up and running already. Like we are wasting time or missing some other opportunity."

"Do you still feel that we should have taken that property in Los Angeles instead? Is that what is bothering you?" Dr. Burton knew that even though both of them were happy with the decision to move their research to this location, part of Martin was still wondering what would have happened if they had chosen to move their research to California instead.

"I'd be lying if I said I didn't think about it. But my frustration truly is based on concentrating on getting this place up and running as soon as possible. I suppose I'll just keep Los Angeles in the back of my mind … for now." Martin said the last part with a smile. Both men knew that he had never just given up on an idea or possibility of "what might have been."

"Up and running will be a realization before you know it. The last of new lab technicians arrive the day after tomorrow. Two of them in the morning, arriving from England. The third one will be arriving later in the evening from Germany. Hopefully the last of the equipment we ordered will have been delivered by then so we can set it up. This Thursday I am scheduling our first staff meeting."

"And if the equipment isn't here?"

"Then we'll handle it when it does arrive. We have enough of our labs set up that they are functional." Dr. Burton spoke with a bit of excitement in his voice now. "Regardless, we need to be sure everyone on staff is ready. Our first patients will be arriving soon," he leaned forward and said with a tremendous smile, "and our PSI Center will be ready for them."

Chapter Twenty-Three
Meetings

Thursday morning was chilly but bright. With barely a cloud in the sky, the sun was shining through the windows of the lobby area of the new PSI Center. Staff members, some of whom had just arrived and others who had already been in the building for a couple of hours, made their way through the lobby toward the cafeteria. They were here for the first official staff meeting. This meeting was to include everyone on staff. Doctors, interns, receptionists, janitorial… all were required to attend. It was not only intended to relay information on the operations of the PSI Center, as most of the staff were already aware of their duties and what was expected of them, but it was also going to be a pep rally of sorts to help strengthen a teamwork mentality among coworkers and for everyone to become familiar with each other. A group meeting like this would most likely not be a common occurrence. After the initial meeting, the heads of each department were going to meet with their teams and go over any last-minute details and double-check that everyone was prepared for the official opening on Monday.

There were already 60 staff members in attendance, with a couple dozen extras still arriving. The cafeteria was large enough to accommodate everyone comfortably. It was quite a large area. The ceiling was raised to open the space up to the first two floors. It created a very open and calming space. One wall was all windows, looking out to a grassy courtyard on the side of the building. A large tree, not too far from the windows, provided afternoon shade. The other walls were white, keeping with the hospital theme. Some of the staff members had been lobbying for a mural to be painted on one of the bare walls to break up the "sterile hospital" feeling. There were tables with attached benches that could seat 6 or 8 adults each, as well as traditional square tables with four separate chairs around them. Not everyone had taken a seat yet, and it appeared that some would have to stand in the back of the room once the meeting started.

Staff members who were familiar with each other found seats next to one another. They greeted each other with the typical "Good morning" and "How are you?" While the newer members searched the unfamiliar faces hoping to recognize that look of awkwardness, of not knowing anyone, and being lost in the crowd. This would usually spur an introduction and some relief of finding others with this newness in common.

Martin noticed these groupings, spotting who the newer people were compared to the veterans on staff. There were groupings of those in white lab coats and those in regular business attire. He also noticed another group. Why was this particular group standing out to him? It was a group of maybe 7 or 8 people. There was a definite mix of both new and old faces. They were from various staff positions and departments. Some of the more familiar faces were even past subjects who stayed on as staff members. Was that it?

The reason suddenly became clear to him. That group consisted of people with various abilities. He couldn't positively identify exactly what ability each person possessed, but he was sure that was the common denominator. He scanned the rest of the crowd, looking at the other groups and couples who were talking and waiting for the meeting to start.

There were other gifted people scattered throughout, but none grouped in as large of a number as the one that caught his eye. Just as he made a mental note to remember who was in that group, Dr. Burton entered the cafeteria and approached a podium. It was positioned at the far end of the cafeteria, facing out to the crowd. He adjusted the microphone that was attached to it and addressed the crowd.

"Good morning, ladies and gentlemen," he said into the microphone. It gave off a little bit of feedback which helped to gain everyone's attention. The sound was clear, not loud enough to echo off of the high ceiling, and his voice carried clearly through the large space.

The whole room turned to face Dr. Burton. Those who were sitting began to stand and the entire room began to applaud.

Dr. Burton blushed at the admiration from the crowd. He smiled, nodded, and gestured for everyone to sit.

"Thank you," he said into the microphone, "thank you, everyone. Please, everyone, take a seat and we will get this underway."

The applause faded out and was replaced by the sound of people moving about to find their seats and get settled. Those who were not able to find empty chairs earlier continued to stand at the far end of the cafeteria.

"Good morning everyone," Dr. Burton started, "I would like to assure those of you standing in the back that this will not be a long speech. A relief to those who know that I can be a bit long-winded at times." The crowd chuckled at his statement.

Martin was seated next to the podium. He looked into the sea of faces that were all paying close attention to Dr. Burton's every word. It took him back to the days of watching the man teach class. He wondered if Dr. Burton knew just how much of a leader and role model he was to so many of these people. If he did, he never alluded to it.

"First, I want to thank you all for being here. Not just for this meeting, but for being a part of this fantastic journey of discovery that we are all going to take together. Some of you have been part of this crew for some time. You are familiar with our systems, our goals, and our work ethic. It is to you people that I ask for help in assisting our newer staff members to get acclimated to how our facility works. Even though many of you have been in this building for a while now assembling offices, lab equipment, and organizing, you may not have had the experience of actual hands-on research. That is why we are here to help each other. That is why we have spent so much time preparing for the opening of this facility. Next week is when all that preparation will pay off.

"As I'm sure you have all noticed, this facility was formerly a hospital. I would like us all to keep that fact in mind as we move forward in the weeks, and hopefully, years to come. I want us all to carry that spirit of helping others in mind when we conduct our research. When we have patients who are confused or scared, we need to hold on to that same compassion that so many doctors and nurses have when caring for patients. Some of you have been in the position of our patients, and know better than anyone how frightening that can be. We are all here to help these people.

"We may have our sights set on making scientific breakthroughs and unlocking medical discoveries… but more than anything else, our goal is to help others."

The cafeteria broke into applause once again. Dr. Burton humbly smiled and again raised his hands to gesture for everyone to be quiet.

"We can, and will, achieve our goals by working together." He adjusted his glasses and removed a folded piece of paper from his pocket. "Now then, on to some updates on important events and visitors to the Center." He unfolded the paper across the top of the podium in front of him.

As Dr. Burton began to read off his list, Martin noticed one of the people in the crowd turn and look back at the exit to the cafeteria. It wouldn't have caught his eye, but everyone else had been facing directly forward, and this one man, seated directly in Martin's line of sight, turned around to look behind him as if he'd heard something. Martin followed the man's gaze to the exit and saw the door closing as if someone had just exited. But he didn't see anyone, just a blurred spot in his vision. As if he'd had something in his eye.

The distracted man was Dr. Rex Wall. He was about the same age as Martin, but the similarity ended there. He had tan skin from outdoor activities and sun-streaked blonde hair, which complimented his blue eyes. His build was tall and broad-shouldered with his square jaw setting off his masculine features. He was a new addition to the team, but he was very familiar with the research and fit into the workings of PSI Center very quickly.

He had come from Australia after contacting Dr. Burton when he'd heard of the work being done at the PSI Department just before it closed down. Dr. Rex, as he was commonly called, had a special interest in the work being done, as he had displayed some telepathic abilities of his own. He wasn't one of the more powerful telepaths. His telepathy was not very strong at all. While he wasn't as capable of sending out specific thoughts, he was better suited to picking up the faint whispers of thoughts in others. His real talent was that his type of telepathy made him excellent at detecting others with abilities. A psychic "bloodhound" of sorts. With practice, he was able to spot those who were gifted, what type of ability they had, and currently how strong their ability was. He speculated that his brain was just more sensitive to the "wavelengths" that other gifted brains emitted.

When Rex turned back from the exit, Martin caught his eye and saw a look that let him know that something wasn't right. This was one of those times that Martin wished Rex had the ability to communicate telepathically. But the look Martin got was clear enough for him to know that he needed to investigate whatever disturbance was at the exit.

Martin got up from his chair as smoothly as possible. He caught Dr. Burton's eye and silently mouthed "Be right back" as he made his way to the edge of the room so he could get to the exit without walking through the center of the cafeteria. The whole room was still paying close attention to Dr. Burton speaking. If anyone had been distracted, they were now focused back on what was being said and not on Martin's movements.

He exited the cafeteria quietly, being careful not to let the doors make too much noise as they swung shut. Just as whoever had exited before him had done. He glanced at both ends of the hallway, not seeing anyone in either direction.

"He's going out through the front," he thought he heard someone whisper in his ear. Like the soft voice of a child. "To the lobby, quickly." A girl's voice, perhaps.

He raced through the halls to the front lobby. As he rounded the corner to the lobby, he scanned the area hoping to find whoever he was looking for. He thought he could see someone. They appeared hazy. His vision was blurred again. As he approached the person they seemed to come into focus. Sure enough, there was a figure standing at the large glass doors. The figure had on a long overcoat which gave it broad shoulders, and what looked like a fedora hat as well. As Martin quickly got closer, he could tell it was a man and that he was just then turning the locks on the doors to let himself out.

"Hold it there," Martin shouted as he broke into a jog to reach the man in time.

The silhouette of the man stopped what he was doing but continued to face the glass doors, looking outside. "Fine," the man said, "you caught me."

Even with the bright daylight behind him, the coat, and the hat, Martin could recognize that voice as Paul Burton. If by nothing else but that smug tone.

"What are you doing here Paul?"

"I came to congratulate my father on the grand opening of the new PSI Center," Paul said as he turned around to face Martin. "I didn't realize I needed a formal invitation, or your permission, to see my father."

"When it's in this building you do." Martin planted his feet, feeling the need to assert his stance. "If that is the real reason you came, then why sneak about? What are you up to Paul?"

"Always so suspicious?" Paul asked with a raised eyebrow and his all-too-familiar smirk on his lips. "I arrived here too late to say a private 'job well done' and leave. I figured I would just stay until his assembly was over to deliver my message. But I know how he tends to drone on and on, so I decided to leave instead."

Martin narrowed his gaze at Paul. He was mindful to keep an image of a bike in his head. If he felt that Paul was prying into his thoughts, he would then envision the wheels of the bike turning, and how the chain and gears worked. He had developed this technique with the help of some of his telepathic subjects. He learned this was an effective way to keep unwanted spies from his thoughts.

"I didn't join in on your little party here because I didn't think I would be very well received. I know I'm not very well-liked here," Paul said. The look on his face changed slightly. The smirk gave way to down-turned pursed lips and flared nostrils. It appeared he just caught the mental image of the bike. "Apparently, I thought correctly."

Martin reached past Paul and finished unlocking the door. He could feel the faint tingling in the back of his skull. He pushed open the door and held it, giving the clear sign that Paul was free to go.

"Feel free to keep your thoughts to yourself," Martin said as he continued to hold the door open. "I don't need you, or your lackeys, playing around in my head again. I'll be sure to pass your well wishes on to your father, so you don't have to feel awkward staying where you're not wanted. Or feel the need to come back."

Paul's smirk returned as he looked into Martin's eyes. He sucked his teeth and sharply exhaled through his nose. He walked through the lobby door into the sunlight outside. Once he was completely outside he turned back around to face Martin, looking up at the building as he spoke.

"It really is a nice building," he said looking up at the windows. "I wonder how long you'll be able to hold on to it."

"Bicycle, bicycle, bicycle," Martin kept repeating in his head. He was trying not to let Paul get to him. If he got angry and lost control, it would give Paul an easy opening into his thoughts.

Paul obviously caught it, as he began to laugh. He flipped his coat collar up around his neck and turned to walk away from the building. Laughing the whole time.

"Smug bastard," Martin thought to himself.

He pulled the door closed and locked it. Even with locked doors, he didn't have a sense of security. How do you protect yourself from someone like Paul? He knew he couldn't walk around with various images in his mind all the time.

The bigger question was: Why was Paul really there? Martin doubted that he was being honest with his reasons. Though it was possible, it wasn't likely. The real reason had to be that he was spying, or checking on someone he had placed in the Center to do the spying for him.

"Great," he thought, "after he'd been silent for so long, now he decides to cause problems. With all of the chaos of a brand new facility, I suppose now would be the perfect time for him to do it."

Martin returned to the cafeteria just as Dr. Burton was finishing his speech.

"Ok, Martin," he thought to himself, "clear your mind, settle down. You don't know who in here might pick up on your thoughts or your emotions."

He approached the podium as Dr. Burton introduced him to the crowd as the next speaker. The room began to applaud for him.

"Thank you, Dr. Burton," he said into the microphone. He looked into the crowd and saw all eyes were on him. He made sure to concentrate on what he was saying and nothing else. "I really don't have much to add to what Dr. Burton had to say. I believe we all know what our goals are here. We all know that we are here to work together and share our findings to achieve those goals. That's how we've made it this far. Even though we don't officially receive any of our patients for a few more days, we will begin running our schedules as if they were here today. In this remaining time, we have our last chance to work out any glitches before those patients walk through the front door. Those of you who have had experience as being patients will once again step into that role. We will begin running mock sessions to ensure we all know where we need to be to have things run as smoothly as possible. This is the time for us to make our mistakes so we can correct them before they have a chance to affect the people we are here to help.

"At this time, team leaders will take your groups to finalize all set-up procedures. Be sure all paperwork and documentation is complete before the end of today. So, as of right now, the PSI Center is functional and operational. Let's get to work!"

The cafeteria erupted in applause. People stood from their seats and continued clapping. The energy of the room was definitely a positive one. Everyone was smiling and eager to get started. They were shaking hands as they broke away to go to their various jobs throughout the building.

Martin stayed close to Dr. Burton. He wanted to speak with him, but not while there were still people coming up to say how excited they were that PSI Center was now up and running. He noticed that Rex was also staying behind, so he motioned to him to join them.

"Dr. Burton," Martin said, "I need to speak with you."

They made their way out of the cafeteria. There were still too many people in there, lingering or getting their morning coffee, to be able to talk freely.

"We need to go to my office," Martin said to the other two men.

They were fairly silent during the elevator ride up, as it had stopped on three different floors to pick up and let out other staff members. Just the occasional "good morning" and "great meeting" from those who rode with them.

The three men exited the elevator and made their way to the end of the floor, where Martin's office was located. They didn't speak as they reached his office and Martin unlocked and opened the door.

Martin entered his office first, then Dr. Burton followed by Rex, who closed the door behind him.

"Paul was here this morning," Martin said as he sat on the corner of his desk. He wanted to stay in close range of the other two when speaking, feeling like anyone could be listening at the door.

"What?" Dr. Burton said in a shocked tone. "I didn't see him."

"Nobody was supposed to," Rex spoke up. His Australian accent was very apparent when compared to the other two men. He stepped in closer so he wouldn't have to speak too loudly. "It was like he was masking his presence. I almost didn't know he was here until that little girl pointed him out to me."

"Little girl?" asked Martin.

"She was just to the left, behind you. She pointed to the back of the cafeteria and whispered in my mind to turn around and look. She said, 'he's trying to hide from you.' When I turned back around she was gone. That's when you locked eyes with me."

"There was no little girl here this morning. There are no children in this building at all," Dr. Burton stated.

"I also heard a child's voice tell me to head to the front lobby to catch him," Martin said in a low voice.

Dr. Burton had a worried expression on his face. "Were you able to catch up to him?"

"Yes," Martin said, "just as he was about to leave the building. He said he was only here to tell you congratulations."

"His only motivation was to see me? I love my son, but I don't trust him. I don't believe that was the true reason for his visit here this morning."

"What concerns me," Martin paused as he stood from the desk and folded his arms. "What if this wasn't the first time he's been here? How long has he been able to hide himself like that? How did he do it?"

Rex had a theory on that. "It seems he's using his telepathic abilities to block anyone's brain from recognizing that their eyes are seeing him. I wouldn't have known he was here if I hadn't been told to look for him. And even then it was hard to see him. Like he was out of focus or the sun was in my eyes."

Dr. Burton looked very troubled by this news. He closed his eyes and sighed heavily. "This raises a lot of questions. Not just the possibility that he may have been here numerous times already, but how did he teach himself this new facet of his abilities? How powerful has my son become?"

"Or even worse," Martin spoke, "did someone teach it to him? And who is the little girl? Do we have a ghost in the building?"

Chapter Twenty-Four
Grief, Pain, Guilt, Torture

The PSI Center opened as scheduled. Though, with less fanfare than they had hoped, it still went smoothly and as planned.

The first month only brought a few new patients to the Center. Most of the people arriving were continuing their sessions from the old PSI Department. Even though the former subjects had been seen before, some were getting fresh new perspectives and results from the newly expanded staff on hand. The new scientists and doctors, with access to new equipment, were able to research even further into possibilities of how to help and understand the patients' abilities.

Some of the improvements implemented in the sessions included adding psychotherapy to some of the more extreme cases, citing a direct link to the control of abilities and the mental well-being of many of the patients. Many of those with abilities had repressed feelings of guilt, resentment, anger, or sadness. Being able to work past those feelings and release them allowed a vast improvement in gaining control of their gifts.

For those who were still showing difficulty in controlling their abilities, to the extent that they could be a danger to themselves or others, the option of pharmaceutical help was enlisted. PSI Center now had experts in the area of drug therapies. From mood enhancers to tranquilizers, there was another path to explore in helping those who couldn't handle their gifts.

A few group training and therapy sessions were started. They incorporated group therapy sessions to give a sense of community to some of the patients who felt isolated by their abilities. This group technique was also applied to the physical assessments and training as well. In the past, there had been sessions with two people at the same time, but this was the first time 3 or more were being attempted. First keeping those with similar talents and ability levels grouped together. Then slowly switching out and integrating others into different groups. Many began to realize they weren't alone in their feelings and struggles.

The family from Spain, who had supplied some of the funding, had arrived for a visit and tour of the Center. They seemed happy with the results and impressed with how it was all devised to understand these amazing gifts. But ultimately, they were more interested in going to New York City to experience a Broadway show and go shopping. It seemed their motivation for helping was more for the good press coverage they would get back in Spain.

The family from India arrived almost six months after the PSI Center opened. To the surprise of Dr. Burton and Martin, they brought five of their family members to stay so they might receive assistance in controlling their abilities. Due to the amount of money the family had given towards their cause, it wasn't a request that would be refused. Luckily, there were rooms that were designed to serve as temporary housing for this very reason. It may not have been the accommodations that these particular guests were used to living in, but they would be comfortable for the duration of their stay.

Three of the Indian visitors were pyrokinetic. None of which were on par with Janet's abilities, but it was one of the rarer of abilities to encounter. It was even more rare to find three in the same family. Two of them were male. One was 16 and one was 18. The 18-year-old was blessed with height, a solid manly frame, physical attractiveness, and the confidence that accompanied possessing such attributes. His confidence carried into his sessions and served him well in mastering the control that is so desperately important to anyone with this fiery gift.

The 16-year-old boy did not have any of those physical qualities, and there was a bitterness that lived in him because of it. Although he wasn't too much shorter than his older brother, he was much skinnier. His body had a frailness to it which seemed to be a reflection of his lack of confidence. His sessions were a combination of training his ability and therapy for his mental well-being. His frustration with himself would lead to outbursts and a loss of control, which would then add even further to the self-esteem problems he already suffered from. His family had informed Dr. Burton that he seemed to be getting stronger, and worse, as he got older.

The third pyrokinetic was a 13-year-old girl. She was friendly but quiet. She had long black hair and round brown eyes that sparkled when she smiled. Her gift was not as strong as her brothers, as she was only able to generate a warming aura around herself. However, she was very good at comforting her 16-year-old brother and keeping him focused.

The other 2 members of the Indian family were telepathic. The first was the oldest sibling, she was 22 (a disappointment to her family that she couldn't be married off due to her "affliction"). She was an attractive young woman with long, straight black hair. Her eyes were almost as dark as her hair and framed in long black lashes. She had an air about her, similar to Paul when he was much younger. Dr. Burton suspected the real reason she had not been married off was that her father was using her telepathic ability to somehow increase the family fortune, and he did not wish to leave that prize in the hands of another family. He reluctantly allowed her to come to PSI Center because she said she was finding it difficult to block out the invading thoughts of those around her. She was a very talented telepath, but for some unknown reason, her control over her telepathy was beginning to wane. One individual she was powerless to block out was her youngest brother.

The youngest sibling, 9, was a telepath as well. His gift came naturally to him. He preferred to communicate via telepathy, only verbally speaking when his parents demanded it. He kept most of his mental chatter confined to his family members, particularly his oldest sister. Initially, his sessions didn't accurately gauge the level of his ability. It became apparent how much he was holding back when during one session he became so frustrated that he began to throw a telepathic tantrum, projecting it to everyone in the building. Fortunately, it only lasted a moment and he was easily calmed down. A telepathic projection on that scale had never been experienced before.

There had been no further sighting of Paul for the first year the PSI Center was open. Dr. Burton had kept most of their communications limited to phone calls and meetings in crowded public places. The first call he made to Paul was that Martin had passed on his message of congratulations and to say thank you. He hadn't mentioned any of the rest of their conversation to Paul. He still avoided that level of confrontation with his son. Not out of fear of Paul's powers or retaliation, but more from the feeling of guilt for not being a good enough father to prevent his son from turning out this way. Regardless of his guilt now, he couldn't ignore what Paul was like, and what he was capable of doing.

One of the rare times they spoke in person was at Carol's funeral. Dr. Burton had always made it a point to stay in contact with his ex-wife. He knew Paul didn't call her as often as he could have. So he would check in with her every so often just to tell her how well Paul was doing. She never knew just how much Paul had used his gifts to gain the position and wealth he had attained. He preferred to let her be proud of her son, thinking he had achieved it all through hard work. Hard work was the excuse why Paul was never able to call or visit her himself. Even when she became ill.

A few months earlier, Dr. Burton had a break in his day. He sat behind his desk in his large office at the PSI Center, looking at the files in front of him. It was the beginning of fall, but the weather still had the warmth of summer in it. The leaves on the trees were still green and the sun was bright in the cloudless sky as it shined through his office windows. He ignored his paperwork as he stared out the window, daydreaming. It reminded him of the warm days of his youth, taking Carol on car rides to the beach for a picnic on the sand. His thoughts turned to his ex-wife. Even through their divorce, her remarriage, and his devotion to his work, they remained close friends. He would always feel love for her.

He picked up the receiver from his phone and listened for the dial tone. He began to dial her phone number. The rotary dial spun back around, clicking after he dialed in each number. After 4 rings, she answered her phone on the other end of the line.

There was a short cough before he heard her wheeze a soft, "Hello?"

"Carol," he asked. "Carol, it's Ross. Are you ok?"

"Oh, hello," she answered back. Her voice was still soft and slightly out of breath. "Yes, I'm fine." She tried to quickly clear her throat away from her receiver before continuing. "I just seem to have a little cold. Or allergies." She used her free hand to tuck some of her soft gray hair back behind her ear. It had shaken loose when she coughed.

"How long have you had that cough? It doesn't sound too good. Do you need to see a doctor?"

"I'm fine Ross. Don't you worry about me. How are things going at the Center? I keep meaning to come and take a tour." He could hear the smile in her voice and noticed she changed the subject. She wasn't one to talk about herself or her problems.

"It's going great here. We've had some fantastic discoveries. I won't bore you with the scientific details, but I think we are close to actually discovering solid proof of why all of this is possible."

"That does sound very exciting, Ross. Have you spoken to Paul at all? I've left messages with his secretary at work, but frankly, I don't think she gives him the messages."

Dr. Burton knew that Paul was getting the messages. He just chose to ignore them. He knew Paul would rather leave his old life behind him. He would wipe it all away if given the chance.

"I've thought the same thing," he lied to Carol. "Many a time I've left messages that I know he hasn't received. Yes, our boy is doing quite well. I was lucky enough to talk to him recently," he lied again, "he's just been extremely busy with work. Sometimes I think all he does is work." He ended with a half-hearted chuckle.

"Like father, like son, eh Ross?" Carol replied with a chuckle of her own. Hers had a genuine sense of humor in it, unlike his. There was a raspy wheeze to her chuckle as well.

"Hmmm, I suppose so," he replied. Although he knew how far off the mark her statement was, he wouldn't let her know just how different her son was from his father.

She began coughing again. "Ross, I need to go get some water. Call me again soon, will you?"

"Of course. Go take care of yourself. I'll check in on you soon."

In between coughing fits she was able to say goodbye and he heard her hang up the phone.

A week later, her cough had gotten worse. She went to see her doctor. He had initially diagnosed her with asthma. When the treatments hadn't alleviated her symptoms, her doctor decided it must be bronchitis and began treatment for that.

A month before she died, they discovered she had lung cancer. It was in a very advanced stage, spanning both lungs and spreading through her body. At this stage, no treatment was going to help her.

There were a few other friends and family members who attended her funeral. Her family had always had a sense of pity towards her. They saw her as the poor woman who had divorced her work-obsessed first husband, was abandoned by her second husband, raised a son on her own, and finally succumbed to lung cancer. "The poor dear," they would whisper among themselves.

Her friends and neighbors adored her as well. Some knew a few details of her life story that she had shared with them over the years. They liked her for her soft heart and gentle words. She was the kindly neighbor who would randomly bring over a plate of cookies or a pie. She would say it was because she just happened to have made too much and didn't want it to go to waste. If they only knew that she would bake such things for the sole purpose of giving them to others and that she would just happen to show up with these baked goods and kind words when her friends and neighbors were in a time of need or despair. She had a knack for knowing when she was needed.

The services were held at the grave site. Her local pastor read a passage from the bible and two of her friends spoke. One friend compared the sunny day to Carol's disposition. Stating that you could feel the warmth of her heart as if standing in the loving rays of the sun.

After all the words were said, and the casket lowered into the ground, the small crowd began to disperse. Some of them approached Paul and Dr. Burton, separately, to convey their condolences. It seemed that Dr. Burton was a bit more grateful in the expression of these gestures than Paul.

When all of her friends had left, Dr. Burton stood next to the open grave, bowed his head in silence, and took a moment to say his last goodbyes to Carol, telling her how much he loved her.

"If you loved her so much," Paul said in a full voice standing behind him, "then why did you let her go?"

Dr. Burton drew in a deep breath. He knew this confrontation was a long time coming. His heart was already aching, and this battle wasn't going to resolve anything.

"Picking a fight with me, Paul," Dr. Burton started saying as he turned around to face his son, "isn't going to bring her back. Or make you feel better about losing her."

"I don't think you know what's going to make me feel better," Paul said, cocking his head to one side as if he was studying his father. "You think being here will give closure to the guilt you feel because you failed your marriage? All of your phone calls and visits over dinner never did that. Is this your one last chance to get that burden off your shoulders?"

"This isn't about burden. This is about closure. It's saying goodbye to someone I loved. If you know I made those calls," Dr. Burton was starting to feel an anger grow in his chest, "then you know the reason why I did it. All you had to do was reach out to her. Let her know you were ok. She was your mother and she loved you!"

"Loved me?" Paul's gaze narrowed as he stared his father directly in the eyes. "She resented me."

"That's a lie!" he said through clenched teeth.

"Think of who you are talking to, father. I know it better than anyone else. I could 'hear' it in her thoughts! She blamed me for Norman leaving us and hated me for being the reason you would never leave your work to come back to her."

"Son, that's not true," his expression softened. "Even if she just thought those things once, it's not how she felt. She loved you."

"Don't call me son." Paul was visibly angry now. Dr. Burton could feel the familiar tingling in his skull which meant Paul's powers were on the rise. "Her kindness to others was her self-imposed penance for how she felt about me. To overcompensate for the whispers of her 'friends' about her 'bachelor' son. She couldn't be viewed as a bad mother, so she would be the shining example of a good friend. As far as I'm concerned I don't have any parents. I haven't for years!"

Dr. Burton felt the pressure behind his eyes. There was a searing white light in his mind, accompanied by high high-pitched whine. It was causing him a headache and he could hear Paul's voice inside his head. His legs began to buckle under the strain of the pain he was feeling and he fell to his knees. He held one hand to his head and the other he placed on the ground to steady himself.

"You're soon to be as irrelevant to the rest of the world as you are to me, old man." It was Paul's words echoing inside his mind. "You're going to outlive your usefulness one day."

Paul slid his shoulders back and raised his chin, releasing his grip on his father's mind. He stood tall above the hunched-over man. Now he chose to speak out loud.

"This is a nice spot," Paul said as he looked around the cemetery. "When your time comes, do you want to be buried next to her?" He turned to walk away, adding, "Not that it matters to me. I won't be coming back here to visit either of you."

Dr. Burton slowly began to stand up. Paul had already crossed the cemetery and was getting into his car. Even with his glasses on, his vision had gone temporarily blurry from Paul's intrusion into his head. He felt something wet on his upper lip.

He touched his lip with his index finger and looked at it. It was blood. Paul had caused his nose to bleed. He removed a handkerchief from his pocket and wiped the blood from his nose. There wasn't much, and the bleeding had stopped, but it still gave him cause for concern. How was Paul doing these things now? Where was he learning these new aspects of his abilities?

He slowly made his way back to his car. His vision was correcting itself and the headache was dissipating. The pain he felt now was the sadness in his soul. He had felt Paul's anger. Paul's hate. His past decisions were coming back to haunt him. He felt alone, stranded with the guilt of so many years. He needed the support of a family. Only now, it seemed, today he would not only be in mourning for the loss of Carol but of Paul as well. His son was lost to him now for sure.

Janet Sellers was just getting ready to pull the pot roast out of the oven when she looked out the kitchen window and saw Dr. Burton's car pull into the driveway.

"Martin," she shouted to the living room, "he's here. Can you ask Margaret to come and help me set the table, please?"

Martin made his way to the front door. Stopping at the end of the hallway, he yelled to Margaret to come help her mother. He opened the front door just as Dr. Burton was walking the stone path up to the front porch.

"Dr. Burton," Martin said. He reached out and gently shook his hand in greeting. He could see the sadness in the man's face and it broke his heart. "How are you holding up?"

"As well as one can in these situations, I suppose," he replied.

"I really wish you would have let us come to the funeral with you."

"I appreciate your support. I do. But I was correct in assuming that Paul would be there and that he would be in a confrontational mood. I think it was best that you and your family did not attend."

Margaret stood in the doorway waiting for her turn to greet him. She was a miniature version of her mother. Long brown hair, with a slight bounce of curl on the ends. She had large brown eyes like her mother as well. Though her features were still soft and rounded like most 7-year-olds, she was taller and thinner than most girls her age.

When Dr. Burton entered the house and saw her, he bent down to look her in the eyes and said "Hello, my dear."

Margaret looked him in the eyes, placed both of her small hands on his face, and said, "You are sad. I'm sorry you are sad, Doctor Grandpa." And she hugged his neck.

She flashed him a sly smile and dashed off to the kitchen to help her mother, as had been requested.

"Sorry about that," Martin said to Dr. Burton as he stood back up. "She has had a lot of questions about what happens when someone passes away. She knows that the people who are left behind are usually very sad."

"It's quite alright, Martin," he said with a little smile. "It's a bit comforting to have the child's sympathies. Just honest concern with no arterial motives."

"Dr. Burton," Janet approached to greet him as she wiped her hands on the apron tied around her waist. "I'm so sorry. How are you doing?" she asked and hugged him.

"Janet," he smiled at her, "I was just telling your husband that I'm doing well. And I want to be sure to thank you again for having me over for this meal."

"It's the least we could do," she said as she clasped his hand in hers. "You truly are like a father to us. I just wish there was more I could do."

They made their way to the dining room and sat down to a wonderful meal. The topics during the meal varied from current events to some of the lighter details of the PSI Center. Janet made sure to put an end to the "shop talk" before it could go too far.

"I hope you don't find this inappropriate of me," Janet interjected, "but I'd like to propose a toast if I may."

The two men took hold of their drinking glasses and raised them. Margaret saw this and took her milk glass and imitated their actions as well.

"I would like to make two toasts, if I may. First, to the wonderful memory of Carol, a sweet and gentle soul who has gone too soon. And also to having such a wonderful man, such as yourself, in our lives. I hope you know just how much you mean to all of us."

"Thank you, Janet," Dr. Burton said, with his glass still raised in the air. "To Carol."

"To Carol," Martin and Janet echoed.

They all drank from their glasses and were silent as they set them back down on the table.

"I remember the first time I met her," Martin said to break the silence.

"When I caught you spying outside of her house," Dr. Burton said. He laughed slightly, recalling the story.

"You were what?" Janet said in shock.

They all laughed as Martin and Dr. Burton both told the story to Janet. The idea of Martin crouched down in the bushes in the freezing snow was a bit funnier now than it was when it originally happened.

The evening continued with them telling stories of important milestones in their lives. Some of these had been shared before, but there was a comfort in sharing them again.

Paul Burton was angry as he drove away from the cemetery. The small amount of dark pleasure he got from forcing his father onto his knees wasn't enough to quiet the rage he could feel inside himself. He knew when he would get this angry it made it difficult for him to have total control over his abilities.

He could hear the faint humming and murmurs in his head from the people who were driving in the cars next to him. Instead of trying to calm himself and regain control, it just infuriated him more. Adding to the already growing noise in his head. It would be deafening soon if he didn't block it out.

He made a few sharp turns down side streets to change the direction he was heading. He now had a specific destination in mind and wanted to get there fast. He wasn't concerned with the speed of his vehicle. If he got pulled over by a police officer, he would simply force his way into their head and make them release him. He had done it before. Another one of the intrusive feats he took pride in.

The trip to the Global Trust Insurance building didn't take long. He sped into the parking lot, his car screeching to a halt as he parked across two parking spaces. He jumped from the car, slammed the door, and dashed as fast as he could towards the building. He could feel the effects of the dampening field even before he reached the building.

As annoying as the mental static that was created inside the building may have been, it was far better than the sea of voices that were invading his head. When he entered the building, the "static" would block him from hearing all those other thoughts. Effectively voiding his abilities.

He sat in one of the chairs in the front lobby for a moment to try and calm himself down. After closing his eyes for a moment, he slowed his breathing back to a normal pace and regained his composure. He opened his eyes and could see the receptionist watching him as she spoke on the phone to someone. He didn't have to hear her thoughts to tell she was talking about him.

Paul got up from his chair and approached the reception desk.

"Are you alright Mr. Burton?" the girl behind the desk asked him.

"Yes, I'm fine. Thank you for your concern," his reply had an apparent sarcastic ring to it.

"Agent Coleman is aware you are in the building and would like to see you. He is on the Medical Level."

"Agent Coleman knows I'm here? I didn't see him here. I wonder how he knows I'm here?" Paul's level of sarcasm wasn't lost on the receptionist. He glared at the girl behind the desk. Even without the use of his abilities, Paul could be a very intimidating man. It was clear that he knew she just placed that call to Agent Coleman.

"Be a dear," he began to say to the girl as he removed his coat, "and take care of this. Would you?" He dropped the coat onto the top of the desk before turning and walking to the elevators. Not waiting for her reply.

He entered the elevator. This time the ride would take him down. Into some lower sub-basement levels. Even as the elevator traveled lower, the static was still present. Always around him, preventing him from using his abilities. It had been made very clear to him that if he was caught attempting to use his "talents" on agents outside of the building, the punishment would be swift and immediate. Something he had witnessed firsthand. So, for now, he decided to play by their rules. It actually suited his long-term goals to do so.

Three levels below the main lobby the elevator stopped and the doors opened. Paul stepped out into what was known as the Medical Level. Though it seemed torture was practiced more than actual medicine, it still yielded some impressive results. The bottom line is what this place was all about.

Agent Coleman was talking to one of the doctors when he saw Paul step out of the elevator. From how freely Paul moved about in this building, and his interaction with Agent Coleman, it would be clear to the general observer that Paul was freely working with them now.

As Paul approached Agent Coleman, he could "feel" with his mind the effect of whatever they were using to negate powers. He hadn't found any spots in the building where it wasn't present, but he would constantly test it, just in case, in the hopes he could discover its origin.

"Paul, we weren't expecting to see you here today."

"No, Agent Coleman, it was an unexpected stop for me. I needed to be someplace where I could be alone with my thoughts. As it were."

"Ah," Agent Coleman understood what Paul meant. "Your mother's funeral was today. I imagine that could have been a bit taxing on keeping your powers in check."

"Her funeral was barely a concern to me. You needn't worry about its effect on me."

Agent Coleman raised one eyebrow and breathed heavily out of his nostrils, "If you say so. But since you are here, we have had some interesting results with our tests based on the hormone research you acquired for us from the PSI Center. If you want to have a look."

Agent Coleman led Paul down a long hallway to a large observation window. It looked into one of the labs where subjects were regularly tested. At this particular time, a man dressed in white scrubs, who looked to be in his early thirties, was strapped onto a reclining padded gurney. He was being injected with fluid from an I.V. bag.

"We are trying various formulas to either diminish or enhance various powers," Agent Coleman began to explain. "We are having a heck of a time getting the dosage right though."

"No successful results so far?" asked Paul.

"Unfortunately, no. Injections for canceling powers have only lasted for a few short moments and have occasionally produced an unwanted permanent side effect."

"Such as?"

Agent Coleman turned to face Paul when he answered, "Death."

"That is permanent," Paul said, turning his attention back to the man behind the glass. "And this test? What is this one for?"

"We are seeing if we can slightly increase this man's telekinetic powers. Or, maybe, greatly increase them. However, the possibility of burning them out completely does exist. Like I said, it has been difficult getting the dosage correct."

"Trial and error, I suppose," Paul said. "You aren't afraid of what he'll do if you make him stronger? You don't think he will try to harm you or escape?"

"He's one of our lower-grade telekinetic subjects. He can roll pens across tables, blow papers around… not enough power to do damage without the proper tools handy."

"And working around the dampening field? How will he have access to his powers?"

"Do you see that collar around his neck? It admits and specific electrical frequency that allows him to access his powers. It also allows us to administer an electric shock. Anywhere from a gentle pinch to act as a reminder to behave or enough shock to drop an elephant. We've had great success in keeping them in line with it. So much so, that we are using them out in the field now." Agent Coleman made no effort to hide the fact he was staring at Paul's neck as he spoke about the use of the collar.

"No need to size me up for one of those, agent. I am not that eager to have access to my abilities here. And I know how to be an obedient boy." Paul stared playfully into Agent Coleman's eyes as he spoke.

They turned their attention back to the scene behind the thick glass. They could hear the muffled cries of the man begging to be released. He yelled, asking where he was and to be set free. No matter how hard he struggled, the straps around his wrists, chest, and ankles held him securely in place.

Paul watched as two men moved around the room. Both of them were in blue doctor's scrubs and surgical masks. They carried clipboards and were making notes as the man in the chair reacted to whatever chemical was being siphoned into his body.

One of the men held up a small glass bottle and inserted a syringe into it. Drawing out a measured amount of the liquid and then injecting it into the I.V. line that would send it into the man's body. After doing so, he stepped back and began writing more notes on his clipboard and taking notice of the time.

The man on the table began to thrash around even more as small objects in the room began to float into the air. One of the clipboards leapt from the doctor's arms and he grabbed it in midair. The table itself began to jump slightly off the floor. It seemed the man strapped to the table was unaware of what he was causing around him. He was in a tremendous amount of pain.

His body became increasingly violent in trying to buck free from the straps of the table, and his screams intensified. He was no longer in control of his body. The man was in pure agony. Paul could see that this sick symphony was about to come to its climatic end.

Larger objects began lifting into the air and swirling around the room. One of the men in doctor's scrubs was even swept off his feet by some unseen force, but only for a moment. The other man rushed to him to help him get back up. Once on his feet, he scrambled to grab a second small bottle of liquid. The second man attempted to help him hold it steady enough to use a syringe to draw the fluid out. They were desperately trying to get this second liquid into his I.V. fluid.

Each attempt failed as the men were swept off of their feet by some invisible force. The man on the table started to spasm violently. While his powers were lashing out at every object in the room, Agent Coleman stood silently, watching, with a small black remote in his hand. Prepared to trigger the collar's shock mechanism at any second. He waited patiently, watching the scene unfold. The results were more important than the patient.

The man on the gurney let out a horrific final howl as his body arched against the straps. He looked as if every muscle in his body had tensed, expelling every last bit of energy he had. Every object that had been circling the room stopped in midair for a split second, then dropped to the ground, as if thrown down with force. The man's body, mimicking the force exerted on the objects, was pushed back down onto the gurney. The gurney's legs had quickly bent under the sudden invisible pressure that pushed down on it, swayed to one side, and fell to the ground.

The man, on his side, still strapped to the gurney, was very still. The room was silent. For just a brief second, it seemed as if the room had been frozen in time. Blood was running out of various points across his body where his skin had split open. Half of his skull looked like it had been crushed. He was dead.

The two men in the surgical masks got up off of the floor and approached the dead man's body. One man was limping, the other was cradling his left arm to his chest. They retrieved their clipboards and began making notes. Their conversation couldn't be heard behind the thick glass as they gestured to various points on the body and continued to make notations.

"One of those side effects I was telling you about." Agent Coleman said to Paul. "It seems, in some of these cases, their powers turn on them. They become amplified so fast that they continue to grow until they self-destruct."

"How interesting," Paul said in a low tone. "Tragic, but interesting." His eyes narrowed as he searched the wreckage in the room and saw the small broken bottle that held the chemical that caused all of this. He looked back up to one of the men in the room, locking eyes with him. He glanced back to the vial on the floor, leading the man's gaze to it, and gave him a small nod.

"Agent Coleman," Paul started as he turned to face Agent Coleman, "if you could perfect this little mystery, you just may have a chance of outpacing my father's research."

"Mr. Burton, if we can perfect this, we can outpower anyone in the world. Our previous attempts to control or enhance with drugs didn't produce results we could work with. Not for long-term agendas, at any rate. Anytime chemicals were used to weaken a subject it would result in making them so stoned that they were useless. Conversely, anything used to enhance powers made them so manic that there was a total lack of focus. In either case, the powers were useless."

"This path seems promising," Paul said as he looked back into the room. The men were now having the body removed from the gurney. "I suppose you can't make the perfect omelet without breaking a few eggs. Provided you can solve this dosage problem before you run out of eggs."

"I don't think finding lab rats to experiment on will be a problem." Agent Coleman stared very intently at Paul.

"It seems you have some cleaning up to supervise," Paul had seen enough. "I'll leave you to it. Always a pleasure, agent."

"Mr. Burton," Agent Coleman said as he extended his right hand. "I look forward to your next visit. Hopefully, with some useful information. And, hopefully, soon."

Paul shook his hand with a smile to conclude his fake pleasantries of good-bye. He left the observation area and made his way back toward the elevator that would take him out of this nightmarish hellhole. Before he left, however, he made a quick detour to one of the rooms in the Medical Level.

He knew the exact room he was looking for. He'd been to it numerous times before, as the patient in this particular room had been here for many, many years. The room was kept dark. The only lights visible were coming from the many medical machines that lined the walls. It was a dark, high-tech, hospital room. He could barely see the body that was occupying the bed, still shrouded in shadow away from the hallway lights from the open door. The many different machines, some with blinking lights, some with stable lights, each making their sounds. Paul stood in the doorway, his eyes adjusting to the darkness inside.

"Oh Emily," he said smugly as he approached the figure in the bed. "You have been a naughty girl, haven't you? Have you been following me?"

The figure didn't move. The machines continued their rhythmic song. One announced heartbeats while another machine pumped air into the slumbering figure's lungs.

"I don't know how you got around their damned dampening field, but I know it was you. You had better not interfere…" he whispered as he gently brushed his hands over the switches on the breathing machine, lightly tapping some of the buttons, mocking the motion of turning them off.

The beeping machine continued its rhythmic count of heartbeats. No change in its song, and no response from the figure.

"I hate to think of what would happen to such a delicate flower if any of these switches were tampered with. I trust you'll be a good girl and stay close to these machines," Paul backed away from the bed and moved towards the door. He paused for a moment, glaring at the figure in the bed. He cursed the invisible barrier that prevented him from prying into her mind. His eyes could confirm her physical presence. But, even though his mind couldn't detect her thoughts, somehow he knew she was there. He knew she was aware, inside her mind.

He brushed his fingers over the buttons and switches of the machine one more time. The idea of actually flipping off the machines was in his mind. He knew he wouldn't get away with it. Not today anyway. The medical level had too many people present, he would be caught for sure, and then probably added to their experiments as punishment. As tempting as it was, the risk was too high.

He left the room closing the door behind him.

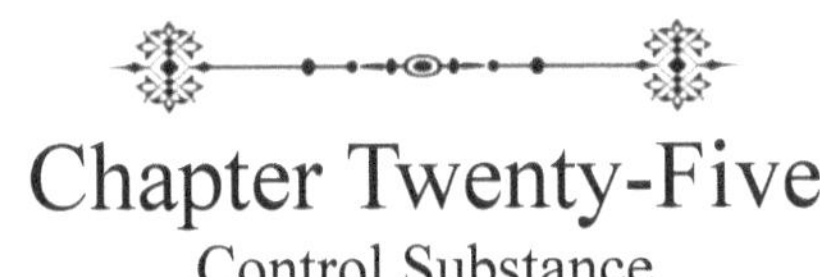

Chapter Twenty-Five
Control Substance

PSI Center had been running smoothly for two years. They had a complete staff, able to work around the clock. The temporary housing rooms were almost all occupied by patients who were either visiting and had no other means of lodging or occupied by patients who needed more constant observation and care. The latter patients were the ones who were not in control of their abilities and were considered to be dangerous to themselves or those around them.

It had seemed obvious to those on staff that the number of people coming to the PSI Center had increased in the last six months, and the age of the average patient was getting younger. More parents were arriving, seeking answers and help for whatever was wrong with their children.

This increase in a new generation of people with abilities coincided with the charts that Martin had plotted out back when he was at Worthington University. It wasn't an exact science, since he had based his figures on tales and fables throughout history, and he still was not able to explain why these fluctuations occurred. If it continued on the path he had charted out, this was just the beginning of what could be the largest amount of people with abilities at a single time.

Martin began looking more and more into the possibility that the answer to how these people were able to do what they did was hidden in their DNA. Maybe certain genetic codes were affected by solar flares, radiation from space, or a shift in the Earth's axis. He tried to compare all those who had telepathic abilities to each other. Then against those with other abilities. Then against those with no abilities. Looking at relatives versus strangers. Nothing was yielding any conclusive results. He could chart the lows and highs in the amount of those with abilities, just not the whys and hows. He was consumed with reviewing his research, even during meals.

Rex saw Martin sitting in the cafeteria. His food sat on the tray, untouched, while he read one of his many files. He looked away from the file, frustrated, just as Rex approached the table. He was carrying his tray of food and stood on the opposite side of the table from Martin.

"Good afternoon doctor. Mind if I have a seat?" His Australian accent was thick and his smile was kind. He had on the normal long, white lab coat. A few various pens and a pair of sunglasses stuck out of the chest pocket of the coat.

Martin gestured for him to have a seat and slid some of his files aside to make room for Rex to set down his tray of food.

"Is the food bad or are you just not hungry?" Rex asked, looking at the untouched tray of food next to Martin. He sat down at the table looking at his tray of food, then back at Martin, waiting for him to answer.

"I've just been distracted. I'm sure the food is fine," he replied with a light chuckle.

"May I?" Rex asked as he took one of the files and began to read the data on the sheet of paper. "This isn't one particular case. This is data encompassing most of our patients."

"I just don't know where the answer is hiding," Martin said. "Where are the reasons why certain people can do these things and others can't? What determines which abilities they'll have?"

"You think the answers for what makes a person who they are is all mapped out in their DNA?"

"If not there, then where?" Martin asked.

Rex closed the file and set it back on the table. "I'm not saying the answers aren't there. But does the DNA tell us who will be smarter? Who will be good at solving puzzles? Who will be partial to the color green?"

"Unfortunately," Martin paused and drew in his breath as he sat back in his chair, "it doesn't look like we have the scientific means available to discover that yet. But I believe it is in there."

Martin finally started eating his lunch as they continued to talk. The debate on whether or not all of someone's characteristics were hidden in their genes was not going to be settled that day.

"Look, Sellers," Rex said as he leaned in closer and lowered his voice. "We have made some great discoveries so far. You were the one who created Thetazine to help numb the abilities of the telepaths and empaths. To be able to block out the thoughts of others without them becoming jelly-brained is a great accomplishment. I'd say that is a much better way to quiet down the voices in their head than telling the parents of a 10-year-old boy to give him 3 fingers of whiskey."

They both chuckled at Rex's comment. It was true that Martin pioneered the creation of Thetazine, an injectable drug that, when administered in the correct dose, could temporarily block or lessen the abilities of telepathic and empathic patients.

"I hate to think of what would happen if that drug got into the wrong hands. It could be synthesized into something much worse." Martin had that look of worry on his face. It was apparent that he shouldered the burden of being responsible for creating Thetazine and what others might do with it.

"You need to stop always looking for doom around every corner. We haven't seen Burton's nasty offspring for almost two years. Do you even know the last time he talked to him? Who knows if he's even still alive? There has been no evidence of spies or turncoats on staff. Aside from my visits from the little 'ghost' girl, everything has been going pretty smoothly. So, stop looking for trouble. Enjoy the calm while it lasts."

"I suppose you're right, Rex. I just can't help but to keep looking over my shoulder. Old habits die hard."

The scientists at Global Trust Insurance had been working hard over the past couple of years to make drugs that could either enhance powers or cancel them out. They had not been successful with either one.

The tests for enhancing powers either ended in the subject not showing any noticeable increase in capabilities, or their powers increased so rapidly and so greatly that it didn't stop until the subject was dead. (In a couple of instances, a few lab technicians were casualties in the experiments.)

The testing for canceling powers hadn't gone any better. Though a few deaths had occurred, it wasn't as common as with the enhancement trials. Results were various degrees of the subjects being intoxicated, high, or stoned until the drug wore off. After that, the powers would return just as they had been before the drug was administered. Except in a couple of cases where the subjects ended up in a permanent vegetative state.

The best their brilliant minds could come up with was the electronic device that could be fastened around a wrist, ankle, or neck. It would deliver various bursts of electrical shock, enough to keep its wearer unable to concentrate and use their abilities effectively. It was also painful enough that it strongly discouraged even attempting to use their abilities. All of these devices were controlled by remotes that the agents carried. They proved efficient in controlling the patients and prisoners. At the first sign of an ability being tapped into, an agent could signal the device to administer either a light zap as a reminder, or a large enough series of jolts to cause a physical collapse.

Even though the static in the building blocked their powers, they were still outfitted with the devices as well. It served as conditioning obedience for maintaining control outside of the building. It was an effective tool in training, as they were warned that agents would be alerted if the devices were removed, and there would be extreme consequences for doing so. A popular, though never openly discussed, rumor was that the devices they invented came about completely by accident. When they were trying to create a machine that would attempt to discover and measure any energy surges present when an ability was used, it instead sent out the electrical frequency that blocked the effects of the dampening field. Presumably from two wires that had been improperly connected. Realizing that they couldn't grant access to powers without a failsafe to regain control of the subjects, they added the various electroshock effects.

Agent Coleman had heard rumors that PSI Center had developed a drug to inhibit a subject's powers. All of the powers, across the spectrum. Unfortunately, for him, he had not been able to acquire a sample of it or verify how accurate these reports were.

His people on the inside informed him that Dr. Sellers kept the only known samples of it, and he administered it himself, because of the very precise dosage amount required. He also knew it was only administered under the direst of circumstances. No one even knew where he kept it. His spies weren't able to move about freely enough to look for it without causing some suspicion. Especially with people there 24 hours a day. The little bit of searching they were able to do hadn't turned up anything.

Agent Coleman was under a great deal of pressure from those above him to deliver results. "A war is coming," they would tell him, "and we must be prepared to stop this threat. If we cannot harness their power, then we will learn how to destroy it."

Most of his superiors were from the military branch. They had no problem in accepting the casualties caused in preparing for the battle they saw in the near future. They had been trying for years to use those gifted individuals to their advantage. A majority of those with abilities were not so willing to just obey the orders and follow the plans of men who did not possess special talents of their own. So they continued to seek the means to control the gifted.

The sessions of brainwashing, torture, and breaking the wills of the gifted subjects were never-ending. Those subjects were viewed as living weapons and assets. The men in charge did not want living weapons to have a will of their own. There was no single process used to train submission and obedience. Various techniques and methods were applied, multiple times, until the desired result was achieved to the satisfaction of those in charge.

They had kept close tabs on Dr. Ross Burton when his early discoveries and research had started. They tracked him as he searched out subjects and conducted his experiments. They had tried to bring him over to their cause numerous times, but he didn't view the impending threat to the world as they did. Even his son provided no advantage in bringing him into the fold.

Their work continued in secret, with no public knowledge of their existence. Even those on staff were not sure of how large the organization was or of the number of other facilities besides the one they worked in. They were kept well paid and made fully aware that they were monitored outside of work. That extra dose of paranoia was insurance that everyone was keeping their mouths shut. They were also told that it was for their own safety that there was never to be contact with other employees outside of the building. There was no use of first names, only Dr., Mr., Ms., or Agent. There would be no way to track down any coworkers. Only those in higher positions had access to personal information.

No one in that building was able to come or go or move around in public, without the organization knowing about it. No one, that is, except for a comatose patient named Emily.

Chapter Twenty-Six
Little Girl Lost

Dr. Rex Wall was finishing a session with Robert Zanetti, the son of Joe and Patty. The boy was now only nine years old but was showing great control over his telekinetic abilities. His training with Rex had been going so well that neither of his parents felt they needed to be present during every session. They were both familiar with the techniques used and comfortable enough with Rex, to know their son was in good hands.

Robert was a little shorter than most boys his age. Though his build was typical, not too slim, not too heavy. His hair was kept short and was the same thick, dark brown hue as both of his parents. Unlike his parents was the color of his eyes. They were no longer the same brown hue as when he was a toddler. They were a much lighter brown now, almost an amber, with flecks of green. It made it difficult to identify the color at first glance. His face was gentle, even though he rarely smiled, and even rarer was a frown. He could usually be seen wearing shirts with some sort of striped pattern on them and corduroy pants, typical of boys his age. Patty said that was something he preferred to wear.

Robert was a very focused little boy. He didn't let emotions affect his control of his power. Even when frustrated, he wouldn't allow himself to become angry and lose sight of what he was trying to accomplish. He was lucky enough to already know how the empaths were trained, thanks to his mother, to keep control of their emotions. Along with learning how to block outside influences, like his telepathic father has to do, he was able to stay focused on the task at hand. The extra training his parents had applied at home, for both empaths and telepaths (because they didn't know which abilities he would develop) had helped him excel even further in his sessions at the PSI Center.

Robert's telekinetic abilities weren't as fine-tuned as some of the other people who shared this particular gift. He had gained considerable control since he had started, but there were still aspects of his ability that eluded him.

Most of those with telekinetic abilities could grasp smaller objects, like books or pencils, and manipulate them with a fair amount of ease. Something simple like moving it from one end of the table to the other end. Or lifting the book, turning it over, and setting it back down.

Robert's telekinesis couldn't simply move the pencil. He would end up crushing it as it moved down the length of the table. A trail of splintered pencil pieces went from one end to the other end, often leaving a groove down the center of the table as well. Even with careful concentration, attempting to lift the book would cause the top half of the book to rip free while the lower portion stayed stationary on the table.

Martin had recalled that Thomas had described his telekinesis as hands that reached out from his mind. He asked Robert if he felt like he also had these phantom hands as well.

"Actually," Robert replied, "they are more like very large tentacles. Only they don't narrow to a point. So, like a really, really thick rope, I suppose. It's hard to describe."

This prompted Rex to have him try to manipulate larger objects. Chairs and tables were handled with ease. He didn't strain as others did to lift, flip, and set down a full-sized table. Robert was eager to try larger objects, hoping to work his way up to a car, or a truck. He thought that would be pretty "groovy."

Rex waited with Robert in the lobby area for his parents to pick him up. He told Robert again that he was making excellent progress and wanted him to continue to practice their "exercises" at home.

"This isn't something you will learn here and then it's over," Rex told Robert. "You will have to continue to practice and keep control of this for your whole life. But, the more you practice, the easier it will be."

"I understand," Robert replied. "I hear it from my parents and watch them practice too. Although they do more meditation than anything else. They said it's important to stay in control of it and not to let everyone know what we can do."

Rex smiled at Robert and saw the boy's father enter the building. He greeted Joe and told him of Robert's progress.

"He's quite a gifted young boy, Joe."

"I know it," Joe said. "He's a good kid. He's dealing with all of this and still keeps his grades up in school and does his chores at home. Without having to be told twice to do them. Sometimes I wonder if that is a whole separate ability!"

The two men laughed at Joe's statement and shook hands before Joe left with Robert. It would be two weeks until Robert's next appointment.

Rex made his way back to his office. He debated on getting another cup of coffee to sip on as he finished up his paperwork. But he figured it was already getting too late in the day and decided against it. There were no more sessions scheduled with him that day and he was eager to head home. He would just sign off on a few items of paperwork and give the rest to his assistants to finish up and file.

He closed his office door so he could hang his lab coat on the hook on the back of it. He sat down at his desk and stacked the papers in order in front of himself. As he began signing the papers, he wondered about Robert's statement about not letting everyone know about what he was capable of doing. It was a thought that had crossed his mind, numerous times, but not a subject he stopped to think about.

He thought back, to about a year and a half ago. He had been sitting in his office, just as he was now. It had been a bit later in the day and his office was more dimly lit then than it was now. His desk lamp had cast odd shadows throughout his office.

While they didn't hide what the purpose of the PSI Center was, they weren't exactly running ads for it in the local paper. It wasn't known to the general public that people with these types of abilities existed. What would happen if that information was to go public? What would the reactions be? Any requests from newspapers, news magazines, or even television interviews had all been turned down. Dr. Burton had made his stance on not going public very clear, even back in the PSI Department days.

Out of the corner of his eye, he thought he spotted a figure standing next to his desk. When he looked up, there was no one there. So, he went back to focusing his attention on the work on his desk.

"It's going to happen someday," said a small voice.

Rex, startled by the sound of the voice, quickly looked up from his desk. There on the other side of the desk stood a little girl. She couldn't have been more than 10 years old. With light blond hair that seemed to shine from some unknown light source. For a brief second, Dr. Rex thought she was wearing some type of hospital gown and that her hair lay loosely around her face. Then, immediately, she was in a light pink dress and her hair was held back by a pink headband.

"What did you say?" Rex stammered out the question, blinking his eyes repeatedly in disbelief that this girl was standing in his office. "Who are you?" he asked. He continued to blink, finding it hard to completely focus on her.

"You can't keep secrets forever. Someday everyone will know. But, not about them." Her voice was clear, but her mouth remained closed. He could see her staring directly into his eyes. And yet, it seemed, that even though she was seeing him, she was looking through him as well.

"You're the little ghost girl, aren't you? The one who warned me about Paul?"

"Yes, but I'm not a ghost," her voice said directly into his mind. "I don't think I am. At least not yet."

"I don't understand. Are you a telepath? Are you here in the building?" He said out loud to her.

"I don't know what that is. I don't know where I am. It was dark and then I saw you from far away. And then I was near you." The sound of her voice became shaky and frightened.

"It's ok. Stay calm. We will figure this out. Let's start from the beginning. My name is Dr. Rex Wall. You may call me Dr. Rex or just Rex if you want. Ok? What is your name?"

"My name is Emily Green," her tone began to even out as she became calmer. "I like how you talk. You sound English."

"Alright then, Ms. Emily Green, it is very nice to meet you," Rex said with a warming smile, just as he would with any frightened child to try and put them at ease. "I am Australian. So, it seems you are projecting yourself into my thoughts. We call that telepathy, and that would make you telepathic. That is very exciting." He broadened his smile and got up from behind the desk to see if he could get closer to her.

She stood in the same spot and turned her head and eyes to follow his movements. He could see her feet did not touch the floor. This physical projection was becoming clearer to him, with only the occasional brief second where she would blur out of focus. As if a wave of water was washing over a pane of glass between them. Her voice was clear but it was not coming from her mouth. Her mouth never moved as she spoke. She appeared to be illuminated by lights that were not located in his office. Her eyes were large and blue, and he could see fear in them.

"Ok, now Emily, I need you to tell me where you are. That is, where is your physical body right now? Are you here in the PSI Center?"

"I don't know," her voice said, with a little fear seeping back into her tone.

"Well, let's see. What do you remember before coming here to see me?"

"Before I got here it was dark. It's always dark. And I could hear people talking."

"It's dark, huh? Is it nighttime? Are you sleeping? Can you open your eyes?"

She paused for a moment. Looking around the room as if searching for the answer beyond the walls of the office. She seemed to fade for a moment and then came back. She looked up at him.

"Dr. Rex, I can't. I can't open my eyes. If I'm not here, it's just all darkness around me." Her eyes began to well up with diamond-like tears.

He moved towards her and reached out to comfort her but to no avail. She wasn't really there. Trying to touch her was like trying to grab onto the spots left in your vision from looking at the sun.

"Shhh-shh-shh," he said to her, trying to calm her once again. "It's ok, Emily. I'm right here. I'm going to help you figure this out. Who were the 'they' you were talking about?"

"The people that Paul works with." Her voice sounded a bit more focused and her expression changed with the mention of Paul's name. "They are the people who are trying to do what you do. Only they are not nice like you. Paul is a bad man."

"Paul Burton?"

"Yes. He's mean. I can see him in the darkness sometimes, but not like I can see you. He talks to me. He says mean things to me."

"What does he say? What things do you hear them saying?"

Emily hesitated before she answered. Almost like she was afraid someone would overhear what she was going to tell him. As she composed herself, and the expression on her face became more serious, it seemed like the pink hue of her dress began to darken slightly.

"They talk about controlling people with powers. Using drugs and medications to get results. I can hear people screaming and yelling for help. It's very scary. And they were talking about keeping secrets in place. They don't want people to know."

"Is that what Paul says to you?"

"No. Paul says stuff to me about turning me off. And unplugging me. He says it like he wants to hurt me. Like I'm a television set. What does that mean?"

It suddenly occurred to Rex why the world was so dark for Emily. He knew why she couldn't open her eyes. But how was he going to explain this to her without sending her into a panic?

"Emily, I want you to listen to me very carefully. You are asleep. What I mean is, that your physical body is sleeping. That is why you are able to project such a clear image of yourself to me. Your brain isn't focused on trying to walk and talk and do all sorts of things, so it's able to use all of its strength to do this wonderful thing." He was saying all of this to her with his warm smile again. "There must be something about my limited telepathic ability that somehow syncs up with yours and acted as a beacon for you to follow to me."

"Is that why I can sometimes see Paul? But his light is not as bright as you are?"

"I think so. Do you see anyone else nearby? Any other lights?"

As Emily looked around the room, her image began to slowly fade a little, again. She seemed to realize it this time and came back suddenly.

"There seem to be some, but I don't want to go to them. When I have before, I saw things I didn't like seeing. And they couldn't see me like you do. I like being here with you."

"That's fine, Emily." Rex paused for a moment. He concentrated on Emily's voice in his head. He hoped his ability could track a trail back to where her body was. He could sense a path leading from the figure before him. He envisioned it like a shining golden thread. He tried to grasp it with his mind, but it only went as far as outside of his office. "You have done a really good job telling me what you know. Say, do you think if I walk to another office in this building you could follow me?"

She was hesitant in answering him. The expression on her face changed to one of worry and questioning.

"It'll be ok, Emily. It's a good friend of mine and a really nice fella. Would you be ok with following me to go see him?"

"Yes. I think I can do that."

Rex had her follow him to Martin's office. Confirming along the way, and again with Martin himself, that no one else could see or hear Emily. She seemed to be keeping herself hidden from others and only revealing herself to Rex. When Rex asked her to try and let Martin see her, she said she would try and began to fade from his sight.

Martin stood patiently, not sure what he expected to happen. He jumped slightly when he heard a very faint "hello" whispered in his head. He recognized the voice as the one who had directed him to the lobby to discover Paul. He wasn't able to see her appear next to him though.

Rex thought it would be best that he relay the story to Martin, so Emily wouldn't exhaust herself trying to do something she wasn't ready to do. Whether she actually couldn't do it or was just too frightened to allow herself to accomplish it, he knew she wasn't ready.

"This is astonishing," Martin exclaimed. He had caught the explanation of how Emily was "asleep," that it was to keep her from being afraid of the situation her physical body was in. "With her brain not having to operate any of her other bodily functions, it can harness all of its potential to actually project an image of herself instead of just a voice!"

"As amazing as it is, Martin, we need to find out where she is and get her out of there. Not to mention this secret… public, whatever plan of theirs."

"You're right," Martin said. "I'll get this info to Dr. Burton, and we'll make a plan on what to do next.

Just then Emily began to panic. "No, he's here! I can hear him in the dark. He can't know I'm not there!" Her image turned around suddenly and then vanished.

"Emily!" Rex shouted, "EMILY! She's gone, Martin! She said someone was there and he couldn't know she wasn't there. And then she disappeared. What does it mean?"

"If she was that scared, I would guess Paul had returned near her body. Probably talking to her and threatening her again. I pray she is safe and we find her in time."

It was almost a week before Emily returned to see Rex again. He was relieved to see she was safe. She was happy to see him as well.

Rex had many visits with Emily. Each time they would try to add another piece to the puzzle of where her physical body was being kept. Rex would attempt to track her using his ability, but each time the trail vanished as before in just a few dozen feet.

He learned more about her with each visit, gaining more knowledge about her while trying to carefully get clues to her whereabouts without panicking her. She remembered liking her mom's scrambled eggs. Spending a lot of time playing with her doll collection. As she recounted the details of her dolls, Rex could see her image changing slightly to resemble what she was describing. She was ever so slightly projecting her memories to him as well.

There were times when she would not fully appear to Rex, similar to a child playing "hide and seek." Other times she would stand quietly in his office while he did his paperwork.

"Is it ok that I just stand quietly? I know work is important. My daddy told me that once. And that sometimes you can have distractions when doing important work. My daddy told me that too."

"Of course, it's ok, Emily," he would tell her. "You are not bothering me in the least. I'm glad for the company, to be honest."

"Me too," she said back to him in his mind. Her image beamed with a smile. "I just like being near you and your light. The darkness was so lonely for such a very long time."

Emily's abilities had their limits. Staying for too long would exhaust her and she would have to leave. Each time she left, his mind would drift back to the time she disappeared in fear of "him" being near.

Emily was surrounded by darkness. She was listening carefully to the whispers of voices that floated around her, peering into the darkness trying to find any faint flicker of light. There was only one dim, foggy light near her. It was him. It was Paul Burton. She didn't get too close to his light, because she was afraid it would allow him to spot her and that he would be able to grab onto her somehow and take her someplace worse than the darkness. She could hear him talking to her. He was saying something about recommending that she be used for some sort of test.

"But they don't think you'd survive it," he continued to say to the shadowed figure lying in the bed. "I may not be able to get right into your head, yet, but I know you are in there. I know you have found a way around this damned static. One way or another, I will find out how you're doing it. And then I'll make sure you take that secret to your grave."

Though she couldn't see him clearly enough to make out the details of his face, it was like she was standing too far away from a frosted window, she could see the way he moved. His hand gestures and his stance showed his arrogance. He enjoyed being a bully.

"If you can hear the things happening in this building," he moved closer to her physical body now. "I suggest you pay close attention tomorrow to the tests concerning Thomas O'Bannon." She could hear the evil grin in his words.

Chapter Twenty-Seven
Testing Family Ties

Katherine O'Bannon had been reporting to the Global Trust Insurance building for a couple of years now. She hadn't always been the most compliant employee of the organization. She had to go through some extensive "retraining" after she had been forcibly brought back into their "employment" four years ago.

Because Agent Coleman had her apartment bugged and under constant surveillance, he knew when to send agents to pick up her and Thomas. It was while she was scrambling to pack their bags after her confrontation and confession with Martin.

After she had influenced Martin into an advanced stage of lethargy, she had returned to the apartment, in a panic, shouting at Thomas to gather the bare essentials of what he needed as fast as he could.

Her apartment was small and modest. She didn't have much in the way of decorations. She couldn't afford too much. Some potted plants hung from hooks in the ceiling. The living room and dining room were in the same area. She had a small television set and a floral print couch that Global Trust Insurance had provided. She and Thomas would often eat their meals on TV trays while sitting on the couch, watching programs on the television. There was a bedroom for her and a separate bedroom for Thomas, though they had to share a bathroom. It was enough to allow her to feel like she was providing Thomas with a loving and stable home. That was what mattered most to her.

She threw her belongings into a small suitcase while her mind raced to think of where they could run. She stopped only for a second to calm herself, knowing her empathic power could influence Thomas and cause him to panic as well. She shouted to him again, telling him to hurry.

As soon as they had enough of their things packed, Katherine grabbed their bags and had Thomas follow her quickly to the door. She still hadn't determined what their destination would be, but she knew they had to get on the road as soon as possible. She handed one of the bags to Thomas so she could open the front door of the apartment. As she swung the door open she discovered their exit was blocked.

"You've been a bad girl, Katherine," Paul Burton said as he stood on the other side of the door. He had one of his telekinetic acolytes standing next to him and 4 agents behind him.

Before she could react, Paul used his telepathy to blast a hot white light into her mind. The pain was so tremendous that she dropped the bag she was carrying and fell to her knees, clutching her head.

"Aunt Kathy," Thomas shouted as he rushed to her side. His anger immediately began to grow and he turned his gaze towards Paul.

"I don't think so, junior," Paul said to Thomas and blasted his mind with the same inner white light. Thomas yelped in pain as he grabbed his head, but continued to stand. Paul turned to the young man next to him, a Hispanic boy in his late teens, and said, "Keep his face planted in the carpet away from us. He needs to focus his eyes on the object he wants to use his power on. So, I would prefer he doesn't get the opportunity to look at me. Understand?"

"Yes, sir," the teenage boy replied. He narrowed his dark eyes on Thomas and exerted his will onto him. The sudden weight on Thomas's head caused him to collapse down onto the floor. The boy stayed focused on Thomas, keeping his face painfully pressed into the carpeted floor. He was enjoying hurting Thomas.

Paul gestured with a single finger to the agents to come forward. They ran up to Katherine and placed a thick collar around her neck. It had a small box on the front of it with a tiny red light. They quickly placed matching cuffs around each wrist, each one had a small box with a red light on it.

"Now then, Katherine," Paul began to speak. "I know you are familiar with these shock restraints. If I sense the slightest use of your power, all I have to do is press this button." He held up a small remote in front of her tear-streamed face. "And Thomas," he directed his words to her nephew with his face still being forcibly pressed into the carpet. "If you try to use your powers or escape, I'm going to shock your aunt with some very painful electricity. Do you understand?"

Thomas's anger was growing. He began to fight against the force of the other telekinetic by using his ability on himself. He was able to lift his head off of the carpet and was trying to shift his line of sight upwards to the other men now.

"Can't you do one simple thing," Paul said with obvious disappointment to the telekinetic boy next to him. "I warned you," he hissed at Thomas.

Paul pressed one of the buttons on the remote in his hand. The small red lights on the collar and wrist cuffs, which had been placed on Katherine, lit up as she screamed out in agony. Her neck muscles, legs, and arms tensed uncontrollably from the electricity surging through her body.

"NO!" Thomas yelled. The focus he needed to fight against the other telekinetic began to fade, replaced by his fear for his aunt.

Paul calmly released the button and Katherine lay flat on the threshold of the doorway. She gasped for air between her fits of sobbing. Thomas stopped his struggle as he watched his aunt lay there, utterly defeated.

"Sir," one of the agents addressed Paul, "we can place those wrist cuffs on him instead. The collar should be sufficient in restraining her."

"No," Paul said with his back to the agent, barely turning his as he spoke. "I want Thomas to understand how much force will be applied to his aunt if he disobeys. He will comply, not for his safety, but for hers. That is more effective than any physical restraint."

Paul stepped over Katherine, becoming fully aware of the ankle device that had been placed on him. He could feel it, slightly weighing down his right ankle. It irritated him to think about how it was also stretching out his sock.

He gestured to two of the agents to take her away. He bent down towards Thomas, getting close to his head, and yelled "Do you understand NOW?"

The other two agents stepped into the apartment and lifted Thomas to his feet, placed a blindfold over his eyes, and took him to the same van where Katherine had been taken.

Paul kicked both pieces of baggage back into the interior of the apartment. He glanced around the small living space and curled his lip in disapproval.

"Tacky," he said out loud. "Tell the agents to call a cleanup crew," he spoke to the Hispanic boy who was inside the apartment, standing next to him again. "I want this place emptied out. No trace of Katherine or Thomas having been here. Do you think you are capable of relaying that message for me?"

"Yes, sir. I'll be sure to get that done."

"See that you do," he said without a hint of warmth. "And try not to fuck it up. I won't be riding back with you. I have business to attend to."

He gave the boy a couple of light taps on the side of his face and walked away. "What a shame," he thought to himself. "Katherine had such potential. Now I'll have to find another use for her."

Katherine would recall that day almost every time she had to go back to that building. Seeing the giant "Global Trust Insurance" sign would send a flash of rage and fear through her. Every time her mind would race to think of a way out. If she could devise some plan to get away… but there were none. They had Thomas, and there was no way she would leave him behind.

As she entered the building she could feel the effects the dampening field had on her empathic power. The only way she could describe it was that it felt like she was walking around with a fishbowl over her head. It was not a pleasant experience, but it seemed to be quite effective in keeping her from influencing the emotions of others. Unfortunately for her.

Her presence had been requested for a testing procedure. Not on her, but on some other poor soul who would have some hellish drug or device tested on them. Why they wanted her here was beyond her. Her abilities would not be effective on any of the subjects as long as she was wearing that ankle device. Unless they were going to switch it out for one of the collars used during testing. She began to panic thinking that she could be the object of one of their hellish experiments.

She had to calm her thoughts. Perhaps it was going to be a field test. Or they wanted her to compare their findings with what she knew from her time working at the PSI Department. She could have been called in for a simple question-and-answer session.

That part of her life seemed like a lifetime ago. She knew she had made poor choices and had done some evil things. Maybe this was a fitting punishment for her. Maybe she knew that and that's why she didn't try to plan a way for her to escape.

She waited in the lobby for an agent to arrive and escort her to her appointed place. Every time they summoned her to this place she would have to wait for an agent to accompany her. They were smart enough to not let her wander through the building alone and she was constantly partnered with an agent. Even with her power neutralized, they didn't want her to roam free, able to snoop or help anyone escape.

Katherine had to resort to wearing slacks instead of dresses, due to the ankle cuff they outfitted her with. The large restraint would draw too much notice if left out in the open, so she hid it underneath long dress pants. Even though it was just one cuff, it was enough to send her into convulsions if they activated it. Strong enough to leave electrical burns around her ankle and leave her unconscious if they used it at full strength. She was entirely aware of its presence, especially when just standing around and waiting for agents to show up.

The elevator doors opened up and a female agent stood inside. She had her dark hair pulled back in a tight, military-style bun. She was wearing a female version of the male agent's dark blue suit. The skirt ended just at her knee, and loose enough to allow her to fight if the occasion called for it. She had black-framed glasses that fit her expressionless face.

"Miss O'Bannon, I'm here to escort you to your appointment," she said in a monotone voice.

Katherine stepped into the elevator. She was aware that she could not read this woman's emotions and that she was wearing the ankle cuff and shouldn't attempt to try. She also noticed that the agent pushed the button for the lower basement floor. All of her appointments to give her reports had taken place on the upper floors. This was a concern for her. Even though she had not been to the lower levels, she was aware of what happened down there. She was afraid her "fight or flight" instincts would be called upon very soon.

A single electrical note sounded, signaling they had reached their floor. The doors of the elevator opened, but Katherine didn't step out immediately. She waited, looking down the corridor outside the elevator. It looked like any number of hospitals in any town. Nothing to connect it to the office-style levels above.

"Miss O'Bannon, please exit the elevator," the female agent said behind her.

Katherine turned and looked at her before stepping out. She saw the agent had a remote in her hand, almost out of sight at her side. She took a deep breath to steady her nerves and stepped into the hallway. The agent followed her as the elevator doors closed and made its ascent back to the upper floors. The hum of the elevator grew more distant as it traveled away. It wasn't a sound she liked to hear. Her escape route getting farther and farther away.

The agent guided her down the hallway and into a room. It was a simple square room. There were 3 rows of chairs, with 5 chairs in each row. It had a large window that looked into what appeared to be a medical examination room. She assumed the window was one of those one-way mirrors, judging by how dimly lit the observation room was kept.

The agent gestured to a chair for Katherine to sit down. The agent took her spot in the back of the room against the wall. It seemed odd that they would have her sit in here with just an agent. What was she supposed to observe?

Just as she was pondering this, the door to the observation room opened. The light outside the doorway was brighter and it made it difficult to immediately tell who was coming in. Two male figures entered the room.

"Katherine, dear, it is so good to see you again," said Paul Burton as he entered the room. "You are looking well." He was so sickly sweet it was obvious he was being snide.

Katherine turned in her chair, prepared to spring to her feet. But as she did, she felt the weight of the ankle cuff, and it reminded her to keep herself calm and to behave. They had reinforced these responses in her with all of their "retraining." She sat back in her chair, lightly clenching her teeth.

"Katherine, I said hello. What? No response back? Kind of rude, don't you think?" Paul said, trying to goad a response from her.

"That is enough Paul," said Agent Coleman. He was the other man who had entered the room. "Katherine, I'm sure you are wondering why you were brought in. Well, for the test that is going to be run today, we need you to keep the test subject calm and focused."

"How do you expect me to do that, sir? I'm wearing the ankle cuff, and even if you don't have it activated, the static keeps my abilities from work…ing," she stopped speaking when she saw the door to the examination room open and the test subject was led in with two men in lab coats.

The subject was a male, who looked to be approximately 19 years old. He had a blindfold wrapped tightly around his head, pressing down his copper hair, keeping his eyes concealed. The men in lab coats sat him in a large chair, one which supported his legs and had him reclining back at a slight angle. The chair had restraints built into it at the points where his hands and feet rested.

Katherine stood from her chair and put her hands up to the glass window. "Thomas?" she whispered. Standing at the window, waiting for the men to remove his blindfold. She knew it was him, but was hoping she was wrong. A couple of years had passed since she last saw him.

The female agent in the back of the room took a step forward, raising the remote, and looked to Agent Coleman awaiting his orders. He closed his eyes, shook his head "no," and nodded for her to return to the back of the room.

Katherine watched as they strapped his wrists and ankles to the chair, making sure he was secure. He lay back in the white chair, in his white scrubs, with his lower arms exposed. Then they wheeled over a tray that had several syringes and vials on it. The men brought their surgical masks up over their mouths and noses and put on rubber gloves to protect their hands.

"You son of bitch," Katherine said as she turned around to face Paul and Agent Coleman. "What are you going to do to him?"

"Thomas is going to test a serum in our latest attempt to control these abilities," Agent Coleman said. "Today, we want to see if it can slightly diminish his telekinetic abilities. Based on some of the past trials, we've seen that some of the subjects tend to panic, and that affects the drug's ability to work. So, we thought it best to have you here to see if you can keep him calm."

"But I can't use my empathy here. You've seen to that. There is no way I can use that to help him. Or you."

"I know this. We aren't going to give you access to your power. Instead, I'm going to allow you to speak to him, to reassure him, and to keep him calm as best you can as his Aunt." Agent Coleman was very cool as he laid this all out to Katherine. He had this all planned out. What wasn't apparent was there still was no reason why Paul was present during all of this.

"And if I don't," Katherine asked Agent Coleman. "If I don't help you in your torture of my nephew?" She was getting visibly upset.

"It would be in yours, and Thomas', best interest to make this test a success," Paul chimed in now. "I've seen these tests first hand, Katherine," Paul paused when he saw Agent Coleman was prepared to object to what he was going to tell her. "She should know what is at stake," Paul continued. "When the subjects can't be controlled, their powers spiral out of hand and usually end up destroying the subject. Death, Katherine. Thomas' life is what is at stake if you can't keep him focused."

Katherine knew there was no real concern in Paul's tone, but she also knew he wasn't lying. She had heard the tales of the tests and the fatalities that took place on the lower levels. She knew that even those who didn't die (and were possibly left in a vegetative state) were usually experimented on again. What choice did she have? Maybe if he survived this, she would be able to free him later.

"Fine," she said. She pressed her forehead to the glass window, trying to be as close to Thomas as she could. "I'll do what I can, though it would be easier if I could use my empathic ability to help him."

"Of course it would," Agent Coleman responded. "But we want to perfect this without using those powers as a backup. We may not always have empaths and telepaths handy to keep these drugs under control. We need to test it against their willpower alone."

Agent Coleman rose from his chair and approached a speaker box on the wall next to the observation window. He pressed a button and the speakers in both rooms made a clicking sound.

"Gentlemen, we are going to start the test. Place the collar on the subject so he can access his powers. Young man, I suggest you behave appropriately. That collar may grant you access to your powers, but will also give you an extremely painful electric shock. This speaker will be left active so communication between both rooms will be possible during the whole process." The men in the examination room nodded to this. "Thomas," Agent Coleman continued, his voice carrying into the examination room, "I want you to pay close attention to what you hear. There is someone here who is going to help you through this."

Thomas, still blindfolded, tilted his head from side to side, struggling against his restraints. He was already agitated as the technicians placed the collar around his neck. Small sweat spots were visible under his arms and beads of sweat were forming on his forehead.

Katherine approached the speaker box, "Thomas, you need to relax."

"Aunt Kathy? Aunt Kathy, is that you?" Thomas strained hard

against the restraints.

Katherine paused, closed her eyes, and tried to reach out to his emotions. But it was no use. The dampening field reached into this room and effectively blocked her. With the collar on, she knew his emotions were out there, beyond her reach. As if he were stranded in the center of a swimming pool, drowning, and she had no way to reach him.

Agent Coleman placed his hand on her shoulder and guided her gaze to the female agent at the back of the room. She stood ready, with the remote in her hand pointed at Katherine.

Agent Coleman pressed the mute button on the speaker box, "Regardless of your powers being nullified, I won't allow you to even try to use them. One more attempt and you will be punished and removed from this room, and the experiment will continue without you being able to help him. Do you understand?"

He depressed the mute button and let Katherine speak to Thomas. "Thomas, it's me. You have to listen to me, ok? Just listen to my voice and let me help you."

Thomas settled down a little, enough that the men in the lab coats were able to prepare his arm for injection.

"Thomas, listen to me. You are going to get an injection that is going to affect your powers. No matter how it feels, I need you to stay calm. Just concentrate on my voice and do as I tell you. Ok? It is very important you remain calm, do you understand?"

"Yes, Aunt Kathy. I hear you. I'll try. Are you using your powers? Do your powers work?"

"No, honey. They don't work here. It is up to you."

One of the men in the lab coats prepared a syringe and the other held down Thomas' arm. As they injected the fluid into Thomas, Katherine could see Paul in the reflection of the widow. He had moved to one of the front row chairs and was leaning forward, watching for the reaction Thomas would have to the drug.

"Thomas," Katherine said into the speaker box, "I want you to talk me through what you are experiencing. So I can help you."

"It's like ice water. It feels like ice water is moving through my body, Aunt Kathy. It's in my arms, and now in my legs." Thomas was silent for a moment, his head moving around like he was trying to see past his blindfold. "It's moving into my chest. Oh god, Aunt Kathy, I can feel it in my head! It feels like it's trying to freeze my brain!" He began to panic.

"Thomas, stop. Thomas, listen to me. Focus on my voice. It's just the drug, it's just a chemical reaction, it's not actually cold." Katherine moved close to the speaker box as if it would bring her closer to him, so he would listen more carefully to what she was saying.

"NO!" Thomas screamed. "It's trying to put me to sleep! It's going to freeze me from the inside out. I'm going to die!"

"Thomas. Thomas!" Katherine screamed into the speaker box. She feared for his life. She had failed him. "Thomas, fight it! Fight for your life. Free yourself!"

Katherine was cut off as the female agent activated the ankle cuff and sent an electrical shock through her body. She screamed and dropped to the floor, trying to fight the muscle spasms and grasped at her ankle.

Thomas could hear her screams coming through the speakers. He began to thrash in the chair, but the restraints held him in place. He suddenly stopped, holding perfectly still, but baring his clenched teeth. He opened his eyes wide and stared at the fabric that blocked his sight. The blindfold that had covered his eyes flew from his face, hitting the observation window with a light thud.

"Crap," Agent Coleman said under his breath. He yelled to the speaker box, "Don't shock him yet. Give him another dose, fast!"

Thomas struggled to focus his vision on his left wrist restraint. The drug was making it difficult to focus. He used his will to unfasten it. Unfortunately, the men in the lab coats were injecting his right arm with another dose of the test drug.

Thomas turned his gaze towards them. One man was flung against the observation window, causing a small crack. The other man was only shoved to the ground, the lack of power was already apparent and Thomas feared the second dose would make him weaker.

Thomas tried to focus on the restraint holding his right arm down. He blinked repeatedly, trying to clear his vision. His head started to sway lightly side to side. He let out a loud, slurred groan. Even as the drug began to take over, he fought it. He used his left hand and his power to try and free his right arm.

The ankle cuff on Katherine had stopped electrocuting her. She sat on the floor, horrified by what was happening to her nephew. She saw Paul, still leaning forward in his chair, watching …no, studying what was happening to Thomas. The female agent and Agent Coleman were also engrossed in the event unfolding in front of them. Katherine watched as Thomas became more sluggish, and now with both hands free, he clumsily struggled to undo his ankle restraints.

"Aunt Katthhhhyyyy," he cried out in slurred agony. It was more than she could bear.

In one smooth motion, Katherine grabbed the leg of the chair she had been sitting on and used it as leverage to get up off the floor. Then in one fluid movement, held on to it as she stood up and slammed it into the window. She connected perfectly with the crack in the window causing it to shatter. All observers instinctively used their arms to shield their faces as the full pane of glass rained down. She leaped through the opening, hoping to reach Thomas before the female agent could activate her ankle cuff.

She raced to Thomas, who was no longer coherent enough to try to free himself. She laid him back onto his chair, hugging him close. No audible words came from his mouth, just mumbles and gurgles. He wasn't able to use his powers, and she knew that meant there was no way either of them could escape now.

"I'm sorry, Thomas," she cried to him. "I'm sorry I couldn't save you. Forgive me." She held him close and cried. He was still alive, but this outcome seemed crueler than if he had died.

As she held him close, her arms cradled the collar around his neck. Being in contact with the collar and that close to him, she could sense her abilities switching on. She could feel his mind, and it was blank. There were no emotions emanating from him.

The others stepped through the window. The female agent helped the men in lab coats to their feet so they could take Thomas back to his holding cell.

Katherine did not want to let him go. She held him tightly, even when threatened with the shock cuff, she would not let go. Paul stood back as the others grabbed her arms and pried Thomas free of her hold.

No one noticed that during this commotion, Paul had spied the vials on the tray. With no one looking, he was able to pocket the unused vile marked "accelerant." He swiftly joined the crowd, remarking, "Just shock her and be done with it." As if he had been standing there the whole time.

Paul leaned over and pressed the female agent's thumb down on the remote trigger. Katherine's muscles tensed involuntarily and she released Thomas. She collapsed to the floor, having fainted from the massive jolt of electricity.

"There, see," Paul said. "Now, what shall we do for lunch?"

Chapter Twenty-Eight
1973

"It's been so long since we've been able to have a dinner out, just the two of us, Martin," Janet said as she reached across the small table and touched his hand.

It was a quaint, little Italian restaurant. Complete with the dim lights, red and white checkered tablecloths, and candles in red jars on each table. Other couples were dining as well, but the place never felt crowded. When they had finished dinner they decided to treat themselves to some dessert.

"Things have just been running so smoothly at the center, that I'm finally able to keep a regular schedule," Martin told her. "I hope I didn't just jinx myself by saying that."

They both chuckled, knowing Martin wasn't the superstitious type. They gazed at each other over the low flame of the candle. He loved her even more now than when they had first been married. And he knew her love and devotion to him was just as strong.

She had been supportive of his work for so many years now. Of course, having experienced it firsthand, she knew how important it all was. Without his help, starting all those years ago, she didn't know if she would have survived this long. Much less have such a wonderful life with a loving husband and beautiful daughter.

Ah, their daughter. That was one of their greatest joys and touchiest subjects. Janet had long suspected that Margaret might have special talents. Luckily, it was not the same talent as her mother, but still along the lines of what her father's work was all about. She knew her daughter was smart. Being a stay-at-home mother, Janet was able to observe a lot of the traits that Martin didn't get the opportunity to see.

Janet saw Margaret sit quietly and observe people when they were at the grocery store. People would compliment her on how well-behaved she was. Janet knew it was more from being preoccupied with watching what other people were doing than just having good manners.

Janet knew that Margaret would stop and think before answering questions. Carefully gauging what the other person's responses might be before she spoke. It was those same calculating looks that she had seen in Paul Burton. That is what worried her so much. Was her daughter a telepath like Paul? Could having both loving parents stop her from becoming the same as Paul? Or was it the fate of all kids born this way to end up on the same path?

"Martin, I don't want to spoil our evening, but…"

"Then don't," Martin cut her off. Smiling, not knowing exactly what she was going to say, but suspecting it had something to do with cutting the evening short so the babysitter wouldn't have to stay too late watching Margaret.

"Martin, please," Janet started again, "I need you to be serious. Just for a moment." She reached across the table to hold his hand with both of hers, to gain his attention. "I think we should have Margaret tested. Just take her to work with you this week, and see if you can run some tests with her."

"Janet, we've talked about this. I think you are seeing something there that doesn't exist. You're looking for it to be there, so you are seeing it. She's just a smart little girl. I think she takes after me, not you." He said the last part with a smile, trying to lighten the mood. It didn't work.

"I'm not seeing shadows, I know it. I want us to know what she's capable of before it's too late. I don't want her to ..." she paused, afraid that saying it out loud might make it happen.

She lowered her voice and leaned in closer to him. "I don't want her to turn out like Paul Burton."

"Honey," he said to her while he stroked her hands to comfort her. "You are a terrific mother. There is no way you would let her turn into a monster like that." He could see the fear in her eyes. He knew the only thing that would bring ease to her worrying would be to grant her request.

The waiter approached their table and brought a tiramisu for them to share and two cups of coffee. They both sat back in their chairs while he placed it all on the table in front of them.

"I'll take her to work with me this week. I'll even ask Ross to sit in on some of the tests, although I think she has a crush on Rex. Will that make you feel any better?"

"It does, Martin. I just need to know for sure. We need to be prepared."

Martin had already started to plot out a course of action while they shared their dessert. When it came to Margaret, he hadn't noticed any odd fires or moving objects. And even though Janet was convinced it was either empathic or telepathic in origin, he couldn't be sure. Even though silence and intelligence were common in people with either one of those abilities. Maybe there was cause for concern, but he would have to wait for conclusive evidence to be sure.

They enjoyed their dessert together. They talked about how Martin enjoys watching "M*A*S*H" and Janet prefers "The Bob Newhart Show." She still gravitated towards shows that were strictly comedies. A habit born from the fear of how her mood affected her control of her ability.

They continued laughing and gazing into each other's eyes. Reaffirming the deep connection they felt for each other. When the check came, Martin paid it, without letting Janet see it. An old habit of his with her, that he never stopped doing. He still treated every time out with her as a proper date. He quickly got up and dashed around to her side of the table to assist in pulling out her chair.

"My my, what a gentleman you are," she said teasingly. "You may just get lucky tonight."

He made a growling noise and they laughed as they made their way to the car. The car ride was spent chatting over the news on the radio. The broadcast announcer had just finished a story about the launch of Skylab 2 and began playing Roberta Flack's "Killing Me Softly with His Song."

Janet leaned forward and, even though she loved that song, turned the volume down a little. She sat back and looked over at Martin while he drove the car.

"Another space launch. It's amazing where science is leading us. Do you think this type of progress will impact what you're doing at all?"

"Who knows," Martin replied. "It could go in so many directions. If we can discover the cause, or if the explorations into space can discover a connection, there is no way of telling. What if it's from ancient aliens who visited our planet? You could be part alien!" He laughed at his joke.

"Oh no you don't! You are not going to live out your Captain Kirk and the green alien lady fantasy with me mister!"

They were still smiling and laughing when they pulled up to their house. As they walked inside they could hear that the television was on and could hear Margaret's voice. She was explaining the television show to the babysitter.

"Jamie," Martin spoke to the young woman, the babysitter, sitting on the couch watching the television. "What is Margaret doing up this late? And eating a popsicle too?"

"I'm sorry Dr. Sellers," she was blinking her eyes as if coming out of some sort of daze. "I just sort of felt bad for her for having to go to bed so early and miss these shows. I… I don't know why I let her stay up."

"It's fine Jamie. Grab your coat, I'll drive you home." He stood by the front door, car keys still in his hand. "Margaret, go brush your teeth and get to bed."

Margaret ran up to Martin and gave him a hug around his waist. "But Daddy, I miss you. Don't you want to spend time with me?"

"Yes, of course I do," Martin began to say.

Janet quickly walked over, scooped Margaret up in her arms, and distracted her with loud kisses all over her face.

"I will tuck you in, and Daddy will drive Jamie home," Janet said in a loving mommy-style voice. Watching Martin blink himself out of whatever type of spell Margaret had just put over him.

"Uh, yes. That's what I'm going to do. And first thing tomorrow, I'm calling Doctor Grandpa. I think we need to spend a little time with him at work." Martin locked eyes with Janet. He now began to think she may be right about their daughter.

On the other side of town, Rex was getting dressed for a night on the town. He enjoyed the bachelor life. He was young and handsome and had a confidence that seemed to easily attract very beautiful women. The fact that he was in exceptional physical condition didn't hurt in adding to that attraction.

He knew how to dress for the shape of his body. His shirt had a tight, tailored fit to it. Not so tight that the material bowed between the buttons that ran down the center of his cream-colored shirt. All neatly tucked into the waist of his pants. He, of course, kept the top 3 buttons of the shirt open to expose a portion of his toned pecs and gold chain.

His dark brown pants fit tight, like his shirt, around his hips and thighs and flared loosely from his calves to the top of his shoes. He made sure that he kept an impressive, but not vulgar, bulge in the front of his pants. He wanted to make sure the ladies could tell they would not be disappointed in his company.

Rex liked the release of going to nightclubs and being out in the crowds. Unlike other telepaths, his ability didn't force him to shy away from others. He was never overwhelmed by the thoughts of large crowds. He was able to scan a crowd and barely pick up on the light whispers of what was in the mind of an individual. Or, if lucky, sense that they were special like him.

Those instances didn't happen too often, but when they did, he was positive about what he had discovered. In his head, he could sense a certain "aura" around people with abilities. The people with empathic talents were the easiest for him to detect because their ability reacted to his like trying to force similar magnetic poles together. He could feel a type of repulsion to them in his head. Tonight, however, his talents were focused on attraction, not repulsion.

He could use his talent to zone in on which women would be receptive to him. To know what kind of approach would work best on certain women. Though he wasn't directly manipulating these women into doing anything they didn't want to do, it did give him inside knowledge on how to be exactly who they were looking for. He never felt any sort of remorse about using his ability in this fashion. He figured he was good-looking enough that he'd probably score at any rate. The ladies never seemed to complain. Well, not until he had to leave the next morning.

On one such night, he was standing at the bar in a crowded nightclub having a drink with a beautiful flight attendant named Debby. Or was it Betty? It was noisy enough that he couldn't properly hear her name. She was giggling at everything he said. With each giggle, she would lightly bounce to attract attention to the ample cleavage exposed by her extremely low-cut red blouse. Her dark blond hair rested in loose curls on her shoulders and across the top of her breasts. She swirled around the olive on the end of the toothpick in her martini glass. Occasionally taking it out of the glass, not to eat it, but to suck the martini off of the olive. She would then swirl it in the drink again and repeat the process.

It was loud and difficult to hear exactly what she was saying. That didn't matter, as he could hear flashes of her inner thoughts moaning in approval of what she was seeing before her. He knew for sure she wanted him and would be ready to leave as soon as he suggested it.

Just as he was leaning in to propose that they leave and head back to her place, he felt a tingle in the back of his skull and spied someone behind her.

Poised, as if sitting on the bar stool, yet not actually touching it, was Emily. The flashing lights of the disco ball strolled across the walls and patrons of the nightclub but never reflected onto her. As always, she was in her pink dress. Along with the pink ribbon headband holding her hair back. She was completely out of place in this setting, though no one could see her. Except for Rex.

Debby (or Betty) caught the change of expression on his face as he suddenly sat back away from her. He was looking back and forth from this woman to the unseen figure behind her.

"Is something wrong? You looked like you wanted to say something to me," she shouted over the music. She turned around to see what he was looking at, but couldn't discern who it could be. "Is your wife here or something?" she shouted to him as she turned back to face him.

"Uh, no," he stammered, trying to think of a quick excuse. "I… I, uh, need to use the restroom." He flashed her his dazzling smile and poured on the Australian accent. "Hang tight, I'll be right back."

He did a small head jerk to his right to Emily, with his lips pursed, to signal her to follow him. He became a bit angrier when he could feel the woman's thoughts in response to how his accent was affecting her.

He began walking to the men's bathroom, stopping just outside the door. It didn't seem the proper place to bring an astral projection of a telepathic little girl. He turned to find an exit and saw Emily standing there, with her hands behind her back, smiling up at him.

"Was that lady a friend of yours?" Emily projected her thoughts into Rex's mind. "Her shirt didn't seem to be covering up her chest very well. She could catch a cold."

"Jesus Christ, Emily," Rex thought to himself. "Your timing couldn't be worse."

"I'm sorry," Emily said into his mind. Her closed-mouth smile quickly turned to a sad frown. "Should I have waited until you left?"

"No. I don't want you seeing… Wait," Rex wasn't speaking out loud. He was using telepathy to speak to Emily. "You can hear my thoughts? Clearly hear me?"

"Yes," Emily replied, and the smile crept back onto her face.

"Em, this is amazing. I haven't ever been able to clearly project my thoughts back to anyone before!"

"See, Dr. Rex, we're best friends." She was beaming now. Her pink dress was bright and vibrant. It was an obvious reflection of her emotions.

Rex suddenly became aware of his body language and facial expressions when he noticed how the people entering and exiting the bathrooms were staring at him. He moved a little further down the hallway away from the bathrooms towards the emergency exit door. He looked at Emily and looked back toward the crowded nightclub.

"Emily, you know this isn't an appropriate place for a little girl. Even if you aren't physically here… well, you're still here. Does that make sense?"

"Are you going to dance with your lady friend?" she asked, ignoring what he had said to her. "Are you a good dancer? I think I would like to see you dance. I wish I could be there to dance."

"Emily, you aren't listening to me," he was attempting to think in an authoritative tone. "This is a place for adults. And since I'm the only one who can see you, having you floating around is a bit distracting."

"I wish I could be an adult." Her smile and curious eyes turned to sadness once again. Her bright pink dress shifted to a duller shade now. "I understand, Dr. Rex. I'll leave so you can talk to your friend."

He could see and hear the loneliness in her. He stole one quick glance back towards where his fun evening was waiting for him. Then he made his choice.

"Wait, Emily. If you leave then I won't have my real friend to talk to." He smiled down at her. "You're my friend. Let's get out of here so we can have a proper conversation. Somewhere I won't be seen and looked at like a crazy person."

He left the nightclub. From the perspective of any casual observer, he left alone. Nodding his head, sometimes shrugging his shoulder in response to a silent conversation. The thing no one else could see was the little girl in the bright pink dress who was literally skipping on air alongside him.

Chapter Twenty-Nine
Plans and Deceptions of '75

D r. Burton had just finished a session with Robert Zanetti. Though he was not the most gifted telekinetic subject, he had an almost hidden secondary ability. It seemed that he could occasionally amplify the abilities of those around him. As if his telekinesis was assisting to strengthen the power of another subject. It was one of the reasons Dr. Burton preferred to run Robert's sessions himself, and not hand him off to any other doctors or assistants.

This other ability explained the fluctuation in power that his mother had experienced after his birth. His natural connection to her automatically had him augmenting her empathic abilities. It wasn't any of the scientific tests that initially discovered it. It was Dr. Rex who sensed it when he sat in on one of Robert's sessions. He could "feel" an extra energy signature coming from him that was unlike any other telekinetic ability.

Even with practice, it was a talent that continued to elude him. He wasn't able to tap into it on command. At only 12 years old, it wasn't something they expected him to master overnight. Or, he may never master control over it. There was no way to know for sure.

Dr. Burton had just celebrated his 62nd birthday. Which also meant that it would soon be two years since he had started tutoring Margaret Sellers with her empathic abilities. Though, he realized, as he'd gotten older, he required some assistance in this task. Especially with a subject as strong-willed and intelligent as Margaret.

That was why he would schedule her session right after Robert's. Patty would come to pick up Robert and could stay to assist in Margaret's training. Having Robert nearby to amplify his mother's ability was handy in keeping Margaret in check.

Margaret wasn't malicious, not like Paul, but like most of the telepathic and empathic children, she did have an air of superiority about her. Especially once these children got a handle on their power. It was important to make sure they knew the importance of being humble and responsible with this gift. Something Margaret seemed to understand as she didn't lash out or throw temper tantrums when she felt frustrated.

The advantage, and disadvantage, was that Margaret already had such amazing control over her own emotions. It almost seemed that was her secondary gift. She could feel joy, sorrow, anger…but she could choose to shut them off. Doing so left her more open to perceiving the emotions of others and what they were feeling, and then, effectively tap into those emotions.

Patty practiced with Margaret on how to recognize foreign emotions by imposing her empathic abilities on her. She would have Margaret concentrate on stopping Patty's influence from taking hold of her emotions. Patty was attempting, in these sessions, to teach her how to block out the emotions of others. She would teach her that it was like spying on people, to look at the emotions others kept inside themselves, and to force those feelings or other foreign feelings onto people was wrong.

Margaret could grasp this concept, but she was very much like her father. She saw others as experiments. Judging reactions and making mental notes of how people responded to various types of stimuli. It seemed the only one who could effortlessly keep her in line was her mother.

For some unknown reason, Janet was immune to Margaret's power. No tests could conclude if it was a natural immunity, or if Margaret's subconscious wouldn't allow her to exercise her will over her mother. Even when she actively tried, Janet could not be influenced by any effort from her daughter. Regardless, Margaret loved her mother unconditionally. She would follow every word, request, command, and suggestion from Janet.

No one needed any empathic influence to become enamored at the sight of the two of them together. Mother and daughter were a stunning sight to behold. Both with long, full-bodied brown hair. Janet would style Margaret's hair similar to her own. Though Margaret had recently insisted on tying a gold ribbon across her forehead, due to the start of her new favorite television show, "Wonder Woman." Perhaps that would help in giving her a positive role model. (Even though the similarity between her mother and Wonder Woman had been pointed out in private conversations.) Using the show as a reward seemed effective as well. It seemed things were progressing smoothly and that

Margaret Sellers was on the right path.

Meanwhile, Katherine paced back and forth in her small room on the lower levels of the Global Trust Insurance building. Things had gotten very difficult for her since the testing on Thomas. They only let her out when they needed her specific empathic abilities for delicate situations. She was still one of the most talented empaths in their stable. They guaranteed her obedience by taking care of her nephew, who was in a vegetative state. He could no longer feed or take care of himself. They promised to keep him comfortable and alive, and away from further testing, as long as she obeyed orders and delivered on their requests. She felt she had no choice but to obey them. She had failed him once, she would not let it happen again.

Now she paced, waiting to be let out so she could sit with Thomas. Which they allowed her to do once a week. She clung to these visits. She couldn't tell if he was still aware, trapped inside his body. Or if he was just a shell, and his soul had moved on. She had to hope he was in there, and that she was doing the right thing by keeping him alive until he could find his way back and wake up. Or until she could get him out of the building and use her empathic ability to lead him back.

The lock to her door made a loud click, signaling it was going to be opened. The agent, a tall man in a dark blue suit, stood on the other side of the doorway.

"Miss O'Bannon, if you will come with me, I will take you to Subject 1491's room."

"His name is Thomas," she hissed at him. "I know where I'm going."

"I've been ordered to escort you there and back, miss."

Which he did. To the elevator, down to the medical level, and to a long hallway. On the way, they passed a room. A room she had passed numerous times, but this time the door was open, and she saw Paul Burton inside. She couldn't see much, the room was very dark inside, but she did see that he had noticed her walking by as well.

"Here we are, Miss O'Bannon. You can go in. You will have 10 minutes, at which point I will escort you back to your room."

"Thank you, I think I know the drill by now." She huffed and flared her nostrils at the man as she entered the room.

It was all white inside. White walls, white chair, white medical instruments, white bed with white sheets. It was surreal to her. It was like a bad dream as her nephew lay there, silent as a statue, in this sea of white. His once bright copper hair was now dull and faded. His face, which should have been that of a handsome 22-year-old, was aged with sunken eyes and cheeks. His bright eyes were gone, and stared into space. Only occasionally slowly blinking. That one act was the only thing that gave her hope that he was still in there. The rhythmic sounds of the machines, keeping him alive because he had been in this state for so long. No, she knew he was still in there despite that.

She sat on the bed next to him. She stroked his hair and talked gently to him, just hoping he would answer her back. In mid-sentence, she was interrupted by the sound of the door to his room opening.

"It hasn't been 10 minutes," she started to say as she turned toward the door.

"Relax," Paul said as he entered the room. "I won't take up too much of your visitation time. I know how much it means to you."

"What the fuck do you want?" She was angry. She blamed him more than anyone else. If he had let them get away, they wouldn't be here now. He had taken pleasure in watching the torture of the experiment. She was painfully aware her power wouldn't work in this room. And she knew, even with all her anger, she couldn't take him in a physical fight.

"Listen, I only have a couple of minutes," Paul approached her, speaking in a hushed tone. "I feel bad about what happened to Thomas. I'll be honest, it's mostly because of the wasted potential he represented. But also because I care for you, Katherine. I always have. That's why I wanted you to come back here. To be close to you."

"What? You expect me to believe this bullshit?"

"It's true. I wouldn't say it was the noblest of reasons. But it's why I did what I did. And I want to help make it right. Look," he held out his hand. He was holding a small bottle, with the label scratched off. "This is one of the experimental drugs they were using to dope up the pyrokinetics. It's a powerful sedative."

"And what am I supposed to do with this?"

"Use it to kidnap Martin Sellers' wife."

"Are you insane? She's a top-notch pyro. She'll flash fry me before I get within 5 feet of her."

"Not if you use your influence. Get close enough to inject this, she'll go down fast, and …"

"And then what? What do I care about kidnapping Janet Sellers?"

"I'm getting to that. She's our bargaining tool to get the medicine we need for Thomas from Martin. He has the formula to counteract what was done to Thomas. It will snap him out of this," Paul said as he gestured to poor, silent Thomas. "They based this drug off of Martin's research. He is the only one who has the antidote to fix this!"

"Then why not just ask him for it?"

"He won't just hand it over. After what you did to him, working with me, and this place. He'll want all sorts of information in exchange, and you know they won't let that happen. This is our best chance to fix Thomas. Take it." He held out his hand, holding the vial.

Katherine looked at it. She knew it was a deal with the devil. But the clock was ticking. She reached out and took the vial from him. She didn't even look at it before she shoved it in her pocket.

"I will get you an assignment that will get you close to PSI Center," Paul told her. "You'll be able to break off from your agent and go get this done instead."

"And just how am I supposed to ditch my escort without getting electrocuted?"

"I'll be following close behind you and take care of that."

"Then why don't you just do this all yourself? If you feel so bad about what happened to Thomas, then just kidnap Janet on your own."

"Because I can't get close to that building. If I'm spotted, by anyone, then everything is ruined. And, my power can't get me close enough to Janet. Your power can. You are the best empath in this organization. That's why they haven't experimented on you. That's why they won't dispose of you. Even if you're caught, they can't replace you. You'll never have a chance to be free if Thomas isn't made better."

It seemed to Katherine that he was right. If he wasn't, it was all going so fast that she didn't have time to debate it or think about it. Her time with Thomas would be up soon, and the agent would be back to escort her back to her room.

"When the agent comes back for you, we have to convince him that I came in here to beg for your forgiveness about Thomas. Scream at me that you'll never forgive me. Make a big show of it."

"I think I can be convincing in that respect," Katherine said, glaring at him. Even if this plan worked, she would never forgive him. She knew he was evil, and suspected there was an angle to this, but she had to try. She owed it to Thomas.

A moment later the agent opened the door and told her it was time to return to her room. He was shocked to see Paul in the room with her.

"NO," she screamed! "He took up all my time with his incessant whining of forgiving him. Monster! I'll never forgive you!" She swung her fist at his chest. "I've lost Thomas forever and it's your fault!"

"Obviously, she's deranged," Paul said to the agent, with his usual arrogance. "I would never need to apologize for this vegetable. I mean, I can't see a difference in his personality, are we sure something is even wrong with him?"

Katherine rushed at Paul and struck him across the face. "You are lucky my power doesn't work in here," she said to him through clenched teeth.

"As are you," he said coolly back to her.

The agent grabbed Katherine by her arm and escorted her out of the room. As the door closed, Paul approached the bed that Thomas was lying in. He glanced at the medical equipment, noticing it was very similar to the ones in Emily's room. He grazed his fingers lightly over the switches and buttons.

"Now, you…. You, I can switch off."

And he did. Thomas O'Bannon slowly closed his eyes as the machines stopped humming. He was, finally, free.

Two days later, Katherine O'Bannon sat in a debriefing meeting. She was going to be sent to a diplomatic meeting, posing as the executive assistant to the U.S. Ambassador. They wanted her to influence the visiting ambassadors into total cooperation and agreement with all the terms that our government was going to propose. She was not given the details of the terms or the specifics of the meeting. Those were not things she needed to know. Only their compliance. That was all.

The agent assigned to her was not her usual escort. She had seen this man before but had never worked with him. For whatever reason, he had been tasked with escorting her to the meeting and keeping hold of her ankle remote. She could see the remote inside his jacket, right above his gun.

As soon as they left Global Trust Insurance and were driving away from the dampening field that surrounded the building, she could pick up on his disdain for her. Regardless of how well-trained he was in keeping his emotions in check and hidden, she was sure he kept his thoughts hidden from the telepaths as well. But, as faint as his emotions were, she could still taste them.

"I was sorry to hear about your nephew." He said it in a very monotone voice.

"I don't have to use my empathic ability to know you don't mean it. So, no need to zap me. Can we just not talk, I need to focus on what's coming up."

She was so concerned with shutting him up and not wanting to converse with him that she didn't realize that he wasn't referring to Thomas' vegetative state. He was talking about his death. Which she was still unaware of.

It was just approaching 3 p.m. Even though PSI Center would be teaming with people, there would be a shift change occurring soon. That would be the perfect time for her to make her way inside.

Paul had left the instructions for her with the agent who was driving the car. It was obvious to her now that Paul had simply bought off this agent to help them in this plan. Playing on people's greed seemed to be another talent of Paul's. The agent gave her a diagram of the building and told her where she would find Janet. This was a weekly routine Janet followed while taking her daughter to the center for her sessions. Luckily, she would be in one of the corner rooms near a stairwell, but it was on the 6th floor. Getting in would be easy. Getting out with a drugged-up Janet, may not be so easy.

She continued to study the diagram and the agent said he would be waiting in the stairwell for her signal, and he would help her get Janet out of the building quickly. They would then take her to a location where Paul would be waiting. Then they could continue to the scheduled ambassadors' meeting, while Paul negotiated the trade for Janet for the drugs he said would cure Thomas' condition.

When they pulled up to the building, Katherine was already putting her hair up into a bun and grabbing a lab coat from the back seat of the car. She took the syringe that was included with the letter and filled it using the vial Paul had given her. She looked at the vial of clear liquid. She noticed the label had been torn off. She replaced the safety tip on the syringe and put it in the lab coat pocket.

"A simple disguise," she thought to herself. "But it should help me blend in a bit better. I don't want to be recognized."

She made her way to one of the side entrances. The place was busy, just as she suspected. It made it easier for her to not stand out as much. She made her way passed various staff and patients and found the stairwell that would lead up to the 6th floor. She paused for a moment. Not only to make sure there wasn't any kind of alarm on the door but to second guess if what she was doing was right.

She thought about going to Martin and telling him what was happening. Telling him everything. All that had happened since she last saw him. She could beg for his help. But she couldn't be sure that he would help her. Or that she could get back to Thomas before Paul discovered her treason, and exacted his revenge on her nephew. Martin might protect her, but he wouldn't be able to protect Thomas.

It was too late to turn back at this point. If she backed out, Paul would sacrifice her to the organization. Or fry her mind. Either way, Thomas would be left defenseless.

She quickly opened the door and closed it behind her. She stopped on the other side to listen for anyone else in the stairwell before she started her ascent. She didn't hear anyone, so up she went. She tried to move as swiftly and as quietly as she could. Just the sound of her own thoughts for the entire journey upwards.

When she saw the placard next to the door that said "Floor 6," she stopped again as she reached for the handle.

"Last chance," she said to herself. But again, she reached the same conclusion. It was too late to stop now. Again she listened to the stairwell. How was the agent going to get in and get out? She paused for a moment to catch her breath and compose herself.

Katherine exited into the 6th-floor hallway. The room she wanted would be to her left. There were only a few people up here, which could make it easier for her to be spotted. She stood up straight and walked with purpose towards her destination.

"Excuse me," a male voice said behind her.

"Yes?" She turned around, putting on the most pleasant face she could conjure up.

"Do you have the proper clearance to be up here?" He was a security guard. He was looking her up and down. "I can't seem to find a badge on you anywhere. Maybe I need to take a closer look."

She thought to herself, "What a pig," but used his primal urges as her weapon. She bore down on him with lustful emotions. Bringing deep desires and yearnings to the surface.

"Mmmm, that sounds groovy," she stroked his face as she pummeled him with continuous waves of sexual need. "Go wait in the nearest utility closet for me. I just need to grab my purse from my office down there and then you can search me for my badge."

"Ok. But hurry, I don't think I can wait." He was sweating and practically shaking with anticipation.

"Oh, then you should go ahead and get naked in there for me too. You'll do that for me, right?"

"Yes," he said, panting with eyes all glazed over. "I'll do anything you want."

He spun around and ran for the utility closet. Lucky for her there was a utility closet on this floor. And she figured if her influence wore off too fast, it would buy her more time if he had to redress himself before he would be able to look for her.

Now, unhindered by the groping hands of a pesky security guard, she was able to find the correct room very quickly. It was an office. The nameplate on the door read "Dr. Ross Burton."

She cleared her mind, preparing to force the same type of lethargic state onto Janet that she had done to Martin. A calmness. She needed to keep her calm so she could inject her with the sedative. She reached into the coat pocket, took out the syringe, and removed the safety cap.

When she entered the office, Janet was sitting in a chair next to the window, reading a magazine. She was alone in the office and hadn't noticed Katherine until it was too late.

In the split second it took for Janet to look up from her magazine, and then to recognize that this woman was Katherine O'Bannon, the effects of Katherine's power were already taking effect. Just as Janet was throwing down the magazine and getting out of the chair, she suddenly fell back into it. The sudden small burst of heat that had been felt in the room quickly dissipated.

Katherine continued to pour the emotions onto Janet as she rushed towards her. She could feel Janet's anger fighting against her influence. She had gotten the drop on Janet, and she was fairly confident that she could hold her until the drug would take effect.

"I'm sorry," Katherine said to Janet, as she knelt next to her and put the syringe next to her arm. "I have to do this for Thomas. Forgive me."

Katherine stuck the needle into Janet's arm and injected the liquid.

She stood up and waited for the drug to start to take effect. But Janet didn't get drowsier. She didn't become more lethargic. Instead, she started to force herself free of Katherine's influence.

Sadness, pain, guilt, sleep… no emotions Katherine could muster up were taking hold of Janet. This drug was having the opposite effect on her. It was giving strength to her rage. A rage that was building quickly.

The temperature in the room shot up quickly. Random items around the room began to smolder and smoke. The magazine burst into flames.

"What have you done to me?" Janet screamed. There were no more audible words. Just screaming as her clothes began to ignite. Her power was consuming her from within.

"No. I didn't know. He tricked me." Katherine was frozen. Stunned, watching this woman's body spontaneously combust. "I didn't mean for this …"

The office door swung open and hit the inside wall of the office. Dr. Burton ran in from the doorway, pulling his lab coat off as he moved towards Janet. Katherine saw a young girl standing in the doorway. She was a miniature version of Janet. Katherine knew it had to be Margaret.

"Oh god, what did I do?" Katherine said to herself.

"MOMMY!" the girl screamed.

"Katherine, get her out of here!" Dr. Burton yelled at her as he was wrapping his lab coat around Janet, trying to extinguish the flames.

Only he didn't realize that the fire couldn't be extinguished from the outside, and was rapidly getting worse. The temperature in the room was unbearable. Katherine bolted for the door, grabbing Margaret, and taking one last look before pulling the door closed behind them.

She saw an office on fire. Everything was on fire. Dr. Burton's clothes were on fire as well. He was still attempting to put out the flames that were consuming Janet. Her screams getting louder and more desperate. Katherine had pulled the door closed just in time. The air itself seemed to ignite causing the whole office to explode. Blowing out the windows and knocking the office door off its hinges.

The door flew back into the main area. Striking Katherine, who fell into Margaret, knocking her to the ground.

PSI Center staff raced towards the office with fire extinguishers.

They rushed in to put out the few remaining items that were on fire. As quickly as it had all started, it was over. Everything was charred black like it had been burning for hours.

On the floor by one of the windows were the burned remains of what was once the most beautiful and powerful pyrokinetics. No clothes, no skin, no features remained of her. Just a vague shape of a human form.

There was a scream from outside the building. Without the windows as a barrier to the outside, the commotion of a gathering crowd could be heard.

"Oh my god," one of the staff members exclaimed. He was standing at the window frame, holding a fire extinguisher, looking down to the ground outside. "Who is that? Who were these people? This was Dr. Burton's office. Were either of these people him?"

Lying on the ground, 6 stories below, next to a tree, were the smoldering remains of Dr. Burton. He had most likely died before being blown out of the window by the last explosive blast of Janet's power before it consumed her.

Katherine sat, stunned, trying to recover from being hit by the flying door. She knew this was all her fault.

"You did this," Margaret said quietly. She stood up next to Katherine. Tears streaming down her face. She could feel Katherine's guilt, and Katherine could feel Margaret's anger swelling up. It was pushing past her sadness and digging its angry claws into Katherine's guilt.

"Margaret!" Martin ran to his daughter and grasped her in his arms. "Thank god, you're ok. Janet?" He yelled for his wife.

"She did it," Margaret said, pointing at Katherine.

"Katherine, what…? What are you doing here? What happened?" Martin asked her.

From behind Martin, Patty and her son Robert approached. They stood next to him, trying to see past the office doorway into the office.

"Oh… Martin, what… what happened?" Patty asked.

"It was her," Margaret's tone thick with anger now. Her accusation of Katherine was clear. "She did it. She killed Doctor Grandpa. She killed my mother!"

Young Robert stood next to his mother, but his power was connecting to Margaret's. His power was amplifying her power. Margaret latched onto Katherine's guilt and fed it back to her, over and over. Her guilt became depression. Her depression became suicidal thoughts. Wave after wave of guilt crashed down on her. Escalating within seconds. With Robert helping Margaret, there was no hope for Katherine to fight against it. She couldn't even try. She no longer wanted to. Underneath it all, she knew the blame was hers, and she was accepting all that Margaret had to give her.

"No. Stop this." Patty said, turning to Margaret. "You can't do this to her." She could feel the empathic power being used. But she wasn't strong enough to push past Margaret's influence and help Katherine. "Robert, Margaret… stop this!"

"She…" Margaret narrowed her gaze onto Katherine. "Killed…" tears streaming down her cheeks. "My…" her mouth downturned with sadness and hatred. She drew a deep breath and screamed at Katherine. "MOTHER!!!"

The emotion forced Katherine to flee. She scrambled to her feet, panicked, with her eyes darting all around her. She was searching for a way out. Her path to the hallway was blocked by people watching the scene unfold, she turned and ran into the office. She was beyond frantic. She ran, screaming, through the office looking for another door that would exit the room. But there were no other doors. There was only one way out. All of the windows had been freed of their glass panes and presented themselves as an exit.

Her eyes saw the remains of Janet, there on the floor beneath the open window frame. Hysterical and crying, she ran to the opening and dived through the window frame to whatever awaited her below.

The tree that was shading the remains of Dr. Burton, helped to interrupt her fall, but it would not save her life. She bounced off some of the tree's sturdier branches as she plummeted to the ground below. There was no time to notice if the cracking she heard was from her bones or the tree's branches.

She hit the ground hard, on her back. She couldn't move. All she could do was sob as she struggled to catch her breath. She began to cough up blood. She could tell she was not going to survive this.

A crowd gathered around her and some of the doctors ran up to her with medical equipment. They were trying to tell her to lay still and that she would be okay. She couldn't really hear them clearly. She could only hear a voice in her head.

"Now, THAT is a very dramatic way to exit a room." Paul's voice rang inside her mind. "Like father, like daughter. Hmmm? Is that irony or karma?"

She couldn't respond verbally without coughing up more blood. With every breath, she spat up more blood. Her hands and feet were feeling very cold, and the sensation was moving up into her limbs.

"I must say," he continued to project his words into her brain, "that went much better than I had hoped. Since you're going to die anyway, I'll go ahead and let you in on a little secret. That wasn't a 'pyro-downer' that I gave you. But I suspect you already know that. I knew it would cause Janet's powers to freak out. I was actually hoping it would take the two of you out. And cause mass destruction in the wake of it. I didn't know my father would get caught up in your colossal blunder as well."

"W…why…" she gurgled out loud.

"Lay still miss," said one of the doctors, thinking she was talking to him.

"Well," Paul continued his monolog into her mind, "I'll tell you why. Because I have people I need to place in certain positions. People like you and Janet are in my way. Taking her out also delivers a crippling blow to Martin. That part is just gravy. Oh oh, looks like you are starting to fade out. But before you go, I want you to know one more thing. I killed Thomas two days ago."

Katherine O'Bannon died on the opposite side of the tree where Dr. Burton's body had landed. She passed away with the doctors trying to save her life. Just as her last breath escaped she gently pulled one of the doctors who was kneeling over her, down to her mouth and whispered a soft "I'm sorry."

As her Irish eyes focused on the blue sky above, tears began to run down the temples of her face. She watched the sky as she faded away and hoped to join Thomas wherever he might have gone.

Chapter Thirty
The Funeral

Dr. Martin Sellers was a broken man. He stood at the grave sight of his beloved wife completely oblivious to the words being spoken by the priest. His thoughts were drowning out any sounds that reached his ears.

He was fully aware that it was not only his sadness he felt, but that of his daughter as well. The tragedy of losing her mother was too much for her to bear, and she didn't have the skill to keep that emotion under control. She was trying her best but she was having little success. Unfortunately, those who stood the closest to her would also be vulnerable to her influence.

Martin's training helped quite a bit in recognizing when her power was active and helped him resist it. Today, however, he felt like he needed to take this pain from her. He hoped that taking it on would help ease her sadness. Deep down, he knew that wasn't true.

Janet's services were kept private. Just family members and a few of their closest friends were in attendance. Martin didn't want to think ahead to four days from now when the services for Dr. Burton would be held. That would be open for all PSI Center staff, patients, colleagues, and friends to attend. Though his body had already been cremated, and Martin had possession of the ashes, the memorial service would be held in the cafeteria at PSI Center, where their first staff meeting was held.

Martin watched as Janet's casket was slowly lowered into the grave. He cursed himself for thinking that it contained the burned, twisted remains of his once beautiful wife. He struggled to picture her soft face, framed by her shining hair. Only to have it replaced by his last sight of her, the charred corpse that had no resemblance to the woman he loved.

He rubbed his eyes, feeling the tears he had been unaware of that he had been crying. He held his daughter close to his side, feeling her tremble as she cried. The loss of a parent is difficult for any child, but how this took place, and seeing her mother's body, was traumatic. Added to this was Margaret's struggle to keep her emotions in control so her ability wouldn't get out of hand.

Martin did not approve of giving children sedatives, but in the first 2 nights following the trauma, he felt it necessary to keep her under control. Her fits of sadness and rage were rampant. At that time, he was having enough trouble dealing with his own emotions and wasn't capable of handling her onslaught of emotions as well. A course of action he knew Janet wouldn't approve of. She'd only been gone a few days, and already he was screwing up.

Joe and Patty Zanetti were in attendance as well. Though partway through the services, Patty had to walk away. She needed distance from all the people and all their emotions.

She felt her grief, and Martin's and Margaret's. She could feel the sadness from Janet's family, and the anger from the blame they placed on Martin. The exact details of the accident were not made public, but they speculated it was somehow his fault. He was the one who brought her into this weird medical practice that he was involved in. He never cured her of this curse she suffered from. It must have been his fault.

Patty wasn't sure if she felt anger or pity for those people. They would never truly know just how much Martin helped Janet. How much good he had done for so many people. She shook her head, cleared her thoughts, took a deep breath, and made her way back to the congregation.

When the service had ended and those in attendance said their condolences and goodbyes, Martin walked Margaret over to Joe and Patty.

"I really appreciate you watching her for me," he said to them both. He looked down at Margaret, tilting her chin up to his face. "You're going to spend the day with Uncle Joe and Aunt Patty and Robert. I need you to be on your best behavior. Ok?"

"No, Daddy," she began to cry in protest. "I want to be with you."

"I have work stuff that I have to do for a little bit. I have a meeting that I have to go to. I'm sorry honey, I won't be too long. I'll be back in time for dinner." He said as he bent down to her and kissed her forehead.

He could feel her sadness and panic begin to creep into him.

"No, Daddy. Please don't go back to that place. I hate it. Don't leave me!" Margaret grabbed onto him as if some invisible force was going to sweep him away from her.

"Margaret, look at me," Martin said to her in as calm of a voice as he could muster. He fought against her emotions as he gently pulled her away so he could kneel down to her. "What happened to your mother won't happen to me. I know you are scared and sad, but right now I need you to try really hard to keep control of your feelings and be as brave as you can. Can you do that for me?"

She stared into his eyes, feeling his need for her to do this for him. She could sense the desperation in his emotions and began to take control of her own emotions. She didn't want to hurt him, so she began to shut off her own emotions.

"I can, Daddy," she said. She wiped the tears from her eyes with the back of her hand and then wiped her hand on her dress.

Patty came to Margaret's side and reached down to take her hand.

"Come on honey," she spoke to Margaret, "let's let your daddy talk to Uncle Joe."

Patty began to walk Margaret back to their car. She told her about some new board games that Robert had and that they could play when they got back to their house.

"What meeting could you have to attend today, Martin?" Joe asked.

"Some investigators are looking into the cause of the fire and explosion. Safety concerns, insurance claims. It's just too much," Martin said as he rubbed his eyes again. "But, it looks like I'm in charge now, and I can't put them off any longer."

"Why in the hell was Katherine there?" Joe felt a little bad for asking, for bringing up the incident again, but he wanted to make sense of what had happened.

"I've asked myself that a hundred times," Martin's gaze shifted off into the distance. He was half-lost in thought as he spoke. "I don't know if that was her goal or if something had gone wrong. I haven't even spoken to Margaret about what she did to Katherine. I don't know if she can handle it. Or if I can handle how she may react."

Joe paused for a moment, carefully considering if he should ask his next question.

"How… I mean, why did Janet's powers go out of control like that? Could Katherine's empathy do that to someone?"

"No," Martin said. He was still looking off into the distance as he replied. "I don't think there was anything empathic to it. There was a crushed syringe in her pocket. I've been testing the little bit of residue

I could find in it. Nearest I can tell, she must have injected Janet with it. It did something to Janet's hormones, amped up her adrenaline or something. I've never known Janet's powers to go to such extremes. It was like nothing we've ever seen before."

"Patty told me that some of the patients and staff left after …after what happened."

"Yes. Whether it was from the explosion, rumors of an attack, or whatever reasons. Some just up and left. They're too scared to come back. I can't say that I haven't thought of walking away from it all myself."

"What? You can't be serious!" Joe put his hand on Martin's shoulder. "Listen, I know this is the worst possible thing that could ever happen, but you have to think of all the people you've helped over the years. All the people you could continue to reach in the years to come. You may have stopped this very thing from happening numerous times in the past with the discoveries you made. There could be more kids out there like Robert, or Margaret," he hesitated on his last words. "Or, like Janet."

"I… I just don't know anymore." Martin sighed. He was exhausted. All of this was taking its toll on him, and he didn't know how much more he could take. He didn't know what the price would be if he continued. Or, the price if he stopped.

"Listen," Joe said, "you go do what you need to. Don't worry about Margaret. We'll take care of her. Between my limited telepathy and Patty, she'll be fine. We work pretty well together." He smiled at Martin. "And you just go answer whatever questions those guys have for you. You've done nothing wrong, so they can't touch you or PSI Center. It'll all work out for the best. You'll see."

They went their separate ways, knowing nothing about the existence of Global Trust Insurance, and that the incident at PSI Center had their property buzzing with activity in speculation over what had happened. Agents and staff alike were gossiping about what they had heard and tried to be the first to come up with plausible conclusions.

Agent Coleman had summoned Paul Burton and 8 other agents to the conference room. He had called the meeting to discuss the events that had occurred at PSI Center. All of the agents had heard of the accident and the rumors circulating about it. Paul had caught the side glances and whispers aimed at him. He again cursed the static field that prevented him from hearing their thoughts.

"Agents," Agent Coleman, standing at the head of the table, spoke to get their attention and start the meeting. "I have gathered you here to give you the details, as we know them, of the events that resulted in a pyrokinetic explosion at PSI Center."

He handed a stack of folders to the agent on his right and gestured for them to be passed down around the table to each person.

"These folders have all the information. I want to be sure any and all loose ends are tied up. I want a full sweep of our facility. I want to make sure this type of thing doesn't happen here."

"Sir," one of the agents interrupted. "I've heard so many different stories and theories as to what happened. How accurate should we assume this information is?"

Paul sat silently, flipping through his folder. Knowing that it was completely inaccurate.

"The facts are this," Agent Coleman now sat in his chair. "Katherine O'Bannon acquired a vial of the Accelerant drug. We suspect it was back when her nephew underwent his testing trials. It had been assumed that the vial had been smashed and trashed during the chaos of that event. She waited for her chance to be paired up with an agent who was unfamiliar with her skills. When she had the opportunity, she must have gotten the drop on him, taken his sidearm, and shot him in the head. His body was discovered about a mile away from PSI Center. She then made her way to PSI Center, we think to ask either Dr. Martin Sellers or Dr. Ross Burton for their help. Instead, she found Mrs. Janet Sellers, wife of Dr. Sellers, who was most likely still very upset about Katherine's betrayal and attack on her husband. She must have tried to use the drug on Mrs. Sellers, mistakenly thinking it was like the inhibitor used on her nephew. When the accelerant became active, Mrs. Sellers either threw her out of the window or Katherine leaped from the window to avoid being burned alive. The impact killed her. Dr. Burton stumbled upon the scene, and blown out of the window as Mrs. Sellers' powers became uncontrollable and killed them both."

Paul was very pleased with himself. There had been no connection to him whatsoever. He had promised the new agent a hefty payoff for escorting Katherine to PSI Center. When Katherine went inside, the agent drove a mile down the road to the designated meeting spot to meet Paul. And that's when Paul shot him. By the time he got back to PSI Center, he heard the explosion and someone exclaimed that Dr.

Burton was dead on the ground. He then got to witness Katherine leap from the open window. Aside from having to shove the murdered agent out of the passenger seat and right into a ditch, he didn't have to do anything too strenuous.

"Agent Coleman, if I may," Paul spoke up. "I happen to know that Martin Sellers is supposed to be interviewed today by an investigator. He's been trying to delay it, but they've given him today as a deadline. I think today might be a perfect opportunity for us to turn this to our advantage."

"How do you mean?"

"Well, the paperwork and reports are already in motion with local authorities. So, it's too late for us to head them off now. But, what if we send in one of our 'negotiators' to help the authorities understand that it was some faulty wiring or some such accident? We save Martin Sellers, we save the PSI Center. He owes us, we own him, and then we take over PSI Center."

"You think it will be that easy to convince him to work with us?" Agent Coleman laced his fingers together and leaned forward on the table. "Our organization approached your father numerous times. We never had any luck with even the slightest consideration of our becoming involved with them. You think that will change now?"

"Yes, but that was when you were dealing with my father. And Martin was at my father's side with his wife for support. Both of which are now gone. He's weak, and it is the perfect time to strike."

Agent Coleman saw the gleam in Paul's eyes. There was no remorse at the loss of his father. He might as well have been reciting chess moves rather than talking about the passing of living people. One of which he was related to. But, he couldn't deny the logic behind it.

"You are correct Mr. Burton. But, as talented of a telepath as you are, there is no way you could go near Dr. Sellers. We'll need another telepath who can handle this task."

"I just happen to have someone in mind," Paul said. Smiling to himself, he continued. "And I think this task would be too important for just any agent to undertake. If I may be so bold, I would think this requires your personal attention."

The meeting had concluded and the agents all began to stand up and gather their folders. Paul remained seated and cleared his throat, loudly, to gain their attention.

"One other thing, agents," he said as they all turned to look at him.

"I thought I might mention, in case it's important, that from what I've heard, Ms. O'Bannon did her swan dive from the window after the explosion that killed my father and ...what's her name? Oh, Janet Sellers." He then stood up from his chair. "I don't know if that's idle gossip, or something worth noting."

The agents, each with a puzzled expression on their face, left the conference room. Only Agent Coleman and Paul remained behind.

"Mr. Burton," Agent Coleman remained seated, "why would you feel it necessary to interject that information if you consider it gossip?"

"You can drop the 'Mr. Burton' crap. We're alone in here and it's not like any telepath can eavesdrop on our conversation."

Paul walked to the head of the table where Agent Coleman was sitting. He used his knee to push Coleman's chair, rolling back away from the large table. Paul straddled his legs and slowly lowered himself on the agent's lap.

"I want to see just how good the agents are," Paul said with a playful tone. "I could have left a trail of neon bread crumbs before, during, and after and they still wouldn't be able to figure it out. I'm just having a little fun with you. Don't worry about it, baby."

"I do worry about it," Agent Coleman said. He had a serious tone and some stress in his words. "I have bosses. And those above me take this all very seriously. If they found out about us ...it would have dire repercussions! Your 'fun' is playing with our lives!"

"Oh, calm down," his words had some bite to them now. Paul stood up and positioned himself behind Coleman's chair. He began rubbing the man's shoulders. "I said I would deliver PSI Center to you, and I will. It's just time and paperwork at this point. Your superiors will be happy. Your job will be secure. We'll be all set."

Chapter Thirty-One
The Meeting and the Minds

Martin met the three men who were sent to investigate the fire in the main lobby of the PSI Center. Two of the men were local law enforcement, dressed in their brown uniforms. The third was a short round man in a poorly tailored dark brown suit, sent from the insurance company to work with law enforcement, and their reports of the accident and deaths, to determine the cause if any charges or claims would be filed.

They shook hands and made the usual introductions. The short man identified himself as Carl Potts. His brown and yellow striped tie continuously led the eye to his fat face, with the perpetual dew of sweat above his upper lip. He was wearing black-framed glasses, that were too large for his round face, and a combed-over hairstyle that was a poor attempt to cover his balding scalp.

The short man adjusted his glasses as he began to speak. "Dr. Sellers, I assume the area in question has not been tampered with and we will be able to inspect it today?"

Martin was taken back a bit by his direct approach. "Of course. The only thing that has been done is the windows have been boarded up."

"I see. Well, let's hope that all the traipsing back and forth to board up windows hasn't disturbed the site too much." Carl Potts began to walk towards the elevators, swinging his small briefcase at his side, leaving the other men behind.

"I'm sorry this has to be done now, Dr. Sellers" one of the policemen spoke to Martin. "I know this is not good timing. With today…well, being what today is and all."

"I understand, officer. It's not your fault, and I suppose I had to face it at some point. I'll take you up to the 6th floor."

As they turned to follow Mr. Potts to the elevators, Martin was being called to by someone entering the lobby.

"Dr. Sellers," they yelled to get his attention. "If you could wait one moment please."

Martin turned around to see two people approaching. He recognized Agent Coleman, though not immediately since it had been some time since he had last seen the man. The other man, as tall as Agent Coleman, though visibly younger and dressed in the same dark blue suit, was someone he did not know. He walked with the same straight posture and purposeful stride as Agent Coleman.

Martin wondered what the reason for their visit could be. He imagined that it couldn't be a coincidence that Agent Coleman happened to be showing up today. He immediately went on the defensive as they approached him.

"What are you …" Martin was interrupted before he could finish. Agent Coleman quickly extended his hand and introduced himself to the two uniformed policemen.

"I'm Mr. Coleman and this is my associate, Mr. Sumner. We're from Global Trust Insurance. We're here to investigate the accident site." His eyes widened slightly, trying to signal Martin not to let on that he knew who they were.

"Dr. Sssellersss," a voice said inside of Martin's head. It had a peculiar echo to it. Almost like a hiss, as if a snake was speaking to his mind. The other agent, Mr. Sumner, caught his eye and nodded. "Yesss, it'sss me. We are only here to expedite their invessstigation. We have our concernsss and reasssonsss to help you keep thisss incident covered up. We want to assure you that we had no involvement in the unfortunate sssituation that took place. We can talk openly once thisss isss over."

Carl Potts had made his way back to them from the elevator. "Gentlemen, I thought we were going up. Who are you?" He said looking at the two new men in dark blue suits.

"We're from Global Trust Insurance," Agent Coleman said with a smile, extending his hand.

"Another insurance company?" Carl Potts ignored the outstretched hand. "Are you trying to file multiple claims on this building Dr. Sellers?"

"Sir," Agent Coleman interjected, "our interest is in some of the specialty equipment that may have been damaged in the fire. Nothing that was covered or any concern to the company you represent." He glanced at Agent Sumner.

Agent Sumner slowly blinked, unnoticed by any of the others. His focus was totally on the round little man, who suddenly seemed to lose his balance for a moment.

"Yes, no concern of mine," Carl Potts said out loud. "Shall we go up then?"

The elevator ride seemed to be taking even longer than normal for Martin. He was careful to guard his thoughts, especially with a telepath so close to him. He couldn't know what would happen if he were to try to alert the police that these men were with a secret government organization. That they could be the ones responsible for the tragedies that took place here. Would he have time to explain it all before the telepath stopped him? Would they believe him? What proof did he have?

The elevator opened to the 6th floor and Martin showed them to the office. The door was gone, but a plastic sheet and some yellow caution tape covered the entry. One of the policemen pulled the yellow tape down and pulled back the plastic sheet so they could enter.

There was one window in the corner of the room that had not been blown out, it was covered in multiple cracks. The sun was shining through it and it provided enough light to clearly see the office.

Martin paused outside of the plastic sheet hanging from the door frame. He hesitated going back into that office. The horrific memories of that day were already flooding back into his mind.

"I can see thisss is hard for you. You can ssstay out here," said Agent Sumner's telepathic voice. "There'sss no need for you to go in there. It won't take long."

"You'd do well to stay the fuck out of my head!" Martin replied in his mind. He had no doubt the telepath received his message loud and clear. He could feel that familiar tingle in the back of his skull fade away, signaling that the telepath had indeed disconnected from his mind.

The men in the office were in awe of the damage they were witnessing. Ashes were all that remained of most of the furnishing and decorations. Nothing had escaped the fire.

"This is unbelievable," said Carl Potts. "I can't begin to think what would cause such destruction. For something to burn like this and that it didn't spread outside of this room." He spoke as he removed a legal pad to start making notes on.

"Seems simple enough to me," said Agent Coleman. "Faulty wiring. Probably a rat that chewed threw a wire, caught on fire, and caused all the electrical devices in the room to ignite." He looked to

Agent Sumner, which signaled him to begin using his abilities on the other men in the room.

"Yes, that seems likely." Said one of the policemen.

"Good enough for me." Said the other.

"What? Wires? Rats? Are you kidding…meh…" Carl Potts' sentence trailed off. He stood silent for a moment, then began talking again. "Yes, I would say that's exactly the cause of this. And a terrible shame that people were trapped in here when it happened." He seemed satisfied with this explanation as he packed his legal pad back into his briefcase and made his way to exit the office.

Martin stayed on the other side of the plastic but could hear everything that was transpiring in the office. He took a step back as Mr. Potts and the two policemen made their way past the plastic and into the main hallway.

"I believe we have all we need, Dr. Sellers." The older of the two policemen said, shaking Martin's hand. "There doesn't seem to be any type of criminal cause to what happened here. Again, I'm sorry for your loss."

"Yup, rats and wires. Always a bad combo." Carl Potts exited the room next. His eyes had a slightly glassy look to them. "I'll have it all in my report. I will expedite your claim immediately, Dr. Sellers." He stood still for a moment as if silently receiving new instructions. "And no need to see us out. We know the way."

The three men walked to the elevator together and rode it down to the lobby. They walked through the lobby and out to the parking lot. Without saying a word to each other, they got into their respective vehicles and drove away.

Both of the agents had exited the office. Martin had no idea what to expect next.

"Now then," said Agent Coleman, "let's talk."

Down the hallway, in his own office, Rex was finalizing some paperwork for more of the patients who had decided to leave PSI Center. He was still in shock over the number of patients and staff who left in the past week. For him, this incident proved even more how important their work was and why they had to be brave and stay and continue working.

Rex stopped what he was doing, and set the paperwork down on his desk. He smiled as he looked up, feeling the familiar tingle in his skull that meant Emily would be appearing to him.

Sure enough, a split second later, there she was. There, but not there. Illuminated by her unknown light source, in her usual pink dress. Her hair was still held back by the pink ribbon headband. Rex had begun to notice, that in these past years of her visiting, and trying to determine her location, she had never changed. Her clothes hadn't changed and she hadn't appeared to age. He wondered, is this the age she was when she fell into her coma? Or was this how her subconscious pictured herself?

"Good afternoon, Emily, my dear," Rex said with a warm smile, greeting her as he usually did.

"They're here," Emily's voice projected, in a frantic whispered tone. As if she was afraid someone would overhear her. She had skipped any of the pleasantries and got right to the point of her visit. "They are here in your building."

"Who's here? Who is in this building, Emily?" Rex began to stand up from his desk chair.

"The men from where I am. I heard people talking about it. So I tried to follow them through the darkness. They are here to try and take over. They want to take over the PSI Center!"

"Where, Emily? Where in the building are they? How do I find them?"

She faded slightly, signifying that she was looking for them. She was carefully looking through the building. "It's hard to pick them out. One of them I know I can't 'see.' He's normal. The other is special, he can read thoughts and mess with people's minds. He's bad like Paul. I don't want him to see me." She continued to fade in and out. Then she came back completely. "Here! Dr. Rex, they are here on this floor! They are talking to your friend, Dr. Sellers, right now!"

Rex tore out of his office. Not bothering to shut his office door behind him or to put his lab coat back on. He looked like one of the patients. Dressed in casual khaki slacks and a simple button-up collared shirt. He cursed the slick soles of his dress shoes as he attempted to run down the hallway. Emily, barely visible to him, seemed to be gliding effortlessly alongside him.

He spotted Martin and the two agents outside of what was left of Dr. Burton's office. Martin had just finished saying something to the men and was using a free hand to rub his forehead and temples.

"I… I'll have to think about all of this. I just can't even start to contemplate this right now," Martin was saying to the agents as Rex rushed up to the men.

"Martin," Rex said in an excited tone, slightly out of breath from the frantic dash down the hallway. "These men, they are the ones holding Emily!"

"Emily Green?" Agent Coleman turned his attention to Rex. "What do you know of Emily Green?"

"I know that she is a telepath and that she is in a coma. And you are keeping her hidden in whatever facility you are running." His Australian accent became more apparent when he was agitated. "Where is she?" He grabbed ahold of Coleman's jacket lapels.

"How do you...," Agent Coleman forced Rex's hands from his jacket. "We are keeping her alive," he responded to the accusations. "She represents a great deal of value to us. And we are making sure she is receiving the best care possible." He glanced at Agent Sumner.

Agent Sumner stepped forward slightly. "He's not reading our minds," he said. He continued searching the air like he smelled something. Or like he saw something. "This man has communicated with her," he said in a stunned voice. "Somehow, she is projecting all the way here. How is she getting passed the..."

Agent Coleman cut him off. "Dr. Sellers, Dr. Rex, as a show of good faith, if you would like to come back and check on Emily Green yourself, you will see we are not some evil warehouse designed to torture and exploit those with gifts."

"Yes, actually," Rex spoke up, "I would very much like to see Emily for myself."

"Rex, are you sure you want to go with them?" Martin was obviously concerned, but there was no way he could go with them, not when he had the safety of his daughter to consider.

"I'll be fine. You have enough to deal with. And if anything were to happen to you... well, you have Margaret to think about. This is one lead I can follow up on." Rex turned to face both agents. "I assume you meant that we would be going right now."

"Of course," Agent Coleman replied. He looked over at Agent Sumner, whose eyes were still darting around, searching for some sign of Emily.

She appeared only to Rex, very faint, down the hallway. She shook her head "no," she was afraid to get any closer to him for fear Sumner would sense her.

All 4 men took the elevator to the lobby. Emily stayed away from Rex, though he could sense her traveling with them, down through each floor, outside of the elevator. When the got to the lobby, Martin stayed behind.

"Are you sure this is a good idea?" Martin asked Rex.

"I have to know she's okay," Rex said to Martin. He placed his hand on his shoulder to reassure him. "I'll be alright. It's about time one of us got to see what they're up to."

They led Rex out of the building and through the parking lot to their car. The agents rode in the front, with Agent Coleman driving, and Rex sat in the back. They rode mostly in silence. Rex would occasionally feel Sumner trying to sneak his way into his mind, but Rex had him effectively blocked. Any non-gifted person might not have noticed him trying to pry, or might not have been able to block him out, but Rex was more than capable of keeping this man out.

"As one telepath to another, mate," Rex spoke loud enough for both men to hear him, "If you try to go poking around in my head again, I'll rewire that noggin of yours until you shit yourself every time someone says 'hello.'" He was bluffing, of course, and he hoped they weren't aware of how limited his abilities were.

Agent Coleman gave Agent Sumner a look and gave a little shake of his head. Rex suspected he didn't want someone shitting in his car.

There was no sign of Emily for the entire ride, which took about an hour until they were pulling into a parking lot with a large single building set at the far end of the lot. Its highly tinted windows acting as a mirror, reflecting a sepia-toned sky. Rex looked up at the "Global Trust Insurance" sign.

"Trust," he thought to himself, "yeah, right."

They all got out of the car. Each keeping a watchful eye on the other.

The agents walked on either side of him now. As he entered the building he began to experience an odd numbing feeling inside his head. He stopped walking and his eyes scanned both the agents for signs of what was happening to him. He tried not to panic, as he had never experienced anything like this before.

"It's the dampening field," said Sumner. "It's blocking your telepathic ability. However, limited as it might be. You'll get used to it."

Even though his abilities were being blocked, and he couldn't see her, Rex thought he could feel Emily's presence again. He looked at

Agent Sumner, and he wasn't showing any signs of sensing her presence this time. Rex wondered if he was imagining it.

The receptionist behind the main desk looked up from whatever she was reading, "Hello, Agent Coleman." She drew in a short breath and flashed a coy smile at Rex. "Well, hello sir. Welcome to Global Trust Insurance." She batted her eyelashes at him.

"Whore," Sumner said under his breath, but still loud enough for her to hear him.

"Pinky dick," she responded and sat back down at her desk. She gave a little wave to Rex as they stood in the elevator and the doors drew closed.

"They used to date." Agent Coleman said with a sour expression on his face. Displeased by the lack of professionalism that had just been displayed.

The elevator took them down. Lower than what should have just been a basement level. It felt to Rex like there was a whole other complex underneath this building. When the elevator came to a stop, he could only guess that there were three floors, maybe more, underground.

Stepping out of the elevator felt like he was in any other hospital if it had been nighttime. No windows, no lights from outside. Just the fluorescent bulbs overhead. Technicians were walking about, in white lab coats, just as in any other clinical setting. At first glance, there was nothing sinister going on here. It was a colder imitation of the PSI Center. The floors were clean, there were no sounds of patients screaming in the distance. He spied nothing so obviously, outwardly evil in this place. That is until he saw Paul Burton twenty feet away.

"What?" Paul exclaimed as he approached the men. "This isn't Martin! This man has no value to us! Why bring him here?"

Agent Coleman was visibly angered by Paul questioning his actions. Especially in front of another agent. "He is going to assess Emily Green's condition and report his findings back to Dr. Sellers."

"I do not think it is wise that he be allowed to see Emily alone," Paul spoke to Agent Coleman as he was glaring at Rex. "I've been overseeing her care for years now."

"I've heard about the type of 'care' you've been giving her, Paul." Rex's accent became more prominent. He began to tighten his jaw. Powers or not, he was sure he could take Paul out in a fistfight. And he so much wanted to punch him in his smug face.

Paul's flash of anger subsided, and his Cheshire grin began to creep back onto his face. Now he knew who Emily had been going to visit. However she was doing it, she was able to find her way to him. Paul knew that fighting with this man wasn't going to give him the answers he wanted.

"Calm yourself, pretty boy," Paul said in his most soothing, and condescending, voice. "There's no need to posture for a physical confrontation. You can see her. Shall we go then? Prove to you she is in the best possible care available."

Paul walked with the agents as they led the way to Emily's room. It was dark. Just the few blinking lights from the machines that kept her alive. Barely a silhouette of the body lying in the bed was visible from the lack of available light.

Paul walked over to the light switch and flipped on all the lights at once. The fluorescent lights seemed to come on with a vengeance. Flooding the room in the white-blue light they gave off, exaggerated by all the white furnishing and white walls in the room. The light bounced and reflected off every surface. All of the men cringed for a moment, letting their eyes adjust to what was before them.

Rex squinted his eyes, blinking as they adjusted to the lights. As they acclimated themselves to the room, objects quickly began to take clear shape. He was immediately drawn to the figure that was in the bed before him.

He approached her. He heard the rhythmic beeping of the machines counting her heartbeat. Another machine made a pumping and whooshing sound, as it breathed for her. He got closer to the bed. Looking down at the frail form that was hooked up to all the tubes and wires. This woman was much older than the form of the little girl who had been visiting him all these years.

Her eyes were closed, sunken beneath the high cheekbones that were barely covered by a delicate layer of skin. Her thin hair was a mix of dull blond tones. Some gentle wisps of gray hair were sprinkled in the thin strands of hair that lay across the pillow. He had no idea how long she had been in this state. He had no way of gauging her true age by seeing her in this state.

Paul stood next to him now. "You see, alive and well. And I'm sure as happy as a clam. Or something slightly less active than a clam. But equally as happy."

Rex turned to face him. His anger was welling up inside of him. He wouldn't stand for Paul disrespecting her like this. "Get away from her."

"Fine, fine. I'll give you some space with your girlfriend." And he stepped back next to Agents Coleman and Sumner. "I guess unrequited love can be touchy."

Rex reached down and took her soft, delicate hand in his. He could feel every bone in her hand and almost feared that this mere touch of his would damage her. He hadn't immediately realized it, but as he held her hand the static that had been present in his mind had faded. And next to him stood a transparent little Emily Green. Still in her pink dress, and shining blond hair.

He could feel it now, they existed in a bubble. A clear bubble, with no static. The 3 others in the room were still surrounded by the static, unable to sense her presence inside the bubble.

"Is that me?" She asked Rex in her small voice. Her delicate lips still not moving, the voice just existing in his mind.

"Yes," he answered her back in his mind. "I'm afraid it is, my dear." He still gently held her hand as he knelt next to the bed.

"I guess I kind of knew it already. I could never see myself. But with you here, I can. And you make me not afraid. Do you think I would have been pretty?"

Rex fought to hold back any tears. "Yes. I have no doubt you would have been a real looker."

The vision of little Emily wavered. "I want to see me as you do. All grown up. Pretty. Can you see me that way?"

The translucent shape next to him began to change. She got taller. And as he imagined her as an adult, with her long shining blond hair, full lips, healthy adult cheekbones, and jawline, this is how she began to appear to him now. She seemed to float, with her hair flowing in an invisible breeze, dressed as an adult woman in her pink dress. He glanced up at the image next to him now. A beautiful woman. Healthy and happy.

"Yes," Rex thought to her, "a real looker."

The shift in Rex's attention did not go unnoticed. Paul watched him look away from the woman on the bed, and up at something invisible that now held his attention.

"She's talking to him now," he thought to himself. "How? How is she getting around the static…" he drew a sharp breath and turned to Agent Sumner. Now he spoke out loud and without haste, "She is the source of the static!"

As quickly as he came to this conclusion, he shoved Agent Coleman to the ground and shouted at Agent Sumner to keep him down. To which Sumner responded by kicking Agent Coleman in the face and stomach.

"You sneaky bitch," Paul said through gritted teeth. "This whole time, you were the source of this damned static!" He dashed forward towards the machines. Grabbing at them and pulling them free of their stands and electrical supplies.

Rex sprang to his feet and grabbed on to Paul, trying to stop his rampage. "You'll kill her! STOP!"

Paul held tight to the square metal box that counted Emily's heartbeats and swung it at Rex. It connected with the side of his face, knocking him to the floor. A small trail of blood began to flow down his left cheek.

"You fucking bitch," Paul kept saying. "All this time… all this time," he kept clawing at the wires and tubes connecting the machines to Emily. Pulling some free from the machine, and violently pulling some from Emily's body.

"Rex!" screamed the image of an adult Emily. "Rex, you have to get up. Run! You have to run!"

Paul stopped, only for a second, to see the vision of Emily standing over Rex. He could almost hear her yelling at him to get up. The static was only slightly fading, somehow she was fighting to keep it up as long as she could.

Rex regained full consciousness and could see Emily yelling to him. He turned and saw that Agent Coleman was on the floor, knocked out and bleeding profusely. Agent Sumner, holding Coleman's remote in hand, was focused on watching Paul's rampage now.

"Rex," Emily pleaded, "you have to get out of here. I'm already fading and I don't know how much longer I can keep the static up." She saw him look towards her body. "I'm unhooked from the machines. I'm going to die. You can't save me. Run. Please, Rex. RUN!"

Rex stopped and looked into her eyes. She was already fading, and slowly shifting back into a child form. She whispered in his mind that she would follow him for as long as she could, but he had to go now!

Rex jumped to his feet, ready to rush and knock Agent Sumner out of his way. It was easy enough as he was focused on Paul. A quick punch to the jaw and Agent Sumner joined Agent Coleman on the floor.

Paul hadn't noticed Rex's escape. He had crossed to the other side of her bed and was too busy trying to disconnect Emily from all of her machines. He was frantic to get that static to stop before any agents discovered what was happening.

Paul turned to Emily's body, seeing the wires that ran under her gown, and the tube in her mouth and throat. He swiped his hands down, clutching them all at once, and yanked them all out. His rage consumed him. Panicking with the thought that he would be discovered before he could succeed in this wicked endeavor. The static began to noticeably fade away. But still, Emily kept it present.

"Why won't you DIE?!?!" Paul screamed at her body, still clutching the disconnected tubes in his hands. He threw the tubes and wires across the room and in his rage, he grabbed the woman in the bed by the shoulders and began to shake her. "Die you bitch," he yelled at the unresponsive body. He shook her and tossed her frail body from the bed. She landed on the floor. Agent Sumner regained consciousness and sat up in the doorway, stunned by the gruesome event he was witnessing. He looked at his hand to see he still held the remote.

The static was gone.

Rex had made it to the elevator without resistance. He rode it to the lobby and burst out of it as soon as the doors opened. He could feel the static was fading in the rest of the building. The childlike vision of Emily still glided next to him. She pleaded for him to hurry his escape.

The receptionist jumped to her feet, startled by his presence, when he made his dash into the lobby and headed towards the doors.

"What's going on," she shouted. "Where are the agents?" She held out her hand as if grabbing the air in front of her. Suddenly, Rex felt as if something had grabbed a hold of his ankle and pulled his feet out from under him.

He began to slide back towards the desk and the receptionist. It was now apparent that the receptionist was a telekinetic.

"No, you have to get away," Emily said to Rex. She flew from his side and towards the receptionist. As she got closer, she became more visible to the receptionist and began to take on a horrific ghost-like appearance of the emaciated woman she really was.

Emily howled into the woman's mind, "Release him!"

The receptionist was horrified at what she had just seen. She fell backward against the wall behind the desk. With her concentration broken, her grip on Rex was released. He was quickly back on his feet, with child Emily at his side again, and racing towards the exit.

Just as he was about to exit the building, he felt the whole wall of static drop. He looked at Emily, fearful of what this meant for her. Her expression was pure fear. No brave face. They both knew it was inevitable. There was no time to contemplate it as they could both hear Paul's voice in their heads announcing the end of the static barrier.

"Attention to all fellow prisoners," he was shouting telepathic orders to all those within the building. "The static is gone. Subdue all agents! Prevent them from using their remotes. Liberate those who cannot free themselves! We are in charge now!"

Rex could feel the use of powers activating throughout the building. The bursts of telekinetic forces being used. He could sense the empaths forcing the foreign emotions onto others. The sudden and intense use of these abilities made it easy for him to detect the sheer number of gifted people in the building now. They were like fireworks exploding all around him. Brilliant lights were seen in his mind and one light he could sense fading away.

Rex looked down at Emily. She reached up with her ghostly little hands. He knelt in front of her to meet her just as she began to fade.

"Thank you, friend. You …" She dispersed like a creature made of smoke. Nothing left of her. No sound, no form.

Rex clenched his teeth, fighting back his tears. He stood and dashed the doors again. He knew he had to make it back to PSI Center. He had to warn Martin about what had happened and what was coming. Paul's wrath and plans were unleashed, and now he'd have an army to back him up.

He vowed that Emily's death would not be in vain.

About the Author

~ 254 ~

Ric Bruce has sought out various forms of creative outlets his whole life. From drawing, painting, sculpting, sewing, and a 20+ year career as a licensed Hair Designer. He currently enjoys life in Las Vegas, Nevada with his husband, Mark, and their 2 dogs.

9 798989 820306